M000170051

The Deeps of the Sea
and other fiction

by the same author

GEORGE STEINER

The Deeps of the Sea

and other fiction

faber and faber

LONDON · BOSTON

First published in 1996
by Faber and Faber Limited
3 Queen Square London WC1N 3AU

Photoset by Parker Typesetting Service, Leicester
Printed in England by Clays Ltd, St Ives plc

'The Deeps of the Sea' was first published in *Botteghe Oscure* in 1956.
The Portage to San Cristobal of A.H. was originally published in the *Kenyon Review* in 1979 and was published in book form by Faber in 1981. 'Return No More', 'Cake' and 'Sweet Mars' were published in *Anno Domini* (Faber, 1964). 'Proofs', 'Desert Island Discs, 'Noël, Noël' and 'Conversation Piece' all first appeared in *Granta* and were published in book form in *Proofs and Three Parables* (Faber, 1992).

A CIP record for this book
is available from the British Library

ISBN 0–571–17764–6

2 4 6 8 10 9 7 5 3 1

Contents

INTRODUCTION

George Steiner's Fiction
by John Banville

The first thing to be remarked about George Steiner's fiction is how much of it there is. Given his enthusiasm for the abstruse, the hermetic and the condensed, one would have expected his stories to be difficult, closed and very, very short. Anyone who had browsed through his criticism (or even his titles: *Language and Silence*, *On Difficulty*, *Extraterritorial*, *Antigones*) could be forgiven for assuming that his fiction (again, the titles: *Anno Domini*, *Proofs and Three Parables*) would fall into the category of 'European', a term which conjures up a text in which an unnamed man in an unnamed city in an unnamed country in *Mitteleuropa* paces the floor of a hotel bedroom in search of his identity, while below his window ignorant armies clash by night. But not a bit of it. This work – a novel, three novellas, a goodly handful of stories – is vigorous, precisely located, broad in reference, accommodating in style and, to re-employ an outmoded designation, *engagé*.

We first encountered George Steiner in *Language and Silence* (1967). This collection of essays, which, if any volume ever did, deserves to be called seminal, was not his first book; there had already been *Tolstoy or Dostoevsky* (an 'Essay in the Old Criticism') (1959) and *The Death of Tragedy* (1961), both of which, as Steiner has acknowledged, not without a certain justified pride, have been 'made use of in schools and universities' and have 'had influence'. However, it was *Language and Silence* that introduced us to Steiner's essential, multifarious concerns. That book, and the critical works that followed, 'take their substance', the author says, 'and much of their "voice", from the legacy of Ernst Bloc, of Adorno, of Walter Benjamin and from the inheritance of Jewish poetic-philosophic investigations of the word as it is evident in Roman Jakobson, in Karl Kraus, in Fritz Mauthner and Noam Chomsky. The mapping of my identity, the inward orientations, remain those

vii

circumscribed by Leningrad, Odessa, Prague and Vienna on the one side, and by Frankfurt, Milan and Paris on the other.' In 1967, many of us had never even heard most of these names, much less read their work, and *our* 'inward orientations' were circumscribed indeed, confined as they were to the anglophone world, with its twin poles at London and New York. Suddenly, in *Language and Silence*, a door was flung open for us on what had been there all the time, at our backs, namely, our European heritage. It was an electrifying moment.

I say *we*, because I think of Steiner's readers as a community – an inclusive, not an exclusive, community. Few critics demand of their readers a commitment to a point of view – or, one might better say, to a vantage point – as Steiner does. He insists on the central significance, historical, political and aesthetic, of the European experience, and specifically, in this most terrible century, the experience of the Jewish people. In his own Introduction to *George Steiner: A Reader* (itself a suggestive title, in which the pun is surely intentional), from which I have quoted above, he speaks of several of the pieces in that collection constituting 'an act of remembrance (a *kaddish*)'. He will yield to none in his conviction that the Holocaust (not a term he favours) is the defining event of our time, although he gives full acknowledgement to the century's other great horrors, from the Turkish massacre of the Armenians through the unimaginable enormities of the Stalinist era, and the many postwar atrocities that have been committed in the name of this or that tribe or ideology. 'These texts,' he writes, 'endeavour to wrest from forgetting one of the very great periods in the history of human thought, of language and of dreams, and to recall the crimes committed upon millions.'

Not everyone thanks him for this endeavour. There are those who will declare that such an act of remembrance, such an effort of recuperation of a history and a culture, is not the business of literary criticism, which should, they hold, confine itself to the elucidation of texts. Steiner is a devotee of the text – he has spoken of the intense pleasure and satisfaction to be derived from sitting with a few students and working down through the onion-skin layering of a poem by Celan, a story by Kafka, or a canticle by the Psalmist – but he is also that increasingly rare phenomenon, a humanist critic, certain of the centrality of humankind's place in the world, and of the writer's moral task to inform man's mind and, in however modest a way, to seek to direct his actions.

It is this moral dimension that is the most striking characteristic of his fiction. *Anno Domini*, first published in 1964, and dedicated to Storm Jameson, comprises three novellas, all of which deal with the aftermath of the Second World War. If the adjective had not been exhausted long ago as a mark of literary praise, these narratives could be called powerful. All three deal with the moral crises precipitated by the inhuman circumstances in which humans find themselves in time of war and its aftermath. In the first tale, 'Return No More', Falk, a former German officer who comes back in peacetime to the French village and the family there whose eldest son he had executed, states the predicament of all the book's survivors and walking wounded: 'I am like a sleepwalker looking for that which kept me alive in the daytime. Looking for the one door that opens on the night. Probably I shan't be allowed anywhere near it.'

The door that opens on the night: there is a peculiar and fitting ambiguity to the phrase. The night that fell over Europe between 1939 and 1945 will not be lifted, no matter what guilt is acknowledged or reparation made; but here and there, through this or that chink dragged open with the greatest pain and difficulty, a little light may fall into the darkness. Art is one such aperture. Even in the work of Paul Celan, one of Steiner's most admired poets, who lost his parents in a Nazi labour camp and whose suicide in 1970 was due in large part to his experiences in the war, there is illumination, as in the tiny, free-standing phrase in what is perhaps Celan's darkest poem, 'Tenebrae': '*Es glänzte*' ('It gleamed'). It is this small flicker of that for which hope is too strong a word that Steiner seeks to locate in these fictions.

His most daring venture in the medium is the novel, *The Portage to San Cristobal of A.H.*, a sort of politico-philosophical adventure story which tells of the capture by a group of Israeli Nazi-hunters of 'the one out of hell', Adolf Hitler, who in Steiner's version has not died in the bunker but escaped to the jungles of South America. In the long, crazed tirade by Hitler that closes the book, Steiner expands on one of his abiding themes, which is that the persecution of the Jews throughout history is the result of gentile rage at a race which invented the doctrine of 'an omnipotent, all seeing, yet invisible, impalpable, inconceivable God'. 'The Jew,' declares A. H., 'emptied the world by setting his God apart, immeasurably apart from man's senses,' and thereby made of himself 'a long cancer of unrest'. More blasphemous still, from the point of view of secular Zionism, is the question Steiner puts into Hitler's mouth: 'Perhaps I *am* the Messiah, the true Messiah, the new Sabbatai whose infamous deeds were allowed by God in order to bring His people home.' This is fiction at its most risky.

But Steiner has always been a taker of risks. It is what makes his work, the criticism as well as the fiction, exciting, infuriating, omnivorous, and impossibly ambitious. Few writers working now, at the fag-end of this theory-tormented century, are as sure of *having something to say*. Nothing daunts him. 'Proofs', the novella, or long short story, published in 1992, is an extraordinarily daring meditation on the fall of communism, executed with brio and a kind of muscular relish. The central character is a master proof-reader, known as *professore*, renowned for his exactitude and obsessive attention to detail, who as the story opens discovers that he is going blind. He is also a doctrinaire communist. At the centre of the tale is a long discussion between the *professore* and Father Carlo, another, less rigidly ideologically convinced party-member, after the fall of the Soviet Union. 'At the heart of Communism is the lie,' says the priest. 'The central, axiomatic lie: a kingdom of justice, a classless brotherhood, a release from servitude here and now. In this world. That's the great lie.' To which the *professore* replies:

> Marxism did man supreme honour. The Moses and Jesus and Marx vision of the just earth, of a neighbour's love, of human universality, the abolition of barriers between lands, classes, races, the abolition of tribal hatreds: *that* vision was . . . a huge impatience. But it was more. It was an overestimate of man. A possibly fatal, possibly deranged but none the less magnificent, jubilant overestimate of man. The highest compliment ever paid him. The Church has held man in doleful contempt. He is a fallen creature, doomed to sweat out his life-sentence. Dust to dust. Marxism has taken him to be almost boundless in his capacities, limitless in his horizons, in the leaps of his spirit. A reacher to the stars. Not mired in original sin, but himself original. Our history is nothing but a savage prologue.'

The dialectic in 'Proofs' takes us to the heart of Steiner's work and of his thought. He recognizes that, as in all intellectuals, there is in him an ineradicable duality: on one side the liberal humanist, on the other the ideologue, with all the fierce vision and vaulting impatience that term implies. But what we also see in 'Proofs' and in the three beautiful little *Parables* that accompany it – indeed, in all his books – is the surprising and yet simple truth that George Steiner is, at a fundamental level, and in the broadest sense, a religious writer. The numinous gleam is there throughout the work, from his first published story, that Jamesian tale out of Melville, 'The Deeps of the Sea', to his most recent critical excursus, the title of which is, and not by accident, *Real Presences*. 'God did seem much about in the city these days,' thinks the *professore*, the seeker after proofs. 'So be it. The real battle with Him lay ahead.'

July 1995

The Deeps of the Sea

1

The deeps of the sea were driving Mr Aaron Tefft to the brink of insanity. On the marine charts papering the walls of his study in Salem, the deeps were marked in tints of mounting stridence, from the quiet blue star encircling Sigsbee Deep, a mere 12,425 feet beneath the Gulf of Mexico to the blood-red figure out of the cabbala which circumscribed the world's abyss, the centre of Mr Tefft's nightmares, Mindanao Deep, 35,400 feet below the glint of the sun. Not that Mr Tefft looked often at the map on which this final pit was so manifestly charted. His brain reeled at the thought of that funnel of night in which Everest would pass unnoticed, its snow plume choked six thousand feet under the silence of the sea.

But the bare certainty that Mindanao Deep exists, that its walls of water spin with the diurnal wandering of the earth, clutched at Mr Tefft's heart and compelled him, now and again, to leap up from his frayed leather chair and face the east wall on which he had fixed his maps of the Pacific. And even if twilight in the room, or the hot reflection of the western sun blurred the details, he knew where Mindanao Deep was and could glimpse above it the purple square marking Ramapo Deep, 34,626 feet of typhoon-familiar sea plunging into a sudden darkness off Japan. To Mr Tefft's perturbed imaginings, Magellan's peaceful ocean disguised the several openings of hell – Nero Deep off Guam, Aldrich Deep windward from Kermadek Island, the Milwaukee Depth, a chasm out-measuring the Himalayas.

To Mr Tefft's mind there was no such thing as an unexplained marine disaster. Why had the *Cyclops* never been heard of after she left Barbados on 4 March 1918? Simply because somewhere in her path lurked an undiscovered deep out of which there had risen a quick stirring, a hunger in the maelstrom, sucking the vessel into darkness. First, the *Cyclops* had passed through the region where the light of the sun still penetrates, a dim soft blue; then into the green jungles where the barracudas hunt; deeper yet where absolute night begins and the inhuman cold, but where luminescent rays throw their darts of fire; finally into the unknown where after centuries of dissolution armadas become dust.

But when his imagination drew near that latter region, Mr Tefft would be seized with a violent tremor and would walk to his window, staring into his garden and fixing his dazzled senses on to the lime tree or Katherine Tefft's straw bonnet until, as if drawn by his wild gaze, she would turn about in her wicker chair, smile towards him and say, 'Are you all right, Aaron? Come down and sit by me, my dear.'

Mr Tefft's obsession had a precise form. He was terrorized and haunted by the fear that he would be buried at sea and swept into one of the great deeps by the ocean currents whose paths he knew with exactitude. With each year of service on the bridge of merchant ships and ocean liners, Mr Tefft's knowledge of these currents grew subtler and his conviction that each dead thing floating somewhere in the sea would ultimately be sucked into one of the chasms more firm. Let a man be cast on to the waters even in the shallower reaches of the Atlantic – his body would drift into one of the currents and be borne towards Bermuda and Nares Deep or east of the Azores to Monaco Deep. There was no escaping it. A man must be buried on land. Otherwise the seas shall suck him to their centre and his journey will be more terrifying than any pilgrimage across the floors of hell. That journey burned in Mr Tefft's mind with such material intensity that it had brought a curious light into his eyes and had charred the edges of his soul.

He could remember when the hallucination had first mastered him. It was a night of clamorous south-west gales, after it had been decided in the downstairs parlour that young Aaron would be apprenticed as cabin boy on a Blue Star liner. He had put the blankets over his head to shut out the storm and then he rolled himself tighter and tighter into the darkness until his feet touched the end of the bed and a drowsy warmth enclosed him. It was then that the nightmare came upon him for the first time, the dread sense of suffocation, of being drawn to some hungry centre by a vast undertow. He recalled the struggle for breath, the mad sense of entanglement and, at last, after what seemed an age of pent-up anguish, the burst into the cold of the night. Aaron had rushed to the window and looked at the sea charging inland. But the old acquaintance was gone, shattered. Somewhere beneath its familiar surface lay the deeps, waiting for his carcass, ready to fill his mouth and nostrils with their masses of water before his soul could find its exit. But it was too late for Master Tefft to draw back from his destined profession.

That was some thirty years ago. With each year of service the terror had grown more insidious. But the sea was Mr Tefft's calling and after his holidays spent with Katherine in Salem it drew him as surely as it drew the rivers. Curiously, moreover, at sea the nightmare seemed less frequent. It was in his house that it cried havoc.

It always began in the same manner: Mr Aaron Tefft, First Mate on the *Hibernia*, was stricken by a tropical disease. After a few nights in the sick bay, under the blue lamps and the whirring fan, the First Mate died. Because his disease was infectious and as the nights were dangerously hot, the Captain and the Chief Medical Officer decided to bury Mr Tefft at sea. The sailors were lined up and the Chaplain intoned that splendid litany for the dead. Then the coffin was lifted above the railing, the Master at Arms seized a corner of the flag and gave the command. Down slid the mortal remains of Mr Aaron Tefft. The coffin struck water with a gash of spray, was drawn momentarily towards the propellers of the receding ship and then floated below the surface on the start of its great voyage.

The prelude was gentle: a few hundred feet under the waves there is still light. Storms are heard and the bright stars leave a shimmering trace. Life is multitudinous: cod, tuna and blue marlin turn about the coffin and brush it with their fins. Portuguese men-of-war sail past in transparent armadas, and sea-flowers, green, mauve and smouldering red deck the coffin in ceremonious grief. It is a region where earthly life has its soft echoes: passing liners leave a taste of oil and the pounding of their engines beats as a dim gong. Debris cast overboard sinks by encrusted with stars of salt and when the fish dart downward, the cry of a gull shrills after them.

3

But after a few weeks, the coffin becomes waterlogged, riddled with sea-worms and top-heavy. Then it begins its descent into the depths and with it Mr Tefft's nightmare becomes more ominous. The sea turns to ink: hammer-heads roll their protruding eyes and the swordfish penetrate the lid of the coffin and stab at Mr Tefft's affrighted bones. Albacores and bonnet-head sharks sharpen their teeth on the decaying wood and as it sinks yet deeper, leviathans nudge it with their lazy humps.

Then the coffin breaks open and out tumbles Mr Tefft. Instead of sinking to the bottom and the oblivion of the sand, he is captured by a passing current and driven towards one of the deeps. Struggle as he may, Mr Tefft cannot awake. The dream holds him with obsessive power. The current becomes swifter as it nears the rim of the abyss. Great fish struggle to escape the suction and the sea jungles are bent in the direction of the deep as by a perpetual hurricane. Now he is only seconds from the plunge. Already he can make out the jagged line where the floor of the ocean opens. On the brink a giant squid is fighting. Some of its venomous arms have already been sucked over the edge, but the others are gripping on and trying to cast anchor. Above them the great eyes of the brute spin wearily, but already it is toppling into the abyss.

As Mr Tefft speeds towards loud oblivion, all his drugged senses struggle to awake. But before they can break the nauseous spell, his dreaming mind glimpses the deep. It is a brief but terrible vision: the dark is so absolute that it illuminates, the cold is so intense that it burns. Monstrous beasts, blind titans and the legions of the drowned are hurled downward, and although Mr Tefft is beginning to awake, some part of him, some fragment of that which gives a man joy of life, is left behind.

Such was his recurrent nightmare. And with time he grew convinced that it was no mere fantasm of his disturbed brain, but reality and sober appraisal of what happened to those damned souls sepulchred in the oceans.

4

2

But only in two ways did Mr Tefft betray to the outside world that he possessed some private vision. In all his contracts with successive shipping lines he insisted upon a clause stating that under no circumstances whatever would he be buried at sea. He declared himself ready to provide money for a first-class, airtight coffin and saw to it that the ship's hospital carried plenty of disinfectant. All employers under whom Mr Tefft served would be compelled to put in writing their assurance that in the event of demise his remains would be returned to dry land. Throughout the merchant service this request came to be known as Aaron's clause.

The second clue of his special insight into the deeps of the sea was his will – a document drawn up many years before with the aid of Mr Horace Brindle, an old friend of the family and a good lawyer.

Mr Tefft's fortune was considerable, inherited in part from his fathers with their interests on the high seas and in the inland textile mills. A good deal of it had gone into the Tefft house, a spacious, hoary structure shaped by generations of gales. It was a fine house, alive to the equinoctial changes and the phases of the moon, moaning in its odorous loft even before the October storms had ridden Cape Ann, distending its rafters before the halcyon had, in fact, built a nest in the Sargasso Sea.

The house was full of nooks and labyrinths, with small flights of stairs leading to corridors and rummage rooms which spilled over with maps, old brass fixtures and sermons bound in faded morocco. There were two silver tankards in the master bedroom reputed to bear Revere's mark and on the main stairs hung a clouded mirror, clasped by an eagle and embossed with stars. Mr Brindle judged it a rare piece of 'early Patriotic work'. In front of the house was a small garden, Katherine Tefft's favourite domain. In it were an old lime tree, a laburnum hedge and blackberry bushes. At the western angle stood a stone pillar with a mottled cannon ball on top of it. Neither Mr Tefft nor Mr Brindle, the prince of local antiquarians, knew whence it came. Katherine's view that it was the petrified cranium of one of Aaron's more austere forefathers elicited from her husband merely a shrug of distaste.

Mr Tefft had drawn up his will shortly after his return from a voyage that took him from the Sunda Islands and through the lone Carolines to Guam. It declared that all of his worldly possessions were to belong to Katherine Langley Tefft, his lawfully wedded spouse – but only when and if the mortal remains of her husband had been buried in firm ground. Should this condition be dishonoured in any way or manner, all the property was to go to a charitable institution.

For a long time Mr Tefft had hesitated over which of the many deserving causes he knew of should benefit in the event of Katherine's negligence. Mr Brindle had, in turn, suggested to his client a home for retired clerks, a school for orphans of men lost at sea, and a small mill staffed by young ladies rescued from Satan. Mr Tefft had expressed courteous interest and given small donations, but it was only after a typhoon had driven his impotent ship through the Djailoto Passage and into the roaring blackness of the Pacific, that he discovered precisely which charity would benefit from his burial at sea.

It was a home for the deaf and dumb a few miles from Gloucester. In its white-washed rooms, with their chintz and flowerpots, Mr Tefft found an oasis remote from his nightmare. The deaf could not hear the oceans rushing to the deeps nor the dumb utter their horror at the thought. So Mr Tefft often visited the home, sat with its softly blinking inmates and poured out his visions to them. They would listen, nodding and smiling at the mere presence of this tall gentleman who came with baskets of fruit and addressed their silence with such seriousness. After having spoken his piece, Mr Tefft would feel less afraid. Yes, either his fortune would be Katherine's or – if by some dread negligence he fell a prey to the deeps – it would profit these men and women over whose brains the sea had no spell.

Mr Brindle duly drafted the will. But on reflection, a difficulty arose in his mind. When his client returned from his next voyage, through the Andaman Sea with its lazy watersnakes, he asked him to come around to the office.

'My dear Aaron,' began the lawyer after having admired a small jade figure which Mr Tefft had acquired in Akyab, 'my dear Aaron, there is an oversight in your will and it threatens Katherine with a grave injustice.' Mr Tefft looked at him enquiringly. 'Well, let us suppose that through some marine tragedy or act of war your entire ship went down! There is then no way in which your afflicted widow could satisfy the condition you have imposed. That, surely, is inadmissible and, believe me, your will would be broken by any court in the land.' Mr Brindle sat back with a certain air of pleasure at his acuity.

Mr Tefft was visibly disturbed. 'You are thinking of the *Titanic*?' he demanded. 'Not only of her, Aaron, but of any number of ships that have gone down with their crews. In fact,' and here Mr Brindle positively smiled, 'in fact, I can even think of a case in which the vessel has been found but the crew had vanished.' 'Ah, the *Marie Céleste*,' said Mr Tefft with a pained expression. 'Yes, yes I grant you that one, Horace. It makes no sense, does it? I've puzzled my brains over it often. I wonder whether there was not some madman on board, some inspired lunatic who mesmerized the passengers and crew, who persuaded them to abandon ship in the face of some imaginary peril.' 'That may be a shrewd guess,' said Mr Brindle, 'but it does not resolve our present difficulty.' Mr Tefft promised to give it earnest thought and left. Mr Brindle could hear his steps retreating down the windy street. He rubbed his small hands and put away Starr's *Manual of Marine Law and Insurance*.

Brindle was right. Mr Tefft admitted as much to himself. Even modern ships foundered in typhoons, struck icebergs or collided in impenetrable fog. Walking homeward, Mr Tefft added the possibility that he would go down with an entire ship to the index of his fears. No time for coffins then, only the great list and shudder that hulls suffer when a vessel surrenders to the sea. Then the water coming in the funnels and the vast iron grave nosing down, with her company, as are the centurions of Pompeii, in attitudes of duty. It was conceivable that the sheer tonnage of the ship would, for a long time, anchor it to the sea-floor. The chronometers would mark time for months to come and as the locks weakened on the galleys, bottles of port and burgundy would float into the green world. Moreover, and this point held Mr Tefft's attention, when the time came for the crew to abandon ship in the true sense, when the woodwork had dissolved and the forests of barnacles and polyps bloomed in the state-rooms, surely things would proceed in orderly fashion.

No decent Captain would let his men stumble out chaotically. Discipline runs deeper than salt water. The crew would go forth in order of rank. And although the thought of being drawn towards the nearest deep in company with his Captain and shipmates terrified Mr Tefft, it seemed to him far less terrible than the vision of journeying to hell in solitude. Yes, Brindle had hit on something, and though he might not know it, it was more than a legal quibble. It was a source of hope and comfort to his client. Should the *Hibernia* sink, her First Mate would play the man and go before the Second Mate even into Mindanao Deep.

Mr Tefft hastened to retrace his steps. 'All right, Horace,' he said, 'let my will state unequivocally that if I am lost with an entire ship or with some substantial part of its crew, then Katherine may inherit. Only if I should die alone must she see to it that I am buried in a cemetery.' Mr Brindle nodded approvingly.

3

At first encounter, Mr Tefft had liked John Talford. Later on he remembered that summer afternoon on which the architect had come to tea and had been introduced by Katherine as 'Mr Talford, fresh out of Harvard, and building some of his first houses hereabouts'. The young man had gone quite red, had bowed and had not known where to put his new straw hat. Mr Tefft had liked this gaucherie in him and the unfeigned interest he had evinced in the old house and the maps on which each successive voyage had been inscribed. If he remembered rightly, that first tea took place after a particularly romantic spell of duty.

Mr Tefft was with a tanker fleet at that time and had been through the Suez Canal, along the spice coasts and into the Indian Ocean. The *River Rouge* had been caught by a near-hurricane in the Strait of Malacca, had met the late winter gales in the South China Seas and had finally reached Valparaiso like a battered sheep-dog parted from his flock. He remembered how Talford had listened to his tales, closely and intelligently, and how he had diffidently misquoted *Othello* to say that it must be fine to have such stories to recount to a lovely woman.

And his bow to Katherine had been so stiff and boyish that Mr Tefft had felt old age steal over him all at once.

John Talford settled down near Marblehead and, imperceptibly, became a part of the Tefft household. The young man had little money of his own and Aaron was only too ready to offer him the run of his house and garden during weekends and the drowsy summer months. Talford would arrive, leaping over the hedge with his shabby suitcase and invariable butterfly net, and settle down like a cat, familiar yet independent. After supper, when the mosquitoes sang around the storm maps, he would play chess with Aaron or draw out of him stories of strange fish glimpsed in the Sunda Seas, or make his host say once again why the South Atlantic is the loneliest quarter of the earth. And Katherine would sit in her rocking chair and fix her large eyes on the boy's head. Like Aaron, she looked forward to Talford's visits.

When he was away on his months-long trips, moreover, Mr Tefft treasured the thought that Katherine would be less lonely and that she had someone to invite other than old Horace and the grey ladies from the neighbourhood. He realized that some people might gossip; around Salem that was unavoidable. But it did not trouble him and he presumed that Katherine would be jealous of proprieties. That was why Brindle's postscript to a letter waiting for Aaron in Singapore nettled him and stuck in his mind. It said simply that he – Brindle – was a man of large views, but did not Aaron think it careless of Katherine to travel in young Talford's company? The very next letter from his wife cleared up the matter; she had merely gone to a fine arts exhibition in Boston and the architect had insisted on escorting her. Nevertheless, Aaron wrote delicately but firmly intimating that she must be careful.

But when he returned to Salem, he asked Talford to come as often as he wished. The young man's nimble imagination fascinated him. Suddenly, one blazing afternoon, when they were close-gathered in the shade of the lime tree, he sat up on the grass and said, 'I wonder what a man of my profession might learn from plumbing the sea!' 'What are you driving at?' asked Mr Tefft, drawing on one of the fine pipes he had brought from Java. 'All those splendid legends of sunken cities and towers,' urged Talford. 'I've been cramming up on them. Cantreus in Cardigan Bay, the City of Ys, Tintagel, the Land of

Lyonesse, the Ile Verte, Atlantis – all those legendary citadels sunk beneath the waves. There must be something in it, you know! Some actual remembrance of a kingdom, full of golden places, reaching from Ireland to the Azores and engulfed in some great burst of ocean.'

Mr Tefft watched a trail of bluish smoke and nodded. 'Yes, John, I think there is something in it. Sailors along those western European coasts will tell you that on clear days, at the hour of the angelus, you can hear bells chiming from sunken steeples. And once, when we were near the Cape Verde islands, on a truly pellucid night, I saw what seemed like lights glimmering below us in the sea. The pilot said it was a sunken city reflecting moonlight in its glass and marble. I think it may have been a shoal of luminescent eels. But I am not certain.' Talford hunched forward, wiping perspiration from his eyes. He said, 'Oh yes, there must be something in it!'

Katherine turned towards him from under her parasol and asked, 'What would you be looking for, John?' 'I don't really know,' he conceded. 'Perhaps some magnificent style of architecture unknown to our learned academics. Some style massive as Karnak, yet building with light and not against it, with air and not around it. Perhaps there were master builders in the lost Atlantis, stylists linking, like their engulfed kingdom, the pillars of Ionia and the pyramids of the Toltecs. What a fashion I could launch! Build your houses in Atlantian style! Mr John Talford, sole begetter!' And he drew his head back and laughed till the others joined in.

Katherine smoothed her dress and asked, 'Do you think there are sunken treasures in those places?' 'Who knows?' said Aaron, shielding his eyes against the light. 'Fishermen have brought up ancient tools and bracelets from the Dogger Banks and there are tales of Portuguese trawlers hauling up ancient gold marked in a language no one has deciphered.' 'Ah, that's for me,' said Talford with sudden intensity. 'That's what I need! A cache of sunken treasure! It's no good being poor and young all at once. You work all the days of your youth building stupid little houses to other men's orders and when you have scraped together enough to be your own master – why old age is upon you and the joy of it is stale! Yes, lead me to that sunken wealth and I shall dive for it like a cormorant and haul it up with my teeth!'

Aaron looked at the architect uneasily and Mrs Tefft bent towards the young man. 'John,' she said, 'you must make a rich marriage.' 'Ah, Katherine, do not urge me to do that!' His eyes met hers full on, and Aaron Tefft saw the remote, cold brilliance in them. His pipe had gone out and his hand fumbled as he sought to light it again. But already Talford had jumped to his feet, stretched his gangly arms and stepped into the sunlight. 'Anyway,' he drawled, 'there may be no treasures at the bottom of the sea, but there are some fine butterflies in that meadow. Care to join me?' 'No,' said Katherine, 'it's too hot for a woman of my age to go gallivanting through the fields. But run along and be sure to be on time for supper.' The architect waved to them from beyond the garden as she remarked, 'What a joy he is, Aaron. You liked him from the first. You have good taste, my dear.' And she placed her hands on his knee.

'I did not know he was so eager to get rich,' observed Mr Tefft. 'Ah, but he is, Aaron. It would allow him to see the world and build the things he dreams of. I wish that I could help him. People like ourselves salt money away as if it was pork. John would spend it! Spend it gloriously! Oh, I can see him now, riding through the streets of Rome in his own carriage. There are people born to turn dead money into sheer delight and they are usually the ones that have none. Take me, Aaron. God knows I don't spend much or beautifully. But without our money I would be miserable. I would become a hateful old woman. But when I have it, what good does it do? John could show me all the wonders that it brings.' She was staring into the distance, towards the meadow where Talford and his net could be seen moving like a speck of glass in the bright sun.

Aaron followed her glance. 'Yes,' he confessed, 'John could show you all the wonders. But there wouldn't be anything left. All squandered, all the labour gone!' 'Oh, Aaron,' she countered with a flash of anger, 'whom should we leave it to? You gave me no children!' He rose and walked away from her. She had not thrown that at him in years. It was true, but he had long believed that she was resigned to it. But once more her voice rang hot: 'Whom are you saving it for? You will roam the seas till you are an old man, Aaron. I cannot hold you back. At night I feel the tides drawing you away from me. Ah, how I hate that sea of yours! I hate it, Aaron Tefft! I hate it!'

When she spoke again she was near his elbow. 'I am sorry, my dear.

These are things that need not be said any more. I lost my head, I'm afraid. It is so hot out here. Please, let us go into the house.' She drew him by the arm and as they stepped into the chill parlour he had to lean on her for guidance, so sudden was the dark. But from far away came Talford's voice; he was singing in a high tenor, singing and striding through the fields in defiance of noon.

4

That day's breach widened. Aaron had always realized, in a blurred and distant way, that in the event of his death Katherine would probably marry again. She was younger than he, and dimly he thought it right. But it angered him that she would pick a man to whom the depths of the sea were not a place of terror but a kind of museum, replete with inspiring ruins and hoards of fairy gold. In all these years, he reflected, he had conveyed nothing to her of the vision that consumed his soul. Only a sense of remoteness and absence. His nightmare had left him a stranger not only to himself but to those nearest him, to Horace Brindle who considered him daft, and now to Katherine. John Talford had made him a stranger to his own house, and beneath a placid mien, Aaron Tefft began nursing jealousy and detestation.

He bade Katherine farewell before setting out on his next voyage. 'I trust you will not see too much of Talford. I hate gossip.' Katherine looked at him quickly: 'You need not worry, Aaron. You have no grounds for jealousy.' He snatched at the word. 'Yes, I am jealous! Why should I be ashamed of it? He's young and attractive and is near you when I am far away. And between us there is, of late, so much silence.' 'Of late?' challenged Katherine. 'Have you not heard it before? Or is it that the sea is always pouring down your ears?' Aaron stared at her: 'Why do you say that? What do you mean by it, Katherine?' 'Oh, Aaron, I've slept by you many and many a night and heard all of the Atlantic roaring between us!' 'That is not my fault. Believe me, people who get their living from the sea bring a bit of it with them, even when they are far inland.' 'Ah yes,' she retorted with a laugh, 'I know that's what the poets say. You are like those shells we used to pick up as children. Put your ear to them in the midst of the Sahara and you will hear the tide. But there is no echo in those shells, Aaron! There is no echo, and it is hard to live without one. It is especially hard for a woman.' He turned away and asked flatly, 'Will you be seeing Talford?' 'I may.' 'Don't, Katherine. I ask you not to. I have a right to ask that.' 'You have a right to ask very little, Aaron. Leave me in peace. I shall not bring disgrace on your fine name.' She threw the promise at him. And then it sprang out of him, meanly: 'I know you, Katherine. You won't have Talford or anyone else that's poor. You'll have to wait until I'm dead and buried. You'll just have to wait, my girl!' She turned on him: 'Aaron Tefft, this is the first time in my life – I swear it – that I have hoped I shall not wait too long.' And she left the room.

On his way to New York, Mr Tefft made a point of visiting the home for the deaf and dumb. He was joyously received and sat down among his friends. He spoke to them softly and they watched his lips like a chorus of conspirators. He begged them to keep watch over his house, told them of his hatred of Talford and of his certainty that there was a world of merry noises between the architect and Katherine – noises he could not hear for having so much ocean in his brain and that they could not perceive for being deaf. Ah, but he would keep her to the will! She could not dare relinquish him to the deeps of the sea. And the patients huddled around him and pressed their moist palms in his hand.

On his voyage the image of Katherine obsessed him. Because another man found her desirable, Aaron lamented the lost years at sea, the nights in which he had brooded over his charts instead of being with her. He had a young man's warm dreams and despised himself. Mrs Tefft's letters were in the old style, gay and courteous. She wrote simply that Mr Talford had proposed alterations for the house and would be pleased to submit his drawings to Aaron when the latter came home. This put Aaron Tefft in a state of frenzy. For he could imagine them exploring the house together, tearing it down in their impatient minds, mutilating the things he treasured.

When the *Hibernia* docked in Halifax, her First Mate asked to be allowed immediate leave instead of completing the voyage back to New York. He did not know exactly what he feared, but the compulsion to reach Salem drove him. He laughed like a rescued child at the mere sight of his house and stood before it in the twilight staring, gathering in each familiar detail. He entered and his eyes struck the antique mirror. In one corner of it, distorted but unmistakable, he glimpsed two figures drawing swiftly apart. Immediately thereupon Katherine's voice hurried towards him: 'Aaron! I didn't expect you. What a magnificent surprise!' 'Yes, I suppose it is,' said Aaron fascinated by his own calm. Talford stood in the door for a moment, then advanced his hand outstretched: 'It's good to see you, Sir. I was impatient to show you some of the plans we've made for the house.' Aaron Tefft stared at him as if the architect were babbling in some remote tongue. 'Come,' urged Katherine, 'take your things off. I shall have supper ready in no time.'

After Talford had gone, Aaron went to his study. He remembered some French joke about cuckolds coming home from a long voyage. It had been told him by a petty officer in Brest many years ago. He heard himself laughing at it, but his voice was so loud and alien that he grew afraid. Katherine too must have heard it, for she knocked on his door and entered before he could answer. 'Don't sit up tonight, Aaron. You will make yourself ill staring at those maps.' He drew away feeling her hands on his shoulders. 'Ah,' she said, 'I know why you hurried down from Halifax. I know what you are thinking.' Someone whose calm seemed remote from him and rather terrible was saying, 'Is it true, Katherine?'

'Would you really care?' she countered after a moment of silence. 'More than I dare admit, even to myself.' She heard the pain in him: 'I am sorry it should hurt you so, Aaron, for had it been true it would really have been the least of what is wrong between us.'

He leaped up. 'How can you stand there talking about it in nicely turned phrases? How dare you stand there and deny to my face that you are Talford's mistress? Have you no shame left, Katherine?' 'Aaron,' and her voice seemed doubly quiet after his shouting, 'perhaps I do have little shame left. For if I did, and if I was not an avaricious, spoiled woman, I would have married John before now. As is, I have not even become his mistress.' 'You expect me to believe that,' he demanded. 'I thought you would be intelligent enough to see it for yourself.' And then she smiled strangely and added, 'But I am grown such a stranger to you that you no longer know anything about me.'

Her calm inflamed him: 'Katherine you are lying! You are trying to make a damn fool of me! I saw you! In the name of God, I saw you!' 'What did you see, Aaron? Two people on a settee looking at a blueprint! You are blind, Aaron Tefft! How could you see?' As he struck her he felt the edge of a tooth against his knuckles. She brought her hand to he mouth and stared at him, uncomprehending.

'You are unhappy, Aaron. You will drive yourself mad. But let me warn you. Hang on, hang on to your senses and to your health. For I am waiting to be rich and free. Free, Aaron, free to go inland, to tear down this house, to go a thousand miles from the smell of the sea, to go where there is wheat and dust enough to choke the wind. So hang on, Aaron, and let us see who shall endure!'

5

But hanging on proved difficult. He could read the patience in her eyes, and the tenacity. He wrote to his employers pleading illness and took a leave of absence until the following spring. Katherine travelled to Boston with him and spent lavishly. A new life was burning in her and she seemed to grow younger. One February morning he saw her dancing in the garden, her fine rich hair unbound. She threw her arms high and called to him, 'Come dance with me, Aaron! I shall bewitch this lime tree and it will bear gold.'

He sought to restore at least the old neutrality. But she was too alive and what drew near her seemed to kindle into a new radiance. 'Katherine,' he pleaded, 'let us try to come to an understanding. I was wrong to mistrust you. I know that now.' 'You were not wrong, Aaron, but what does it matter? It is too late for the two of us. Let us live our lives, each in our own way.' And she bought jewels and wore bracelets on her strong arms.

Aaron felt his own vitality ebbing in the struggle and resolved to return to the *Hibernia*. He was to join her in San Francisco on the spring cruise which took her to Hawaii and Japan. On the long train journey across the United States, and in his quarters on board ship, the image of Katherine , as he had last seen her, haunted him. She was standing on the porch, in her great sun-hat, waving to him. But she was actually looking past him, far beyond his own receding figure. He had said, 'Goodbye, Katherine, keep well.' And she had said, 'Oh, I shall, Aaron, I shall, and I want you to do the same. The sea is full of shoals.' And he had come back to ask, 'Will I find you here when I return?' 'I shall be here, Aaron, but only you can tell whether you will find me.'

In his heart, Aaron Tefft believed that she loved Talford and that they were waiting for him to die. Their own vitality was sapping him. It was an unequal contest for the deeps of the sea were drawing at his strength. He raged at the thought of their impatience and even if they were innocent in flesh, he knew that they had made love in their hearts and had lain together, mind to mind. It drove him mad to think on it. It drained him of all feeling save a desire to thwart them, to undo their bright expectations.

In Honolulu, Mr Tefft got ferociously drunk and tore up and down the beach in the moonlight, driven in a donkey-cart by a young woman in a yellow chemise. But neither the night air, nor the witches' sabbath that followed – when the First Mate of the *Hibernia* pranced up the brothel stairs holding a bit in his mouth – brought him relief. What kept him alive now was the thought of the future Mr and Mrs Talford tearing down his house, selling his charts and travelling westward, into some land-strangled place like Kansas to spawn their happy brood. He would defeat them yet, and it filled him with rapture to think of Brindle reading the will and of Katherine being evicted by a patient procession of the deaf and the dumb. Then let Talford woo her! Katherine would turn mean without money, mean and old. Yes, he would defeat them! And through the iridescent night of the mid-Pacific, the *Hibernia* steamed towards Japan.

Mr Tefft was no longer afraid, only desperately tired. His life's great nightmare and recent hatred had gutted him. Now he was like an empty house, its windows staring into blank air. He stood on the bridge and let the waters dazzle him. That night, the *Hibernia* would pass Ramapo Deep. Reflecting on it, Mr Tefft had made what seemed to him an odd discovery: in Latin the word *altus* signified both high and deep. It described Everest as well as the great chasm off Japan. Perhaps, in some transcendent way, vastly beyond his numbed imagining, the two dimensions were the same, or were only infinitesimally apart when measured on a greater plumb-line. The deeps of the sea were mountain summits reversed. Make the earth smooth again and they would vanish. Aaron Tefft treasured the thought and waited for night.

It was near on one in the morning when he went topside. The *Hibernia* was steaming under her blue lights and the sea was like incandescent velvet. When he peered into it, Mr Tefft could perceive the image of the stars, and beneath them yet other stars. And looking upwards, he could not distinguish between the real stars and their images. The night world was like a turning mirror, reality sometimes beneath and sometimes above the muffled pounding of the ship. He checked his watch and glanced at the bridge to make certain that the Second Mate was at his station. Now the stars hung so low and brilliant that the water seemed to burn at the horizon. *Altus* could describe the deeps of the sea – and the most distant constellations.

Mr Aaron Tefft walked swiftly towards the railing.

The Portage to San Cristobal of A.H.

1

– You.

The very old man chewed his lip.

– You. Is it really? *Shema*. In God's name. Look at you. Look at you now. You. The one out of hell.

And saying it the young man, almost a boy, tightened his calves and tried to drive his worn boots into the ground. To be implacable. But the voice shook inside him.

– It is you. Isn't it? We have you. We have you. Simeon is sending the signal. Everyone will know. The whole world. But not yet. We have to get you out of here. Ours. You are ours. You know that, don't you. The living God. Into our hands. He delivered you into our hands. And it came to pass. You.

And the boy forced himself to laugh, but couldn't hear the echo. The still air lay between them, the rain shaking out of its hot, still folds.

– Silent now? Whose voice. They say your voice could.

The boy had never heard it.

– Burn cities. They say that when you spoke. Leaves turning to ash and men weeping. They say that women, just to hear your voice, that women.

He stopped. The last woman they had seen was on the river bank at Jiaro. Endless marches back. With no teeth. Squatting by the green pool and not waving to them.

– Would tear their clothes off, just to hear your voice.

And now the rage came. At last.

– Why don't you speak? Why don't you answer me? They'll make you speak. They'll tear it out of you. Ours. We have you. Thirty years hunting. Kaplan dead. And Weiss and Amsel. Oh, you'll talk. Till we have the skin off you. The soulskin.

The boy was shouting now. Sucking at the air and shouting. The very old man looked up and blinked.

– *Ich?*

2

Ryder passed his fingers over the crack in the leather binding. The lot would have to be oiled again. The recollection of the day on which he bought that particular book came up sharp. At Wells, not far from the wide glory of the cathedral porch. In a shop as brown and fine-grained as the book itself. Then he turned from the shelves and walked to the window.

– Yes. Yes, I know they've been hunting for him. They've never stopped. Started almost immediately after the war. Small parties sworn to get him. To give their lives. Never to rest until he was found. And they've been at it since, I dare say. Lost some men doing it. That shooting business at Paraña. When was it? Late fifties, as I recall. That was when Amsel was killed. Oh, it was never mentioned, of course. But some of your chaps saw him at São Paolo on the way in. One of the best of them, you know. Worked with us during the war. In and out of Poland. Twice, I believe. Trying to get Bomber Command to do something about the rail lines. Wanted me to go to the old man and tell him about the ovens. The old man wouldn't have believed me, you know. Not his kind of war really. So Amsel got out. Wishing us in hell, I imagine. After that he helped run the blockade. I wonder what went wrong at Paraña. He was frightfully good at his job. Alpha, I'd say.

Ryder peered out the window. Though the delicate whorls and shadows of tower and lodge were as familiar to him as breath, he found it difficult to turn back to his two visitors. It struck him that their shoes looked oddly large in the light of the fire.

– As you say, Bennett, they've never believed either us or the Russians. Despite the dentures. They've always thought he decamped a few days before the bunker was surrounded. And that plane did take off, you know, with a passenger. We've got an eyewitness to that. It need not have been Bormann. No proof that he was in Berlin at the time. It could have been someone else. Never a trace of that plane. Anywhere. Just the testimony that it got away through the smoke, and turned south.

Evelyn Ryder was pacing now, rapidly, between the cabinet and the window, the curve of his high shadow brushing over the bookshelves.

– Mark you, I don't think there's much in it. I've been certain from the start. Almost certain. ('Almost is a very good word, Ryder.' It had been Strakes's last and only bit of advice before Ryder went off to give his first tutorial.) I don't think he wanted to get out. Not then. Not with the whole crazy thing blazing around him. Actor to the end. That's the secret of him, you know, mad keen on theatre. Impresario, drama of history and all that. Supreme judge of an audience. Too great an artist in his own insane way to throw away that curtain. And I've gone over the evidence with a fine-tooth comb. Every bit of it. The Russians made off with the chauffeur and the doctor. Did them to death later so far as we know. But the identification looked pretty certain. And there are the teeth.

– We've only got one statement on that. The woman who said she had helped make the plate. I've got a report on her from Smithson. He didn't think she was all that much to go on.

– I know, Bennett, I know, but I'm inclined to believe she's telling the truth. All the evidence points that way. We've mapped his last days in detail. We can account for every hour. We know what he ate, whom he saw, when he last saw the sky. I can tell you when he went to the lavatory if you care to know. If he had really got away someone would have told us. Those that survived came up like frightened rats.

– But suppose

It was Hoving speaking, the younger of the two men who had come up from London on that autumn afternoon. He had not worked with Professor Ryder during the war.

– there was a double. That there was someone whom they wanted us to find in the Chancellery courtyard. It must have been hard enough to tell them apart when alive. If you had only the charred remains, bits of bone. How could you be sure?

– We thought of that. I kept turning it over in my mind. Just possible, of course. But this whole business of a double. Very interesting, I don't deny it. But little we really know about it. Bennett will correct me on this, but there were only two occasions on which we had any real evidence that a double was being used. In Prague once, and then in the last year, during one of those hospital visits on the eastern front. I've thought about the man. Oh, interminably. Tried to get inside a bit of his skin as it were. And I don't see it. Using a double at that point, where it mattered so that the ghastly show be done right. The high note and Valhalla. And how could he be that sure of any other human being, leaving another man to step into his own fire? When everything around him was betrayal.

– He thought he would come back, didn't he? That the Reich would rise again if only he could survive, make his voice heard.

– Quite so. I remember when we first talked about that, Bennett. Just before I went out to look at the stuff. The Barbarossa dream. The storm king in the mountain lair. And out to vengeance when his people call. He may have believed that sometimes. But not at the last. I don't suppose he wanted time to go on, not after him. And history and the cities and the chosen race were to perish with him. In the last fire. Sardanapalus. There's a lot of that in German romantic poetry, you know. And he was a romantic. A romantic mountebank. Mad to the heart but with a brightness –

Ryder stopped, embarrassed. *Le mot juste*. But not exactly. Rather than search for it, he glanced over at Bennett. How Bennett had aged since the war. How heavy the skin lay under his eyes. In that instant Ryder felt the whole of his own body. Time had dealt more lightly with it. He stretched his arm to pour the sherry.

– Are you sure about that signal? Have you got the code right?

He went back to his desk and peered again at the small sheet of blue paper with its familiar blazons of high secrecy.

– As you know, sir,

It was Hoving.

– we've been following the operation for some time. And picked up a fair number of messages as they went up river. We're pretty sure we've got the cipher right. Not a very difficult one, actually. In fact, I'd say it was almost too easy. As if they didn't care who listened in. A Concordance to the Old Testament and a pretty elementary set of permutations. We've got a local chap, in Orosso, one of the last airstrips. A man called Kulken. He's been listening in steadily. Their transmitter isn't much. Signals have been getting weaker. Of course, there is the weather there. Pure hell, I'd imagine. Clouds never off the ground and the wet eating through your wires. No one really knows. No white man that is. So far as we can tell there's never been a party beyond the falls. They call them the Chevaqua falls: the waters of boiling teeth. And they're a thousand miles from nowhere.

– Yes, but this particular message. Garbled.

– Quite. But not hard to reconstruct.

Bennett reached over for it and read slowly.

– First word indecipherable. Then: Praise be to Him. Thou art remembered, O Jerusalem. It looks as if the first word was a short one. Monosyllable, I'd say.

– *Found*.

Ryder was startled at the sharpness of his own voice.

– Yes, I should have thought so. Found.

And Bennett folded the paper and slipped it back in his waistcoat pocket. Sir Evelyn Ryder drummed his fingers against the decanter. The cool exact feel of the glass flattered him.

– It's a pretty queer business, I'll grant you that. And just possible. Just. Million-to-one shot. I'm certain in my own mind that we know what happened. He shot himself in that warren of his and they burned the holy remains in the yard. As fast as they knew how. With the shells detonating all around them. I've never thought that plane could have got very far. The sky was like a furnace in those last days. And I just don't believe he was on it. Not his style. No, Bennett, if you ask me, I don't think the thing is on. They've been tracking down other men out there. Minor butchers. All the chaps that were at Wannsee when the Jewish question was settled. We never laid hands on the half of them. I dare say they've found *somebody*. Very likely it's someone important. Dietrichsen or Sepner or Pirveč, the insane devil who came into Carinthia in '43. And good luck to them. But *him?* I shouldn't have thought so.

The three men were on their feet, their shadows tinged by the reddening coal.

– But you will keep me posted, won't you? Anything you pick up. I'm anxious to know. It brings back the old days, doesn't it, Bennett.

You remember that balls-up in Tunis. I thought they'd have our hide for that.

The slow chimes were ringing for hall. Ryder was halfway into his gown, when he stopped.

– That point you made earlier, Hoving. Suppose

His fine-boned features opened to an expression of gross enchantment.

– that the one they've caught is the double. Yes. Yes. Don't you see it? The poor devil looked so like his master that he wouldn't dare be captured. No one would believe him. He had to get away. To the ends of the earth. If they've got someone it's the shadow, the mask of him. Who must be very old now. And how can *they* believe him? Having crawled a thousand miles through that green hell to fetch him out. If that's what's happened, Bennett, I'd say –

And they started down the spiral staircase.

3

Simeon bit at his broken nail and tasted oil. The anatomy of transistors and close-threaded wires lay before him intricately hurt. The delicate beast corroded by the incessant damp, until its voice had dimmed to an unsteady croak under the larger voice of the rain. He braided the wire around the bent screw, but where the insulation was gone the metal itself seemed to sweat under a fine web of decay. Bending close over the set he could see the spreading life of the fungus. He had cleaned the circuit-boards a dozen times over. Now the soldering came apart in his sweating fingers. He turned his shoulders slightly to get out of Benasseraf's near shadow.

– Did you get through?

– I think so. I'm not sure. There's almost no juice. Look at the wiring here. Rotten all the way through.

– But you think they picked up the signal?

– I hope so. I can't be certain. Look for yourself. Turn the crank

Simeon bent close, listening for the voice of the broken thing.

– and nothing happens. Dead. I don't think I can patch it again. But something did get through. It must have. Part of it, at least.

– If I forget thee, O Jerusalem.

The words sang under Benasseraf's breath.

– They *must* have heard us. If we're to get him out alive. If they didn't get your signal, there'll be no one to get us out. They've heard us, Simeon. The plane will be in San Cristobal. To fly us home. To fly. After the years of walking. Lieber will be there to meet us. He knows now. That we've found him. My God, Simeon, we've found him.

But Simeon wasn't listening. Not after the word Lieber. It brought back to him, with a pressure sudden and more blurring than the rawness of his sweating face, the notion of a world beyond the clearing, beyond the barbed, dripping wall of trees. Emmanuel Lieber, whose fingers they were, often fumbling and ten thousand miles from his arm's length, but his as surely as if he were now standing with them, dreaming the web, spinning and tightening it over the grid of the jungle, directing their racked, unbelieving bodies to the quarry, as he had for thirty years from London, then from Turin (where they had first, in worlds past it seemed, picked up the scent) and now from the small, unmarked office in Lavra Street in Tel Aviv. They were his creatures, the animate embers of his calm, just madness. Of a will so single, so inviolate to any other claim of life, that its thread went through Lieber's sleep producing one incessant dream. That of this capture. Emmanuel Lieber in San Cristobal, waiting at the landing-strip which they had hacked out of the lianas and then covered over with brush and vine leaves. Waiting to fly them out, the lost hunters and their game. An image almost absurd, because of the silence, the necessary absence of Lieber's person and the loud waste of the jungle. There was next to nothing left of Emmanuel Lieber when he crawled out from under the burnt flesh in the death pit of Bialka. And he had never taken the time to mend, so that his will raged visible beneath the grey, splotched skin, and behind the thick glasses. Yet he was beautiful. Simeon remembered that now and was startled. His eyes. Marked by the things seen. As if the fires at Bialka, the children hung alive, the bird droppings glistening on the shorn heads of the dying, had filled Lieber's eyes with a secret light. No, that was kitsch. Not a secret light. But a perception so outside the focus of man's customary vision had given Lieber's broken features and low voice, and the shy rigour of his motions, a piercing strangeness. The stench went from

Lazarus but even long after no one could take their eyes from him.

Beyond Lieber and San Cristobal waited the great tumult of voices, of those who would soon hear the news and not believe.

– Found him, Simeon. Found him.

Now he looked at Benasseraf and the dead weight of the radio-transmitter came back into his shoulders. Yes, they had found him. But the shock of the last hours was too new. And the memory of the near abandonments. First when Stroessner's hooligans had drawn Amsel into a death-trap at Paraña. Then when a whole squad of hunters (my dervishes, said Lieber) had disappeared, almost without human trace, in the swamplands south of the Cordilla Nera. Was his the last party left? Simeon was no longer certain. And what of their own surrenders, of the innumerable times they had resolved to turn back, doubting, deriding the quiet mania of Lieber's conviction? Only a year ago, not five hundred miles in from the coast, when Father Giron had explained to them, speaking out of the knowledge of his own skin, parchment yellow and bruised by countless journeys, that no man, be he devil's spawn, could live in the unmapped quicksand and green bogs beyond the falls. And a hundred times after that. Nearly every day. When Benasseraf fell ill in the encampment at the headwaters of the Bororo and danced in the heat of his fever. When the rains, black stampedes of water, swept away their supplies, split their boots open as with rat's teeth and all but lashed the clothing off their backs. When the maps went mute.

As they did about two hundred miles south-south-west of Jiaro. Where cartographers had marked, with pale-blue strokes and wavelets, a blank of uncharted swampland. No man could live beyond the falls, in the quaking marsh and sulphurous air. So said Father Giron, and the Chava Indians who had watched them pass with hungry derision. But had lent them a guide, a hollow-ribbed heron of a creature who could throw slivers of bark on to the green scum of the morass and tell where there was footing.

Perhaps that had been the nearest point to rout. When, only ten days ago, yet it seemed to Simeon much much longer, the Indian had melted away from them, refusing to wade a step further into the stinking water, his mouth set with panic. And the five of them had stood, up to the armpits in the green heat of the living mud, the swamp sucking at their blistered skins like the pale-bellied leeches. They had stood single file, trying to hold their packs over their heads, the midges swarming at their swollen eyelids. And Simeon knew that if he faced about, if he turned his shoulders under the suffocating canvas of dead, poisoned air, they would turn back, to Jiaro, and the crossing of the Cordillera and the wonder of cold beer and open sky that waited at San Cristobal. The next step had been everything. Hosannah, though he had almost fallen into the shifting ooze and his bones had frozen at the sudden slither of the snake. He had taken that step because Lieber was at his back. Whose voice, as they read the cipher, insisted, with an insistence deeper, more binding than even the swamp, that the man was in there, that this was his lair and desolation, that another thirty miles.

They had crawled those thirty miles. Inchwise. On their knees and with loosening bowels. Until the clearing, and the point of light. The insect-swarming oil lamp in his window.

– Yes. We've found him. Praise be to God and peace on our souls.

But as he said it and reached out to touch Benasseraf's hand, Simeon knew that he was deceiving himself. About the exhaustions and physical barriers that had so nearly made them turn back. It had not been Amsel's death, or the disappearance of Kaplan, or the hideousness of jungle and swamp. These things had made them maniacs and browned skeletons. But the true obstacle, each of them carrying it inside himself like hidden leprosy, was far greater. Indifference. Common sense with its fine, sharp bite. A boredom with vengeance so acute that it rose in them, during the fever marches or stinging nights, like the taste of vomit. So what? Even if he is alive. Why drag the aged swine out of this stretch of hell? Who cares, now, thirty years after, or is it more? We're doing his bidding here, emptying our lives in this stinking jungle when we could be building, when we could be knitting ourselves new and forgetting. No one cares any more. Even if we find him alive, if we get him out, who'll want the stinking carcass? And what will they do to him? He's no more than a poisonous ghost now, and we're mad to hunt him down. Mad as he is. Exactly what is it he did to man? What is it they say he did? Who will be left alive to remember?

They had not spoken these sentences aloud. Not since they had taken the oath just before their ship sailed from Genoa, Lieber touching each one of them on the forehead and then lost in the crowd at the bottom of the gangplank. To find him, be it at the cost of their lives. Not to return until they had found him or had absolute proof that he was dead. Simeon remembered the plangent tumult of Italian partings. And John Asher, next to him at the railing, saying: Immigrants, like ourselves. We're immigrants out of life.

So they had not said any of these things out loud. But had thought them so intensely, with such deepening bitterness, that Simeon could make out each question, doubt, crisis of self-mockery or forgetting, in their sleeping faces, in their rebellious stumbling, in the rages that had all but torn them apart during the final year of the chase.

– It was time we did. High time.

Benasseraf eased the strap on his sweat-blackened shirt and nodded. It seemed to Simeon that they had spoken very little of late. All of them. As if they were afraid of the poisoned gnats that might enter their mouths. But he was trying to get the thing clear, those last hours and the capture. As Lieber had dreamed it. It was in his dream that they had moved, in the insane, unwavering certitude of Lieber's dream. Right to the edge of the clearing.

They had stumbled on it at twilight, the sudden break of sky over the circle of charred stumps. And crouched at the rim, in the insect-loud grass, like men overwhelmed. They had crouched the whole night through, their bones knotted by the cold breath of the swamp. Not saying a word. Their thoughts numb at the fantastic nearness of the end. Believing Lieber now, yet unable to believe that he had actually mapped this minute rent in the forest, that he had drawn this last small circle around the man, unravelling the sinuous logic of his successive flights, deeper and deeper into the interior, from one foul cover to the next. They had crouched there till the sour note of a tucca bird signalled the dim, wet rise of day. Two men had come out of the hut. An old man, one-armed and in a grey tunic, and a much younger, dark-faced guard, carrying a fowling-piece, which he pointed vaguely at the sky before sitting down.

Isaac Amsel, to whom the enterprise had become a vengeance too narrow, too selfish, and whom they had tried to send back since first he hung around them in the marshalling yard at São Paolo, rushed forward, against Simeon's order. And fired. So that the sound of the shot rebounded in an absurd, thunderous echo from the green wall of the forest. The guard had risen, spun histrionically and fallen dead. What had killed the other man as he scratched at the thin bed of lettuce was not clear. Fright, perhaps, or the end of the long wait.

They had raced across the open ground, each momentarily lost to the others. Mindless of Lieber's warnings, of the curare-tipped staves which they found outside the abode in the Sangra cañon, of the trip-wires and anti-personnel mines sown around the first bunker, his opulent lair in the hills above Paraña.

There had in fact been a wire, and Asher tripped over it. But it ended in a pit of sodden leaves, the firing-pin long since rotten.

Beyond Benasseraf's heavy breathing, the fever was often at him, Simeon could hear the click of the spade. Striking the patch of gravel which was the lone bit of solid ground in the waterlogged clearing. They were burying the old gardener and the man with the gun. There was no ammunition. They knew that now. He had spent the last shot, long ago perhaps, on the marmots and rubber-bellied lizards whose blueish bones they had found behind the stove.

Simeon and Benasseraf walked over to the grave. Asher was smoothing down the broken grass and grey mud. The grave was shallow and Simeon could make out the contour of the guard's foot. It was slightly deformed and where the spade had struck the toes had come wide apart. He could not take his eyes off the vague shape and it filled his mind with ugly, tattered images. They cut across the film of sweat which seemed to close around him at every motion and the raw edge of the transmitter pressing on the small of his back. Asher looked up.

– Did you get through, *Capitano*?

– I think so. Not the whole of it. But enough to let them know.

He wanted to explain about the transmitter and the corroded generator coils. But Elie Barach had begun his prayers for the dead. Had stepped back from the hurried pit and begun the rise and fall of his prayer. Over the months of heat and jungle drippings, the forest sticking to them like resin, Barach's cap had become a blacker patch in the tangled blackness of his hair. The morning shone through his threadbare shawl and his body swayed gently with the words. His eyes were closed and he appeared to move outward with the tide of his prayer, easily, being so light a guest in his own flesh.

– And may You take their souls into Your keeping. And give rest unto those who had none upon earth. May they find peace who brought none. And forgiveness who so need it. Amen.

But the prayer began anew.

– For Thou alone art judge. Thine is the vengeance and Thine the pardon. It behooves not us. It is not ours. Guard us, O Lord, from the temptations of righteousness. Guard us from certitude. From dealing in Thy name when that name, hallowed be it, is a secret beyond secrets. *Selah*. From doing Thy will when we know it not. Or only, O God, such small part of it. Make us thine instrument but not Thy replacers. For we stand in exceeding peril. We who have striven so long that we have become our single purpose. Who are less than we were because Thou has given us beyond our deserving. Do not ask of us, O Lord, that we do vengeance or show mercy. The task is greater than we are. It passes understanding. And whom Thou hast now delivered into our hands, may he be Thine utterly. Amen.

– Yes, said Simeon,

– they must have picked up our call. Can you imagine Lieber. In this hour, when he knows.

– If we manage to get him out. To bring him out alive.

And Asher repeated it, giving a last tug at his spade.

If he did it a little less well, thought Benasseraf, if the words were a little less round. Like the gold coins when we dug up the jar in Caesarea.

Elie passed his hands over his moist forehead and smiled, still in the wake of his prayer.

– We'll get him out. If we have to carry him. Every stinking mile.

Benasseraf spoke loudly.

– Just as we said in our oath. With our lives if need be. We'll hand him over to Lieber. If he has to ride on our backs to get there.

– That might be the only way.

Asher said it brushing the rust-grey hair out of his eyes.

– Because I don't see him walking. Not far. He's an old man now. I thought of that last night, when we were in the grass, freezing our balls off. Born in 1889. That's it, isn't it? It says so on Lieber's warrant. I remembered that last night. Walk through the swamp, at his age?

– And over the moraine, said Elie.

– And how strong do you think he is? I mean, look at what they've been eating. Mice and raw beans and lots of muck scratched off the trees. We'll be lucky if we can *carry* him out alive. He shakes, even out here in the sun.

He said it without looking back at the hut.

– Ninety years old. That's as old as he is. Men and women ninety years old. The crippled and the blind and the ones spitting blood. They made them walk barefoot, over the cobbles. And whoever fell behind, they threw water over their feet. So that they would freeze to the stones. And stand there till they died. Burning alive in their skins. At Chelmno, there was a rabbi, a man of wonders. A hundred years old. And they tore out his tongue

Benasseraf brought his hands to his mouth.

– and made him hold it before him, and walk. A mile. More than that. Till he came to the fire-pit. And they told him: Sing. Sing, you man of wonder.

He went on picturing the device in his own mind.

– When he can't walk, we'll carry him. In a litter. We can use one of the hammocks and tie it between two poles. We'll put a poncho on top to keep his carcass dry. We'll take turns carrying him. Like the ark.

– And dance before it, said Asher.

– Are you being serious, Ben? Carry a man through the swamp, when we can barely keep our heads above the filth? And Elie is right. What of the rock-fall? Most of our ropes are gone. Swept down the bloody falls or torn to shreds. It can take hours to go a hundred yards in that stinging hell. Imagine trying to get a hammock through. He isn't all that light. There's a paunch on the bleeding old ghost. No. We need help. And fast.

Simeon looked up at Asher, entranced, as so often, by his sober fantasies.

– They've got to get supplies to us. Blankets, guy-ropes, Benzedrine, iodine, crampons, a new transmitter, we could do with two more sleeping-bags, batteries are rotten in two of the flashlights, quinine. The lot. We need cocoa and fishing-lines. I've got one decent lure left. And we could do with more fuel for the Primus. I say we wait here, until they drop some of the stuff. And skirt the swamp. I don't know that we can get ourselves back through that ordure, let alone carry the old devil. Track along the western edge, until we find open ground. I don't think we can make San Cristobal. Not in a month of Sundays. It's all very well on Lieber's map. Red arrow in and blue arrow out. He hasn't been here. He hasn't seen the poisonous muck. Or the Chavas. If we try to slog out there won't be enough left of our bones to fill a matchbox. Look here, Capo, you try and get a supply drop, and then we can make it to the scrub. And wait till they lift us out. Or ferry him at least. Look at the rabbi's boots. I can see his bleeding corns.

Elie smiled and shifted his foot.

– We'd be mad to try. Stark raving mad. And he'd die on us inside a week. Turn over and die like a bloated water-rat. They owe us that much. I mean we've found him, haven't we? Found him alive at the bottom of nowhere. The four of us and that nit. Why shouldn't they get us out? Helicopters, medics, the whole shooting-match. To drown in that hell bog? After all this. After we've gone and dug him up alive. Or freeze to death on the bloody col? I won't do it.

– Even if I can get the transmitter working

Elie leaned forward and interrupted Simeon.

– they won't come for us. No one will. Perhaps Emmanuel will be waiting in San Cristobal. Perhaps he won't even be there. We don't know that he's still alive. That his life has outlasted our news. There was only one thing left of him: his waiting. That was his soul and nerve and bone. Just like this man. Waiting. He too must have known that we would find him, some day, when he closed his eyes for an instant at the bottom of his warren. Two men will know that Simeon was not lying when he sent his message. He and Lieber. Who else will believe us? Even if they remember, why should they believe that the dead come to life, and in a hammock yet, carried out of the jungle. Even before we left they thought Emmanuel was sick in the head, that he had death and ashes in his brain. They wouldn't give him any help. Our own people. 'Stop it, Lieber. Stop telling ghost stories. The beast is dead. Those rumours from the Chaco, those spoors in Paraguay, the telephoto bought from Major Gomez – and at what a staggering price, dear Lieber – all journalist's gossip. Trash. Someone trying to make a fool of us or start a diplomatic incident. Look what it's got us. Amsel murdered. The best agent we had. A professional, Lieber, and no offence meant. Murdered in a mousetrap. And for what? A wild whisper, a map which is probably a fake. Stop haunting us. Stop waiting outside our offices. We won't back you another inch. Not a penny. No more false papers and consular immunities. *Genug*, Emmanuel. If you find any men left *meschuga* enough to believe you, to go out there on a fool's errand, we don't want to know about it. If they die, their blood be on your head.' That's what they said to Lieber. In the Ministry, at Military Intelligence, wherever he turned. 'You're crazy, Lieber. Get out of the sun.' If Emmanuel got our message, if he's still alive, he will meet us. His boots may be shabbier than mine. But he'll meet us. The others. May God wake them.

Asher caught the note of invocation: – and flay them alive.

Simeon marked the words pouring out after the long quiet. Gideon Benasseraf, John Asher, Elie Barach. Taking on their own shapes again in the better light of late morning. He spoke slowly, making them draw near.

– It isn't that. Or it wouldn't be now. There *would* be help. And a helicopter coming in as far as Jiaro. If the news could be released. Oh, if everyone knew, there'd be an airfield dug here, bigger than Lod. And roads bulldozed. And a million television cameras. And a Hilton. They wouldn't believe us, not at first, and not all of them. But if they heard his voice and we described just what he looks like, they'd come like locusts. And take him from us. That's the whole point. They'd take him to New York or Moscow or Nuremberg. And we'd be lucky if they allowed us to stand in the anteroom peering over a million heads. That's how it is in the museum, at Auschwitz. 'Here perished the heroic Polish combatants against Fascism. Here the vanguard of the heroic Communist partisans were executed.' And then in the corner: 'Eighty Jewish women from the Warsaw Postal Service were deported here and died.' *Eighty*. No. He'd be theirs to try, or parade around the world, or pension off. They wouldn't let us near him. We'd have waded up to our eyes in the filth and death of this place, so that *they* could take him out. That's what Lieber fears most. And he's right. That story about the man and the large fish. The largest ever. But the sharks hammering at it, stripping it to the bone before he could reach the dock. If we call for help, if Lieber went to the Ministry and they were to send planes to get us out, or drop supplies, everyone would know. From São Paolo to Lima. And swarm at us. To take him away, to kick us on to the garbage heap. 'Now we take over. This is too big for you to handle. Much too big. Mr Hurok will handle it. And the International Court. We might call you to say your piece. Or we might not. Off with you now. No loitering.' Eighty women. Subtract eighty from six million, and what do you get? Zero. The mathematics of the *goy*. *This* is the time when we must move fast, and keep most silent, and be secret to all. Don't you see? Until we have him home. Then go to the four corners of the city and blow your trumpets. But not now. If they knew we had him, if they could follow us in here, they wouldn't leave us his shadow.

Simeon looked up, with sudden comfort, at the steaming mist.

– The way we came? There must be another way. We won't get out alive. Not any of us.

– I haven't had time to think about it, Gideon. There may be another route. At least for part of the way.

He unfolded the map from its waterproof case.

– But not at the start. The swamp is everywhere around us. That's why he came here. Because no man could follow. Except through the black water and the quicksand. He crouched in the dead centre, on this mud bank, and we've got to wade through the thing if we want to get out.

– Bleeding Jesus. I'd rather rot here.

Asher's terminology, and the rich variants on it, always brought an elfin, secret expression to Elie Barach's face.

– Look for yourself. There's no other way. And after that we've got to reach Jiaro and see what we can dig up of our stores. I've left some spare circuit-boards there, and wiring.

– Supper for termites, said Asher.

Simeon was bending over the map.

– But after Jiaro there *might* be an easier way. If we could turn the falls on the north side and avoid that portage. Here. About half a degree south of the Querracho. Do you remember what Giron said? That there was some kind of very large ruin in the valley. A lost city. Known to the Indians, and bits of it seen from the air. There was thought to be a road leading from it, stone slabs laid down by the

Mayanos and leading to the quarries, to the blue-stone quarries here, just above Orosso. If there's any kind of paving, it'll be easier to get through. And if we have to carry him –

– Isn't there a landing-strip at Orosso?

Benasseraf pointed at the faintly drawn propeller in the middle of the green hatchings.

– I think so. Probably used by surveyors. But Lieber warned us not to use it. We'd be seen there. And we wouldn't have the range to fly out. It's got to be San Cristobal.

– That means the mountains, and as he said it, Barach swayed on his heels.

– The rock-fall, and the two pitches below the col. Without crampons or axes. And carrying the old swine on our backs. You're mad.

Simeon nodded, puzzled by his own gaiety, by the delight he took in Asher's rebellious good sense.

– We'll rest up somewhere outside Orosso. Perhaps there's another track. To the right of the glacier. Perhaps we don't need to go as high. And once we're over that

His finger straightened out to touch San Cristobal. Though the easy unbending was a lie. The breadth of his oil-blackened nail covered ten thousand steps. The shadow of his finger spanned interminable hours hacking through jungle, thick as leather, and marching through the razor grass of the uplands. The map was an ambush, set to catch dreams. Extended eastward from the swamp his hand reached well into the blue void of the South Pacific, into safety and the long flight home. It should not be so easy to place a hand across a map where our feet must follow. An hour of sweat and fear to a thousandth of an inch.

– we're almost in reach. One or two of us can go ahead to contact Lieber. You and the boy. We'll see. Once we're off the mountains

– the soulskin.

The word was so loud and ludicrous that the four men started up from the map and turned to look at the hut. Isaac Amsel saw them staring at him, flushed, and stepped back from his prisoner.

Simeon folded the map carefully, cradled the transmitter against his back and walked slowly towards the door of the hut. The others followed. He had not yet looked at the man. Not directly. He knew he would have to now. In his throat the air seemed to close like a fist. The sweat lay cold and prickly at the corners of his mouth. He was near to gagging, but bound himself tight lest he make some stupid, irremediable gesture.

The old man had been looking at the boy. Seeing Simeon's shadow lengthen towards him he turned. And raised his head. Simeon choked. The caged air hammered at his ribs. He saw the man's eyes. For the first time. He saw the grey-green pupils under the puffed lids and the vein which rimmed them like a livid thread. The eyes were dead. But suddenly, in the cold ash, a minute, sharp crystal of light blazed. Then the grey smoke passed again over the man's glance. But in that instant Simeon found breath. The voice sprang out of him harsh and pent-up. The words spoke him and he trembled.

– AUFSTEHEN. LOS. I have a warrant here. Born 20 April, 1889. In the name of man. For crimes herewith listed. In the face of God. AUFSTEHEN. We're starting out. We're starting now. To take you home, Herr Hitler.

4

Because it had been a long time, a very long time, since he had travelled in an official car, and because his early-morning cigarette had a tart, pleasant edge, Nikolai Maximovitch Gruzdev had forgotten his fear. Or folded it somewhere in the back of his mind, away from the brilliance of the windows flashing by in the morning sun and the epaulettes of his escort. The fear came back as they passed under the sudden bar of shadow at the gates. But it was not wholly unpleasant, and ascending in the silent lift, Nikolai Maximovitch felt his bowels shift comfortably.

Offices had not changed very much since his day, but the file cabinets were of a much improved model and there were two vases with flowers on the window-sill. Both men rose, momentarily cutting out the morning brightness, and even across the wide desk Gruzdev could smell the prickling scent of shaving lotion. His mind dwelt on that for an instant. Then he realized, with embarrassment, that he was meant to sit down.

The desk was heaped with dossiers. But their bright plastic tabs were entirely different from those he had known.

– It was good of you to come, Nikolai Maximovitch,

The shorter man spoke first.

– so early in the morning. I regret the inconvenience. The matter is of no great importance.

– No. I understand. Of course.

The moment he said these words, not knowing why he had spoken, and realizing how inept, how damaging they might prove, Gruzdev felt afraid. It was an abrupt fear near to panic. Worse than any he had known since the first afternoon of the interrogation. But the short man, only his shoulders seemed impressive, went on as if nothing had been said.

– A few small details. Matters of history. We are historians here, Nikolai Maximovitch. Bookworms. All these mountains of paper.

He swept his hand delicately over the desk.

– From time to time we try to do a house-cleaning. To put a period to things. That is what historians should do. Put to rest. Do you agree?

The fear had ebbed. Gruzdev lit a fresh cigarette and inhaled. He did not do that often. Not before lunch.

– That is an interesting way of putting it. I agree, Comrade Colonel. Naturally.

– Where there is untidiness we must sometimes go back over things. Small things.

– Yes. The small things.

Colonel Shepilov looked at his visitor. But Gruzdev was staring past him, at the lit, cloudless sky. And thinking. Why is it so like Gogol? All such interviews. Even when death is very near. Everyone speaks as if they were quoting Gogol. The wonder of it carried his mind back. During the journey, and after, he had clung to the thought. It would all end bearably because Gogol had imagined it far ahead. They were merely acting it out. *The small things*. It was a quotation, of course. But from which tale? He would look it up, as soon as he came home.

– As I said, Nikolai Maximovitch, it is good of you to come and assist us. In one or two small points. Please feel at ease. The sun is very bright this morning. The light. I trust it does not inconvenience you.

Shepilov riffled his papers and paused, his thumb bearing heavily on the margin of a photostat.

– There are a few details we should like to verify. In the testimony you gave. Particularly before the 'interrogations'.

– But that was thirty years ago, Comrade Colonel. My memory is no longer of the best.

Gruzdev said it not because it was relevant, but because it seemed the proper form.

– We understand that. But the file is here. I have your signature before me. It is quite plain.

And he turned to the other man, who was a good deal taller than he, wore a brown suit and sometimes drew a handkerchief from his breast pocket to wipe the corner of his mouth.

– Tell us, Nikolai Maximovitch, why were you so certain? We are historians, not psychologists. We are puzzled. Your certitude interests us greatly.

– I was wrong, said Gruzdev. Surely that too is in your file. I was utterly mistaken. And made a full statement of my errors. You will find it in the court records. If you will allow me, Comrade Colonel

But he did not reach out towards the desk.

– Even after the two confrontations with Mengershausen. Even after SS adjutant Rattenhuber confirmed to you, in front of witnesses, that Hitler and the woman Braun had killed themselves, that he had helped burn their bodies. Here is a transcript of your interview with Heinz Linge, Hitler's valet. Your initials are at the right-hand lower corner of each page, Nikolai Maximovitch. 'Linge is in error. I continue to believe that the body shown me by Captain Fyodor Pavlovich Vassiliki on 11 May last is not that of Adolf Hitler.' And there is more of this.

Shepilov's fingers tugged at a bundle of foolscap.

– Yes. Here is the testimony of SS man Otto Guensche. A remarkable witness. He had helped carry the bodies into the yard. And what do I read here. 'Dr Nikolai Maximovitch Gruzdev affirms that the said Otto Guensche is lying or mistaken.' Your certitude, Gruzdev. It puzzles me.

– Comrade Colonel, I beg to observe

The voice was flat and servile. They had all acquired it, whether tenor or bass, during the interrogations. It bound them together however diverse their natural tone. Hearing it again in his own mouth, the last syllable of each word overstressed, Gruzdev flinched. He had not known that that voice remained in his throat, packed away with its echoes of pain and humiliation, but so ready for use.

– I beg to observe that all the denials you refer to, all my erroneous depositions, occurred during the preliminary inquiries. Indeed, the extent of my confusion is shown by the improper designation I then gave to witness Rattenhuber. The rank was not adjutant but *Brigadenführer*. I feel certain, Comrade Colonel, that the matter was corrected in my later statements.

Suddenly he realized that he remembered every detail. Like sharp pebbles in a shoe. His memory had betrayed him with a fierce precision. It would not mend, though ten years had passed since his return from the camp. Gruzdev felt sweat itching under his thin beard.

– You withdrew all these statements subsequently. That is correct. You concurred unreservedly in the findings of the official tribunal: to wit, that the bodies of Hitler and the woman Braun had been identified beyond any possible doubt by Captain Vassiliki and dental mechanic Fritz Echtmann. Asked to give reasons for your earlier obstinacy, you admitted that propaganda originating from western intelligence services had infiltrated General Chuikov's staff and your own department. The fullness of your testimony and the completeness of your retraction were taken into account when sentence was passed.

– Is all this necessary, Comrade Colonel?

The question had seemed unanswerable, even to himself, when it came from Gruzdev's blood-stained mouth during the last of the interrogations, and innumerable times thereafter, in the trains and in the arctic clearing. Why ask it again? But Shepilov seemed pleased, as if some prefatory, laborious rite of courtesy had been absolved.

– No. It is, as you say Nikolai Maximovitch, unnecessary. We are busy men, you and I, not children. Your later testimony, your recantations, the report you submitted on Fascist influences in the official American war history,

Shepilov's palm brushed idly over the green-covered notebook, the child's exercise book in which Gruzdev had written his additional confessions in the fourth winter at Vorkuta, and seeing it there, so casually naked, as had been his brain and body under the lights of the barrack, Gruzdev felt a hammering in his throat. He couldn't speak. Not without crying out.

– all these things are not of much concern to us, now. The illegality of certain proceedings is, unfortunately, quite plain. The persuasions used to make you change your mind . . . but surely there is no need to go into that. To remember certain things too well is wasteful. What interests us now

Shepilov bent forward for the first time, shifting out of the direct brilliance of the morning light.

– are your reasons at the start. Before you were questioned by Major Berkoff and his assistants. What made you so certain that Hitler was alive, that all the evidence submitted to your medical judgement was inadequate? 'The documents as enumerated above, together with my own examination, suggest to me that the evidence points to a very different conclusion.' These are your own words, Comrade Doctor, recorded by the secretary of the commission of preliminary investigation on 17 June.

Who was the man in the brown suit? Trying to remember, Gruzdev frowned.

– These matters happened some years ago. We understand that. But the Historical Commission attaches importance to your present answers. Bear that in mind.

Why *had* he been so certain?

– I must ask the Comrade Colonel to remember that Stalin himself believed that Hitler had survived. He stated at the Potsdam conference that Hitler was being sheltered by Fascism in Spain or Latin America. When Major Berkoff informed me that Stalin had changed his mind, my last doubts were resolved.

The informing had been graphic. It burned still, when the weather changed, in Gruzdev's knit fingers. Sometimes it went through his kidneys like a long needle.

– There is no need to extend this inquiry beyond our competence. It is your reasons, not Stalin's, that concern us. Please feel free to continue smoking.

Gruzdev's cigarette had gone out. Why had he been so certain? Even after the first beating. It puzzled him now. Not because his

39

recollections were vague, but because their exactitude had a distant finality.

– I do not recall the full details, Comrade Colonel. How could I?

After which he said something that seemed to come from another language, possibly lost.

– The cold, Colonel Shepilov. It stays in the brain.

– I was there too, said Shepilov, and waited.

– You were there too.

Gruzdev repeated the words mechanically. The taste of tobacco had turned acid on his lips. He had breakfasted too hurriedly, standing up, with the man in the epaulettes watching.

– Why was I so obstinate? It is strange, to be sure. I remember how they brought in the dentist.

– Käte Heusemann.

– Yes. Heusemann. And she said I was mad. That I knew nothing about dental fittings. But that was the point. If a man shoots himself in the mouth his dentures will be smashed, or at least damaged. If the angle of trajectory was such as the X-rays showed, and Captain Vassiliki affirmed, then the bridge on the upper jaw and the window-crown on the incisor would almost certainly have been broken. The fittings shown to me were intact, with the exception of some crude scratches on the metal clip. It was these scratches that stuck in my mind. They were white at the edges, as if they had been made very recently, by a nail-file and in haste. Then there was the right arm. We know from Dr Morell's files precisely where Hitler's arm was injured in the 21 July explosion, and how the bones set. On the body submitted to my department for autopsy, the right arm was badly charred. The wrist and elbow-joint were like powdered ash. So my reconstruction could only be partial. But it seemed to accord too perfectly with the pathology as recorded by Morell. This is difficult to explain. But evidence that is too clear makes one uneasy. The cracks in the metacarpus, the sutures, the chipping of the bone immediately below the shoulder, were too perfectly apparent. Things that mend naturally, or that retain a partial dislocation, are more blurred. There are always markings and local complications which do not fit the case. Only death composes a perfectly coherent image. Again, as with the dental fittings, it seemed possible – did I say more than that? – that the lesions had been recently and deliberately plotted. That we were meant to observe them and be deceived. Forensic medicine is well acquainted with such devices: toxic substances introduced where there has been no actual poisoning, bones broken after the fact to produce false leads, scars incised in dead tissue in order to conceal identity or suggest false identity. One of my first cases, in Kharkov. I was very young then, and did not know that a tattoo has a peculiar yellowness at the edges when it has been made recently, and on a dead man. I was lucky that Trenin was in charge of the case. Wise as an old fox. He taught me everything. I hear him now: 'When the facts are too plain, Nikolai Maximovitch, there is something amiss. There's more in heaven and earth, Horatio. The blind can smell dirt before the wind rises.'

And seeing Trenin before him, in his olive-drab cashmere shawl, Gruzdev paused, enchanted. Shepilov looked up from the dossier and said nothing.

– What else can I tell you, Comrade Colonel? It is all there in the records of the preliminary inquiry. The dental fittings and certain aspects of the brachial anatomy. Those were the points which misled me. I withdrew my objections entirely during the hearings before the tribunal.

– But today. Speaking freely, Doctor. As a historian. What would you say now?

The man in the brown suit had spoken so softly that Gruzdev bent forward, almost bowing. And the man's voice, though muffled by the handkerchief at the corner of his mouth, seemed to come out of some dim but irrevocable remembrance, out of a distant gallery or mine-shaft of hellish pain. Gruzdev almost panicked.

– Today? I do not understand. What is it you gentlemen wish me to say? I am an old man, Comrade Colonel. I have made a complete statement of my errors. Several times.

Then his eyes glimpsed the book, with its familiar red dust-jacket, under a sheaf of papers on Shepilov's desk. He could scarcely contain his relief.

– Academician Ryder's book. I see you have it on your desk, Comrade Colonel. A most remarkable work. The English bloodhound. A veritable Sherlock Holmes. Its account of Hitler's last days is

41

conclusive. Had I known at the time of Academician Ryder's analysis, I would not have been so foolish.

The voice bore in on Gruzdev, nearly inaudible.

– Ryder and British Intelligence are of no concern to us. You will answer my question. Thinking back on all the evidence, do you regard it as possible that you were right? That the body shown to you by Captain Vassiliki's detail was not that of Adolf Hitler?

You will answer my question. Gruzdev knew now where he had heard the voice. In what blinding room and nightmare. But he kept his eyes on Shepilov and breathed noisily.

– Possible?

Gruzdev moved his arms as he had seen actors do in *The Revizor*. If he did not find that gesture out of Gogol he would suffocate.

– That Academician Ryder is wrong? That all the proofs obtained from Linge, Rattenhuber, Hans Baur are false? I appeal to you, Comrade Colonel. Possible? How is a man to answer?

Shepilov loosened a typewritten page from a large bundle.

– Nikolai Maximovitch, you say here that there is a hypothesis to account for the fresh scratches on the dentures, for the clean fractures in the third phalange.

– A double. That the body so clumsily burnt and then left for us to find was that of a double. That the man's bones had been broken just before they shot him in the mouth, and a set of dentures made and carefully preserved.

Gruzdev spoke the words in a monotone, remembering the last time he had dared say them, under Major Berkoff's lashing fist. He was feeling faint. The taste of his own blood seemed in his throat.

The man in brown had risen.

– That hypothesis, Doctor. What is your judgement of it now? Do you regard it as probable?

Gruzdev closed his eyes and asked for a glass of water. He smelled the rank sweat under his arms and between his fingers. It offended him.

– I do not know. I will say whatever you wish me to say. Possible, gentlemen? Everything is possible. *Everything.* I am an old man. *Credo quia absurdum.* Do not torment me. Academician Ryder –

Then he stopped speaking, and Colonel Shepilov of the Historical Section motioned him to the door. But they held him there for a moment to tell him that the matter under discussion was not to be referred to in any way. That it was a state secret and that any indiscretion, however slight, would be dealt with as a criminal act.

Gruzdev crossed the bridge and entered the park. He sat on a bench breathing hard but not getting enough air. The light was colder now and he shivered. So it had all been for nothing, the hours in the cellar and the eight years in the camp. He had been right from the start. But why had they called him in now?

A child's rubber ball came bounding toward Gruzdev. Before his eyes it twisted into an insane mask, spitting out yellow, scarlet and silver words. Words that tore the skin off his sweating body. Grusdev covered his face and gave a cry. The child stared at the old man and whimpered, afraid to pick up the ball. Two women turned sharply on a neighbouring bench.

Gruzdev got up and walked away. Hitler was alive. They knew it now. And they wanted him, Nikolai Maximovitch Gruzdev, to tell them it was not so. *Ergo est*. Because he is. Because he is they ripped out my nails, and sent me to the ice forest. Because he is I carry in me the memories of the living dead.

Standing on the gravel path Gruzdev laughed aloud and shook with fear.

– Hitler is alive.

He bent low, saying the words to a sparrow, which stood, its pale eyes glittering a few inches from his foot. And repeated them in a wild whisper until the bird moved away.

5

A drawing from his biology textbook, committed to memory in the year in which he left school in a Boy-Scout mania for vengeance, crystallized in Isaac Amsel's brain. It pressed on the far edges of his consciousness, barring the wild jabs of panic, the thought, which seemed alive in every bone and fibre, that he would let go at the next step and pitch headfirst into the swamp. It was a histological plate, a vertical cut of an inch of human skin. Through the adipose tissue branched the lacework of capillaries. The white mist of lymph lay in the follicles. And spread among the sinuous roots of hair which, through multitudinous apertures, broke the membrane to form, a fraction of an inch outside ourselves yet inseparably ours, a soft myriad-branched layer. Far beneath, in an interior of hexagonal cells, the candelabrum of veins arched back to its stem and entered the red mouth of the artery.

His own skin must be like that. The exact square inches of it on his left shoulder under the pole of the hammock. But suffocating with sweat, the pores so strangled that the beads of acrid moisture were stiffening into venomous thorns. The raking weight of the pole had flattened the down, pressing each minute hair back into his broken, blistered hide. He imagined the beehive of cells rent of shape, the blood seeping through its sluice-gates and the whole landscape of that torn piece of himself bright with the nameless colour of pain.

He would concentrate on that image for the next five steps. Empty his sweating bent skull of every other awareness. He would fill his breath with the remembered smell, linoleum and cool, of the paper in the biology text. He would stop his ears with what his teacher had called the 'whisper of lymph' and keep out the sickening sough of water in his boots. Five steps. Then he would void his lungs of the heat and stench and cry out.

– I can't go on. I can't. Take the litter. Before I let go. Not another step. Take the pain from me and the heat and needles under my eyelids. I don't care that we've found him. That we must carry him out alive. I can't go on. Not a yard. I will count to ten and get my left foot to touch that floating branch. Then open my hand and let the fire slip from my shoulder. I want to die. Shema. Here. Elohim. To stretch out till the burning stops.

Isaac Amsel slid his leg forward pressing his numb fingers to the pole. He knew that he must not commit his full weight until Asher and Benasseraf, the two front bearers, had gained secure footing. They were still in motion; he could see Asher's back trembling, trying to steady, his neck askew like that of a puppet towards the heavy pack which trailed from his right shoulder. Elie was beginning to step forward on the other side of the hammock. The economy of effort in that thin body, the tautness in reserve, had startled the boy on their first marches through the jungle.

The pole dragged along his raw skin and he followed. Towards the sodden branch.

There was a foot and a half of water intervening. Minute darts skimmed across its steaming surface. Dead leaves, matted berries stung open to their grey pulp drew the putrid wash into momentary solidity, but then the bubbles rose catching the dim light, and the fronds of moss drifted apart. Inches above the muck the smell hung visible. Dragon-flies and cuara insects hummed through it, their high stilts scarcely brushing the scum. Over the dead leeches gnats swarmed in a rage.

Bending forward to place his boot, the boy saw a sudden clearing of the water. An insect shrilled upwards and brushed his mouth. A shape was gliding out of the green fog. Rising towards his leg with a blurred flash of silver.

Isaac Amsel cried out. His cry seemed lost in the lash of water and vine as the four men stumbled.

Simeon spun around. He saw the litter tilt above the boy's frozen face and Asher lurch sideways under the shifting weight. The poncho loosened into the wings of a large bat. With his free hand Elie Barach reached for the half-submerged branch. Feeling the hammock drag away from him, Benasseraf had gripped the pole with both palms. Now his wrists were turning and the carbine, whose strap had slid to his elbow, was slapping against his thigh. Hitler fell out of the blanket.

The swamp was not deep at this point. But crumbling sideways, his right arm pinned to his body, the old man went under. Asher lunged at the tuft of grey hair and pulled him up. He surfaced, shedding water and the sticky filaments of the bog from his eyes and the spare growth above his upper lip. Blinking into the light he shook like a wet mole.

Asher loosened his grip and Elie Barach began laughing. Under his breath but then louder. Benasseraf laughed, shaking water from the hammock. Then Asher. The boy watched, outraged. They were laughing with *him* in their midst, his lips moving strangely. Then the boy laughed also. It seemed easier.

Hitler's arm shot out stiffly, a finger pointing. A braid of silver circled the branch and swayed, weaving and breaking its own image in the dead water. Its mauve hood opened and closed with a pulsing motion. Seeing the man's finger dart at it, the snake stood unmoving. A moment later the thread unwound and vanished with a single flick into the green depths.

Isaac Amsel threw his head back and laughed again. This time at the top of his lungs.

6

Ajalon to Nimrud. Message received. Can you hear me? Ajalon to Nimrud. Glory to God. In the highest. And for ever. The sun stood still over Ajalon so that we could prevail. But then the night stood still. For twelve years. Darkness unmoving. Over us and our children. Can you hear me? Over. But now there is light again, at Gilead and in Hebron, and to the ends of the earth. I tell you there is light as never before. And tonight the stars will dance over Arad. And the world stand still to draw breath, and the dew be like cymbals in the grass. Because he is ours. Because he is in the hands of the living. In your hands. Ajalon to Nimrud. Listen to me. You must not let him speak, or only few words. To say his needs, to say that which will keep him alive. But no more. Gag him if necessary, or stop your ears as did the sailor. If he is allowed speech he will trick you and escape. Or find easy death. His tongue is like no other. It is the tongue of the basilisk, a hundred-forked and quick as flame. As it is written in the learned Nathaniel of Mainz: there shall come upon the earth in the time of night a man surpassing eloquent. All that is God's, hallowed be His name, must have its counterpart, its backside of evil and negation. So it is with the Word, with the gift of speech that is the glory of man and distinguishes him everlastingly from the silence or animal noises of creation. When He made the Word, God made possible also its contrary. Silence is not the contrary of the Word but its guardian. No, he created on the night-side of language a speech for hell. Whose words mean hatred and vomit of life. Few men can learn that speech or speak it for long. It burns their mouths. It draws them into death. But there shall come a man whose mouth shall be as a furnace and whose tongue as a sword laying waste. He will know the grammar of hell and teach it to others.

He will know the sounds of madness and loathing and make them seem music. Where God said, let there be, he will unsay. And there is *one* word – so taught the blessed Rabbi Menasseh of Leyden – *one* word amid the million sounds that make the secret sum of all language, which if spoken in hatred, may end creation, as there was one that brought creation into being. Ajalon to Nimrud. Are you getting me? Perhaps *he* knows that word, he who very nearly did us to death, who deafened God so that the covenant seemed broken and our children given to ash. Do not let him speak freely. You will hear the crack of age in his voice. He is old. Old as the loathing which dogs us since Abraham. Let him speak to you and you will think of him as a man. With sores on his skin and need in his bowels, sweating and hungering like yourselves, short of sleep. If he asks for water fill the cup. If he asked twice he would no longer be a stranger. Give him fresh linen before he needs it. Those who speak to us of their dirt and the itch in the groin are no longer enemies. Do not listen to his sleep. Over. If you think of him as a man, sodden when the rains come, shaking to the bone when you reach the Cordilla, you will grow uncertain. You will not forget. Oh, I know you will never forget. Rememberers for Jacob. But the memory will turn alien and cold. A man's smell can break the heart. You will be so close now, so terribly close. You will think him a man and no longer believe what he did. That he almost drove us from the face of the earth. That his words tore up our lives by the root. Listen to me. Ajalon calling. Can you hear me? This is an order. Gag him if you must. Words are warmer than fresh bread; share them with him and your hate will grow to a burden. Do not look too much at him. He wears a human mask. Let him sit apart and move at the end of a long rope. Do not stare at his nakedness lest it be like yours. Over to you. Are you receiving me, Simeon? I am not mad. There are thousands of miles to go before he is safely in Jerusalem. You will come to know him as you do your own stench. Look away from his eyes. They say that his eyes have a strange light. Do not leave the boy alone with him. The boy knows but does not remember, not in his own flesh. What this man did. Ajalon calling. Come in, Nimrud. Tell me that you remember. The garden in Salonika, where Mordechai Zathsmar, the cantor's youngest child, ate excrement, the Hoofstraat in Arnheim where they took Leah Burstein and made her watch while her father, the two lime trees where the road to Montrouge turns south, 8 November 1942, on which they hung the meathooks, the pantry on the third floor, Nowy Swiat xi, where Jakov Kaplan, author of the *History of Algebraic Thought in Eastern Europe 1280–1655*, had to dance over the body of, in White Springs, Ohio, Rahel Nadelmann who wakes each night, sweat in her mouth because thirty-one years earlier in the Mauerallee in Hannover three louts drifting home from an SS recruitment spree had tied her legs and with a truncheon, the latrine in the police station in Wörgel which Doktor Ruth Levin and her niece had to clean with their hair, the fire-raid on Engstaad and the Jakobsons made to kneel outside the shelter until the incendiaries, Sternowitz caught in the woods near Sibor talking to Ludmilla, an Aryan woman, and filled with water and a piano-wire wound tight around his, Branka seeing them burn the dolls near the ramp and when she sought to hide hers being taken to the fire and, Elias Kornfeld, Sarah Ellbogen, Robert Heimann in front of the biology class, Neuwald Gymnasium lower Saxony, stripped to the waist, mouths wide open so that Professor Horst Küntzer could demonstrate to his pupils the obvious racial, an hour of school which Heimann remembered when at Matthausen naked again, Lilian Gourevitch given two work-passes for her three children in Tver Street and ordered to choose which of the children was to go on the next transport, Lilian Gourevitch given two work-passes, yellow-coloured, serial numbers BJ7732781 and 2, for her three children in Tver Street and ordered to choose, Lilian Gourevitch, the marsh six kilometres from Noverra where the dogs found Aldo Mattei and his family in hiding, only a week before the Waffen-SS retreated northward, thus completing the register of fugitives, five Jews, one Gypsy, one hydrocephalic, drawn up at the *prefettura* in Rovigo, the last Purim in Vilna and the man who played Haman cutting his throat, remember him, Moritz the caretaker whose beard they had torn out almost hair by hair, pasting on a false beard and after the play taking the razor in the boiler-room, Dorfmann, George Benjamin Dorfmann, collector of prints of the late seventeenth century, doctor and player on the viola, lying, no kneeling, no squatting in the punishment cell at Buchenwald, six feet by four and one half, the concrete cracked with ice, watching the pus break from his torn nails and whispering the catalogue numbers of the Hobbemas in the Albertina, so far as he could remember them in the raw pain of his shaven skull, until the guard took a whip, Ann Casanova, 21 rue du Chapon, Liège, called to the door, asking the two men to wait outside so that her mother would not know and the old woman falling on to the bonnet of the starting car, from the fourth-floor window, her dentures scattered in the road, Hannah, the silken-haired bitch dying of hunger in the locked apartment after the Küllmans had been taken, sinking her teeth into the master's houseshoes, custom-made to the measure of his handsome foot by Samuel Rossbach, Hagadio, who in the shoe-factory at Treblinka was caught splitting leather, sabotage, and made to crawl alive into the quicklime while at the edge Reuben Cohen, aged eleven, had to proclaim 'so shall all saboteurs and subverters of the united front', Hagadio, Hagadio, until the neighbours, Ebert and Ilse Schmidt, today Ebert Schmidt City Engineer, broke down the door, found the dog almost dead, dropped it in the garbage pit and rifled Küllman's closets, his wife's dressing-table, the children's attic with its rocking horse, jack-in-the-box and chemistry set, while on the railway siding near Dornbach, Hagadio, the child, thrown from the train by its parents, with money sewn in its jacket and a note begging for water and help was found by two men coming home from seeding and laid on the tracks, a hundred yards from the north switch, gagged, feet tied, till the next train, which it heard a long way off in the still of the summer evening, the two men watching and eating and then voiding their bowels, Hagadio, the Küllmans knowing that the smell of gas was the smell of gas but thinking the child safe, which, as the thundering air blew nearer spoke into its gag, twice, the name of the silken-haired bitch Hannah, and then could not close its eyes against the rushing shadow; at Maidanek ten thousand a day, I am not mad, Ajalon calling, can you hear me, unimaginable because innumerable, in one corner of Treblinka seven hundred thousand bodies. I will count them now, Aaron, Aaronowitch, Aaronson, Abilech, Abraham, I will count seven hundred thousand names and you must listen, and watch Asher, I do not know him as well as I do you, Simeon, and Elie Barach and the boy, I will say *kaddish* to the end of time and when time ceases shall not have reached the millionth name, at Belzec three hundred thousand, Friedberg, Friedman, Friedmann, Friedstein, the names gone in fire and gas, ash in the wind at Chelmno, the long black wind at Chelmno, Israel Meyer, Ida Meyer, the four children in the pit at Sobivor, four hundred and eleven thousand three hundred and eighty-one in section three at Belsen, the one being Salomon Rheinfeld who left on his desk in Mainz the uncorrected proofs of the grammar of Hittite which Egon Schleicher, his assistant newly promoted Ordinarius, claimed for his own but cannot complete, the one being Belin the tanner whose face they sprinkled with acid from the vat and who was dragged through the streets of Kershon behind a dung-cart but sang, the one being Georges Walter when they called him from supper in the rue Marot, from the *blanquette de veau* finely seasoned, could not understand and spoke to his family of an administrative error and refused to pack more than one shirt and asked still why why through his smashed teeth when the shower doors closed and the whisper started in the ceiling, the one being David Pollachek whose fingers they broke in the quarry at Leutach when they heard that he had been first violin and who in the loud burning of each blow could think only of the elder bush in his yard at Slanič, each leaf of which he had tried to touch once more on the last evening in his house after the summons came, the one not being Nathaniel Steiner who was taken to America in time but goes maimed nevertheless for not having been at the roll call, the being all because unnumbered hence unrememberable, because buried alive at Grodny, because hung by the feet at Bialistok like Nathansohn, nine hours fourteen minutes under the whip (timed by *Wachtmeister* Ottmar Prantl now hotelier in Steyerbrück), the blood, Prantl, reporting, splashing out of his hair and mouth like new wine; two million at, unspeakable because beyond imagining, two million suffocated at, outside Cracow of the gracious towers, the signpost on the airport road pointing to it still, Oszwiecin in sight of the low hills, because we can imagine the cry of one, the hunger of two, the burning of ten, but past a hundred there is no clear imagining; he understood that, take a million and belief will not follow nor the mind contain, and if each and every one of us, Ajalon calling, were to rise before morning and speak out ten names that day, ten from the ninety-six thousand graven on the wall in Prague, ten from the thirty-one thousand in the crypt at Rome, ten from those at Matthausen Drancy Birkenau Buchenwald Theresienstadt or Babi-Yar, ten out of six million, we should never finish the task, not if we spoke the night through, not till the close of time, nor bring back a single breath, not that of Isaac Löwy, Berlin, Isaac Löwy, Danzig (with the birthmark on his left shoulder), Isaac Löwy, Zagreb, Isaac Löwy, Vilna, the baker who cried of yeast when the door closed, Isaac Löwy, Toulouse, almost safe, the visa almost granted, I am not mad but the *kaddish* which is like a shadow of lilac after the dust of the day is withered now, empty of remembrance, he has made ash of prayer, AND UNTIL EACH NAME is recalled and spoken again, EACH, the names of the nameless in the orphan's house at Szeged, the name of the mute in the sewer at Katowic, the names of the unborn in the women ripped at Matthausen, the name of the girl with the yellow star seen hammering on the door of the shelter at Hamburg and of whom there is no record but a brown shadow burned into the pavement, until each name is remembered and spoken to the LAST SYLLABLE, man will have no peace on earth, do you hear me Simeon, no place, no liberation from hatred, not until every name, for when spoken each after the other, with not a single letter omitted, do you hear me, the syllables will make up the hidden name of GOD.

He did it.

The man next to you now. Whose thirst and sour breath are exactly like yours.

Oh, they helped. Nearly all of them. Who would not give visas and put barbed wire on their borders. Who threw stones through the window and spat. Who when six hundred escaped from Treblinka hunted down and killed all but thirty-nine – Polish farmers, irregulars, partisans, charcoal burners in the forest – saying Jews belong in Treblinka. He could not have done it alone. I know that. Not without the helpers and the indifferent, not without the hooligans who laughed and the soft men who took over the shops and moved into the houses. Not without those who said in Belgravia and Marly, in Stresa and in Shaker Heights that the news was exaggerated, that the Jews were whining again and peddling horrors. Not without D. initialling a memo to B-W. at Printing House Square: *No more atrocity stories. Probably overplayed.* Or Foggy Bottom offering seventy-five visas above the quota when one hundred thousand children could have been saved. Not alone.

But it was he who made real the old dream of murder. Everyman's itch to clear his throat of us. Because we have lasted too long. Because we foisted Christ on them. Because we smell other.

It was he who turned the dream into day. Read what he said to his familiars, what he spoke in his dancing hours. He never alludes to the barracks or the gas, to the lime-pits or the whipping-blocks. Never. As if the will to murder and the knowledge were so deep inside him, so much the core of his being that he had no more need to point to them. Our ruin was the air he moved in. We do not stop to count our breaths.

It was he. With his scourge of speech and divining rod. His wrist breaking each time he passed over other men's weakness. With his nose for the bestial and the boredom in men's bones. His words made the venom spill. Over to you, Simeon. Can you hear me?

Do you remember the photograph in the archive in Humboldt-strasse? Munich, August 1914, the crowd listening to the declaration of war. The faces surging around the plinth. Among them, partially obscured by a waving arm, but, unmistakable, his. The eyes upturned, shining. Within twenty-four months nearly every man in the photograph was dead. Had a shell found him out, a bullet, a grenade splinter, one of millions, the night would not have stood still over us. We would have grown old in our houses, there would be children to know our graves.

It was he. The sweating carcass by your side. The man picking his nose as you listen to me or dropping his trousers.

None of the others could have done it. Not the fat bully or the adder. He took garbage and made it into wolves. Where his words fell lives petty or broken grew tall as hate. He.

Do not listen to him now. Guard him better than eyesight. We must have him alive. Knit the skin to the bones. Carry him if you must. Let him lie in the sun and in dry places. Force his mouth open if he won't eat. Search his teeth for poison and smear ointment on his boils. Tend him more dearly than if he were the last child of Jacob.

Skirt Orosso if you can. The ground is not sure. And keep from men's sight. If it was known that we had him they would snatch him from us. And mock us again.

I shall wait for you in San Cristobal. Send me news of your position. Each day at the agreed hour. I shall leave here in good time. Life is new in me now. I shall wait for you at the edge of the forest. Ajalon calling. Come in, Nimrud. Come in. Can you hear me?

Simeon, answer me. Over to you. Over. This is Lieber calling
this is Lieber
this is

7

Trapped, the black tick had stung Simeon's ear. The lobe had swollen. Now a warm cotton hum lay between him and the world.

His attention, moreover, strained to interpret the new rhythms of the march. For months there had been at his back, grown familiar to him as the wince of his own muscles, a four-stress motion. By ear, by the antennae sharper than hearing which seemed to pulse from the nape of his neck, Simeon had learned to register the forward progress, the falterings, of Elie Barach, John Asher, the boy, and Gideon Benasseraf who usually held the rear. After bending a liana he could distinguish, without having to turn around, the four-fold interval during which each man bent the vine in turn for the next to grasp until Gideon let it lash away behind him into the thorny weave of the forest. In the sucking stench of the bog he had been able to mark the position of his four companions as sharply as if he had eyes in his spine.

Now the beat had totally altered.

His thin arms tugging at their shoulders, the right hand jabbing in a constant palsy, Hitler, after his fall from the hammock, had been half-carried and half-drawn through the steaming water by Asher and Benasseraf. At moments Hitler's head brushed against Gideon's cheek like a clump of wet leaves. Where footing was steadier – snake-grass plaited to spongy mats, vines cut and wound to a spiral around submerged branches, humps of packed mud iridescent with the sheen of sulphur, formed brief shoals and dykes even in the heart of the swamp – Hitler's grip loosened and he came forward on his own.

But whether borne, dragged or labouring at his own pace, the old man had broken the habitual pattern of heavy breathing and snapped branch which Simeon had come to locate in the wake of his every motion. Nearly at each step he wanted to turn around to make out the

53

meaning of unfamiliar shufflings and sudden leaps of water. His back prickled with the sense of a new presence. Behind the slither and frequent pauses in Hitler's progress he could not locate the lighter gait of Isaac Amsel. Who now came last and had added a part of Benasseraf's gear, and the carbine, to his own pack. Yet Simeon knew he must not turn his head.

The yards ahead, more often it was a matter of a few feet, exacted his total attention. He could hardly think of reality any more except as dark green. To exist was to guard one's sweating mouth and hands against an unbroken rush of spiked and thrashing shapes, against blotting creepers that left filaments and small burning shards in one's skin and hair. To Simeon breathing had become a smell musky and heavy as dead water. Unknowing, he had grown new feelers. The scent of rot had only to thicken a little, to steam more densely from the moss, for Simeon to know that rain was near and from which quarter in the green cage of the world it would hammer down. A leathery slide in the barbed grass, an abrupt whorl of stillness in the saw of the swamp-cicadas, and he would keep his foot poised waiting for the adder to whip away. A dimpled swelling of the bark told Simeon of the tree scorpion. He could hear the woodpecker in the unseen thicket. That there might be another order of life, where one step followed unheeding on the other, where breath passed cool through open lips, seemed knowledge as distant, as irrelevant to his present being as was Simeon's remembrance – was it still within his reach? – of the last sabbath of peace in Lemberg, when the end of summer air lay blue around the candles and the grain of cinnamon shone on the white cloth.

The new, often alarming shapes of sound at his back, the lure of Hitler's feet ten yards behind him and the utter watchfulness demanded of him by the swamp, made Simeon insensible to the wisps of noise from the transmitter. He carried the thing with him still, gutted as it was, its delicate skein of wires dishevelled. If the damp had not eaten through the canvas wrappings, there were spare coils and circuit-boards waiting at Jiaro. Now it was only a weight, a hot rub across his left shoulder and a frequent jab in the small of his back.

Nevertheless, some part of his brain, inexplicably idling or numb to the pressure of the swamp, *had* registered the bursts of static. He understood that the set was alive and picking up a signal though it could no longer amplify or sort it out. When they had taken a break after the collapse of the hammock to let Hitler wring the water out of his trousers, Simeon had swung the receiver nearer to his good ear and listened.

The fret and whine had come through in staccato fusillades. Simeon remembered the double rasp of shotguns in the arcade in October, when he was a small boy. He strained to hear. And imagined Lieber's voice saying urgent words, giving precise indications of help, instructing the party of the planes under way, of the supply-drops being marshalled on the edge of the swamp. But instead of being in a frenzy over the failure of the set, over the betrayal of rubber and metal which cut him off from Lieber's guiding genius and assurance of relief, Simeon found himself drifting. The needling at his ear was not being produced by Emmanuel Lieber. The rhythm was wrong. It was not Lieber speaking at the other end of the transmitter, or if these pricks of sound were indeed Lieber's they had been emitted a long time ago. They were reaching Simeon like light waves from a burnt-out star. Lieber was dead. Or had given them up for lost. He had left the airless room in Lavra Street locked, gathering dirt. The mice were at the maps and a large fly lay dead on the silicone mouthpiece. There would be no one at San Cristobal, no sulpha tablets at Jiaro. Lieber had not been there to receive his call. Who was trying to reach him now?

The thought must have shown. Asher had stopped laughing and was staring at him across the dripping poncho. Simeon pulled himself up, swung the transmitter back over his shoulder and stopped listening.

Or almost. Now, in sight of the day's goal, he could still make out below the shrilling of the bugs the obstinate pulse of static. Simeon let the strap slide down his arm as he lurched the last few yards towards the sand-spit.

He had marked the place on the way in but was too preoccupied to celebrate the precision of his bearings. Here the basket-weave of water and shifting ooze had widened to a large pool. Though the drag of swamp continued in the deeps and everywhere around, the water in the pool had a clear black stillness. Forming an almost regular circle it mirrored a round patch of sky unbroken by the sway of vines and the close knit of tree tops. The high sun skimmed over the pool like a gold sovereign. Though the winds did not reach them, the waters reflected, in a strange fixity, the tearing of rain-clouds and the green and copper of dawn as it streamed across the Cordillera. On one side the pool was rimmed by a crescent of fine sand. From it a spit of ground extended a few hundred yards into the dark funnel of water. Neither the salt stench of strangled vegetation nor the vapour of insects intruded on this small peninsula. Simeon had seen only one sign of life when they passed the sand-spit on the march in, a tree-toad no larger than the flat of his hand, its horns and sharp ridge of its spine glinting like pale silver.

Though he had been in the rear, Isaac Amsel splashed past Simeon at a run and was the first to dump his pack and blanket-roll at the edge of the pool. In the dimming light the figures jostled and appeared to move without aim. Hitler's presence, he stood on the verge of the jungle almost invisible against the soft stuff of leaf and nightfall, had splintered the order of march and the close-hammered drill of encampment.

Asher's question woke Simeon from his trance.

– Shall we tie him up? Not that he'd get very far.

Simeon panicked momentarily. Hitler had vanished. Then he saw him, a few feet inside the undergrowth, urinating. A final streak of daylight had caught the old man's face as he bent forward. It lay like a white moth against the flatness of the leaves.

– Yes. Tie him up.

Elie Barach began laying out the Primus stove. He blew on the wick and brushed the grid with his sleeve. The sounds, coming in their right sequence as they did with each sunset, braced Simeon.

– Tie him securely. Use one of the guy-ropes.

– Use a long rope, said Elie.

– Tie one end to his leg and the other to one of us or the hammock-pole. We can hammer it into the ground. That way he can move a bit and be on his own. I don't suppose he sleeps much. And Nebuchad-nezzar shall graze, yea like a tethered goat.

– He won't run away, said Benasseraf,

– I'll guard him. I couldn't sleep. I'll stand watch.

And Isaac Amsel flourished the carbine above his head. He had seen the gesture on a poster advertising an American film of espionage and liberation in São Paulo.

– He wouldn't last the night in that bog. He'd die alone not knowing who he was. In a thousand square miles we're the only ones to know. He needs us.

And Benasseraf unrolled the canvas sheets and staked out the pegs for the lean-to.

When Asher knelt before him and tied the rope to his ankle Hitler moved his lips. He made a hoarse sound but said nothing. Asher knotted the other end to a peg and drove it into the ground between his and Simeon's bedding. Then he dipped his hands in the water and said to no one in particular

– Cold. The water's really quite cold.

Blackness had fallen from the sky at a single stroke. Meeting the blackness of the pool it formed an opaque pillar. It muted the beat of Benasseraf's mallet and the crinkle of the stove. Simeon had noticed before how the sudden night took sounds with it. Only smells stayed distinct. He inhaled the rust sweetness of the tea even before Elie came out of the shadows to hand him the mug. The boy lit the hurricane lamp but its light seemed to recoil from the pressure of darkness. It was only in the shelter that a stain of red showed against the ground and the taut canvas.

The rope had moved a little when Elie carried a mug of tea into the outer darkness. Now it lay still, coiling away from the faint sheen of light. Isaac Amsel crouched next to Elie and opened the tins of meat and noodles. Simeon could see the points of light on the opener but heard no crack of metal. At that instant, from far in the jungle, the cry of a parakeet came high and piercing. The rope quivered, then slackened again.

– I'll take the food to him, said Benasseraf,

– He'll want more salt than that. He's sweating his bones away.

Each man ate inside his own cone of blackness. The line between earth and black had vanished. Though there was no motion in the air a soft booming, as from some quarry many marches away, reverberated now and again in the deeps of the pool. Benasseraf came back into the patch of light. He drank avidly. Simeon stopped chewing and listened. Now the transmitter was really mute. He tried to recapture the inflection of Lieber's voice, the exact shade of his skin. He couldn't. The darkness sucked everything from him except the sour odour and chill of his own body. He saw Asher look towards the water and pucker his lips. Asher could whistle like a yellow finch, liquid obbligatos that woke the forest to a chatter. But he kept silent and turned back to the shelter, testing the rope with his foot.

– I'll get his plate, said Elie.

The boy felt for the water's edge and rinsed the mugs and spoons, His bowels were churning and he farted. Quickly he rattled the tin plates, but they made hardly any noise. He was breathing fast. The night closed on his eyes and mouth like a blotter. When Elie Barach's shadow cut across the lamp, Amsel couldn't even see his own hands. He put down the canteens and hurried to the bushes sweating. The depths of the pool sounded again, a muffled stroke, long drawn out. It went through him like a cramp.

When he returned to the bivouac, stepping wide over the rope, Isaac Amsel saw that Asher and Simeon had rolled themselves inside their sleeping-bags. Next to Simeon, seeming to form an enclosure against the reaching chaos of the jungle, lay his revolver, the holster strap unfastened, the short-wave transmitter, the zinc box of snake-serum and novocaine, and Simeon's large flashlight. The mosquito netting was so near Asher's face that it followed the contour of his nose and cheek-bone like a cobweb on the effigy of an armoured personage, tensed to spring from repose. An egg-shaped hump of shadow, barely distinguishable from the surrounding dark, told Isaac that Barach was at prayers, wrapped in his shawl, his knees close-pressed under his bowed chin. By the outermost lamp, at the point of the sand-pit, a red ember brightened and dipped in abrupt arcs. Benasseraf had lit one of his coarse-leaved cigarillos. The ashes flaked into the pool. The boy went to him and sat down in the sand. He saw the stock of the carbine resting against Benasseraf's knee. Gideon's face was turned away from him staring at the night air which dragged on the water like black felt.

– I can't sleep either. Not with him out there.

Benasseraf didn't answer. He didn't want the boy near him. It was a cliché, part of the scenario Lieber had contrived and whose pages they were now turning probably at the cost of their souls. It was part of every bad novel. There had been a time for bad novels. Paper escarpments of them guarding his unmade bed in the Rue de Rennes. The drug of pulp, drowsier than mandragora. Bad novels that packed his brain like sawdust in an art-gallery crate and kept the jagged, twisted objects of his memory from crashing about, from piercing the walls of his skull. It was he who resented Amsel most. Who had tried hardest to get rid of him, first in São Paulo, then at Orosso where the boy should have stayed to watch over the stores of the botanical expedition. It was Benasseraf who found Isaac's flourishes and turns of heroic phrase – confetti out of old war-films – most aggravating. Nevertheless, or because of this, the boy would seek him out on the march and when they made camp. He could have entered into Elie's tabernacle, into that complicity of prayer and parable which seemed to advance so fluently even through the jungle. Or learned from Asher how to drink life through a straw, barely cutting the rind of the orange. Instead he came to him in patient blackmail. Setting traps for recognition. Precisely as a banal fiction would have it. The son choosing the father.

– You can't sleep either, either, can you, Gideon? Is it loaded?

– No. Why should it be?

– You don't think he'll try to escape?

– Where to? The bog is alive almost everywhere around us. If he didn't drown there are the ants. Did you see the mud move back there? Simeon saw it. As if a cloud of red pepper was blowing along the ground. They'd scour the bones.

– If I was he I'd try to escape. No matter what. I'd saw the rope with my teeth. Because he must know what we'll do to him. Or be thinking about it all the time.

It was easier to talk than to say nothing. The words blew away with the ash of the cigar.

– And what will we do with him?

– Ah, said the boy throwing his head back. The night soot was in his hair.

– Ah, that's up to Lieber, isn't it? And all the others. They must be running wild with excitement. Getting everything ready. They'll try him in the high court. In the highest. And hang him. After breakfast. That's not what I would do. I've thought about it. I wouldn't do it that way at all. Quiet and clean. You don't feel anything. I've read about it.

Just a hammer blow, with the hammer in a rag. I'd do it so that he knew it was being done. Every thousandth of a second. And done many times. Not all at once. Snap and it's all over. So he'd wonder about the next time, that's how I'd do it, and hear himself howl. I'd chain him to a stake on top of a pile of wood. So high that he could see beyond the city. And lay a trail of powder or a wick a hundred miles long, winding through every street and coiling around the square. And light it. He'd see the flame travelling nearer. He'd have to watch it for hours. Closer and closer. Just before it reached the faggots I'd jump in front of the crowd and stamp it out. I'd stamp it out with my own heel. And have them light the fuse all over again, at the far end. Or hang him on a pulley just above a vat of acid. Each day someone would come, there'd be tickets or numbers drawn, and turn the crank so that some bit of him would dip in the acid. One turn if you've lost a wife, two for each child. I'd jam a prop in his mouth so that he couldn't scream. Till his eyes burst. Or set his balls in a carpenter's vice. For a few minutes each day. Until he fainted. Putting a timetable on his wall so that he would know exactly when the next session came. And skin his leg to make the lampshade in his cell. How does a man live with the smell of his own skin outside him? Or have a jar with rats, starved rats behind a grate.

– You've got that out of a book. You're not talking about *him*. You're emptying your own mind. Of garbage.

– No, said Isaac Amsel,

– I'd do all those things. I'd do all those things. And keep him alive. And start all over again. What would you do, Gideon, what would you do?

– I haven't thought about it. I'd let him go.

The boy's images were like the sour breath of the pool.

– I'd let him go wherever he wanted inside Israel. With only the clothing on his back. Every single time he wanted food or water or shelter he'd have to ask for it and say who he was. Everyone would know, of course. But I would make him repeat it each time, very loud. 'I am Adolf Hitler. I am Adolf Hitler. I beg bread of you, a cup of water. Give me shelter in your house.' I'd make him say it loud.

– What would be the good of that? If that's what you want why not let him die in the jungle? Why not turn him loose?

– Why not? I don't know. Imagine it. He'd die a very old man. Well fed. A fat old tourist in the land of Israel.

Amsel slid his knuckles over the butt of the carbine.

– If you feel that way, Gideon, why are you here? You're not telling me the truth. You want him, just like the rest of us.

– You're stupid. No one wants him like anyone else. Each in his own little way. You because. Because you'll pretend you're making good your father's death. Because you've seen too many movies. Brave boy. Sunset. Father avenged.

He tried to flick the ash into the water. But it seemed to catch in the net of the dark and fell on his boot.

– How do you want him?

– I don't know. Not now. Not like Lieber and Simeon. I don't think it was that way for me even at the start. To me he isn't Elie's Beast of the Seven Fiery Heads. I never wanted him that way.

The boy leaned back, content. Night talk, closer than he had ever had with Gideon. Whom he worshipped. Who was the strongest of the lot. Stronger even than Simeon, or different. Whom they would never have drawn into that cheap death-trap at Paraña.

– Not to get even. For what? You wouldn't understand. But when I hear about vengeance, about his eye for an eye, I want to vomit. There can be no vengeance, no making good. Why should history apologize, just to the Jews? Don't stare at me, Amsel, as if you knew what I was trying to say. You don't. You think it's a game, ten points to each side. Because we've got Hitler and can tear his nails out and wait for them to grow again the dead will sit up and give themselves a dusting. They won't. Not one of them. Not if you parade him over every grave, over every ash-pit, not if you dip him in boiling oil six million times. Do you really believe a man can get even for murder of his children? For what a six-year-old girl saw before she died, for the fear which was so great that she dirtied herself, that she was driven down to the street in her –

He had been told, years after. By Moritz Levenfisch who, inexplicably, survived. Who had sniffed him out in Paris and was a liar and *shnorrer*. It might not be true. Or perhaps it was. Benasseraf had locked out memory and come to Lieber empty. He had brought only himself. Why remember now? The three children were not clear in his mind.

How old would they be this night? Shlomo had been eight when. What was the colour of Rebecca's hair? A burnt brown. Even before the fire. He felt frightened and nauseated. As if his foot had missed two steps in a black staircase. He almost turned on Isaac Amsel.

– own dirt. You think that can be made good? You can't be that much of a fool. It doesn't matter. The rest of us aren't any wiser. There are two kinds of Jews left, the dead and those who are a bit crazy.

This time the ash flicked away but went out long before it reached the surface of the pool.

– That's why I don't want anyone to touch him. To torment him, to hang him would be to pretend that something of what he has done can be made good, that even a millionth of it can be cancelled. If we hang him history will draw a line. Accounts settled. And forget even faster. That's just what they want. They want us to do the job for them and put the whole guilt on him. Like a great crown. *He's* the one to blame. Let the Jews hang him high. *He* did it all. They must be the ones who know. We're acquitted now. First they nailed up Christ and now Hitler. God has chosen the Jew. For his hangman. Let them carry the blood. We're in the clear. You don't understand, do you? I'm talking mad talk. The leeches have sucked my brain. At the first town we come to we should leave him. Go to the hotel, put him in an armchair and leave him. Then we should scatter, turning away from each other on the run. Not looking back. Let them try him and do what they will. He's *theirs*!

Gideon thought he had shouted the word. Perhaps he had. In his first drift of sleep Asher felt the rope move momentarily. He had looped it across his waist.

– He's theirs.

Saying it once more he almost touched the boy. Isaac Amsel smiled in the dark.

– Gideon,

He didn't have to hurry now.

– where will you go? I mean afterwards. After we hand him over.

– Afterwards? I'll go look for Adolf Hitler.

Isaac tried to choose the right laugh.

– You don't think that's him? You think we've got the wrong man? Are you serious?

He wanted to take the lamp and swing it close to Gideon's face.

– I don't know whether that's Hitler. Have you smelt him? He smelt too much like a man. He's got diarrhoea. The scourge of God shouldn't smell that way. The real Hitler is inside the mountain. You haven't ever seen the *Riesengebirge*, like the mouth of an old leopard, white and grey teeth curving into the sky. The cold breath of those mountains hits you miles away. Listen to the pool, Amsel, listen.

The muffled booming of the gong passed just below them and drummed away into the unechoing forest.

– It's much louder than that in the mountains. That's where he's hiding, in the mouth of the black winds with the Redbeard and his armoured men. They were Jew-killers too. You can draw gold out of a Jew's bladder if you squeeze hard enough. I read that, carved on the wall in the prison tower at Schwarzberg. I don't think he'd let himself be caught and done to death, not by a few scarecrows wading through a swamp. When a grenade bursts the sharp bits scatter. This is one of his splinters. Perhaps there are many flying about. The thousand-year Reich has hardly begun, count for yourself. I know when Hitler will die. I know the day. When the last Jew is dead. Then he'll shout once more, one last bellow, so loud that the mountains will.crack, and he'll smile and fall dead on the stone table. But not until then. To be a Jew is to keep Hitler alive.

They heard Elie Barach's steps scuffing the sand as he went to the shelter, still mantled in his shawl.

– Why do you listen to me? Go to sleep. Check the paraffin and go to sleep.

– I want to go with you. Afterwards.

– Where?

– To Paris.

Isaac felt such lightness in himself, piercing through the weight of sleep and the churn of his bowels that he fluttered his hands before the hurricane lamp, a moth beating against the glass.

– To Paris. Where I'll study to become a film director. Oh, I know it takes a long time. You've got to know languages; they make you spend six months in the cutting-room just watching. But I'll become a director and write my own scripts. Like Jean Renoir. He's the greatest. I've seen everything he's done. I've seen *The River* five times. You remember when the flute stops sounding and you know that the snake has come? I'm going to make a picture about us, how Lieber's men went into the jungle and found Hitler. *Journey into the Green Hell*. Wide screen. No one has learned how to use a wide screen yet, not really. Antonioni faked it. I think he's really a still photographer. No film sense. I'll show how the Chavas surround us and won't let us go until we leave a hostage. Or until one of us fights against their best warrior using a spear set with piranha teeth. Long panning-shot of the fight and the circle of spectators. I think I'll cast you in the part of the fighter. You'll win, of course, but we'll have to show a great scar. At the end we'll be seen staggering out of the jungle, bearded, limping, almost delirious, and a great crowd will surge towards us. I'll use a zooming lens to show a sea of faces, ecstatic, unbelieving. We'll hand Hitler over to the waiting guards. Press helicopters overhead, painted bright yellow, cameras looking at my camera. But I'll never show Hitler's face, not full-on. Only from the side or in a shadow. In the last frame there'll be the back of his head and Lieber moving towards him.

– And the two heads will become as one.

– Yes. As one. Do you remember *Umberto D.*? Made years ago. I saw it at a festival of old films. There was an old man in that. I don't remember his name. I want him to play Lieber, if he's still alive.

– And use the back of his head for Hitler?

– Yes. No. I don't know why you say that.

Gideon's voice was almost too near.

– I want that old man to play Lieber. There was a marvellous close-up, the light glinting off the rim of his glasses. I'll never forget that. The camera must have been angled from below.

Benasseraf tapped the ash. His cigar was nearly out.

– Why should I go to Paris?

– Because you said you would. I heard you say it to John, on the train. That it was the only place where you could forgive. No. Not forgive. Not exactly. I don't remember the word. But something like that.

Isaac Amsel rocked gently on his heels. It warmed him and made him feel strangely housed to try to remember. They were old friends now labouring to get things right.

– And during the fever you said

Too many things. He carried the still in his mind, perfectly framed, ready for the long touch of his senses. A table fifty yards from the corner of the Place Fürstenberg, the trefoil silhouette of the streetlamps almost touching the red and white tablecloth. A little while earlier he had walked past the Librairie des Saint-Pères and seen his monograph newly displayed in the window. G. Benasseraf, *agrégé*, *Le Silence et le poète*, Editions de Minuit, the characteristic font, tight and a little forbidding, on the off-white jacket. Now, at the restaurant, he had ordered lunch: *pâté de campagne*, *brochette de fruits de mer sauce béarnaise* with *pommes pailles*, to be followed by the Boursin with its shade of garlic and a pear, speckled gold and burnt to the touch as was the sunlight of early afternoon. Before him the early edition of *Le Monde* with a *feuilleton* on his book. '*M. Benasseraf, dont la plume vive et érudite . . . cette page admirable de probité et d'intelligence sur Valéry . . . qui quoique de souche étrangère maîtrise la sensibilité française comme ne le font que trop peu de nos critiques en vogue . . . dont la lecture de René Char est témoignage philosophique non moins que poétique . . .*' The cold-earth savour of pâté was in his nostrils, the sunlight shivered into small eddies and crystals of red fire as it passed through the glass of Gigondas, the bread was new as morning, the chimes of St Etienne were striking half past one, their dry ivory note still clear behind the splash of the fountain. *Werd' ich zum Augenblicke sagen.* This perfect moment outweighing eternity, richer than damnation. And she was sitting across the table from him, waiting for Gideon to take the first bite, her hair smoke-brown as September grass, hooded in the soft dartings and quivering of the sun, her hand laid next to his, the cuff of her blouse closed with a charm, an ancient hammered thing of silver which, only an hour hence, in the sudden dark of their room, he would fumble at and unclasp. Her eyes were on the newspaper article mirroring his name but changing it, as her mouth changed his mouth, as the silent weight of her breasts changed his hand when he held them. In a moment he would bring the bread to his teeth and set the reel in motion again. But so long as his being dwelt on that image, on that convergence of all dreams, the chimes marked one-thirty and the sun danced untiring in the burning of the wine.

It was a glossy postcard, tourist-bait. Made up of all the miracles and reawakenings of his three years in Paris after his release from the sanatorium in Lündfjord. *Silence and the Poet* was unwritten though tenaciously projected. He had been to that restaurant once, but only to watch a friend eat, a shallow friend. He no longer knew his name. The breasts in his hand had been light, tired after short sleep. There had been no one to transmute him. He had not wanted to give that much of himself lest some ineradicable message in the blood carry over to a child his own memories, lest a child be born and grow up carrying with it his knowledge of pain or the monstrous shapes of fear and the inhuman which filled him. The cuff-links were real. He had broken a nail toying with their intricate clasp. Who had worn them? A man or a woman? Gideon was no longer certain.

Yet the snapshot glittered inside him with a weird pressure of life. It arrested in a waking dream the otherness of the world, the illusion of total possibility without which the soul falls to a dusty heap. To sit at that particular table and smell the summer in the wine, to write that book and hear the rustle of paper and fireman's fanfare of literary acclaim – *gloire* has the shape of a fireman's helmet – to lie with such a woman in the sea-noises of a Paris afternoon, these were indispensable longings. That postcard, sharp in every line, was Gideon's remembrance of the life to come.

He hated its banality, the fact that so many other men had taken the same view. It was a bright chromo, common as tinsel. It belonged to every young man in Paris who had read Balzac, who had seen Sartre pause to wipe his glasses in the Rue Jacob. Hope as cliché, as the uplifted finger of the street photographer. Why did these common wonders possess him? Who had been housed in hell. Why had his fantasies not been ennobled and made immune? Benasseraf loathed the quick sensuality of his day-dreams. A piece of cheese and its garlic tang sat more solid in his memory than the long hunger in the forest south of Grodny. When he turned imagination on his wife and the three children the focus was blurred and the light too naked. The montage of his unwritten book and of a woman's hand poised over the tablecloth had a wondrous precision. A man whose child has been burned alive and who has eaten dung in a sewer should know rarer, more exigent temptations.

– No. Not forgive. Not exactly. I don't remember the word. And during the fever you said

Amsel was near enough the truth. Not 'forgive'. He had never said that word to Asher on the journey from São Paulo. He had said 'become spurious like a child's tantrum'. That was the trap of his life in Paris. His hatred and the memories which made up the substance of his life were being nudged away. One by one the words in his mouth were beginning to drift into the future tense. A man whose child has been burned alive, whose wife has led another of his children into the gas, should use the future tense sparingly. Only to harry time, to make it ripen into vengeance. In Paris it had ripened into books and garlic cheese and the silver skein of cuff-link. That was why Benasseraf decamped and sought out Lieber.

– Back to Paris? Why should I? I'm not going back anywhere. I'm setting up a trading post at Jiaro. Kosher meals and shrunken heads.

Isaac could make out that Gideon had turned to him, that he was speaking to him more directly then ever before. But he knew he was losing him. Gideon cracked stupid jokes whenever his thoughts were distant.

– Look, said Isaac,

– look what I've been hiding. Even Simeon doesn't know.

He had got to his knees and was rummaging furiously in his pack.

– Look, Gideon.

He was on his feet, swaying and coiling like a wisp of smoke. He was clutching something, a small oblong. He gyrated, teasing and triumphant, beating a tattoo in the muffling sand. Suddenly, it was the first glint of light, Benasseraf caught a flash of metal. Still arching to and fro, Isaac Amsel began pulling out a thin, bending stalk.

– Look, Gideon, look. A transistor. A Japanese one. Nakima. I bought it in São Paulo. It picks up short-wave. Sometimes. When the nights are clear.

– Why have you been hiding it?

– Mine, said the boy,

– mine. Not yours, not even Simeon 's.

He was laughing, darting out of reach.

– No one would steal it from you. And stop dancing. Why are you dancing? You're a fool, Isaac.

– I bought it with the money father left me. Before he went. It took nearly all I had.

– What good will it do you? You won't pick up anything. Not out here.

The boy was still laughing and shushing and putting his finger to his lips. He turned the little radio around and around, now above his head, now at arm's length, whipping the antenna through the heavy air.

– Listen. Can't you hear?

His whisper was startling. It carried. Sounds were beginning to lift and take shape. The pool had stopped booming. Somewhere, quite near, a bubble broke and the rings glinted in the water.

The whisper had turned to a burst of static, needles showering a distant forest in the Cordillera. Isaac stood frozen. Only his wrists moved, banking the transistor now to the side. Now upwards, the antenna tracing delicate loops like a fly-rod.

– Listen, Gideon. Can't you hear it now?

And in the same moment in which he looked up at the break of light, Benasseraf heard it.

– *hombre hombre hombre mío*

Light tided in a sudden bright stain from the centre of the pool. The dark spilled along the edge of the jungle. Gideon was on his feet watching the canvas flap, the banana trees and the bodies of the sleeping men surface, their black forms edged with a silver contour. In the light of the sudden moon the air cleared and sounds quickened A sand-crab scuttled past his foot leaving a braided spoor.

– I've got something. Listen.

From one of the senders on the vast perimeter of the Amazon Basin.

– *hombre hombre hombre mío*

A woman singing, and behind her the oily slide of the tango. Late-night music. Incessant, always the same and inescapable up and down the entire continent, from Guyana to the Cape. Greasy as the *cantina* floor.

– Now you can hear it.

From San Martin. Or Orosso. No, there was no station in Orosso, only the wireless in the shack by the airstrip. But the new radio tower at Vila Branca might reach. It seemed almost impossible. Across the desolation of the grasslands, the web of the falls, the Cordillera, the muffling rag of the swamp.

– bésame bésame hombre mío

The boy stood rigid, the transistor away from his body. His eyes were on Gideon's; they had gathered the new light and were dancing.

– míoooooii

Her trill lifted and flexed like a monkey's tail before vanishing in the hot thump of the saxophone. Then, at once, the voice started again.

– salida del sol salida d'amor

The rope was moving.

Asher jerked up out of his first sleep feeling it slide across his wrist. Simeon lifted his head. In the moonlight the hurricane lamps had dimmed to a candle-flame. The rope was moving on the sand.

– flores de mí corazón flores.

The voice reached them. Asher remembered the butter gone rancid on the march to Jiaro. Simeon sat up. A slow shadow passed across the tent-cloth. Benasseraf saw him, his face like a plaster mask, the hair glued to it. He was shuffling toward Amsel, his hand cupped to his ear. The top button on his fly was undone.

– Music. Music, said Hitler.

The boy turned and sprang back. He swung the radio away from Hitler in a wild toss. It dangled from his wrist and the strap twisted.

– Let me hear the music. I haven't heard music. Oh, in a long time. Many years perhaps. *Blumen*. It is a long time since I have heard a woman sing.

– No. No.

Amsel was yelling. Yelling so the forest rang.

– No!

Hitler stood, staring at him.

– I won't harm the radio. I want to hear the music. Only the music.

The box had gone silent, but the minute sphere at the tip of the antenna continued to vibrate.

– Stop shouting, said Benasseraf,

– stop it.

He was shivering and threw his cold cigar into the pool.

8

– flores de mí corazón flores.

– Shit

Rodriguez Kulken, coming to and shaking off the sour netting of his sleep, said it to himself. Then again

– Shit

under his breath, spitting it languidly at the back of the neck of the woman who lay beside him snoring. He hated the song. He hated the singer, Carmelita Rosa, whose treacle voice choked his earphones nightly as he cut across the sender from Brasilia. He hated that song because the syrup of its tune, tum tum ta ta tum ta, stuck to his brain. As the mango seeds stuck to the roof of his mouth. Now, more awake, Kulken passed his tongue over the stump and cavity on the upper left side. But together with the taste of singed rubber and sleep – the woman's coffee was a foul thing, an outrage here where the upland bean could be had dirt-cheap – came the thrum of the song. *Flores* ta ta tum ta tum *mío cor mío cor.* It had been the last thing in his earphones. And had stayed trapped under the net buzzing deep down into his heavy sleep.

Rodriguez Kulken caught the full scent of himself and said

– *Merde*

but no longer in uncertain consciousness. Across the rancid shoulder of the woman who lay beside him snoring he could see the milk-grey light of early morning. Kulken kept his front door ajar and only the screen-door closed. The Indians and Ruiz Manola, who ran the commissary and was *imperador* as far as his paunch and drugged eyes could reach, told him that he was loco. To keep his door open at night when the jungle exhaled – you could hear the first long sough of breath at sundown – and the poisonous air blew into Orosso. But Indians were shit and Ruiz Manola a loud-mouthed pile of ordure. Kulken knew about malaria. All you had to do was take plenty of quinine and keep your bowels open. Fresh air never killed a man. As it was, the house stank. Scour it, break your nails in the cracks between the floorboards, the fungus thrives. At night you can hear the damp crawl, hungrier than termites.

– Orosso is a cesspool in hell. *Una latrina nell'inferno. Ein Scheissloch in der Hölle. Une pissottière en enfer*.

Rodriguez Kulken said the litany each morning. Sometimes he added responsions in Portuguese, in Dutch, or in what he knew of Bororo. He said it before emptying his bladder. To affirm his erudition, to tune the fine strings of his worldliness and remind himself, in the scum and bog of his present sojourn, of loftier stations. He knew the tongues of men and their several nations, he was a condor among mice. And once more, but this time like an *aubade* bugled in his own honour, Kulken said

– *Merde*

whereupon he rose and stepped across the sleeping woman not kicking her. He would do that later, grinding the cork sole of his sandal into the small of her back. She would wake, extract the ball of gum from between her teeth and grin to know him there. Now he wanted to be alone. The tune was still buzzing in his skull but growing faint. He would be free of the filthy thing in a moment.

Kulken watched the bronze stream foam into the mottled bowl. By the time it reached Orosso beer was flat. Or Manola had spat in it. And the greasy bitch still snoring under the raised mosquito netting couldn't keep the ice from melting in Kulken's cooler, not if he showed her a dozen times and bloodied her mouth in the bargain. Indians were dung. Whatever Father Giron might say. The ones that looked human were dangerous. They made it hard to tell. Like Teku, the mongrel, who slithered in from Jiaro with soft monkey-skins and carved fishbone and had contacts with the Chavas – or so it was said. Kulken shook his member thoughtfully and straightened up, his back tingling with the new emptiness of morning. When he remembered.

He had dreamt of a motorcycle. It had barrelled through his sleep just before the song had come back. The rest of the dream was a blur but the tattoo of the engine stayed loud like one of the 500-cc Hondas he had seen lashing around the circuit in Montevideo. Why should Rodriguez K. dream of a motorcycle? he enquired of himself with solicitude still stroking his foreskin. Of course: his spell as a dispatch-rider for ITT in Barcelona just after the war.

Kulken belched and inhaled the acid freshness of the outhouse.

Barcelona in the late spring of '45. Gunning the engine on the dilapidated Harley, the pride of the ITT stable, out of the chill courtyard into the white sun of the Calle Mayor. Up the sugar-loaf and down the hairpins, twisting around the eucalyptus gardens and through a crazy chute to the harbour. Kulken had been *el diablo*, the red spark. No other rider could touch him. He had driven by smell, knowing that he must change gear and throw his leather-encased body to the left at the precise instant when the eucalyptus faded and the first whiff of fried oil charged to meet him from the Ramblas.

His legs still apart on the cold dirt-floor, Rodriguez Kulken threw back his head. Memory breached the dyke.

False papers. Real people carry false papers. Only queers and Belgians travel under their own names. R. Kulken had been many tints and delicate stipples. He knew how to coax the metal prongs through the stiff paper in a Danish driving-licence so as not to betray a change of photograph. Or where the gum loosened in a *Livret militaire* (he had carried one in Metz). The filigree of an Irish passport enchanted him and he retained in his left thumb the remembrance of the perforations, so intricate yet easy to counterfeit, of a Moroccan *permis de séjour*. It had almost cost him his balls to get that piece of pasteboard. The stapler with which the Consul General of Ecuador in Antwerp affixed his seal to a visa was locked away in a cabinet – *Compagnie des coffre-forts de Liège 1911* – set between the two east windows in the back room. The lock yielded to a hairpin.

To know this was knowledge. Kulken's brain was packed with sharp-edged monads of exact wisdom. He knew where the night-express from Oporto, the 9:14, slowed down before entering Lisbon. He knew that the lack of proper lighting at the south end of the customs shed at Fishguard made it easy for a man to squat in the pools of shadow and wait for the tea-break which came at 10:55 after the second ferry. Knowledge. Not the spindrift that fogs the minds of ordinary men. But nuggets, fine as Björnske ball-bearings, and gathered at a price. Kulken kept them polished for instant use by a study, more exhaustive than that of the Mayanos runes, of the only real truths that men have set down: timetables, shipping registers, customs regulations, ordinances from the Bureau of Standards, visa applications, questionnaires addressed by the Principality of Liechtenstein to all who would incorporate, triplicate certifications obtainable from the

Panamanian office of flag registry, the *Bulletin commercial de la Banque du Nigère* invaluable for its schedules, more evocative of the scent of forest and sea than any verse, of soya and coco transfers. Kulken had flicked the gnats out of the maelstrom of his reading lamp and pored over the monthly newsletter of the Agence Havas and the *Zettel für Devisenhandel* of the Düsseldorf Finanzamt. He knew how thirty-day bills were discounted in Trieste and the name of the daughter of the widowed dispatcher at the Bergen marshalling yards. She had a passion for nylons and yellow plastic raincoats.

Mí corazón flores de mí

That was garbage. False as an import licence for Honduran teak. The truths of life spoke from ruled paper and columns of incorruptible figures. No man was himself for long, but hollow and veering as a windsock. The fact – rooted in the taste for peyote of the sheriff of Small Springs, Texas – that the easy ford into Mexico 19.4 miles south-east of Juarez was never patrolled before midnight on the second Wednesday of the months between October and June, was a solid, beauteous thing. It would not crumble in one's palm. A man could stake his mortal soul on it. Rodriguez Kulken had, twice.

Not that his papers were, in the ordinary sense, false. How could they have been true? Kulken remembered his mother. She owned a green cardigan which enveloped his entire sense of childhood and there had been an almond smell in her hair. He could not sever that smell from the recollection of a gravel path behind the pension in Ostend where they had, for reasons unfathomable, mouldered during the early 1930s. Who was his father? A Flem, said the chiromancer in the fairground in Cincinnati, squinting at the touch of pepper and flax in Kulken's eyebrows. But the barber in the Posthotel in Solothurn had opined, through the steaming caress of the towel, that, 'Monsieur has a fine mouth, a Semitic mouth.' No matter. He had shed his skin whenever necessary. He had left it in station lockers and on coat-hangers in empty hotel closets. What had they made of the Homburg, still quite new, he had left deliberately on the top shelf in the King's Arms at Bradford, or of the hair-dye flushed imperfectly down the toilet in the entresol WC of the Hotel Astoria in Belgrade? This was the century of the borrowed skin. Men who knew their fathers or had come of age in a single house were freaks. The poplars were down, their roots a dead tangle sticking out of ditches. It was a good time for the long-legged and those who could make a bundle of their shadows. The roads themselves had begun to move under the persuasion of the bombs.

They had almost speared him, at the poste restante counter in the main post office in Geneva. He had forgot the number of his *casier*. He hesitated a minute and the sirens of the police cars had started up in the Rue des Bergues. 832. Kulken hated that number but would never again forget it. He had made the Rosière tramcar on a dead run. Where had he switched to the North line and shaken them off?

Kulken narrowed his eyes and sucked in his cheeks in fierce concentration. A fire-ball exploded only a yard from his stretched skin. He flinched and grabbed for his crotch. A cold shaft passed through his kidneys.

Again the rooster crowed and bright knives spun in the morning air. Kulken gathered up his pyjama bottoms and heaved out of the privy. The stinking fowl. Its cry had dried up the past; all the rich shades were receding.

When he wanted to Kulken could move fast. On the floor of the yard his shadow grew to a thunderous fist. The bird shot its neck to one side and flounced away in a puff of red and dusty orange.

Kulken aimed a high kick. His sandal slapped the wall of the shed. The rooster lifted a leg and Kulken wondered momentarily at the cruel, ancient shape of the thing. His rage ebbed and he turned towards the house feeling the night-damp of the clay between his toes.

– *Cojones*

He breathed the word in a salute to the sun now spilling against the horned spine of the Cordillera and dispersing the haze which drifted across Orosso from the falls. He straddled the woman's jumbled form, saw that the shift had bunched well above her buttocks and lay down.

He had been keeping late hours.

For three weeks he had been listening. Till his eyeballs ached. The leather arc of his head-set was black with perspiration and left a swath in Kulken's thin hair. Monitoring Nimrud and Ajalon. Gleaning through the static and the oily wash of music from Pernambuco, from Rio or Brasilia, as its loud, ghostly amours criss-crossed the pampa and the Amazonian forest, a code out of Revelation, an alphabet reversed and permuted out of Chronicles and Malachi. He had picked up, his skull hammering, the weave of names out of Joshua 15

– *Kirjath-baal which is Kirjath-jearim and Dannah and Kirjath-sannah which is Debir and El-tolad and Chesil and Hormah*

(the latter repeated and followed by a signal reading Exodus 30, xxiv)

– *And of cassia four hundred skekels*

(as his contact had pointed out the text should read *five* hundred)

– *after the shekel of the sanctuary and of olive oil a hin*

At which monosyllable Rodriguez Kulken had found himself staring like a man drugged.

At one point, when the rain swashing against the roof had made it almost impossible to hear anything clearly, the message had been some kind of acrostic threading between Numbers 33

– *and they departed from Kibroth-hattaavah and encamped at Hazeroth and they departed from Moseroth and pitched in Bene-jaakan and they removed from Bene-jaakan and encamped at Hor-hagidgad*

and Matthew 1, xii–xv. In which latter text the begettings had been scrambled so that Achim begat Salathiel and Sadoc found himself to be great-grandfather to Jechonias.

Not that Kulken had to do the deciphering. Let the office in Montevideo break its balls over *Golan in Bashan with her suburbs*, and London figure out why Samuel 9, x, had been flashed thrice, on the night after the transmitter had moved three degrees south-east of Jiaro, but with a change in the canonic number of servants

– *Mephibo-seth thy master's son shall eat bread never at my table. Now Ziba had fifteen sons and twenty-three servants*

For the rat's fodder they gave him Kulken was doing enough. More than enough. There were nights when his fingers had swollen to pale grubs just transcribing the stuff, trying to separate the syllables as they crackled or whispered out of the jungle. There had been thorns in his ears; he had felt them bleed.

Kulken had understood. Oh, right from the start. Even that turd Manolo had understood. Orchid-hunter? Not this lot. Not for all their botanical atlases and best-quality butterfly nets and Leyden jars. Hunters for men. Jew-hunters. Manolo had known almost as soon as the boy had come into the commissary with his supply-list. Fish-hooks, nylon line, Zippo windproof lighters (United States Army surplus), Benzedrine, bricquettes, quinine, 38-calibre ammunition, sulpha. When the boy and the other man, the thin one with the greasy locks, had asked for a stretcher, with extra carrying-poles, Manolo, who had none to sell, said

– Those must be heavy orchids you're after, orchids with a backache.

But neither the boy nor the man had laughed.

There had been other botanical forays. They had plucked Eichmann and Stangler. Ottmar Kühnhardt's body had turned up at the municipal dump in Punta Blanca. The man's eyes had been gouged out. Or so it was noised. They had almost trapped Mengele.

But there was bigger game. Kulken knew, even before that pimply nit of a contact in Montevideo had told him. They were after Bormann, still. They wouldn't let go. Not after all the false leads and the killing of their best man in Paraña. Martin Bormann. He was a fishbone in their throats.

So Kulken had been instructed to take leave of absence – recurrent jaundice – from the flea-circus in which he was employed, the Stella Maris Travel & Shipping agency, and had come to Orosso. Which was the world's anus. He had been there, in it up to his eyebrows, for three weeks, monitoring, passing back to Montevideo the weird chatter of Nimrud and what he could bug of distant Ajalon.

He didn't think they'd get him. Not in that patch of hell. Not alive, that is. Perhaps they'd find his jaw-bone on a Chava bracelet or spoon guava from his polished skull. They were fools. They had bartered the face for the dream and it had made their breaths rancid. Not that Rodriguez Kulken hated Jews. He had made up his mind about them a long time ago when he had seen them whore and beg for visas in Lisbon. They were the snot of the human race. From time to time every man had to pick his nose and suck his fingers clean. Kulken liked to pick his own nose, particularly after sex, and had perfected a delicate probing. If it hadn't been the Jews it would have been someone else – the Sinhalese, for instance, or half-breed Flemings. Killing Jews was a piece of stupid ingratitude. Like scraping one's nose *too* clean.

So he didn't wish the poor bastards ill as they burrowed into the jungle but only prayed they would hurry and give up their fool's errand.

That cordial wish had soured to a dull rage as he found himself nailed, night after stinking night, to his transmitter, either snatching at the wisps of speech from beyond Jiaro or being plagued by queries and commands from London (that, of course, was where the queer from the *Review of the River Plate* got *his* orders).

Kulken was on the point of spewing up the whole business; he had eaten his fill. He was going to pack up his gear and return to the coast. Signals had been growing fainter and more riddling. Remote Ajalon hardly responded or only in wild bursts. One whole night there had been nothing to monitor except the disc jockeys out of Brasilia. Before his smarting eyes the needle swung through an arc of tangos and static. When suddenly.

In the first hour of morning.

Recumbent now, his hand idling in his crotch, Rodriguez Kulken remembered. He was not a man lightly stirred. But this had made the skin tighten over his temples. A cry out of the forest. White and sharp as a snow-crystal.

– *One thirty-six. One thirty-six. O give thanks unto the God of gods.*

As if a near fire sang in his earphones.

– *and slew famous kings; for his mercy endureth forever.*

No cipher now. Only that cry of triumph lancing the morning air and vibrant in him still.

– *Sun stand thou still upon Gibeon, and thou Moon in the valley of Ajalon.*

The cry was in his marrow, blinding.

– *And there was not a day like that before it or after it that the Lord harkened unto the voice of a man.*

Kulken had strained to catch the answering sound, the ring of pipe and timbrel from the east. He had held his breath till the veins hammered in his neck. Nothing had come. Not another syllable. He had passed the news to Montevideo where the squit would get off his soft ass, preen himself, and send the message to London: *Orchidacis muscata amazonia.* And take the credit.

Kulken had been told to keep listening, to chart the movements of the party as it headed back to Jiaro. He'd listened till his spine creaked.

Nada. As if their sender had failed. He'd slept and listened again. Nothing on the second night. *Flores del mío cor flores*. And slumped under the netting, numb with exhaustion.

Kulken closed his puffed lids. A pleasant warmth rose between his thighs. His hand strayed to the woman's buttocks, paddling the brown half moons and exploring the cleft. Kulken loosened his pyjamas and began to turn sideways. Just then his drowsy thoughts missed a step and a sharp jolt went through him. That was no dream of a motor cycle. There had been an engine hacking and whining above the roof. It had woken him. Motor cycle, hell. A plane had landed in Orosso. Just after sunrise.

The figure bulked in the doorway cutting off the light. Kulken's eyes opened wide. He saw the neatly creased whipcords and the yellow leather of the pilot's boots. American. And this time Rodriguez Kulken said quite loud

Scheisse

9

When to Rabbi Jehudah Ben Levi God, hallowed be His Name, dictated the Torah, greatly against His instincts, for the Word had been until then living, seed burning in the flesh because unwritten, might there have been an error made? Because the stylus slipped or the wax of the tablet flaked in the bronze heat of the Babylonian day. Because a gnat had lodged in Jehudah's ear. Because, for a millionth of a second, the Master had drowsed. Because God, may He forgive the libel of my thought, chose to plant one tare in the harvest of His giving, one false accent, one letter wrong, one word out of place, out of which speck has grown till it smothers man the black tree of our hurts. Out of which has sprouted the knife between my toes and the pus hammering at my heel, where the pack rubs. Out of which have swarmed the green flies that hang on the wet sore in my crotch. The black tree of life whose shadows are like nets around my feet and sicken the brain. Whose roots rear out of the swamp to trip me, whose vines will slap my face at the next step, now, O God, hallowed be Thy Name I am falling, whose droppings are the slime in my hair and the stench the stench the stench. I have not fallen.

But *which* word? Which letter or vowel sign or number? It may be only one digit in the numbering of the people or of the cubits of terebinth prescribed for the outward pillars of the tabernacle. Which *iod* has been omitted, which *gimel* misplaced in the three million and eleven characters of Torah. Which being thus imperfect has brought to man not peace not love not clean water but the stench the razor under my sole the needles in my shoulders where the strap burns. Not linen to lie in at evening but the rubber sheet stinking in my hand. Not the child's step in the lit house but *his*, just behind me now, at the root where I fell. Almost fell. Praised be Thou that hast led us.

Which word, which word?

The most learned Isaac of Saragossa declared that the error was in Genesis 22, i. God would command an old man to slay his child but not *tempt* him to do so. Temptation is vile, like a memory of blue air and open sea here in the cauldron of the swamp. Nathaniel Ben Nathaniel of Gdansk had, in 1709, conjectured that Rabbi Jehudah had misheard, O ugly mystery of misprision, Exodus 15, xx, for though it be right to dance before the eyes of Pharaoh's drowning host it is wrong to *strike timbrels*. That dance must have been a heavy and silent thing like the hover of the honey-wasp in the jungle.

I can't go on much further,

thought Elie,

the sweat blinds me and draws the flies. They cover my mouth.

In Mainz, Ephraim the Cabbalist had taught his disciples that the mistake was to be found in the seventy-eighth letter of the thirty-third verse of the twenty-sixth chapter of Numbers, seventy-eight being the cipher of Tammuz the hanged one, thirty-three that of the degree of Mercury when it is in the house of the crab and twenty-six

O God, let me take twenty-six steps more before I fall and take the knife from under my feet and let cold water

But Ephraim had been burned and Gamaliel of Messina, the learned of the learned had written, in a hand disguised and in a Midrash found only after his death, that the Name of God in the Torah, be it sanctified for ever and evermore, was a false name, that even that Name which no man may pronounce was, as compared with the true Name, no more than the dust of dung when set beside rubies. Each time we call upon Him we call in error and cough like toads in the green scum. Lance the boil under my arm whatever be Thy name. Bring me to firm ground. Simeon is falling. Simeon. And the boy is shouting. The flies are in my breath. My breath is like a stink. My own master, Shelomoh Bartov, said to us that the unfathomable error, the breach through which evil has rushed on man was the word *and* in Leviticus 10, v. He said it with such sadness that none of us dared question him. We pored over the text in feverish wonder. A word without shadow, a word lighter than a mote in a sunbeam.

Why *that* word? So I asked. Whereupon the Master called me a dunce, one who understands less than a *goy*, and answered, as in a song to himself, why that *and*? For the reason deeper than reason that it could be any other. And had begun to sing louder and driven us out of *cheder*, like mice, before the song would lift him from the ground. Shelomoh Bartov who was a just man and who danced in the fire-pit at Grodny.

Where I ought to have been with him. It would have been quicker. Than this red scratch in my neck. Quicker than this march which is like many deaths. Death up to the groin, death where the pus hammers, where the buckle scraps across the blistered skin. Blasphemy. The flies are on my tongue. If Simeon doesn't call a halt. But *he* is keeping up. I heard his step behind me. Stronger than yesterday. He takes small hops like an old frightened man. He *is* frightened of the swamp and the fright pricks him. Like an old puppet of a man in little hops. The thorns have scratched his cheek. Now I know which word it is. 2 Deuteronomy xxv: and shall *tremble*.

Benasseraf's trembling had not stopped. The shakes began as he turned from the pool that morning, a slow pounding out of some broken, feverish place beneath the skin. It jerked at the corners of his mouth and made the sweat cold between his fingers. Elie Barach had watched Gideon's back as they set out. Under the blackened shirt, under the carbine strap and the lanyard on which he carried two water-flasks, Gideon's ribs and backbone quivered. At every few steps a drum-roll beat under Gideon's skin from the neck down and the flasks tinkled. Elie could smell the sweat in Gideon's hair. And sourer than sweat the smell of the fever. It made his own heart race. Simeon knew. Elie could tell by the frequent short halts. By Simeon's decision that Asher bring up the rear.

The fever had passed to the forest. The ooze shook under their feet. Daylight vibrated in sharp jabs, out of reach above the dank, shivering vines. Benasseraf had his teeth set and walked in a hunch as if carrying through the mist of the bog a fragile, knife-edged burden. Now and again he would bend low and emit a choked cry.

They stopped where a hummock of swamp-grass, its thorny blades high as a man, protruded from the morass. Isaac Amsel sat down in the green cage and picked at a bleeding scab. Simeon had his hand on Benasseraf's left shoulder. He felt the tremors pass through his own arm. Their faces were close in the thick air.

– Gideon. *Mensch.*

The electric eel was loose in Gideon. He clenched his teeth against the next jolt.

– Have you taken?

Early that morning Asher had tapped the powder into his unsteady palm.

– You've got to take more. You'll break in pieces. Do you want us to carry you? *He* can walk. He's been nimble as a goat. Stop it. You'll break if we go on.

The low cry and Gideon's teeth unlocked.

– I've had worse attacks. I. I. Don't stop. Not here. It's the swamp. It makes the fever

A spasm shot through him. Simeon tightened his grip. He smelt Gideon's sick breath.

– makes the fever worse. I can make it. If we reach dry ground. I

They swayed and argued, close as wrestlers.

– We're getting you out of here alive. If we have to camp a week.

– Let me be, Simeon. I'm better when I keep going.

He fumbled for the quinine and the chain of the flask tinkled loud.

– I am better. Let me. We have to move.

Gideon tensed his body and swallowed the drug. As he straightened a cold current passed down his spine. He dropped the water bottle. Simeon bent down and their cheeks brushed.

– We're stopping here until you're better.

– If we stop here I'll. Get us to dry ground. We can't be too far. I'm better already. Not here.

A bird's egg lay in the mud near Asher's foot. He looked closely. It was teeming with red dots, minuscule, devouring swamp-lice. He bent lower still. He thought he heard a sound, like the scratch of a nail far off. A smell of sulphur rose at him.

They hacked their way through the dripping net. For the first time Amsel was front man. Simeon had dropped back to be with Benasseraf.

When he swung the machete Isaac pivoted on his hips and forced his shoulders down as Gideon had taught him. His wrists were swollen. When the blade tore through nothing but dead vines or tree-moss it wrenched him off his feet. At other strokes it cut clean and the white sap spurted. At every few yards Isaac wiped the edge. Sodden fibres and thorns stuck to his fingers. Once, absently, he touched his muddied knuckles to his mouth and spat violently. Something jellied had moved across his lips. The vegetation arched above his head.

The six men slogged knee-deep through the swamp. In the fitful light the water gave off an oily sheen. The cutlass slashed a windless tunnel through the lianas. Rats slid away their eyes blind and blood-rimmed. Between strokes the boy spoke to himself.

We are in the sewers. They run west-south-west under the ghetto wall and come up in Nowy Swiat. But we've missed the right grate. If I lift the cover now there'll be a boot standing on my face.

He hacked faster. Too fast. Wasting motion and slicing too high so that the spikes whipped back and tore their legs. His lungs hurt. There was no touch of life in the air. As if the bog had drawn and exhaled the same dead breath over a million years. The harder he breathed the more he seemed to choke. A rubber mask pressing down.

Isaac Amsel lashed out with his free arm but the leaves lay heavy on his face. He bent double, panting. Behind him Simeon waited. The boy felt a drilling inside his head. The sound rose to a white screech and filled his ears. He swung his head groping for air. The machete dragged him down. He was going to faint. But the sound was too loud. It spiralled above him and behind. It drowned the chattering of Gideon's teeth and the slither of the rats. Hitler was jabbering and pointing upwards.

– Like Stukas, Rrrrrrr. Blitzing.

The fever had opened the sores on Gideon's legs. High in the massaranduba tree a brown cluster, lice-ridden and mantled in sleep, had caught the odour of blood. The brown furry grape burst. The bats plummeted, their wings flaring. They found a rent in the canopy of leaves. They careened in the hot shadows shrilling. Their brown leather wings slapped the cane-grass and crazy for flight they wheeled from the thrashing men. But the thorn-brakes and hollow of vines held them caged. They dived at the hot smell in the trodden grass and screeched.

– Rrrrrrr

said Hitler, ducking. The bat veered away, a strand of grey hair in its crooked thumb. A brown shape tore at Asher's knee. He kicked wildly and for a moment the bat lay on its back, its belly the colour of smoke. Then it flew straight up, inches from his face, its screech like a file across his teeth.

– *Die Vampire*

cried Hitler

– the drinkers of blood

and fluttered his hands in front of his face. A bat skimmed Isaac's hair. The sound whipped like wire across his skull. Now the leech came in again. He could see its eyes, green as mould, and the skin pinched around its wet nostrils. Its foxes' ears were taut in flight. He stood paralysed, his throat muscles pounding. The bat was drivelling. As it swerved its spittle flecked the boy's cheek. Amsel cried loud. The air rushed out of him as from a man drowning. He swung the machete in a crazy arc and cried again.

A small bat writhed in the leaves, its wing pinned under Simeon's foot. Its other wing slashed the air. A wild piping came through its teeth. Simeon bent down. He wanted to touch the raging thing, to pass his finger over the quivering stays. The bat watched him, its eyes bursting at the rim. For a second it lay motionless, its claw open. Simeon wondered at the delicate curve of the nails. Hands of a blind child. Then the biter exploded under his foot. The animal foamed at the muzzle and Simeon felt the wing raking his leg. He brought down the butt of his carbine. He heard the bat's skull splinter. The wing leaped up and fell broken. Simeon drew back his shoe. Where the bat lay the ground sprang alive. In a moment the white maggots were at its belly and a dung-beetle had its scissors in the dead wing.

Then he heard Amsel's cry and flinched from the wheeling blade.

– Stop that. Stop swinging that thing. You'll take my head off. They won't kill you.

The bats ripped loose from the tangle of hair and the flailing bodies. They swarmed through a break in the palm fronds and out of sight. Only their screech lingered and a randy smell.

Hitler made a warbling noise and said

– All clear.

– Put that thing down. You'll cut yourself.

Isaac heard his own cry and stopped, bewildered. The machete hung in a knot of tree-moss and ferns.

– All clear,

said Hitler,

– finished. At sunset the Stukas go home.

But the raid had infected the march. A thrashing looseness possessed the legs and bodies of the six travellers. Even Simeon, who had taken the machete from the boy's flapping wrists and was again in the lead, heaved and stumbled forward breathing loud through his open mouth. He could hear the hiccups pummelling at Benasseraf's body and the sound drove him. Asher caught the scent of disarray, muskier than the fur of the tree-bat. He knew that Simeon had altered course, that the sun, where it scorched through the tunnel of leaves, had slid abruptly from his left shoulder. But he did not halloo or ask Simeon for a reason. The urge to quit the swamp, the conviction that it would be death to spend another night on the gaseous slew harried the marchers. They kicked their raw stinking legs through the scum, slashed blindly at the shapes which rose and bobbed before their faces, each man labouring in the net of his own panic, in the wild fear of being left behind.

They moved fast, waist-deep in a trough of grey mud, then through tassels of tree-moss, the braids swarming with aninga-beetles, armoured creatures suspended by their precise claw.

– Thy works are manifold

said Elie Barach, and slogged on. Once Hitler cried out, pointing at Gideon.

– We must stop. That man has the fever. He will make us all sick.

But no one seemed to hear and Hitler hopped forward lest Asher, lurching through the creepers just behind him, stomp on his heel.

Towards evening the air lightened. Simeon felt a distant coolness, a puff of living breath on his lips. The wall of vegetation began thinning. The light steadied and for the first time since they had waded into the morass Isaac Amsel saw his shadow whole. The sapucaias and swamp-sycamores drew apart. The water threaded into weedy channels; the green slick ebbed from their boots. Snapping a dry stalk, its top browned by the sun, Barach praised God. Soon they could hear each other's steps. The soughing of gas and oily water, the slap of vines, the blotted rasp of their own breath receded. A cicada sang bright as tin.

Twice Gideon tried to say

– wind, there's a fresh wind from the south

but his teeth were clenched against the fever.

Elie tripped and fell. His body was so worn that it lay like smoke on the coarse grass. He smiled and started to his feet. Simeon said they were almost out of the great bog and would halt for the night. Asher said he could smell fresh water. Beyond the stockade of trees the western sky was bright. The cockades of the calliandras seemed on fire.

– That man has the fever. He will infect us. He must be treated.

Simeon froze. It was the old voice. Now. For the first time.

– I know about the fever. That is how Körber died. I tell you that man must have rest. And quinine. And hot liquids. I tell you

The old voice. It passed over them like a scythe.

– Look at him. If we catch the fever we will die. Just so. Like the rats. We didn't have to hunt them. They gnawed their way into the hut. To get near the fire. And swelled up. Körber could swing them by his teeth. The tail between his teeth. But he caught the fever. You. Come and lie down here. Cover yourself up.

The voice as it had been, high-pitched, incessant. Like a vampire's wing but heavier, bending their necks.

– That's right. Just so,

said Hitler,

– *so geht es besser*

as Gideon Benasseraf put down his pack and slumped heavily to the ground.

It took time to get the drug down his pulsing throat. A woman's fingers, thought the boy watching Hitler tap the powder into Simeon's palm, the fingers of an old woman. Now the shadows lay close; shapes grew indistinct in the light of the small flame. The hunters were too winded to pitch a tent and even here, at the edge of the swamp, the earth was like a sponge. Only Asher stood apart trying to make out, through the screen of toquillas, acacias and charred grass the rise of the stars in the southern sky. They were off-course, he supposed, by almost ten degrees. But Simeon's back was to him, arched over the shivering, loud-breathing man.

– I tell you how it is. That man will die,

whispered Hitler,

– even if we reach help. Too late. The fever. It is in his bowels.

– Shut up, said Simeon speaking low,

– *Mund halten.*

The prisoner sidled away and fumbled at a button on his sere-grey tunic.

The cane-stalks cracked. Simeon glimpsed the gold in the otter's eye momentarily held by the fire. The wet scent hung on after the stalks closed. Asher found it difficult to read the constellations. Behind the tree-fronds the stars flickered and melted out of shape. Somewhere out of the far south, out of the burnt pampa, clouds were piling up.

Barach pictured the fever as a lizard, a spiny quick thing free from its cage in Gideon's body. Through his swollen lids he watched it dart up Gideon's thigh and scrabble in his groin. Sometimes it shot its venom into Gideon's mouth; a trickle of saliva came from the corner of his lips. Elie Barach bent close, tensing his will, the love he bore Gideon, against the lashings of the worm. He reached into Gideon's flesh with the strength of his own stillness. When the body is at prayer it weighs more than cedar, said Ithiel Ben Tov at Salamanca when the flames reached him.

The tremors lessened. Gideon's teeth opened and the vein in his temple grew flatter. Elie watched, immobile, his back like a strung bow.

– Elie. Elie.

Barach jumped. Had he fallen asleep? In the house of need? The fire was almost out and a blackness thicker than night towered in the south.

– Elie, is it you?

Gideon's eyes were open and fever-lit.

– Elie. Where are we?

– Almost out. Out of the swamp.

– Out? Too soon. We shouldn't be. Not yet. Not if we want to reach Jiaro. We're off-course. We must be.

– Simeon knows. If we hadn't cut east, if we were still in there, we would never get out alive. Look at me. I fell down and sat like a sick child when we reached here. And you. God be praised we're out of that. Like being buried.

– Perhaps we should have. I mean we should have stayed in there. Guarding *him*. Keeping sleep from him. Keeping the wind from his face. He would have outlived us. But our bones would have kept watch. He would have died slowly in the circle of our bones. And not heard sleep again or the fresh wind. Do you hear it now? We are wrong to be out of the swamp. To be out so quickly. Now he is asleep. Just like a man. The south wind. Do you feel it rising? I can almost reach it.

– Cover yourself. Try to sleep. Cover yourself, Gideon. When we're in Jiaro

– When?

– we'll have you well again. Soon now. But you must rest.

– Good as new, Elie?

– Better. Yes.

– I am tired. I am tired of me. Of the smell of me. In the swamp I knew where I was. And what he was. Now I

The fever snapped at Benasseraf's wrist. On the blanket his fingers jerked open.

– Now Hitler sleeps like any man. He can look at the stars. That's all we've done. Look there. The red one low in the north-east. In the swamp he could see nothing. Only the yellow air and the stench on the water. Why go to Jiaro?

– Stay covered. You'll be on your feet soon. We'll have help. And cold beer. The way your toes stick out, Gideon. We'll get new boots. And soap. I want a thick bar in each hand. Lieber is waiting in San Cristobal. Perhaps nearer.

– Lieber? Have you ever seen Lieber?

– Of course. That day on the ship. When you saw him. Of course I've seen Lieber.

– What did he look like?

– What did he look like?

Elie laughed or thought he had.

– Don't you remember? He was wearing glasses. The sun was like a knife. So he wore dark glasses. And a round hat. And an old raincoat with a belt.

– What was his face like?

– His face? Why, ordinary. Yes, perfectly ordinary. I didn't notice. Keep the blanket on you. It was dark in the cabin.

– Elie,

The noises of the bog were still loud in the cane-brake and Elie Barach leaned nearer. His back ached and he wanted to rub it.

– Elie, said Benasseraf,

– about Lieber. Simeon knows who Lieber is. He's the one that needs Hitler most. Lieber. They need each other like the breath of life. Lieber couldn't rest, couldn't breathe till he was found. And marched out of hell to where there is light. It had to be done, even if our bones rotted on the way. Without Hitler where is Lieber? Elie, try to understand. I'm not brain-sick, not yet. A man strangling his own shadow. Because without Lieber there would be no Hitler. Not any more. Listen to me. Don't turn away. I don't say there would never be Hitler. Or have been. But not now, sleeping next to us, the stars over him as they are over you. That's why we haven't seen Lieber's face. Not the whole of it. Supposing they were, supposing

Gideon's jaw quivered as the fever rose. Elie rolled the blanket under his armpits.

– I'm not saying. I'm not out of my head. But Lieber's need is a terrible need. It tastes of vomit. I don't want to see them. Not together. By the time you reach San Cristobal I won't be alive. Don't shake your dirty locks in my face. San Cristobal? I want no part of it. The job is done. We should stop here or go back into the swamp and there

– We pray for the coming of the Messiah. Interminably. Somewhere in the world, at every moment, a Jew is calling on the Messiah, wailing for him to come, to hurry. But not every Jew. There are those, oh, they are not many, and they are the secret ones, who whisper to him *not* to come. Who know that judgement and the end of time will be more dreadful, more hideous to man than all his afflictions. Jews are the lightning-rod. God's fires go through them, into their roots. We are made ash. Through our cunning the Messiah is delayed. Lest His justice and His vengeance consume mankind. Lieber is one of the secret ones. Lieber.

– Crap. Golden words. You make your bread of them. To you they smell sweet like your own shit. You sing to yourself. Even in the swamp. I heard you. When the rest of us were crazy for water you drank words. The secret ones, the parables of the masters, the seventy-two Names of the Unnameable. Words. Air out of the furnace. We are the people of the word. That's what they call us isn't it? Well, listen to me, O secret one,

– Don't, Gideon. Don't pull the blanket way. You're shivering.

– he too, *he*, the sleeper under the stars, he is a master of words. Greater than Hillel, greater than Akibah, greater by far than the thirty-six just ones.

– Try to keep warm. The night is turning

– Why, there is nothing he could not do with words. They danced for him. They set fire to stone. They made men drunk or battered them to death. We talk too much, Elie. For five thousand years we've talked too much. Talked ourselves and the world half to death. That's why he turned on us, that's why he could tear the guts out of us. Because he too is a man who made words louder than life. He and us. He and Lieber. Oh, such need of each other. A dog and his puke.

– You'll make the fever worse, said Elie Barach, and smoothed the blanket and the rubber groundsheet. They were soggy with dew. For a time Gideon said nothing. Then

– Elie, where are you?

– Here, Gideon. Right here beside you.

– The night is blacker, blacker than night. You see, I can talk like you.

– There are clouds behind us. They're mountainous.

– There were those who said

– Who said what?

– that he is one of us.

– A lie. A sick, stupid lie.

– Every file burned. The village where his father was born razed. The archives in Linz sacked the week after he became Chancellor. And a tombstone in Bucharest. The name Hitler under a star of David. Adolf Hitler.

– Lies. Journalists' gossip.

– A tramp out of nowhere. An actor. A master of words. Look at his mouth, even when he's asleep, look

– There's nothing to see. It's too dark. Nothing. He has his arm across his face.

– it moves. He speaks in his sleep. An actor's mouth. A Jew's mouth. Like yours. The words crowding behind his rotten teeth. Making his teeth hum.

– He's got his arm across his face. You can't see his mouth. I can't see my own hands. Stay covered, Gideon. You're shaking.

– That is why he had to kill all of us. He could not rest so long as one of us was left alive anywhere on earth to recognize him, to say, 'Welcome *Spieler*, word-spinner, mountebank.'

– All craziness. There is not a grain of truth in it. Fever and lies.

– How else could he have understood us so perfectly? Found us in the hidden places? Known that we would walk into the fire-pit, with just a dozen butchers, lame men, dogs gone in the teeth, herding a thousand Jews, a hundred thousand? How else would he have known?

– Madness, Gideon. Fantasies. You must try to sleep. You must sleep off your fever. We must press on in the morning. Before the rains come.

And Elie Barach turned to look into the nearing blackness.

– To be the final Adam. That's what he wanted, the old *Spieler*. What's the use of being a Jew, one of the chosen people, if there are millions of others? That's nothing to shout about. But to be the only one left. The last Jew. Kill all the others. And be the last. World with end. Can you hear me, *schlemiel*? Your lips are moving. I know they are. Moving in the dark. You murdering ham.

In the ferns a rat's foot crackled.

After a while, perhaps longer, Elie said

– the Other Messiah.

He said it not to Gideon Benasseraf, short of breath under his sodden blanket, not even to himself, but under dim compulsion, as if to reach his own hands, two grey patches divorced from him in the airless, totally still blackness.

– the Second One, foretold by Malchiel. There shall spring from the seed of Abraham, from the tree of Jesse, absolute good and absolute evil. Light out of Jacob and dark. Only one of our number could have accomplished what he brought to pass. Only a Jew could make of the Jew a man halfway to the house of death. His lips *are* moving. Even in sleep he says the incessant prayer, the other *kaddish*, no one dared speak of it in *cheder*, whose one hundred and nine syllables bring death and the end of time. Hitler the Jew.

Gideon, now propped on his elbow, could not make out all of Elie's words but heard the desolation.

– Don't. Elie. *Petit frère*. Don't cry. I am talking balls. I've got a fever in my head. It's all nonsense, fantasy. A sick man playing games.

He reached out but Elie shrank away.

– Don't listen to me. I was talking stupidly. Just talking to keep my teeth from rattling. That one over there? A hooligan. A mad dauber. Shit-brown. He'll be off our hands soon. We'll hand him over and act sane again. Listen, *zadik*, we'll go to the seaside, you and I. Sit on a bench all day till the wind blows us clean. And say marvellous words like, 'What time is it,' or, 'Stop picking your nose,' or, 'Do you want chocolate ice or vanilla?' Words human beings use. Not the lofty, poisonous *Dreck* we've been mouthing at one another in the swamp. Elie, don't cry like that. We're hysterical, we need a cold bath, the lot of us. I was saying anything that came through my poor head. Don't believe a word of it. It's lies just like you said, foul gossip. Him a Jew? And *so* stupid? To be caught by the likes of us? It's only that I thought that once we had him *everything* would be different. I don't know what I thought. That the stars would sing in their course, that's how it goes, isn't it, and the moon stand still over Rio. That we would step out of our own stink and be like men reborn. It's all foolishness. Even if there is no light anywhere else, anywhere in this stinking world, there should be light here so that I could see you, *petit rabbin*. I don't know what I imagined. Fevertalk. But you've stopped whining. I can't get the taste out of my mouth, like cabbage and chloroform. Like the smell of the open pits at Orosso. Do you remember? You turned green as piss. Give me some water, Elie. I know it makes the fever come on. But the taste is driving me crazy. Have you ever tasted yourself, I mean in small bits? That's why I talk stupid.

And Gideon talked on in a hoarse murmur drawing on what he had left of friendship and foul-mouthed ease. Until the thirst made his tongue stick.

– Come on, Elie. Give me some water. There's some left in my canteen. But Asher said there was a spring. I heard him say it. Elie. Can't you hear me?

Elie Barach sat hunched up, swaying a little. Gideon wondered at his soft breathing.

– You're fast asleep, little brother. I'll have to get my own water.

As Gideon pushed back the covers and shuffled the poncho from his feet, a numbness took hold. He pulled himself to his knees and rubbed his leaden calves. The damp lay on him like a sack. Gideon lumbered to his feet but could hardly feel the ground. He extended his stiff arms to keep from falling. The dark spun slowly around him and he bent forward. His dry mouth laboured.

– They're all asleep. *Les cons.* Asher said. He said there was a spring near by. I need a fucking light.

Gideon lurched and spread his fingers as if the night had pillars to lean against. He shuffled towards the tall grass. He pounded his foot on the ground trying to get the blood going. Under the black towering clouds, thicker than walls, the air stood absolutely still. A branch snapped in the far heart of the swamp. Gideon staggered and beat his heel on the sodden earth. Out of his numbness came the fever, its blade edging up his spine. His body slapped against the reeds and the sound carried like a shot. His arms and legs were strangers to him, wild hammers.

Gideon danced. The slow, tottering dance of his fever. His drumming steps boomed hollow.

Beyond the sycamores and tagua palms, in the thorn-bushes which marked the edge of the scrub, the Indian froze. The white men had seen him melt away. But he had shadowed their tracks. Now Teku heard the drumming. And whispered to himself that it was madness, evil madness, to dance the rain-dance when the clouds were coming on thicker than he had ever seen them, when they might, provoked by his false magic, swallow the earth. He looked up and gave a loud cry.

The east was gone. Where first light should have been there was now a fantastic smoking blackness.

The night burst in the south. A wall of thunder higher, louder than the great falls was boiling towards him. The dark raced at him in a blinding thrust. It slammed the air out of his ribs. Teku spun and ran for the trees. The first icy drop caught him in the neck. Then the cold black deluge was on him and he yelled for breath.

Gideon was still dancing. The earth steamed under his tread.

10

– Niiice

The pilot made three syllables of it, brushed his fingers across the amplifier and gave the rotary antenna a delicate turn.

– Very nice. A 207 rangefinder!

Appreciative, muted whistle.

– Haven't seen one of those before. Not mounted on a d-k circuit.

He flicked a switch. The blips came on dim, then contracted to points of humming brightness.

– I'm nuts about this stuff. I'm a radio ham. Just like you, Mr Kulken. You've got yourself some nice hardware. The man's glance shifted. But bleeding Jeeesus, what a dump.

Gathering her smock the Indian woman had, in motions amphibious, retreated to the far corner of the shack.

– No offence meant, lady. You got a nice place here I guess. But Orosso.

He had trouble with the word. It was new to him.

– Keerist, I've landed on some crummy strips in my day. But this field takes the cake. I almost cracked up taxiing in. And get a whiff of the joint. No drains?

The enquiry was solicitous.

– What kind of Indians you got here? I left one of 'em guarding the single. Gave him half a dollar. I told him I'd bust his ass if anything was stolen. That I'd skin his greasy hide. What kind of Indians you got, Mr Kulken?

He moved closer. There was liquor on his breath, but not much.

93

– God-damn bugs.

He slapped his forearm and peered thoughtfully at the squelch.

– Haven't you got any DDT, Mr Kulken?

Kulken was on his feet, his erection undermined. Who in hell are you? What do you want here? Who let you in? He couldn't have asked these stupid questions, couldn't actually have blurted them out, his cheeks rounded and sweating, in the bewildered stance of a grade-C thriller. Not Rodriguez Kulken who had, in settings infinitely more tortuous, in imbroglios more sinuous by far, kept his cool, not unmasked his batteries. Perhaps it was the pyjama bottoms that had precipitated him to so banal an exhibit of enraged wonder, the fact that he had not, in the haste of his rising, tied them properly and that they kept slipping from his shrunk but aching nakedness.

– Marvin Crownbacker. Pleased to meet you, Mr Kulken. And the lady. But everyone calls me Charlie.

This time Kulken heard himself say, 'Why.' Why Charlie? And the grossness of his query, the way in which each cliché of alarm made the ambush tighter brought sweat to his eyes.

– God-damn it. The bugs around here. Like crazy.

The intruder swiped at his chin but the insect was gone.

– This is a hot town you've got here. You bet, Mr Kulken. Why Charlie? Wish I knew. I was born and raised in Muncie, Indiana. They've called me that since I was knee-high to a grasshopper. You call me Charlie, Mr Kulken. It's friendlier that way.

And Marvin Crownbacker offered a warm, crooked smile.

Kulken tugged furiously at his pyjamas.

– What do you want? How did you get here? Get out of my house.

Which behest insinuated into Kulken's fuddled brain, with mournful, numbing clarity, the remembrance of a play seen long ago in a flea-ridden casino hall somewhere on the Belgian coast. The white-faced actor had cried, 'Get out of my house!' and pointed his long index finger.

– I flew in about an hour ago. You must have heard me coming down. Mist was covering the whole valley. Like flying through clam chowder. I nearly peeled the roofs off looking for the strip. And the engine was hotting on me. Mr Kulken, do you mind if I sit down?

Charlie swept from under the table the metal stool in which his host

94

had, for the past three weeks, sat each night, his bones stiff as wire, plucking the cries and turnings of the hunt from the loud secret weave of the air.

– I'm a radio ham. This kind of gear bugs me. Just like you, friend. So how about a cup of coffee. I've come a long way to see you, *amigo*, a very long way.

He'll show his hand, thought Kulken.

Charlie did. Over three cups of coffee with three lumps of sugar in each, two fried eggs, their yolks faintly mottled as they inevitably are in Orosso, and over a plate of seedcakes which the Indian woman, for all her brooding sloth, made beautifully. The gentleman from Muncie talked in a rush, his intimacies and casual foulness of speech like a smokescreen on a dun sea. The start of the affair was slippery. Charlie was a radio buff, oh, not on Mr Kulken's sumptuous scale, but pretty hot in his own small way. He had picked up some of the stuff Kulken had sent Montevideo and once or twice he had got a fix on the transmitter in the rain forest. Nothing like Mr K's precisions and range, but enough to put two and two together and find that they added up to – what shall we say? – a million, no make it two or three million bucks. Which wasn't hay, whichever way you chose to look at it. So he'd high-tailed it down to San Cristobal and hired an old crate of a Fokker, two-seater job, put in an extra fuel-tank and flown to Orosso. The god-damn sewing-machine had almost ditched him a hundred miles out of nowhere.

Where had he monitored Kulken in the first place?

Hadn't he said? He'd been in Brasilia, freelancing.

The word was to cover zigzags of life and a body of knowledge sudden, cascading, remote from Kulken's but in whose confident jargon Kulken could recognize an appetite for expertise, a feel for the grain and yield of things matching his own. 'When our friends hot-foot it out of the jungle (it must be hell's ass-hole in there) we'll be the first to say how-de-do, won't we Mr Kulken?' They hadn't been doing much transmitting over the last days and towards the end their signals had been barely audible. 'You bet you they're out of juice.' Which deprivation signified that there was only one link with the outside world: 'All that sweet circuitry of yours.' Why, they were sitting on a gusher, sitting on it right this minute. They'd need a truck to cart the money to Fort Knox. It was, forgive the expression, the biggest piece of fuckin' good luck that had ever happened to Marvin Crownbacker and he was going to make sure that Mr Kulken got more than his cut, say twelve per cent more, 'Seeing as to how you're Johnny-on-the-spot and got the old mike just waiting, pretty as can be.' Because this was the biggest story of the century. Bigger than Lindbergh. Bigger than John Fitzgerald and welcome to Dallas, the friendly hub. Bigger than Jonestown – and that had been a honey of a PR set-up if Charlie had ever seen one. God Almighty! this was the hottest news-break since Jesus got off his slab. This was like being at tombside and getting an exclusive from Him on the way upstairs. A couple of million dollars? More, Sir, perhaps more. First there'd be the interview with the old motherfucker himself. They'd have US, Canadian and world rights on that and all reproduction thereof, live, canned, videotaped. 'How does it feel being back out? What were your first thoughts when you saw these gentlemen dropping in on you? Do you think they'll try you in Jerusalem like the other guy? Anything you want to tell the folks out there about life in the jungle? Any dietary problems? It's a while back, but now that they may hang you, any regrets? Any thoughts about how your mother would feel?' Let Mr Kulken imagine it if he could. World rights on *that* with a hundred million people out there waiting to hear every word and a hook-up on satellite. After which there'd be hour-by hour flashes and feature fill-ins. What's he eating? How's he sleeping? A special word to the Krauts. An appeal to the Vatican. Who's going to be his mouthpiece at the trial? Then there'd be the good guys. How many did Mr Kulken reckon there were? Three, four, half a dozen? Hadn't they been seen slipping into the forest? The full treatment for each man in the party: life-story with serial rights (Charlie had brought along the contracts, the agent's release forms, the whole legal crap). Background stuff: what brought you here, Mr Cohn? How does it feel being a world hero? Was it the greatest thrill of your life, I mean when you spotted him? What will the missus say and the kids? You have a sweetheart in Tel Aviv? OK, Mr Kulken here will hook in a circuit and you can talk to her. All rights reserved. Charlie wasn't any Cartier-Bresson. But he'd taken along a couple of Leicas and a Graphlex 400. They'd have the first pictures, the only pics for the agencies, at least during the first forty-eight hours. Any TV outfit wanting to show them would have to pay, through the nose. Two thousand for each individual snap, ten thousand for a group shot of old *Shitgruber* and the rover boys against a jungle background. Charlie had brought colour film, 'so maybe we can throw in a few Indians'. He figured they had forty-eight hours, maybe a bit more if they played it smart, once the party was out of the jungle. Two days before Orosso turned to Coney Island, before every god-damn journalist, cameraman and publisher from Kalamazoo to Ulan Bator came in by helicopter or go-kart. By which time

– they'll have to come to us, Mr Kulken, 'cause we'll have the contracts, the sole and exclusive right to deal with and negotiate for the sale of subsidiary and other rights within all territories covered by said agreement, i.e. newspaper and magazine serialization, anthology digest quotation and abridgement, dramatic, film, radio and television, microphotographic reproduction and picturization, reproduction by gramophone records and other mechanical means whether by sight, sound or a combination thereof, translation into any foreign language and that, Sir, includes Bantu, Toltec, Easter Island and/or Yiddish. If the publishers have not sold paperback rights two weeks after publication of the hardcover edition or agreed to publish a paperback themselves, the said sole agents and representatives for the said motherfucker and our heroes will have the option to negotiate with a publisher of their own choice for said paperback edition the publisher's share then being reduced to fifteen per cent.

Some of which rights, especially to more recondite portions of humanity, Messrs Crownbacker & Kulken, otherwise entitled C-K Universal, would resell, because greed was a vile thing and because they had no hankering to spend the rest of their affluent lives signing releases to bushmen.

– Millions, pal, millions. Sweet Jesus above!

At which invocation the gentleman from Indiana surged out of his seat exultant, threw his head back and whipped a sugar-cube into his mouth. But Kulken too was on his feet attempting a dry, superior laugh.

– You're crazy, Mr Whatsyourname. Loco. You have jungle fever, that's what you have. A million dollars? For an interview with Martin Bormann?

– Martin Bormann? Who's he? Who the hell is Martin Bormann?

The two men stared at each other. Crownbacker spat the sugar from his mouth and forced Kulken to his seat. He thrust his face close and spoke slowly. As to a very stupid or very cunning child.

– Listen to me, Mr Kulken. Let's not waste time playing games. Listen to Charlie. He's your friend. When Adolf Hitler walks out of that jungle

Kulken went white and sagged forward. Charlie yelled at the Indian woman in a voice loud enough to wake Manolo at the other end of the village.

– Get me a glass of water. Water, you stupid bitch. *Agua*.

Kulken came around soon enough and shoved away the proffered mug. But he was shaking. The enormity of the proposal, the image it conjured up of his blind nonentity, of his fly-speck role in a web vast, consequential beyond even his own most flamboyant reveries, made him hot and cold and nauseous in quick succession. It *had* brushed the far edge of his mind as a fancy lighter, sooner dropped than dust; he *had* made some remark over the chill pungent soup in the Casa Popo to the effect, 'Who do you think they'll turn up, the old carpet-chewer himself?' only to have his host (*now* he remembered that the man *was* more senior than any he had met before) frown at him with lordly distaste. The queer had kept him in the dark. No one had even hinted to R. Kulken, Esq., what the game was. A 'routine snoop'. Somebody's hobby-horse in Whitehall. 'A loose end worth tying up. Possibly. And only if Señor K. had nothing more pressing on his hands and cared to pick up a little something.' Which was precisely what it was. A pittance. An infamous *pour-boire*, grossly inadequate to the skull-splitting labour of the last weeks, but niggardly, insulting, humiliating beyond belief when set beside the immensity of the stake. So they'd let him sweat his ass off for their own incalculable profit and glory. The last message. The sun standing still. Ajalon and Hosannah. They'd bagged him. Mother of God, they'd gone into the green hell and found him. Now London knew and the jackals were on their way. The lean ones with the tight grey skins and the talcum powder. With accents like an open razor and a lemon in their teeth. To bugger him once again, to scratch him off like a dry scab while they pulled in the catch, the immeasurable dizzying prize.

– You okay, *amigo*? Take a deep breath.

But suppose Crownbacker was lying? Or mistaken, taken in by his own circus patter?

Kulken snatched at the possibility. He sat up and forced a condescending smile.

– Hitler? Hitler died a long time ago. Thirty years or something like that. It's Bormann they're after. Everyone knows that. You've come on a wild-goose chase, Mr Charlie.

– Have I, asked the man in the yellow leather flying-boots and gulped the last of the seedcakes.

Kulken nodded and made a gesture of dismissal. But he did not look at friend Charlie and his bent smile. The truth pressed on him. In school they had held him to the wall and set the point of a compass inches from his eyes. He needed time. Morning air to clear his beating head. Kulken remembered his pyjama bottoms. They were soaked with perspiration. Crownbacker wasn't half as smart as he made out. If it really was Adolf Hitler. Why, that meant

and Kulken almost laughed out loud with a sense of insight, of a global perception far more sophisticated than the crude eldorados offered by his unwanted guest.

If Adolf Hitler walked out of that jungle toothless, lame, blind, palsied, in any form, husk, shadow of his ancient self, there wouldn't only be press agents and candid cameras waiting. Crownbacker was a poor ponce if he really thought that. The thing was political, deeper than adder-pits, more crammed with danger and occasion than anything Rodriguez Kulken had ever had a finger in. Even with the shakes and with the stinking pyjama stuck to his private parts, Kulken could make out, as in a doorway suddenly darkened, a future of clandestine offers and handsome betrayals, of razzias and conversaziones in summit places far richer, far better attuned to his, Kulken's, alchemy of life than all the vulgar loot dreamt up by Charlie boy.

Kulken drew a long, voluptuous breath.

But the man had to be got rid of. Kulken needed time, a zone to manoeuvre in freely.

– Get out, Mr Crownbacker. I don't know what you're talking about. I don't know what you think you picked up. And what's more, I don't give a fart.

Charlie stood still. His eyes were a watery green. Kulken's voice rose.

– What the hell do you think you're doing barging into a man's house? Get out. Just like I told you. Shove it.

In her corner the Indian woman moved heavily.

– You asked me what kind of Indians we have here. I'll tell you, Mister. The kind I can whistle for and who can strip a plane so fine there won't be a bolt left. Beat it, and *buenos días*.

The American shook his head, gently, as if there had been some trifling error.

– I'm not going, Mr Kulken. You know that. I know that. So why get in a lather? Anyway, I couldn't. Not now.

As Kulken rose at him Marvin Crownbacker moved away with a cat-like spring. He kicked the door of the hut wide open. The morning was gone, eclipsed. Two streaks of yellow light smouldered on the wall of the outhouse. Beyond them, billowing towards Orosso, came a blackness high as the sky. A flogging sound was advancing through the forest, louder than the churn of the falls. The Indian woman clapped her hands to her mouth. The rains had begun.

– I couldn't leave now, partner, could I?

said Charlie.

11

'Reger. The Humoresque in B minor. She plays it well. Very well. But not brilliantly. Like everything she does. A barrier at the edge where feeling should flow free. Music = freedom in time, freedom from time.'

Gervinus Röthling took pride in his ability, achieved over years of unwavering alertness to the casual drift and anarchic insubordination of human consciousness, to think in an orderly fashion while listening to music. So far as Doktor Röthling was aware there were not many people who could do so. Music was the prime loosener; with it thought slipped its moorings and meandered in lethargic maelstroms over deeps of after-dinner ease. When Dr Röthling listened fully, when he became 'all ear', he voided the rummage-room of his ordinary self of any intrusive awareness; he could make his soul silent, open-armed as death. But when he listened with only a part of himself, the precise degree of attention being one that Dr Röthling could select, when he allowed a current of thought to flow as it were between the music and that compact node of identity which he guarded above all things, he saw to it that his reflections were orderly and complete. Not a halfway possession: to reflect, to feel without syntax while listening was to make of music an opiate, an aspirin for the élite.

'Music is freedom in/from time. All other human activities and sensations have in them a temporal axis. A linear thread of time-sequence runs through them. But it is a thread from outside, from a system of co-ordinates already established and often alien to their nature. Even a dream, even a bout of delirium does not create its own time. It merely compresses or distorts an outwardly determined temporality. Time pulsates in a crystal and flattens space in the centre of the galaxy. No reality is accessible to human understanding outside the *a priori* grid of time, says Immanuel Kant. No reality except one. That of music. Each piece of music whether it is the *Ring* or one of Webern's cello studies scarcely over a minute long recreates time. It creates its own time, an expressive sequence unique and proper to itself. Other chronometries, that of the actual time required for performance, are only marginally relevant. The true time of music is a construct interior to the particular composition. A piece of music *takes time* but not in the ordinary sense, not in reference to the clock. It sets itself across the general flow of time in which we conduct our regimented lives with a specific assertion of freedom so absolute as to dwarf other pretences at liberty be they political, private, orgiastic. Music is the only reality perceptible to man that governs time. It draws out of our flesh that arrow of past-present-future implanted at the instant of birth and speeding away from us in outrageous anonymity at the moment of death. Each piece of music generates its own temporal sphere, its own alpha and omega of complete existence. When we listen to music we are at once within and wholly outside the banal sovereignty of our clocks. An inverse canon such as that of Tallis or the reverse counterpoint in *The Well-Tempered Clavier* 1, 6, does what mystics dream of and addicts strive after by the use of drugs: they create time-systems which reverse themselves, in which the future, in the full concrete sense of thematic logic, can precede the past or in which two arrows fly in opposite directions yet remain parallel. When a man composes music, when he invents a melody – such invention, such passage from one plane of energy to another being perhaps the *ultimum mysterium* of human existence – he performs a rite of freedom like no other. That rite is the definition of music. It is that which makes music irreducible to language. In speech lies our slavery, our obeisance, manifest every time we use a verb, to the tyranny of tense. Speech compels us to submit our experience, however intimate, however ecstatic, to the universal vulgate of time-past, the blur of presentness and time-future. In fact, our resort to the future tense is a feeble squib, a sling-shot loosed at the fact of our inescapable, unforeseeable death. To speak is to swim and finally drown in the murky, inhuman because unmastered river of time. In true silence there is no time, or at least a brief leap out of time. Thus it is through its silences that language comes nearest to music. *La musique est la liberté dans le temps.*'

When one changed languages was one doing the same as when one changed keys? Doktor Röthling was uncertain. But he had often felt the curious finality of French, its capacity to round off a movement of thought. He heard the closing pedal-point of the Humoresque.

'She plays well, of course. An honest touch. But not brilliantly.'

Anna Elisabeth Röthling glanced at her father. The intensity of his audience, the way in which even his fingers seemed to listen, always moved her strangely. She brushed her fine dark hair from the nape of her neck and played again. Schumann's Toccata in C major. It had an awkward passage for the left hand. Anna Elisabeth concentrated but her father's presence surrounded her like the walls of the study.

'The Schumann Toccata. Not one of my favourite composers. A genius, to be sure. But was he totally committed to music? A translator into music of other things. His music is a mask. There are other forms underneath. Words, theatrical bits, Clara's morning coffee. Does Anna notice that? Probably not. It isn't that she lacks technique or intelligence. But there is always a barrier. She is like the others, her whole generation. Circling on a lead-rein round and round in the manège, never tearing loose. Not one of them shows any skin for the wind to blow on. They walk muffled. Why? They have led solid lives, warm and lit as this room. Some of them pretend that they are carrying our national burden, that the past lies on their shoulders and the blood on their forehead. Mere hysteria. Melodrama. Whoever was not in it can have no real knowledge of what it was like, of why we acted or did not act. Those who claim they feel remorse on our behalf are swindlers. They invested nothing of their own conscience in that terrible account. What right have they to draw on it? Any man can say 'Auschwitz', and if he says it loud enough everyone has to cast their eyes down and listen. Like smashing a glass in the middle of dinner. So easy to do if you were a child at the time or not even born. When you can have no idea of what it was really like, for most of us, for the decent, educated class trying to survive on that other side of the moon. Go ahead, say Auschwitz, Belsen, what have you, put ash on your head, shake your fists in our faces and demand that we do eternal penance. There's a tidy sum in remorse, TV serials to be produced, books for the autumn trade. I have only one question, my dear young ladies and gentlemen: What would *you* have done, what fine words would *you* have cried out at the time? When the brown men stomped by, the bravest of us wet our pants. But I am letting my mind wander. Anna isn't like that, nor are her friends. They drink life in small sips with just a touch of sugar, thank you, and perhaps a dash of milk. As if there was only a little left in the pot. Like trapped miners saving air. They who have grown up secure, who have had everything.'

The monitor in Doktor Röthling's consciousness, that part of his attention which had beneath or rather to one side of his ordered stream of thought been following the piece, signalled the proximity of the difficult passage. The left hand had to cross over. He voided his mind of all but response and smiled as the harmony, momentarily rent, almost out of control in a *salto mortale*, returned through a modulation of startling yet perfect logic to unison. Anna Elisabeth did not look away from the keys but Röthling fancied that his smile had reached her.

'Nicely done. But so little edge, so few risks taken. How they sit, the lot of them, their knees tightly pressed together. Her mother was different. Elisabeth was free as open water. When she moved through a room the light danced. Is it our fault? Have we taught them too much about the past or too little? Are they afraid it will happen again and think it best to go by the back stairs softly? How they ration themselves. Perhaps that's it. Perhaps we *have* left them very little. We drank so deep of history that there can't be much left in the bottle. By God, we took a mouthful! The catkin bursting into bud at Bryansk, cold furry pellets filling the air after the sudden thaw. The dead horses in the gorge south of Mycenae stinking to heaven, but purple cliffs on either side of us.'

Röthling recalled his thirty-six-hour leave in Delft in the autumn of '42 when he had taken men of his company on a tour of the sights, shown them the hunched postern through which William the Silent stepped into present death, and gone on alone after seeing his charges properly fed in an *estaminet* near the station.

'Two perfect rows of poplars, one on each side of the canal. The vesper bells rang from somewhere in the town. The sound and the fallen leaves came towards me down the dusky water. A moment out of time. Two bodies swinging high on the unbleached gallows by the roadside.'

His column was dragging south out of Norway. The crows had been at the partisans' eyes and stripped their cheeks, but a spring light sharp as broken glass had caught the two faces. They were beautiful to look on, marbled, folded in sleep. He remembered his first taste of calvados in a tin measuring-cup handed to him by – by whom? – another officer, a gunner with whom he shared a bunker outside Stralsund. An apple fire blazed inside him and the warm fog blanketed their stiff bones. Each time the Stalin organs loosed a barrage and the rockets lashed overhead, the liqueur shook in the cup. *Les très riches heures*. To have heard Gieseking play the *Waldstein* in Munich, almost at the end. Despite brave efforts at ventilation smoke hung in the concert hall and an odour of fire and burst mains blew in through the gilt and stucco foyer. He had sat at the back of the stalls in a wheelchair, coffined from the hip down. The plush couloir was reserved for wounded military personnel, for invalid *Frontkämpfer* home from a front already smashed, fictitious. Feeling the hand of the young woman from the Auxiliary Nursing Corps on his shoulder, Gervinus had turned in the dark to make out her tall form. After the recital, in the brief mercy of an all-clear, Elisabeth had wheeled him back to the sanatorium, manoeuvring the chair over blistered pavements and deep ruts to what was left of a garden pavilion. She was not as young as he had supposed. She had married at the outbreak of war, seen her husband on two furloughs and received news of his death outside Narvik during the easy war, the one before the real. The sirens had started again and she had stayed by him in the blacked-out room. She knelt by his chair. He edged the uniform cape off her shoulders and unbuttoned her blouse. Already then, as they slipped behind her back to undo a hook, he had noticed how alive her hands were. He found her breasts. Their weight startled him. An old warmth came up in his broken thighs. Just then a stick of incendiaries splattered the branches in the far corner of the park. In the abrupt white sheen beyond the black-out drapes he saw how near her face was and that she had let her skirt slide to the quivering floor.

'I drank deep that night. As everybody was trying to do all around us, in open places, in the crazy houses with no windows, no roofs. I let go. Of everything. As one can when death is no longer private, no longer one's own business.'

She had left her mouth on his trembling arms until sleep came. Would he rather have lived in some other time in some other land? Would it have been better to miss the long holiday in hell? That was what they were saying now, making pious faces over the horror of it. It was a lie or only a part of the truth.

'I, Gervinus Röthling, have emptied life not from a glass but from a magnum. Have known history as I know my own skin. Have crossed and recrossed Europe like Napoleon's hordes, have seen Salonika burning and the face of an old man floating, smiling in the Grand Canal. I have smelt new wheat in the Carpathians and eaten eel, fresh, salt-cold from the Tyrrhenian sea. I have passed my hands over the stone roses in the cloister at Albi and over a woman's hair in a cellar in Kharkov. A magnum, a jeroboam, till it was empty. I wouldn't trade. I wouldn't put my memories on sale or flaunt them like leprosy. God, how we lived! Each terrible year like a hundred ordinary years, like a thousand. He was true to his word. A thousand-year Reich inside each of us, a millennium of remembered life. We have left nothing for those who came after. That's our real crime. They are ghosts, plump ghosts, lean ghosts, the whole generation of them. Not their fault. We left them the cold ash of history, the skin of the grape. But I wouldn't trade. I wouldn't.'

Doktor Röthling came to with an unpleasant jerk. The music had stopped. He had let his thoughts run loose. For a bewildering instant he stared at the young woman in the room without precise recognition or rather with a queer pang of desire, observing the fullness of her shape, the full breasts turned towards him. Anna Elisabeth was smiling.

– I think you have been dozing, papa. Was I that bad?

– Of course not. I have been fully awake. You took the difficult bit, the one for the left hand, well. Excellently, Anna. A little more bite, perhaps. Yes, that's what's needed.

He was talking too rapidly, trying to clear his head of a bizarre, numbing exultation. He flushed at the remembrance of the unseemly lust which had seeped out of his past.

– I should like a cup of coffee, Anna. A cup of strong black coffee would be just right.

As Anna stood up from the piano and pressed the bell-button by the door, Röthling glanced around the room. Everything was back in place, the book-lined alcove, the ivory paper-cutter which F. had sent him from Benghazi, the photograph of Elisabeth in its heavy silver frame, taken only a year before her death when a disorder of excessive life had already made itself felt in her body and carved hollows under her eyes. (At the clinic Rademacher had said, 'My dear Gervinus, we all suffer from some form of cancer; anyone who has gone through the Hitler years carries inside him a heightened, anarchic life force. What shall we do to house the pathological energies and powers of adaptation loosed within us during this insane decade? Cancer is an unfocused excess of life, no more and no less. Your wife's illness is merely the most visible type.') Suddenly, as if it had been stored in some lone oasis of the mind, the close of the Toccata, the last modulation and final chord sounded in his ear, vibrant and distinct, as if Anna was still at the keyboard. 'A trained memory is a wondrous miser,' thought Dr Röthling, shivered a little and straightened up in his cavernous armchair.

Over coffee they talked. Elisabeth chafed at the petty encumbrances of her job at the *Staatsbibliothek*. But was this plaint, her father wondered, more than conventional, more than a figured bass above which the young woman led her essentially harmonious, satisfied existence? That contentment, though muted, had been present even on a late afternoon in Ascona when, during a holiday they had taken together, Anna had stood on a ridge, with the western sky turning mauve, and declared her unalterable intent to resume her lapsed study of Russian, prepare her *Staatsexamen* and launch on a fuller course. At that hour her resolve had been such as to draw her whole being towards the darkening horizon. But soon her resolution subsided, as had so many precedent gusts of high purpose, into that discreet nostalgia which was so clearly a part of her charm.

There was Thaddeus Binswanger, her immediate superior, with his spinsterish foibles and catarrh. Only this morning he had had a scene with Fräulein Schalktritt the archivist. Their voices had spiralled to such a forte of officious snorts and falsettos that Anna had sped from her desk and closed the door to the reading-room. But it was not the occasional fracas which fretted her nerves (at bottom Miss Anna Elisabeth found vulgarity rather compelling); it was the monotony, the snail-pace hours she spent behind the high grey windows, especially now that the chestnut trees were dropping their glory and the afternoons were turning to smoke and fine rain. In the library, winter seemed to come a little earlier than anywhere else. She could tell by looking at the bust of Humboldt in the north corner; after three o'clock the plinth stood in a pool of shadows. She must pull herself together and look to other opportunities, that was certain. But it would be wrong, almost indecent to quit before the new children's section with its gay linoleum and adjustable reading-lamps (her own idea, carried through in the face of Binswanger's carping and Miss Schalktritt's petty treasons) was properly installed and in use. To which resolve, so comforting in its indistinct futurity, Dr Röthling vigorously assented, adding that the New Year was an excellent time for a fresh start, 'for a thorough dusting inside', a mood which the coming season's municipal concerts with their rich sprinkling of Beethoven and Mahler could only reinforce. He whistled with that exactitude of pitch she envied the trumpet call from Mahler's Second. The clarion echoed around the room and died away in the magenta drapes.

Such was their intimacy that Gervinus Röthling and his daughter could fall into a kind of shorthand, grasping each other's intimations perfectly while eliding those connectives, prefatory signals and otiose stresses which make our ordinary use of speech so wasteful. Thus when Anna Elisabeth pondered her father's sudden enquiry,

– Tell me, my dear Anna, what would you do if Adolf Hitler walked into the room?

the reason lay not in any vulgar surprise or confusion at so unheralded a theme but simply in her wish to give the matter due scrutiny.

– I should get up, said Anna Elisabeth.

– Yes, I should certainly get up from my chair.

This interested her father.

– Why?

– Not out of common courtesy. Not to do him honour, God forbid. Perhaps out of shock at actually *seeing* him. But that's not it really.

She paused.

– If a man walked in who had loomed so large, so enormously in the lives of others, who had drawn to himself such a fantastic mass of hate, of love, of fear, simply of daily thought . . . I don't know that I can explain it. But how could one stay seated if such a terrible fullness of life, in him of course but even more in others, came through the door?

Röthling lit an English cigarette. He had developed a taste for them during his brief internment in a POW stockade near Hannover. He associated their grainy flavour with survival and the possibility, so remote in the last hellish weeks of the Reich, of thinking in the future tense.

– You mean that decent folk don't stay on their bottoms in front of history?

– Something like that. But you know I'm no good at putting things in precise words. You remember the time in the mountain railway, when we were going up the Schwarzhorn with Mother and someone thought they heard an avalanche far off. Everybody got up. Some were trying to see out the frozen windows. Others just stood listening, not to that bit of thunder so far away. But stood. One couldn't just sit in one's chair and look up at him, could one?

– And you'd curtsy, Anna, wouldn't you? The way you used to in school, just a very small curtsy.

– Certainly not, Papa. What an idea.

She flushed at the recollection, both awkward and somehow consoling, of how she had curtsied to Herr *Studienrat* Probst when he called her out of class and told her to put on her long blue overcoat and go home because Frau Doktor Röthling, because Mummy had taken a turn for the worse. She had raced through the streets full of March light and a new wind.

– Of course I wouldn't! But what would I do? Just stand there like a mesmerized goose? I couldn't touch him, I couldn't bear to do that. Spit in his face, call him foul names, take your knife and fling it at him? None of that sounds right. I don't think I could do any of those things.

Trying to enter the game, Anna Elisabeth found her resources meagre and the image of herself out of focus. She stopped talking and stared at her empty coffee cup. After a while she shrugged faintly and looked up at her father. She resented his untroubled mien.

– Have they given you the file again?

Dr Röthling nodded. It had, in fact, happened every few years. A thick, intractable dossier on the juridical aspects of extradition and arraignment, on the competence of the courts both *Länder* and Federal, on the question of national vs. international jurisdiction in the eventuality that Adolf Hitler, sometime Reichschancellor, be found alive outside the territories of the German Federal Republic, the which territories had been held to include – held most emphatically by Röthling's lifelong friend, patron and predecessor, the late *Staatsprokurist* Gerlach – to include all lands proclaimed *Reichsdeutsch* up to and explicitly including the *Anschluss* of 1938. A point about which Gervinus himself felt intermittent but mournful doubts. It was, he deemed, a file whose convolutions, proliferating codices, minority reports and thousand-page addendum made in the murky light of the Eichmann affair he now knew better than any man alive, in whose ghostly landscape he could thread his way as no other member of the *Landesgericht*, let alone an outsider (and that included his esteemed correspondent, Sir Evelyn Ryder), could ever hope to. There were no doubt similar files at the Hague but less complete, less omnivorous in their imaginings of possible circumstance (i.e. let us suppose *ex hypothesi*, or as Ulpian put it *per tentare lex*, that the said A. Hitler be discovered on the high seas, on board a carrier flying a flag of convenience and holding Liberian registry, or in Vatican territory, in some country not party to the International Court, in a locality under disputation such as the nether reaches of the Argentine–Chilean frontier, the north-east corner of Basutoland or in the former German lands beyond the Oder-Neisse). No, the prodigality of conjectured happening, the ramifications of invoked precedent and counter-example docketed in his file were such as no other legal body could hope to equal.

They had asked him to refresh his knowledge of the whole matter and minute any views additional to those he had already set down in a series of memoranda since Gerlach's retirement and that disorderly escapade in Jerusalem – not that the Israeli case for *main haute et forte* had been quite as weak as some of his vociferous colleagues in the *Länderamt* and Ministry of Foreign Affairs would have it.

– Why had he been given the file now? asked Anna, leaning her head to one side. It was a gesture which reminded Röthling of her mother, but Elisabeth's neck had been more svelte.

Instructions had come from Bonn marked 'urgent'. There was always someone in that Ministry throwing his weight around. Rumours that Herr Hitler had been found alive cropped up regularly after the war. In more recent years Dr Röthling could recall at least two false alarms (one of which alleged that the Führer had had himself circumcised and was now to be seen in an old-age home in upstate New York). Remnants of the one-time Israeli search organization, tiny groups of individuals probably half-crazed and privately comman-deered, were thought to be operating still in the Amazonian hinterland hunting for Bormann, Menhardt or whomever they could flush from cover on the long register of vanished killers. So much was established. The rest had always proved gossip and astrologers' *Tratsch*.

– Surely it's impossible that he should still be alive. Even if he did escape from the bunker.

No, it was not impossible. Dr Röthling begged to remind Anna that the Federal Republic had been governed after the war and, might he add, 'governed in exemplary style' by a man almost as old as Adolf Hitler would be even now. But it was, to say the very least, unlikely. The so-called evidence of an escape from Berlin had never stood up to serious examination. The theory of a double was probably as nonsensical now as it had been during the Führer's lifetime. Gervinus had caught a glimpse of the man once bestowing decorations and hoarse inaudible condolences in a military hospital on the eastern front. It was he, there could be no doubt. The sallow, drawn skin was his and the rimmed eyes. Nevertheless this latest report had a queer insistence or at least it had produced distinct ripples in high quarters. Ryder was said to be interested, there had been two top-secret signals from Washington, and the usual vulgar flap in Pankow. Only the Russians had let it leak that they regarded the whole affair as a boring canard.

– And what do *you* think papa?

That there's nothing in it. Though it was not Röthling's concern, his old friend Berndt Dietrich had been helpfully indiscreet. A series of short-wave messages, the last fragmentary but exultant, had been emanating out of the jungle and half-explored swamplands beyond Rio Branco, wherever that was. The only curious feature was that so flimsy an affair should be taken at all seriously, that it should have provoked so marked a reaction in various nerve-centres. Not that that proved much. Dr Röthling's war-time experiences suggested that intelligence services manufacture news where there is none.

– Though from my own point of view the whole business is not, I must admit, unsatisfactory. You will remember, my dear, I am sure you do remember the strong reservations I expressed when the Munich courts pronounced Hitler dead – *re* the estate of Paula Hitler, the alleged deceased's next of kin. I said at the time, the records will show how emphatically I said it, that such a declaration was either superfluous or premature: superfluous in view of the attestations of demise made jointly by the four-power Commission of Liquidation in Berlin, yet premature, from a more rigorous and forensic point of view in respect of the absence of incontrovertible proof. I argued at the time, an argument, if I may say so, of some theoretic and even metaphysical import, that it would be far better to invoke the doctrine of *ratio mortalis*, of reasonably expected span of mortal life, and not proceed to any final certification of death until that length had been wholly exhausted. In brief, I proposed that biological truth be set in place of missing legal evidence. But the gentlemen in Munich would not listen. They were in a hurry. Now there's a pretty kettle of fish. Questions of extradition, indeed of our participation in any preliminary inquest or process of legal identification, become somewhat thorny when the person involved has been declared well and properly defunct! Even if there is nothing in the present rumours, and I agree with you, Anna, that there really can't be, the Munich judgment will have to be reviewed. The law makes no provision for phantoms, for those who, as our French friends so nicely put it, 'come back'. I've drafted some notes on the matter and asked Rolf to drop over and discuss one or two points. He should be here any moment.

Anna Röthling smiled. Rolf Hanfmann's perennial courtship was more real to her father than to herself or, she supposed, than it had ever been to Rolf. How safely they had agreed to postpone any official betrothal until after Rolf's completion of his legal studies. How right it had seemed to them both that nothing save tacit understanding should bind them during Rolf's year at Oxford and that their engagement, pledged almost casually here in this room in her father's smiling but somehow edgy presence, should remain strictly a family concern until Rolf felt that his career had reached a requisite level of income and stable prospects. That was well over a year ago. Now Rolf's regular calls and presence on the Röthling agenda had an obbligato quality. The tall, bespectacled young lawyer was to be her father's successor as he was already his assiduous adjunct. Perhaps something might come of it after all but it no longer seemed to matter very much and in the meantime the mild tension that came with Dr Hanfmann's visits, the touch, so subdued, of frustration and unspoken reproach that intruded on their frequent meetings was, itself, not unpleasant. Certainly her father seemed to find it so.

As Rolf entered, a quick warmth tinged Dr Röthling's cheeks. Anna saw that both men wanted to get on with the sheaf of papers which Rolf pulled out of his briefcase (she had given it to him on the evening before he left for England and remembered the feel of the monogram, newly incised, under her fingers). After a few minutes she gathered the coffee cups and said goodnight.

Röthling noted with pleasure how entirely Rolf had mastered the points he had put to him that afternoon, how closely his own vein of argument and even turns of phrase were reflected in Rolf's amendments or additions to the draft. Between them they would have the proposed abrogation of the Munich ruling and a further appendix

112

dealing with certain vexed aspects of Adolf Hitler's Austrian nationality ready in a matter of days. It was at his mentor's invitation, conveyed by the fact that Röthling lit a fresh cigarette and leaned back expansively, that Rolf Hanfmann ventured beyond the immediate brief.

– I know it won't surprise you, Sir, if I say again that there might be a case here for a more striking procedure. The indictment is necessarily without genuine precedent. This allows us to consider the institution of a unique court. I don't only mean an international tribunal – there is nothing new in that. I mean, for example, a court in which those of us who had no direct part in the events, who were too young at the time or indeed unborn could have a role to play. The accused stands outside the norms of law either common or specifically promulgated. Beyond any aim of judicial retribution – imagine, Sir, how old the man must be if he does exist at all, how absurdly beyond correction – there is the hope that things can be got right. Facts, I mean, not motives. It is not so much a high and solemn bench we need as we do a school open to the world.

The young man's warmth of feeling, his bias towards the large and philosophic contour of things, did not displease Dr Röthling, but the implication of a reality beyond the relevance of law could not pass. Either the law is an ontological totality, both central in human institutions and capable by internal logic of extension to all human phenomena, or it is merely and inevitably a corpus of local ordinance, an ephemeral fiat in this or that corner of history. Even as rights of eminent domain, of safe passage, of territoriality could be extrapolated to the deeps of the sea and the outermost reaches of interplanetary space, so a legal code covering murder, the ravage of property, the breach of constitutional oaths, must be capable of extension to the case of the sometime Reichschancellor.

– If the codex does not apply to Herr Hitler, *Junge*, then he was absolutely right in claiming that he stood above the law, that the law is a bundle of mouse-eaten parchment with no authority over the superman or the will of the *Volk*. You are arguing nobly, I grant you, but most dangerously. I can conceive of no instance in the entire history of criminal pursuit in which it is more important that the forms, traditions and nuances of legality and judicial procedure be fully invoked. History has too long been extra-legal, the atrocities which despots and nations commit have too long enjoyed immunity in some special fictional zone of 'inevitable fact'. There are laws, dear boy, not laws of history. History is man-made, like this pair of shoes, though it pinches more.

– You, best of anyone, know my reservations in regard to Nuremberg. *Post facto* law badly drafted and argued. But the underlying truth was there nevertheless. If there is a law for the drunken homicide down the street there must be one for Attila.

Rolf did not dispute that. But the crimes of Attila were not really those of one man. This was even truer in the case of Hitlerism. It was not for those of his generation to judge – 'What right have we, what qualifications?' – but manifestly the rise and deeds of Nazism involved the active support, the initiative of many other men, perhaps of millions. It was the relationship of Hitler's person to that support, the way in which he obtained and harnessed it, the question of whether responsibility could ever be localized which needed clarification. Could existing law do the job?

– I answer yes, my dear Rolf, a hundred times yes. And what I have in mind is no recent doctrine, no *ad hoc* psychologizing or supermarket sociology such as some of our esteemed colleagues in Bonn seem to favour. Your objection is met by a concept of *Staatsrecht* older than our Minister, by a body of legal thought

Gervinus Röthling came forward in his chair.

– richer, more subtly flavoured than old wine. I refer of course to the concept of the *corpus mysticum* of the ruler, to that solid fiction so admirably worked out by our Hohenstauffen and their jurists whereby the identity and liability of the body politic is taken to reside in the body of the monarch. There is in him a twofold being, a duplicity of life: the one private and mortal, the other collective and if power be legitimate, eternal. During the period in which the sovereign reigns the earthly is joined to the transcendent in a perfect *incorporation*, at once mystical and down to earth. It is not poetry, Rolf, that has produced the most vivid fictions or complex metaphors! A mystic carnality of statehood subsists even in the sleeping king, a *deus absconditus*, distasteful, perplexing to vulgar common sense as that may seem, endures in Hitler drugged or even demented. There is nothing in the difficulties you raise which old Henri de Bracton would have found surprising or outside the exact anticipations of the law.

In celebration of which fact Dr Röthling poured a generous snifter of brandy for himself and young Hanfmann. But Rolf shook his head slowly. He acknowledged the force of his master's logic, he always did, yet was left dissatisfied. To him and doubtless to most other people in the world Hitler had become unreal, a spectre trundled out on All Souls' Night. The judicial machinery envisaged by Dr Röthling would bring him no nearer. There was, however, no need to push the argument any further because

– we surely agree, don't we Sir, that these latest rumours are unfounded, that the thing is wellnigh impossible.

– Quite. I can tell you, in strictest confidence of course, that the very location of the purported transmitter is in dispute. Some of our intelligence wizards think it's in Madre de Dios, on the Bolivian side. Others are confident that the messages come from the Ipiruna basin in Brazil. Moreover if this was a clandestine search operation why should the party, unless they all are brain-sick, use so transparent a cipher? As you say, the whole affair is probably a fairy-tale. How refreshingly sober our own trade is.

On the downstairs landing Dr Röthling reminded Rolf that Bonn wanted a draft-text as quickly as possible.

– Though in my humble opinion there is absolutely no ground for haste. My old friend *Staatssekretär* Dietrich tells me that the rains have begun in that God-forsaken part of the world. Not rains such as we know them, my dear Rolf, but black cataracts streaming down for days and nights, stripping giant trees, turning parched dust into a foaming lake. During the rains no one gets very far. The Indians hole up and drug themselves into a long stupor. Not a patch of sunlight for days. So I don't imagine there'll be much news out of there for a while, if ever there was any. But that's Bonn for you. First they make a hash of things, then they're in a great hurry.

Röthling showed his guest to the door. The last strokes of eleven had rung from the *Domkirche* and the sound seemed to reverberate along the pavement. Röthling looked past the raw contours of the new concrete apartment buildings. In the moonlight above the sheen of the arc-lamps rose the mitred crest of the belfry and the high roofs of the old city only partially burnt during the raids and scrupulously restored long since. It seemed to him that the night air in the thinning beeches made precisely the same drifting sibilant noise as it had in his boyhood. Unthinking, Dr Röthling found himself clasping Rolf's shoulder.

– Things haven't changed all that much, have they? Despite the bombing and all the rest. This whole Hitler business, perhaps one exaggerates its importance. Perhaps it's nonsense, a kind of upside-down sentimentality to think back on it, to worry about how or why it happened. Like a terrier scratching for old bones. People who do too much of that go queer, they think they're making deep and terrible statements on behalf of the dead. They aren't. They're puffing up their own little lives. Oh, it was hell, we were in it up to our eyes – while it lasted. And for a few years more. You can't remember, you were a baby. But now, looking back, don't misunderstand me, *Junge*, I can't help wondering whether it was very important.

Closing the front door – that sound too had scarcely changed since first he had tripped up the stairs of his parents' house, lacquered pumps in hand after the *Juristenball*, was it forty years ago? – Gervinus Röthling murmured to himself that proportion was the supreme virtue.

– Measure is the final aristocracy of man.

He said it aloud in the dark stairwell and wondered, as he neared the warm light of his bedroom, whether he was quoting one of Lichtenberg's aphorisms or, perhaps, one of his own.

12

Teku smelt them. Through air so sodden it hung before him like fur. The rains had driven him north. Much further than he had ever been. The blackness and the winds had been crazy, blinding him, almost splitting his skull. He had been swept downriver and had clawed his way to the loosening banks when he had heard the thunder of the falls, a second thunder inside the drumming wind. He had had to keep moving to stay alive, to escape the racing sheets of flood-water. Scissored in the akuba trees, trying to fight sleep and the fetid cold, he had heard animals hump past in a crazed wallowing. The rains had lightened, but he was stunned and uncertain of his bearings. Who were these men? A Brazilian patrol, one of the minute fistfuls of armed men being flung far into the interior to mark future roads? Freelancers lost from an oil or rubber party? They stank like Sr. Kulken, only worse. Their lean-to had been punished by the storms, the leaf-fronds carelessly joined and now gaping. But they had not been camping long in this spot. Teku considered the ash and the footmarked grass between the shelter and the high scrub. Two days, three at most. They must have run before the rains as he had. Stinking devils. How many? He moved his head in a tight arc shaking the rain-dreams, the panics, towards his left ear whence they would spill once the sun was fully risen. His sight cleared. Two men at the east point, against the new light, a boy near the fire, a third man hunched by the hut, trying to steady a pole, wasting motion because the earth had not been properly tamped. Teku grinned and rubbed spittle against the scar above his left nipple. It smouldered after rain. As it was purposed to, calling up the pain of the great thorn and the rasping of the magic men in the long hut when he, Teku son of the anteater, had been made adult. Three men and the young one shivering by the fire. Ghosts rather than men, so sere the light seemed to go through them. Sr. Kulken was dense as a sow. Even his shadow weighed.

But where was the crazy devil who had danced the rain into its fury, and where was the old man? Because Teku's brain had woken and the numbness was passing from him, to the left, as must the tree-frog when he follows night. This was the same party, hunters or rubber-tappers or men sick in the head, whom he had surprised at the edge of the great bog just before the skies had hammered down. He moved closer. The boy was not only shivering. There were tears on his grimed face. Teku parted the clotted grass and studied the whole site. He had been a fool not to observe at once, the rain had addled his wits. It was a poor piece of work; even the coypu would dig it up. A small barrow of earth where the ground was still drinking. No platform, no vines plaited to keep mud in place till it settled in the sun. You could almost make out the dead man's shape under the mound, his feet pointing eastward. Those dancing feet and torn boots. Teku shivered at the memory. Had the rains doomed him for his presumption? Had he died on the march here, somewhere in the intervening floods and ripped savannah? The carbine had been planted in the grave, its stock silhouetted against the sharpening light. How many guns did they carry, wondered the Indian, and felt his cheeks tighten. Then he saw the old man, in the entrance to the lean-to, bent, blinking into the morning. His skin was like that of a dried marmot or of a woman after famine. Teku was not certain whether he had ever seen anyone so old, not even among those who were now speechless, who crouched in the sacred hut inhaling the crushed seeds and who were thought to have seen the shadow of the gods.

– How do you keep the thread

Compacted as they were, each enmeshed in the others' needs and smells, so often out of breath or their mouths fouled with insects and lianas, Simeon, Elie, Gideon, John Asher and the boy had come to grasp one another's meaning, through half-sentences, through words truncated by the slap of vines. But Asher had fallen short of a final immediacy. There were nuances which eluded him, elisions that had to be filled in later. He knew almost no Yiddish: 'You are a dumb *schlemiel*,' Elie had said, 'the ox sits on your tongue.' He had not experienced the Holocaust, but had been a schoolboy at the time in England where green lay open as the sea and was not, as here, a sweating rag against the light.

– unbroken? You are connected to the outside world. Still.

Asher considered.

– The rest of us. What's left. I suppose we're more or less off our heads. The way we talk. As if Elie had dreamed us, made us up of a piece out of one of his parables. I can't picture the outside any more. Not since we have found him. And now Gideon dead. Crazy talk, isn't it? But you.

It was almost accusing.

– It still relates, doesn't it? I mean the politics, if we get to San Cristobal. The people out there. Not only Lieber. The press, the microphones

and saying the words Simeon trailed off, mesmerized, then vacant.

– You've kept the thread. What's that story, the man in the labyrinth unwinding a strong thread and finding his way out again. You haven't tangled it or let it snap. Not on the thorns, not in the swamp. You're a careful man, John. Get him out, and the boy.

The sobs were strangled but audible. Simeon stole a glance at Isaac.

– He'll manage. He's lucky. Not every man loses two fathers, both heroes. And friend Hitler. You've noticed, haven't you. Getting stronger somehow, walking better, keeping his bowels open, brushing the fever from his skin while we

Asher had noticed. Outwardly the prisoner had withered. Even out of the wind his clothes flapped. The rains had whipped through him as through loose straw. But he had been gaining stamina, tapping recondite strengths as his escort sickened. When the fever hollowed Gideon's bones, making that tempered, adroit body a shambling, smelling wrack, the old man had looked on with gloomy interest, prescribed arrowroot and hellebore and had prognosticated, with a fair measure of precision, the moment of final convulsion. The vampire-bat. He would make it out of the jungle leaving their bleached carcasses behind. Asher dwelt on the thought.

– The *rebbe* and I don't have anything to do out there. Not after this. I've heard that often it isn't the fire which destroys, but the water they pour in. Fire-stains fade. But the water and the smoke soak in. So that the room feels dank years after. And has a dead smell like Elie and I. Not all the perfumes of Arabia. *Nebich*, Arabia. Did you learn the line in school? This little, little hand. You must have. At Bishop Romney's Grammar School in Hertfordshire. All in Lieber's file. He made me recite those files till I knew them blind. A dossier on each one of you, down to the final millimetre of past and private life. And then he incinerated the lot, so that no one would know or follow up. Melodrama.

Simeon said the word twice more, testing his rage and the emptiness.

– Melodrama. What was it like? I mean in Hertfordshire.

Asher translated. 'Who are you, really? Why did you volunteer, bulling through every impediment, setting aside every implausibility? And why, after everything we've been through, are you not one of us, not in the ways that matter?' The same question, since the first night in Wiesenthal's study in Vienna all those wasted years ago. Then on the interminable, absurdly clandestine by-paths which led to Lieber. Every hour thereafter, until Genoa – even there, in the cabin, when Lieber turned to go, having voiced benedictions and auguries under his breath yet looking up suddenly, once again, with his flat eyes, to try to read on Asher's face the elusive meaning of his presence in the affair. The answer always the same, and straightforward enough. A man could be of use precisely because he was intact, because he had no true grounds for possession. He was one in whom interest was stronger than love or hatred or hunger. 'To be interested in something' to the limit of one's stretched being, to be interested *in extremis*. The problem being enough to fill every cranny of the day. An algebraist's voracity. Asher had noticed his capacity for absolute appetite early, in the misery of home after his parents' divorce (the mixed marriage whose improper pairing made him technically, legally, Talmudically a gentile, though it was to the father, abruptly denuded, that the boy had gone on school holidays and most Sunday afternoons, in Ladbroke Grove where the leaves drifted). A capacity for orderly drowning. In a schoolboy craze, later in Lepidoptera, later still in Ordnance Survey maps. Concentrations so knotted that they left the world to one side. Sometimes at the level of a parlour trick: extracting cube roots mentally to prevent erection. But gathering subconsciously, out of loose bits of reading, puzzling, devouring old newsreels, towards a master theme. The capture of Bormann and then, sprung from a rumour, from a tangential allusion heard during his stint in army intelligence, the lunatic notion of tracking Hitler himself. A passion as total as Gideon's had been. But rooted in the brain, irresponsible to anything but the vexation of the problem, autistic. It was this passion he had proffered his questioners, together with a marksman's skills, attainments in mountaineering and cross-country, an insolent ease at languages. No metaphysical lusts, no cravings for retribution. And they had finally included him because the laws of coherence in a distant patrol demand delicate asymmetries. Being an outsider to Lieber's monomania and the raging hurts it woke in Simeon or Elie or the boy, being, rather, monomaniacal but in his own hedonistic guise – 'This, Mr Lieber, is the most interesting task now available to anyone with my avocations,' at which point the hammering had reappeared under Lieber's stubbled cheeks – Asher counterbalanced. But now the topology had been wrenched out of relation. With Benasseraf in his shallow grave, the finely spun poise and checks which had welded the hunting-party were twisted. The cadence of the march, the manoeuvres of survival had to be recast. Hence Simeon's question. Yes, the same question. But different now.

– I played Macduff. In the school production. All of whose family is wiped out by the fell kite – something like that, isn't it? – the dam and her chicks at one fell swoop. The hell-kite. That's it. It comes back to one. The boy who played Lady Macduff had a falsetto which could peel the skin off an apple. I remember his scream. Enter murderers

Simeon spun around.

Teku had broken cover. The blowpipe over his shoulder was absurdly long, but he swung it with routine grace. He was moving towards the lean-to, his right hand out-thrust. In it he held an offering, a strip of dried meat. The Indian went directly to where Hitler was standing, crooked over his own shadow. Teku bowed and placed his gift at the old man's feet. He knew that we must honour the old, and that the very old, like this bent man, are precious beyond topaz. 'Ancient one,' said Teku, 'commend me to your spirits.' And looked up warily. Thus saluted, Sr. Kulken had kicked him for his pains. But Kulken was garbage and a man must sometimes gamble. The parchment lips were making a magical motion. *'Blumen.'* The Indian listened avidly.

13

(from the diaries of Blaise Josquin, *Sous-sécrétaire d'état* in the Political Intelligence section of the Palais Matignon)

8 May: Why do I flinch at my own detestation of disorder? When it has served me so well. When it has, in truth, been the mainspring of my career. Josquin *la règle*. Already in school. Then at the *École*. Where my desk drawers were the only ones in the entire *promotion* not overflowing with ash, paper-clips, lozenges. Why the staleness now when, more than ever, rigour is needed? Because nothing else, *mon vieux*, will throw any light into this muddle. I am bone-weary. It has been a bastard of a winter with R. H. ailing and 'Attila' in a foul mood. Not

that he rides me any more, not since the weekend at Rambouillet and the President's memo on my performance over the Libyan note. Bless E. F. I owe the old witch a lot. But it's more than just tiredness. Looking at myself in the mirror: *bonjour, Seigneur Cliché*. The skull finely chiselled but not dramatic. The touch of silver at my temples. The fingernails unbroken. Everything as it ought to be: Anne-Estienne, our three children, the grange at Lavergne, the beige coupé, my age and rank, these two high windows with south exposure reserved for those above the rank of assistant counsellor. Every last orderly bit. *En place*. As it was on my night-table when *maman* came in to say, 'Goodnight, *petit préfet*.' Even V. But yesterday afternoon she was foul. I *wanted* to leave her. Listening to her high-class vulgarities (does she know what the words mean?), smelling her breath, I wanted to be back here, at my desk. Wanted it so much I would have given up the whole marvellous business in exchange for levitation. To be dressed instantaneously and float through the wall of that 'little jewel' of an apartment. Which I've never had a taste for, but which she cherishes and now heaps full of her bric-à-brac. Perhaps *that's* why I'm feeling so down. 'V. my dearest, *mon heure bleue*, perhaps it is time for us

11 May: I have always resented Berdier. Since first we met at the seminar on fuel policies in Rotterdam. When was that? '64 or 5? The bluff exterior. The English worsteds, the Italian loafers. Another cliché figure. Down to the cork-tipped cigarettes and the new 'atomic' lighter. God, he makes me sick. Because he's not like that at all. Underneath the talcum powder comes the sandpaper. Aphorism #3456 by the celebrated wit and moralist Blaise Josquin. Berdier is a brute, through and through. A gorilla. Should have been a bouncer or six-day bicycle racer. He is a crude killer. Probably was at some point in his meteoric ascent. *Who* is his patron? Not Ménestière. Too subtle, and a physical coward. Can it be P.? I was not at my best. Far from it. Berdier coming on strong and smooth. All that spurious deference to our department. He despises it. But we made an impression. Undoubtedly. 'Attila' and his precious phrases about the 'occasional need for direct, or even unattractive methods of procedure'. His annoyance at my 'provisionality' (one of his favourite pieces of jargon). Who the devil wouldn't be 'provisional' in the face of the

evidence? And what evidence? That Semyonov has been seen arriving in Recife and has been tracked as far as Manaos – *if* the identification is correct, at that distance across the airport and with a telephoto lens which Berdier himself qualified as not of the best? Hoving's visit? A nice young man & well-trained. They order these matters in England . . . But who could have been more tentative? 'Ah, that's the very point. Our Britannic friends are being *too* nonchalant. They must be on to something big, too big to share . . .' I find Berdier intolerable when he puts on his Levantine airs. But there *may* be some merit to the point. At least 'Attila' seemed to think so. And Hoving did seem to be holding back. But on what? Make a précis, Josquin; let the skeleton appear from under the skin, luminous. Not my idiom, but Follard's. The only great teacher I have ever been taught by. Great teachers are terribly rare. Killed in a road accident. Near Tarbes, trying to avoid a drunken motor-cyclist. The skeleton, luminous. Oh God, I am tired.

17 May: No time for the diary. They want a protocol 'gathering all the threads'. A minute covering possible courses of action. Is there information I haven't been given? In which event only the President and the 'inner cabinet' are in the picture. V. is sometimes oddly acute. It wasn't that xf was bad yesterday. On the contrary: explosive. But afterwards she said, 'Your body was fine today because it came alone. Your stuffed mind is elsewhere. Completely immersed in something. Good riddance.' The tiny scratch above her nipple.

21 May: Tocsins ringing. 'Attila' having to give up his weekend. His face was a study. I had never seen General D. A legend in the bureau and looked the part. Theroux set out the legal niceties. A brilliant memorandum. That youngster will go far. Now I have three days to pull the thing together, to weave the strands into a coherent pattern. What would F. have said: 'Make of attention a closed fist, and remember that God lies in the detail.' He didn't make up that aphorism. I recall him telling us who had. I forget now. But what details have we?

What are our objectives? a) *if* it is Hitler, the Jewish organization must not be allowed to claim rights over his person, let alone transport him to Israel. Which had no status either *de jure* or *de facto* at the time of the said crimes or of the Nuremberg trials. Which, under the law of nations, cannot be considered a party to the case, though possibly a 'friend of the court' or 'interested observer' (point to be elucidated). Nor must he be handed over to the local authorities in view of the notorious tangle over extradition. Our American friends will probably attempt a snatch. Orosso (??) looks the logical point of rendezvous and if the aerial photos can be trusted there is a light plane already waiting. But the strip looks totally waterlogged and we may have time. To what end? To arrive at a concerted policy along lines laid down at Potsdam. This is a four-power concern, precisely as is Hess's maintenance at Spandau. I can see Whitehall taking this obvious view. But what about Ivan? Our cables suggest that they are being bloody-minded, per usual: denying even the mildest interest in the story, while preparing what will undoubtedly be the most obstructive and divisive of attitudes. Our stance is plain & I see every benefit in stating it early. As co-signatory of the Four Power protocols, as one of the principals in the matter of indemnification and reparation for war-crimes, the French Republic, via the legal agencies accredited both to the Nuremberg high court (have said agencies a successor, a continuing identity? Theroux was sketchy on this) and to the Hague, declares that etc. The venue for the hearings and actual trial? Delicate question. The European Court in Strasbourg! An inspiration, *vieux*.

b) But do we want a trial? If it is Herr Hitler – and why has Sir Evelyn Ryder come around to thinking it is? – the old devil must by now be a half-crazed scarecrow. The proceedings could turn farcical, and it is precisely our antennae for the ridiculous which distinguish us from other nations. Even if the man they're dragging out of that jungle is still lucid, why open the old wounds? Things would get said, which all of us know and can, therefore, let be. That Vichy was not his creation, but a structure out of the heart of French history, out of an agrarian, clerical, patriarchal France which has never accepted the Revolution, which loathes the Jew and the Mason, which would, with a shrug, consign Paris to the devil. That to so many of my beloved countrymen – including my esteemed father and uncle Xavier – it was the wrong war in the first place. 'Perfidious Albion' and Jewish finance being the real enemies. On which point there was a queer unwritten concordat between Pétain and Le Grand Charles: both trying to preserve what they could of the French Empire from British and American 'liberations' – Madagascar, North Africa, the Antilles, St Pierre and Miquelon. Vichy hoping Free France would get there before the 'allies' and Free France anxious lest Vichy lose its grip too soon on Syria and Algeria. With all of which the Reich had precious little to do. And the larger design: a more or less united Europe, with central organs, from the Mediterranean to the Baltic, cemented by its fear of the Russian bear and of Asia beyond him, and embodying a United Kingdom cut down to continental size. Chancellor Hitler's dream and our current ideal, the very goal we are meant to be striving for. Drieux's testament; still worth reading. 'Millions will have died through a hideous misunderstanding before Europe moves towards that unity which Fascism envisioned, that unity of the Teutonic–Latin genius in the face of the materialist barbarism of the United States and its grotesque imitator, the Soviet Union.' Do we really want that stuff pouring out all over the front pages once again, reminding us of our grosser indiscretions? The mass killings – for that's what they were – at the time of the 'liberation'? The betrayals before that? The years of the *milice*, no Germans in that bunch, and of the *French* camps?

c) But if he's not to be put on trial, what then? That, of course, is where friend Berdier comes into the picture, he and his charming thugs in the *section spéciale*. Get to them first, says Berdier. And save ourselves immeasurable trouble and expense. 'Pandora's box,' said Berdier – his allusions are not recondite. 'Let those crazy Jews and their find out of the woods and political nightmares will swarm.' At which point the Chef de Cabinet listened. Too closely, I thought. 'Special operations' are outside my competence. Not even 'Attila' has to be informed. Perhaps the dossier I've been asked to prepare, Theroux's legal brief, the Minister's position-paper are only a smokescreen. Berdier or someone even uglier could be under way now. I wash my hands of that. In any case, it would be political folly. The Americans must be there already. Four days without V., nearly five. I miss her, the smell of her instep, of the perspiration between her blunt fingers. But feel better than I have in months. More indifferent. It is soon midnight. 'Attila' is waiting to see an outline of my report. Let him wait. I love my wife. She will believe me, she will know how deeply, when we are older. Just how old would *he* be now? The

'biography of the accused' – cretinous jargon – is here somewhere. 20
April 1889: which makes him exactly

25 May: A shock last night when, as we were finishing supper,
Edmond asked me whether I had ever seen Hitler. Had there been a
press leak? The file is, of course, classified top security, but that means
little nowadays. In fact, the boy had simply seen old newsreels being
run on a television show, part of the waves of morbid nostalgia that
now swamps film screens, television, bookstores. I had glimpsed the
Führer once, at Montoire. Xavier had taken me along, as the most
junior clerk in the Maréchal's suite: 'Something to bore your grand-
children with, *mon petit*.' We already knew that things had gone
awkwardly at Hendaye, that Franco had been all smiles and not given
an inch. *That*, surely, was the turning-point in the war. Not Stalingrad,
not Alamein, not, certainly, the landings. But the Caudillo's refusal to
let his precious allies and companions-in-arms have right of transit to
Gibraltar. After which the Reich couldn't win. A classic war, really, a
vintage-European war over access to and control of Mediterranean
routes. A problem ancient as Alcibiades' Sicilian débâcle, and
insoluble still. So our high guest was in a black mood. He lit up,
momentarily, as would any tourist, on meeting the Maréchal, but the
animation faded quickly. I watched him on the station platform,
shuffling, bobbing about amid his staff – he rarely stood still – and
stretching his legs during a break in the conference. I have a distinct
recollection of a terrible tedium surrounding his person, streaming
outward from him like a draft out of a cold sealed place. As if he was
unspeakably bored, with his fame, with the machinery he had set in
motion, with all the performances he would have to go through before
an end whose futility he may already have intuited. I know this has a
romantic, psychologizing ring to it. But I don't think I was fantasizing.
The man was ennui incarnate. When he jerked into motion or rapid
speech, it was obvious that he had tapped great springs of energy. But
one supposed that these were somehow implanted in him, almost
mechanically. The centre was inert, probably lucid. Uncle Xavier said
there had been a man just like that in his company, who had, at some
point early in the war, imagined death with such hysterical intensity
that he was never afraid again, merely empty and lashed on by

126

occasional daring. How would he strike one now, after the years on the run? Has he wanted to survive or did that too 'happen to him', coming from outside? How much does he remember of the giant, vacant thing he was? It *would* be fascinating to know, to hear that voice again. If Berdier gets there first, the occasion will hardly rise. If the Americans do, the psychologists will have their day. 'The rehabilitation of Adolf Hitler; the elucidation of his childhood traumas.' The triumph of the therapeutic. To Edmond, the Reichschancellor is a figure out of the dim past, somewhere between the neolithic and the almost equally remote day-before-yesterday. Tarquin, Ivan the Terrible, Hitler, the Hundred Years' War – was it in Europe or in diverse unpronounceable parts of South-East Asia? – all part of a school syllabus and television-past. Totally unreal. Categorized for examination purposes or entertainment. If I had told the boy that Hitler was thought to be alive, that he might emerge on the box in the flesh, he wouldn't really have believed me. Is he wrong? I don't know myself. But this bizarre ghost hunt *has* got under my skin. More than I realized. V. is fed up. Not with the hurried sessions and sudden cancellations (this is the first hour I've had to myself in ten days), but because she finds even my body 'absent', 'up the Amazon' – her oddly apposite turn of phrase. The affair will soon be spent. I know that, and don't mind very much, and don't know why I don't mind. This whole flap at the Ministry and the chance that I may soon be under way to South America (the presence of this branch is 'quintessential', as 'Attila' likes to put it), seem providential. Yes, that's the word. Providential. When I get back, Edmond must see a skin-doctor. There is no reason for the boy to be disadvantaged. His mother has been so wrapped in herself recently. Or is it herself? I wonder, of course. *Bon soir, Seigneur Cliché*. Why do I so hate disorder? Those memoranda-folders askew on the shelf, when I have told my secretary a dozen times

14

– Do you believe me now, you dumb bastard? Well, do you?

Kulken had an appetite for abjection. Within limits. He also had a flair for detestation. But his loathing of Martin Crownbacker 'call me

Charlie' was of a disinterested purity, of a constancy, which made him wonder. The stench of the man, of his bare presence, choked him. Their intimacies had grown manifold. That Crownbacker had moved in on him body and soul, that he had taken his share of the Indian woman, that his harsh mobile manner had electrified Orosso, these vulgarities seemed to Kulken commonplace and vaguely fated. It was the elusiveness in 'ole Charlie-boy', yet another of the tinny sobriquets his guest thrust upon him, that fixed Kulken's hatred, the interleaving of grating banality – loud, caricatural, inescapable – with a strain dramatically contrasting. Just what the latter consisted of was an enigma which gnawed at Kulken, kept him off-balance and hateful. He had, provisionally, settled on some rubric tantamount to 'authority', to a covert, implausible yet central authority. Whether of knowledge, clandestine rank or solid purpose, he knew not. This ignorance, playing as it did on his nerves, had come on top of chaos.

First the airplanes: a jet of the Brazilian Air Force making two passes over the landing-strip, then a light spotter aircraft racketing in at tree-top level and circling Orosso in sluggish sweeps, next that dazzling job, a small commercial or company jet trying for a landing, twice, which was lunacy in view of the sodden, pockmarked state of the runway, then lifting away towards the jungle. With these incursions had come pandemonium on his receiver. A torrent of instructions, puzzling and otiose, from his employers, who demanded with shrilling impatience that the airfield (what an inflated name for it, thought Kulken) be drained and made ready, that a salubrious quarter (the blithering idiots) be reserved for 'senior personnel', that Kulken, to whom a bonus was felt to be due, prepare to hand over. To all of which Kulken had, on Crownbacker's hoarse insistence, acquiesced, gaining time, gaining back-breaking nights in which to pick out of the air, drier now, lighter after the great rains, a gaggle of other voices. Many were code, others sawed off by static and attempts at jamming. But some were plain enough. First they had criss-crossed the continent, weaving an imprecise grid, but then, as in an exercise in orienteering, they had zeroed in on Orosso, using his, Kulken's, transmitter as a focus. ('That, you poor crud, happens to be Russian' – one of Crownbacker's elucidations of the night before which had inspired in Kulken a particular jangle of worry and hatred.) It was

merely the state of the runway – the winds had also savaged old
Charlie's flying-machine – which lay between Orosso and an outside
world gone seemingly loco. But the margin of immunity was
shrinking fast. Kulken had made out enough to know that bulldozers
were at work, that the jungle track from Akonqui, the furthest point
accessible to a landrover, was being thrashed open. During bouts of
fretful sleep he thought he could hear the distant fall of trees. It would
not be long now. Only yesterday, through heavy mist, they had heard,
or at least thought they had, the clatter of a helicopter. A helicopter
might land even now, though Crownbacker's plane was parked,
oddly enough, across the centre of the oozing strip. (Pounded with
queries on just this point – 'who the blazes is with you in Orosso,
what's he come for, can you get this bleeding plane off the runway' –
Kulken had omitted to answer, an omission the more decorous as
Crownbacker, apparently indefatigable, hovered next to the splayed
earphones, monitoring these enquiries with satisfied contempt.) But
what now? What of their hopes, momentarily allied, once the mob
poured in?

– What did I tell you, turd? What did Uncle Charlie tell you?
Bormann . . . Oh Jeeesus, don't make me laugh.

Hilarity, opined Kulken, was hardly on the agenda. He was, he felt,
too finely honed to be taken in altogether by Crownbacker's sordid
imaginings of bonanza. None the less, if Herr Adolf did come mincing
out of the bush in *propria persona*, and if Crownbacker–Kulken Wire
Services Limited did have the world rights, horns of plenty would
gush. Characteristically offensive as the turn of phrase might well be,
amigo Charlie's assurance that the event would 'make that old epic on
Golgotha look like a filler' had its grain of truth. But Kulken had
ruminated further. The crass self-evidence of Crownbacker's design
had left him restive. The strange beauty of this affair lay with politics,
with the warp and weft of statescraft, with potentialities of international barratry or ransom to whose very existence Crownbacker
appeared to be ludicrously obtuse. These filaments were Kulken's
meat. He envisioned the sum of his past career, menace, humiliation
and all, as a didactic prelude to this hour. Hold Hitler and the
chancelleries would hop to one's piping. Not one but would have
pressing grounds for direct or covert approaches, for competitive

bidding. Washington, of course, and with immediate overreaching, lest Moscow get in first. London and Paris acting in concert at first, but soon at secret odds, labouring to meet Kulken's price. The two Germanies, almost by compulsive right. The Jews, both in Israel and abroad, to whom the prize must, by now, be an indispensable talisman. It was less the money, though Kulken's sense of prodigality was material and far-flung. It was the commerce with high places, indeed the highest, the Byzantine delicacies of threat and cajolement, the savour of elevation above, of retribution on, the oily bastards who had in so many back rooms ridden him, that filled Kulken's soul with vertigo, that made him breathe quick and deep as the earphones crackled.

But either eventuality – the richest carnival and scoop on record or the most arcane, remunerative of diplomatic imbroglios – required monopoly. Schickelgruber, alias A. H., must be safely in hand, his finders disposed of, and the world kept at bay. The first two points lay in reach (Crownbacker had sounded the Indians and found them amenable to what would, after all, be a trivial ambush). It was item three which looked desperate. So many signals were pouring in, so many indices of feverish advance somewhere just beyond the horizon, that Kulken felt literally entrapped. How many more days before the pack barged in, high and mighty, scented with cologne and costly tobacco, thrusting Kulken aside, filching the credit, oblivious to the fact that it was he, Kulken, who had, by dint of tireless cunning, reeled in the leviathan out of the inviolate swamps? The injustice of it took Kulken by the throat and he half-rose out of his steaming chair. Crownbacker had also turned towards the door. The Indians stood there, three or four of them, brown as their shadows.

The jungle is strangely osmotic. Impenetrable in one sense, it is, in another, rifted by tunnels of communication. Explorers' postulates about totally isolated tribes, about corners of tropical forest or mountain innocent of any contact with the outside, are largely spurious. Good shivery stuff for the glossy magazines, Kulken reckoned. Real isolation was formidably rare, if in fact it existed at all. How word sped across the barbed lines of mutually incomprehensible tongues, how iron utensils from the distant fringe-stations came to be found in the inmost of the Matto Grosso, was something of a riddle.

But the facts were certain. News could tear like invisible fire through thicket and across cataracts. You had only to listen and it came humming back.

The party had been shadowed by Indians for at least a fortnight. Four white men with heavy loads, Teku and the Old One. They had been observed marching north-north-west, away from the shallow grave and towards the spur of the Cordillera. The ash of their night-fires had been combed, their excrement pondered, their eviscerated food tins smelt and lifted to the light. The Cinxgu had communicated their notice to the Nambikwa, from whom the news had travelled down the Peranja, somehow arching the nine rapids, from where, in turn, the Jiaro had culled it for display in Orosso. Here it harvested fish-hooks, lengths of rope, two bales of rough linen. So more news came. Of how the party was seeking to avoid the pass, now snow-blocked, and find a circumvention to the south, of how Teku appeared to be leading the actual march, of how he foraged for game. And now?

They had halted. Almost in sight of the mountains. They had been camping for several days, four, perhaps five. They no longer kept the Old One tethered. And Teku was carving a chair.

– A chair?

The Indians repeated the word.

Crownbacker did not wait for translation.

– Well, you dumb turd, do you believe me now?

Kulken reflected on the matter of the chair.

– Yes, he said,

– I believe you now.

15

– Marvin Crownbacker's red, white and blue right down to his jockstrap. I'd take an oath on that.

– Maybe. But this is a lot bigger than anything he's ever been involved in. We should have sent a senior man, like Truscott. I was overruled.

– He's been doing fine up to now, Chief. He's a real broken field runner, and that's what we needed. At least in the early stages.

– But who the hell is Rodriguez Kulken? The file stinks.

– I know, Chief, I know

It was hard to keep stride with the big man, in the crowded, interminable corridor that led to the press room.

– but he got there ahead of us. Johnny on the spot. Nine points of the law. And I'd be surprised if he'd blown Chuck's cover. Kulken's pretty small stuff. Just a stringer. Not even on the supplementary roster. I've got MI6's word for that.

The Chief tried to snort audibly but the sound was lost in the hustle of feet.

– They were just lucky getting in there before we did. They took a chance. But Crownbacker's been in on the action almost from the word go.

The crowd was thickening and both men waved their passes.

– Let us through, please. 'Scuse me, ma'am. OK, OK. Sorry. Coming through. No sweat, Sergeant, but just you keep that door closed once the Secretary begins.

The Chief had hefty shoulders, suddenly haloed by the blaze of klieg lights as they inched their way into the packed chamber.

– The whole god-damn mob. Just look at 'em. The Washington press corps. Pretty, aren't they?

– Well, Earl

The younger man was gripped by excitement, but immediately regretted his recourse to an informality which the Chief had often proffered but, no doubt, preferred to leave conditional.

– it is the biggest news break since

He was struggling for decisive analogy as the throng rose to its feet.

– Battle dress, muttered the Chief as he scanned the Secretary of State's alpaca suit and raw-silk tie.

The voices and waving arms surged as from a sea-anemone, bobbing impatiently.

– Ladies and gentlemen. Please. One at a time. Please.

– Riffler. *St Louis Post-Dispatch*. Mr Secretary, is it true . . .

The echoing buzz subsided slowly.

– I wish we could finalize our answer to that, Mr Riffler, but we aren't absolutely certain. What I would say is this: on the basis of available evidence, and in view of the assessment made both by our own intelligence and that of the other sovereign states with whom we have been in touch, there is a reasonable expectation that the man found by what we understand to be – and I underline this point – an unofficial pursuit-party is indeed the Head of State of the so-called Third Reich.

The voices and flash-bulbs burst chaotically.

– Miss Marten . . .

– Thank you, Mr Secretary. Regina Marten, Southern News Syndicate. When do you expect Hitler to come out of those woods and who'll be there to receive him?

– Again, I'm afraid, the question is open to some doubt. According to the latest information we have, and you must realize, ladies and gentlemen, that communications from the heart of the Amazonian rain forests are somewhat circuitous

(Nice word that, thought the young man)

the party and the alleged Mr Hitler have halted. South by south-west of Orosso, at the approaches to a high plateau beyond which our maps locate a native hamlet designated as Jiaro.

(The Secretary of State was glancing at his notes.)

Under optimal conditions the party could be expected to reach civilization, that is to say the airstrip and radio-transmitter thought to be operative at Orosso, in something on the order of ten days. But I am given to understand that there have been early rains of exceptional intensity resulting in flash-floods and fresh snow on the high places. As to the question of the status and identity of personnel at the presumed meeting-point, I would prefer to reserve our position. As you can readily imagine, Miss Marten, this is an issue of extreme diplomatic nicety, involving as it does the local authorities as well as those foreign governments who may or may not have a valid claim to be regarded as interested parties.

– Escomb. *Time* magazine. Sir, do we have anybody on the spot, right now?

– You will understand, Bill, that it would be against the best interests of our government to go into details, at a moment when the relevant issues remain somewhat confused. But I think I could say this: the degree of surveillance we have been able to exercise over the day-to-day course of events should suggest to you that our position is one of readiness at both the local and global levels.

– Mr Secretary, you've referred . . . sorry: Cord Dwyer, *Milwaukee Tribune*. You've referred to contacts with other governments. Can you elaborate on that?

– Gladly. As is obvious to everyone concerned, the discovery of Herr Hitler, if identification turns out to be positive, is a matter for international response. The sovereign states party to the Berlin agreements and to the Nuremberg tribunal are naturally involved. So is Brazil, on whose territory the putative Reichschancellor was found and which he had, it is to be presumed, entered illegally. Since the time when the indictments for war-crimes were drawn up, moreover, the political map has greatly changed. Both the German Democratic Republic and the German Federal Republic have declared their strong interest in the case. It is conceivable also that the Republic of Austria, in which the subject was born and, at different times of his life, domiciled, may wish to be a party to the proceedings of identification and to what are, unavoidably I fear, bound to be the intricacies of extradition. Though the issue is one on which our government has, as yet, evolved no firm view, there would appear to be a *prima-facie* case for referral to the United Nations. I have instructed members of the United States delegation to solicit the views of the Secretary-General and of his legal staff on this very point.

– What about Israel?

The voice was strained and the thick accent cut in above the chorus of questioners.

– Why haven't you mentioned Israel, Mr Secretary of State? He's our prisoner, isn't he?

– Believe me, Mr Simon, it is Mr Simon, isn't it?

and the Secretary shaded his eyes for a moment against the hot banked lights.

– I would be only too pleased if I could give you an unequivocal answer. But our exchanges with your government on this entire matter have been less than satisfactory. It is no longer a secret to reveal that our first communications, transmitted as soon as expert opinion regarded the matter as potentially of substance, received nothing but routine acknowledgement. When we pressed for reply at a most senior level – the President himself has, of course, kept developments under daily review – the response from Tel Aviv was, to say the least, disappointing. So far as we are aware – and that comprises cables submitted to me this morning – your government has not taken any official note of the reports of Mr Hitler's capture. It has neither acknowledged nor denied any participation in the recruitment, dispatch or future utilization of the search-team. Enquiries on our part as to the position the State of Israel might take in respect of a possible trial before a multinational court have, hitherto, met with no clarification. So far as this Administration goes, efforts to elucidate and give the most favourable possible construction to Israeli concerns in the matter and to those of the Jewish community as a whole, will of course continue.

– What if we get him out on our own, and transport him to Israel?

The same voice, hectoring.

– I would, I'm afraid, find it irresponsible to comment on so hypothetical a question. The precedent which you may have in mind, Mr Simon, I refer to the Eichmann case, has, I feel, left a legacy of serious doubt with regard to international law and agreed usage among nations.

Out of the gaggle of voices an alto.

– Gene Jefferson, *Atlanta News-Times*. Mr Secretary, in view of your previous answer, would you care to comment on whether or not a statute of limitations applies to Hitler's crimes. And what of the man's mental state? Suppose he is no longer fit to plead.

The Hon. Avery Lockyer dabbed his cheek.

– As many of you ladies and gentlemen are aware, I have spent a good deal of my life in the law. I am well aware of the fact that even at this considerable remove in time uneasiness over judicial aspects of the Nuremberg proceedings persists. This Administration and I personally hold no brief for special retroactive law. The ideal of common-law precedents is enshrined in our way of life in these United States and, I would hope, in the policies of this Department. But you will recall that the statute of limitations was specifically voided with regard to what have been defined as 'crimes against humanity'. The current eventuality would appear to exemplify this category in an emphatic way. As to the issue of the accused's mental condition and degree of responsibility, it is obviously too early to express an opinion. I remind you that no identification has yet been validated nor any personal contact made by any agent of your government. We would hope that thorough psychiatric checks can be initiated, under proper conditions, and as soon as possible.

– Tylden. AP. Do the Russians see it that way?

– I'd prefer to withhold comment on that, Ed.

– Mr Secretary. Ann Carey. *Miami Herald*. Surely it would be possible to fly that party out. To pick them up by helicopter. Why all the delay?

(– Watch this, breathed the Chief, whose corner-of-the-mouth *sotto voce* was notorious throughout the service.)

– I wish it were that simple, Miss Carey. To the best of our knowledge the most proximate landing facility, at Orosso, has, until a few days ago, been waterlogged. Even from there, a helicopter pick-up presents severe technical problems. It is, moreover, by no means evident what the attitude of the search-party would be to intervention at this point. Perhaps Mr Simon would care to enlighten us.

Mild laughter in the stifling room and a shuffle of metal chairs.

– Big deal, muttered the Chief, let's get back to the salt-mines.

The younger man followed as they shouldered their way through the close-packed spectators and made for the exit. Just before they reached it and caught the cold draught from the now-empty corridor, the young man registered an arresting voice, almost Gregorian.

– Sir, can you give us an assurance, an emphatic assurance, that due process will be followed and, most especially, that the accused will be given every legal aid for his defence?

Shutting behind them the baize door cut off the answer.

16

– Yes. But why me?

The antique banality. Its utterance submerged John Asher with leaden exasperation. For the very first time in the crazed meanderings of the entire enterprise, his heart gave out. The broken plain with its hummocks of saguaro, now in violent bloom, the rock abutments with their pale carpet of new snow, went grey.

Elie Barach began his customary motion of persuasion and humble rapture, a miniature dance-step back and forth. But Asher cut him short.

– I know. I don't really need an answer to that, do I?

– Friend Asher, you misconstrue. Do you know what the wisdom books say of the tribe of Aser, of your tribe? That they are a stubborn folk and sleep a serpent's long winter slumber. Who else can it be? Simeon has emptied himself, made himself a mirror so blank it no longer holds his own image. So that he can judge. I must read the Law, blessed be its Name. The boy Isaac? Since Gideon's death he is full of self-importance; grief has made him swell. It has to be my brother Jonathan. Who knows about fairness, and how they deem a man innocent until proved guilty, out there, in the real world.

Elie half-pirouetted towards the horizon, the little dance starting in his hollowed frame.

– In the real world. He reiterated the phrase.

And from just beyond the cliffs phantasms of a sane, populous existence seemed to tide across the fell.

The cry was in Asher's throat. But he said evenly

– I am no lawyer.

– True. True. Where there is a temple let the rabbi speak. Where there is only a rabbi let the unlearned hold their peace. Where there are ten simple men left, let them join in counsel. Where there is but one man left, let him be steadfast as the temple was, let him seek out the meaning of the Law as the rabbi did, let him take counsel with himself as if a score of just men inhabited his heart. We have only ash in hand to kindle a great fire.

And he set his fingers lightly on Asher's arm.

– He of Aser whose name is also in Manasseh.

– We don't have that far to go. They must be looking for us now. Perhaps Lieber is in Orosso already or nearer. When we get out the thing can be done properly, as it should be. Elie, we're play-acting and I'm sick of it.

Elie Barach, as to an obstinate child.

– No. We've been through all that. A hundred times in these last few days. Since Gideon and the storms. By now those that are looking for us or waiting over the mountains are not ours. Simeon will hold out a while longer, but now he is like a tree in its last season. Rooted here. Move him and he will break. As for me, enough! 'For I am ready to halt,' says the Psalmist. Teku is as a sign sent us. To be a witness to the man's trial. An Indian guest come out of Eden to see the trying of one who sought to banish God, blessed be His Name, from creation.

– Out of Eden?

– Oh, I know. The stench, the bats, the leeches. But it is the nearest thing to the Garden left on the earth. By now men have wasted all the rest, pulping, scarring, dirtying the forests so as not to be reminded of that first Garden. But out here, there are instants.

And Asher recalled the unnamed bloom, sultry gold and with leaves delicate as gossamer, which had shone before them at the edge of the swamps, or the silent rush of stars into the perfect concavity of the drumming lake, or the Tenebrae of a bird, out of sight in the canopies of high moss, the notes arrowing towards nightfall, velvet and swift. A guest out of Eden.

Teku had crushed a kada nut and rubbed the oil into the palm of his hand. Now he was giving a final polish to the carved legs of the ceremonial stool, sliding his fingers along the curved and spiralling motif which signified, in abstract yet unmistakable representation, the anteater sigil. Where his hand passed the black wood glowed indigo. Teku had selected the heavy timber, testing the grain against his cheek. He had burned the necessary hollows out of the living trunk and planed them to a lucent finish. The labour had to be perfect, for he knew himself to be watched. Not by the white men who walked like the blind, but by the Cinxgu and, now, by two Jiaro scouts well out of their own territory. At first, to be sure, the stalkers had done much to mask their presence. It had taken Teku several days and a nocturnal sweep of his own to be certain that the party was indeed being tracked, that each successive bivouac was being deciphered and culled for useful leavings. But in these last days, the watchers had dropped all but the most perfunctory pretence. A child would have made out the spoors of their approach to the edge of the encampment, the grass flattened where they had squatted, the russet traces left on the ground and leaves where they had chewed and spat. At moments they were so careless or scornful as to let themselves be heard. Four foot-beats: a heavy man and his slighter companion. Teku had caught the sound just before dawn. None of his company had stirred. Deaf too.

He squinted at his art. Another pass with his flat hand and the wood shone back at the light of the early sun. It was a regal furnishing, a seat fit for an old man whose language Teku could not make out, whose skin sagged and splotched like that of a swamp-rat three days gone, but in whose eyes the carver had seen two points of cold silver such as only the greatest of the tale-tellers, of the spirit-raisers possess.

Now he lifted the stool and carried it to the circle of swept earth, almost at the midpoint of the camp, as Simeon had ordered him to do. Let those Jiaro scarecrows gape. Let word of this throne travel as far as the nine falls.

Isaac Amsel could not take his eyes off this lambent handiwork. Uncertainly he slid his fingers over the subtly rounded seat. Teku's cunning, on the march, at food-gathering, in the clearing of camp-sites filled them with troubled wonder. He had known of such skills, he had seen them acted in films of exploration and jungle romance. It was a different feeling altogether to witness them at first hand, adroitly enfolded, as it seemed, in the flesh of this small brown visitor, so brittle, so unprepossessing when compared with the stature of Benasseraf or that of Isaac's father. The Indian, in turn, prized the boy's endurance, the way he dogged and sometimes defied the older men. He was teaching him to handle the blow-gun, to make of his pent breath a whistling rush, to spot the change of shadows behind shadows which signified game.

Elie had sat on the ground, halfway between the ceremonial stool and the seat Simeon had made for himself of an empty crate and grey blanket. For the first time since the capture, Simeon had unwrapped and opened the waterproof metal tube, so like a botanist's sampler, in which Lieber had stored the articles of attainder. He thought it would be best to read them aloud, then to give them to John Asher and the accused; after which he, Simeon, leader of the party and agent plenipotentiary, would set forth, with all deliberation and clarity, the grounds, reasons, motives which had caused him to institute proceedings here, at latitude x and longitude y, between the rain forest and the Cordillera, with himself as presiding judge, Elie Barach as explicator of the Law, Asher as defence counsel, and Isaac and Teku as witnesses. To state reasons for a procedure which ordinary good sense and world opinion would doubtless condemn as irregular, indeed mad, but which Simeon knew, upon searching examination, to be conclusive. In regard to the facts of the material and psychological reserves (now fast dwindling) of the party, in regard to their relation to the prisoner and the past, in regard to that indecent and piratical tumult which, they had every cause to expect, lay at the planned end of the march. Simeon had resolved to enunciate these propositions with condign solemnity. He had turned over in his mind phrases which, he knew, could be voiced this one and singular time only in human history. Elie had considered the pronouncement and suggested illustrative citations.

Now everything appeared to be ready. The accused was leaving the shelter with Asher at his heels. Simeon's mouth went dry as he waited for the two men to take up their appointed place. But already, as he came forward with his withered arm crooked to his side, Mr Asher's client had begun to speak.

17

Erster Punkt. Article one. Because you must understand that I did not invent. It was Adolf Hitler who dreamed up the master race. Who conceived of enslaving inferior peoples. Lies. Lies. It was in the doss-house, in the *Männerheim* that I first understood. It was in, God help me, but that was long ago. And the lice. Large as a thumbnail. 1910, 1911. What does it matter now? It was there that I first understood your secret power. The secret power of your teaching. Of *yours*. A chosen people. Chosen by God for His own. The only race on earth chosen, exalted, made singular among mankind. It was Grill who taught me. Do you know about Grill? No. You know nothing about me. Jahn Grill. But that wasn't his name. Do you hear me? Called himself Jahn, said he was a defrocked priest. For all I know he may have been. That too. But his real name was Jacob. Jacob Grill, son of a rabbi, from Poland. Or Galicia. Or. What does it matter? One of yours, yours, yours. We lived close. One soap-sliver between us. It was Grill who taught me, who showed me the words. The chosen people. God's own and elect amid the unclean, amid the welter of nations. Who shall be chastised for impurity, for taking a heathen to wife, who shall have

140

bondsmen and bondswomen from among the *goyim*, but stay apart. My promise was only a thousand years. 'To eternity,' said Grill; lo, it is written here. In letters of white fire. The covenant of election, the setting apart of the race, *das heilige Volk*, like unto no other. Under the iron law. Circumcision and the sign on your forehead. One law, one race, one destiny unto the end of the end of time. 'And Joshua burnt Ai, and made it an heap for ever, even a desolation unto this day.' 'And Joshua made them that day hewers of wood and drawers of water for the congregation.' All of them. Men, women, children. To serve Israel in bondage. But more often there was no one to enslave. 'And they utterly destroyed all that was in the city, both man and woman, young and old, and ox, and sheep, and ass, with the edge of the sword.' Your holy books. The smell of blood. Jacob Grill, friend Grill, and Neumann, for whom I painted postcards, they smelt of shit. But they taught me. That a people must be chosen to fulfil its destiny, that there can be no other thus made glorious. That a true nation is a mystery, a single body willed by God, by history, by the unmingled burning of its blood. It does not matter what you call the roots of the dream. A mystery of will, of chosenness. To conquer its promised land, to cut down or lay in bondage all who stand in its path, to proclaim itself eternal. 'Let the trumpet blow in Zion. Let the Cherubim of the Lord bring fire and plague unto our enemies.' You could hear the lice crack between Grill's fingers. God, how his breath stank. But he read from the book. Your book. Of which every letter is sacred, and every mite of every letter. That's so, isn't it? Read till lights out, and after, singsong through the nose, because he knew it by heart, from his schooldays, and had heard his father. The rabbi. 'They utterly destroyed all that was in the city.' In Samaria. Because the Samaritans read a different scripture. Because they had built a sanctuary of their own. Of terebinth. Six cubits to the left. They had made it seven or five or God knows. Put to the sword. The first time. Every man, woman, child, she-ox, the dogs too. No. No dogs. They are of the unclean of Moab, the lepers of Sidon. To slaughter a city because of an idea, because of a vexation over words. Oh, that was a high invention, a device to alter the human soul. Your invention. One Israel, one *Volk*, one leader. Moses, Joshua, the anointed king who has slain his thousands, no his ten thousands, and dances before the ark. It was in

Compiègne, wasn't it? They say I danced there. Only a small dance.

The pride of it, the brute cunning. Whatever you are, wherever, be it ulcerous as Job, or Neumann scratching his stinking crotch. You should have seen the two of us peddling those postcards, like starved dogs. But what does it matter if you're one of the chosen people? One of God's familiars, above all other men, set apart for His rages and His love. In a covenant, a singling out, a consecration never to be lost. Grill told me that. Jahn Jacob Grillschmuhl Grill or whatever his greasy name was, reeking of piss when he crawled up the stairs. Even he. The apostate. The outcast from Zion. Was still of the chosen, a private vexation to the Almighty. 'Listen,' he said, 'listen Adi,' no man else ever called me that, 'you think you see me as I am, Grill the loser, the doss-house bum. But you're blind. All you *goyim* are blind. For all you know, Adi, I am one of the seventy-two chosen, chosen even above the chosen. One of the secret just ones on whom the earth rests. And while you snore tonight or swallow your spit, listen to me, Adi, here in this barrack right here, my blind friend, the Messiah may come to me and know me for his own.' And he would roll his eyes and give a little laugh, a yellow Jew-laugh. It went through me like a knife. But I learnt.

From you. Everything. To set a race apart. To keep it from defilement. To hold before it a promised land. To scour that land of its inhabitants or place them in servitude. Your beliefs. Your arrogance. In Nuremberg, the searchlights. That clever beaver Speer. Straight into the night. Do you remember them? The pillar of fire. That shall lead you to Canaan. And woe unto the Amorites, the Jebusites, the Kenites, the half-men outside God's pact. My 'Superman'? Second-hand stuff. Rosenberg's philosophic garbage. They whispered to me that *he* too. The name. My racism was a parody of yours, a hungry imitation. What is a thousand-year Reich compared to the eternity of Zion? Perhaps I was the false messiah sent before. Judge me and you must judge yourself. *Übermenschen*, chosen ones!

– What my client means, began Asher

Punkt II. There had to be a solution, a *final* solution. For what is the Jew if he is not a long cancer of unrest? Gentlemen, I beg your attention, I demand it. Was there ever a crueller invention, a contrivance more calculated to harrow human existence, than that of an omnipotent, all-seeing, yet invisible, impalpable, inconceivable

God? Gentlemen, I pray you, consider the case, consider it closely. The pagan earth was crowded with small deities, malicious or consoling, winged or pot-bellied in leaf and branch, in rock and river. Giving companionship to man, pinching his bottom or caressing him, but of his measure. Delighting in honey-cakes and roast meat. Gods after our own image and necessities. And even the great deities, the Olympians, would come down in mortal visitation, to do war and lechery. Mightier than we, I grant you, but tangible and taking on the skin of things. The Jew emptied the world by setting his God apart, immeasurably apart from man's senses. No image. No concrete embodiment. No imagining even. A blank emptier than the desert. Yet with a terrible nearness. Spying on our every misdeed, searching out the heart of our heart for motive. A God of vengeance unto the thirtieth generation (those are the Jews' words, not mine). A God of contracts and petty bargains, of indentures and bribes. 'And the Lord gave Job twice as much as he had before.' A thousand she-asses where the crazed, boiled old man had had only five hundred to start with. It makes one vomit, doesn't it? *Twice* as much. Gentlemen, do you grasp the sliminess of it, the moral trickery? Cast your guiltless servant into hell, thunder at him out of the whirlwind, draw leviathan by the nose, and then? Double his income, declare a dividend, slip him a lordly tip. Why did Job not spit at that cattle-dealer of a God? Yet the holy of holies was an empty room, a silence in a silence. And the Jew mocks those who have pictures of their god. *His* God is purer than any other. The very thought of Him exceeds the powers of the human minds. We are as blown dust to His immensity. But because we are His creatures, we must be better than ourselves, love our neighbour, be continent, give of what we have to the beggar. Because His inconceivable, unimaginable presence envelops us, we must obey every jot of the law. We must bottle up our rages and desires, chastise the flesh and walk bent in the rain. You call me a tyrant, an enslaver. What tyranny, what enslavement has been more oppressive, has branded the skin and soul of man more deeply, than the sick fantasies of the Jew? You are not Godkillers, but *God-makers*. And that is infinitely worse. The Jew invented conscience and left man a guilty serf.

But that was only the first piece of blackmail. There was worse to come. The white-faced Nazarite. Gentlemen, I find it difficult to contain myself. But the facts must speak for themselves. What did that epileptic rabbi ask of man? That he renounce the world, that he leave mother and father behind, that he offer the other cheek when slapped, that he render good for evil, that he love his neighbour as himself, no, far better, for self-love is an evil thing to be overcome. O grand castration! Note the cunning of it. Demand of human beings more than they can give, demand that they give up their stained, selfish humanity in the name of a higher ideal and you will make of them cripples, hypocrites, mendicants for salvation. The Nazarite said that his kingdom, his purities were not of this world. Lies, honeyed lies. It was here on earth that he founded his slave-church. It was men and women, creatures of flesh, he abandoned to the blackmail of hell, of eternal punishment. What were our camps compared to *that*? Ask of man more than he is, hold before his tired eyes an image of altruism, of compassion, of self-denial which only the saint or the madman can touch, and you stretch him on the rack. Till his soul bursts. What can be crueller than the Jew's addiction to the ideal?

First, the invisible but all-seeing, the unattainable but all-demanding God of Sinai. Second, the terrible sweetness of Christ. Had the Jew not done enough to sicken man? No, gentlemen, there is a third act to our story.

'Sacrifice yourself for the good of your fellow-man. Relinquish your possessions so that there may be equality for all. Hammer yourself hard as steel, strangle emotion, loyalty, mercy, gratitude. Denounce parent or lover. So that justice may be achieved on earth. So that history be fulfilled and society be purged of all imperfections.' Do you recognize the sermon, gentlemen? The litany of hatred? Rabbi Marx on the day of atonement. Was there ever a greater promise? 'The classless society, to each according to his needs, brotherhood for all mankind, the earth made a garden again, a rational Eden.' In the name of which promise tyranny, torture, war, extermination were a necessity, an historical necessity! It is no accident that Marx and his minions were Jews, that the congregations of Bolshevism – Trotsky, Rosa Luxemburg, Kamenev, the whole fanatic, murderous pack – were of Israel. Look at them: prophets, martyrs, smashers of images, word-spinners drunk with the terror of the absolute. It was only a step, gentlemen, a small, inevitable step, from Sinai to Nazareth, from Nazareth to the covenant of Marxism. The Jew had grown impatient, his dreams had gone rancid. Let the kingdom of justice come here and now, next Monday morning. Let us have a secular Messiah instead. But with a long beard and his bowels full of vengeance.

Three times the Jew has pressed on us the blackmail of transcendence. Three times he has infected our blood and brains with the bacillus of perfection. Go to your rest and the voice of the Jew cries out in the night. 'Wake up! God's eye is upon you. Has He not made you in His image? Lose your life so that you may gain it. Sacrifice yourself to the truth, to justice, to the good of mankind.' That cry has been in our ears too long, gentlemen, far too long. Men had grown sick of it, sick to death. When I turned on the Jew, no one came to his rescue. No one. France, England, Russia, even Jew-ridden America did nothing. They were glad that the exterminator had come. Oh, they did not say so openly, I allow you that. But secretly they rejoiced. We had to find, to burn out the virus of utopia before the whole of our western civilization sickened. To return to man as he is, selfish, greedy, short-sighted, but warm and housed, so marvellously housed, in his own stench. 'We were chosen to be the conscience of man,' said the Jew. And I answered him, yes, I, gentlemen, who now stand before you: 'You are not man's conscience, Jew. You are only his bad conscience. And we shall vomit you so we may live and have peace.' A final solution. How could there be any other?

– The question the defendant is raising, rasped Asher

Do not interrupt. I will not tolerate interruption. I am an old man. My voice tires. Gentlemen, I appeal to your sense of justice, your notorious sense of justice. Hear me out. Consider my third point. Which is that you have exaggerated. Grossly. Hysterically. That you have made of me some kind of mad devil, the quintessence of evil, hell embodied. When I was, in truth, only a man of my time. Oh, inspired, I will grant you, with a certain – how shall I put it? – nose for the supreme political possibility. A master of human moods, perhaps, but a man of my time.

Average, if you will. Had it been otherwise, had I been the singular demon of your rhetorical fantasies, how then could millions of ordinary men and women have found in me the mirror, the plain mirror of their needs and appetites? And it was, I will allow you that, an ugly time. But I did not create its ugliness, and I was not the worst. Far from it. How many wretched little men of the forests did your Belgian friends murder outright or leave to starvation and syphilis when they raped the Congo? Answer me that, gentlemen. Or must I remind you? Some *twenty* million. That picnic was under way when I was new-born. What were Rotterdam or Coventry compared to Dresden and Hiroshima? I do not come out worst in that black game of numbers. Did I invent the camps? Ask of the Boers. But let us be serious. Who was it that broke the Reich? To whom did you hand over millions, tens of millions of men and women from Prague to the Baltic? Set them like a bowl of milk before an insatiable cat? I was a man of a murderous time, but a small man compared to *him*. You think of me as a satanic liar. Very well. Do not take my word for it. Choose what sainted, unimpeachable witness you will. The holy writer, the great bearded one who came out of Russia and preached to the world. It is long ago now. My memory aches. The man of the archipelago. Yes, that word sticks in the mind. What did he say? That Stalin had slaughtered *thirty* million. That he had perfected genocide when I was still a nameless scribbler in Munich. My boys used their fists and their whips. I won't deny it. The times stank of hunger and blood. But when a man spat out the truth they would stop their fun. Stalin's torturers worked for the pleasure of the thing. To make men befoul themselves, to obtain confessions which are lies, insanities, jokes. The truth only made them more bestial. It is not I who assert these things: it is your own survivors, your historians, the sage of the Gulag. Who, then, was the greater destroyer, whose blood-lust was the more implacable? Stalin's or mine? Ribbentrop told me: of the man's contempt for *us*. Whom he found amateurish, corrupt with mercy. Our terrors were a village carnival compared to his. Our camps covered absurd acres; he had strung wire and death-pits around a continent. Who survived among those who had fought with him, brought him to power, executed his will? Not one. He smashed their bones to the last splinter. When my fall came my good companions were alive, fat, scuttling for safety or recompense, cavorting towards you with their contritions and their memories. How many Jews did Stalin kill, your saviour, your ally Stalin? Answer me that. Had he not died when he did, there would not have been one of you left alive between Berlin and Vladivostok. Yet Stalin died in bed, and the world stood hushed before the tiger's rest. Whereas you hunt me down like a rabid dog, put me on trial (by what right, by what mandate?), drag me through the swamps, tie me up at night. Who am a very old man and uncertain of recollection. Small game, gentlemen, hardly worthy of your skills. In a world that has tortured political prisoners and poured napalm on naked villagers, that has stripped the earth of plant and animal. That has done these things and continues to do them quite without my help and long after I, 'the one out of hell' – oh , ludicrous, histrionic phrase – was thought to have been extinct.

Asher's breath came loud and empty.

Do not trouble yourself, *Herr Advokat*. I have only one more point to make. The last. That strange book *Der Judenstaat*. I read it carefully. Straight out of Bismarck. The language, the ideas, the tone of it. A clever book, I agree. Shaping Zionism, in the image of the new German nation. But did Herzl create Israel or did I? Examine the question fairly. Would Palestine have become Israel, would the Jews have come to that barren patch of the Levant, would the United States *and* the Soviet Union, *Stalin's* Soviet Union, have given you recognition and guaranteed your survival, had it not been for the Holocaust? It was the Holocaust that gave you the courage of injustice, that made you drive the Arab out of his home, out of his field, because he was lice-eaten and without resource, because he was in your divinely ordered way. That made you endure knowing that those whom you had driven out were rotting in refugee camps, not ten miles away, buried alive in despair and lunatic dreams of vengeance. Perhaps I *am* the Messiah, the true Messiah, the new Sabbatai whose infamous deeds were allowed by God in order to bring His people home. 'The Holocaust was the necessary mystery before Israel could come into its strength.' It is not I who have said it: but your own visionaries, your unravellers of God's meaning when it is Friday night in Jerusalem. Should you not honour me who have made you into men of war, who have made of the long, vacuous day-dream of Zion a reality? Should you not be a comfort to my old age?

Gentlemen of the tribunal: I took my doctrines from you. I fought the blackmail of the ideal with which you have hounded mankind. My crimes were matched and surpassed by those of others. The Reich begat Israel. These are my last words. The last words of a dying man against the last words of those who suffered; and in the midst of incertitude must matters be left till the great revelation of all secrets.

Teku had not understood the words, only their meaning. Whose brazen pulse carried all before it. He had leapt up to cry out, 'Proven.' To cry it to the earth twice and twice to the north, as is the custom. But the air seemed to be exploding around him. Loud drum-beats hammering closer and closer, driving his voice back into his throat. He looked up, his ears pounding.

The first helicopter was hovering above the clearing. The second

Return No More

He paused by the edge of the road until the truck had curved out of sight and the rasp of the motor had died in the cold salt air.

Then he shifted his rubber-tipped cane to his right hand and stooped down with the left to pick up his suitcase, torn at the hinges and lashed with string.

He advanced in spasms down the gravelled side road to the village. His right leg was dead to the hip and swung on the socket of his straining body in a slow arc. The foot, shod in a blunt shoe and raised on a bulky leather heel, slid gratingly with each step. Whereupon the man would again thrust cane and body forward and draw the leg after him.

The twist of effort had hunched his neck and shoulders as if he wore armour, and at every lunge sweat shone at the edge of his fine, reddish hair. Pain and the constant observance of precarious footing fogged his eyes to an uncertain grey. But when he gathered breath, setting his suitcase on the ground and stilting on his cane like a long-legged heron, his eyes resumed their natural colour, a deep harsh blue. The port of his head, with its fine-drawn mouth and delicate structure, mocked the gnarled contortion of his gait. The man was handsome in a worn, arresting way.

Ordinarily, trucks did not stop in the highroad but churned by between the dunes and the cliffline, either inland to Rouen, or farther along the coast to Le Havre. Yvebecques lay off the road, on the escarpment of the cliffs and along a half-moon of stone beach. High yellow buses stopped on their way from Honfleur, turning into the market-place. They unloaded under the wide-flung eaves of the Norman market hall. Beyond its pillared arcade ran a street, narrow and high-gabled, and at the end of it the beach, merging into the wavering light of the sea.

On the market-place stood a three-spouted brass fountain. It bore a scroll filled with names and garlanded with ceremonious laurel. Each spout curved like a desolate gargoyle over a date, heavily incised: 1870, 1914, 1939, *pro domo*.

Hearing the truck stop and shift gears, the men who stood among the market stalls or by the fountain looked up. A coldness and stiffness came over their easy stance. The fishmonger, who was hosing down his marbled stall, let the water race unchecked across his boots.

The traveller was now very near. Once again he rested his suitcase and straightened his back, letting the strain ebb from his shoulders. At the verge of the market-place, where the gravel turns to cobblestones, he paused and looked about. His mouth softened into a smile. He had not heard the brusque silence and made for the fountain. He hastened his step by sheer bent of will.

He brought his face under the live spout. The chill, rusty water spilled over his mouth and throat. Then he pushed himself upwards, pivoting adroitly on his good leg. He limped towards the red and yellow awning of the café. But a mass of long, unmoving shadows fell across his way. Three of the men wore the heavy smocks of fishermen; one was round, close-cropped and in a dark suit. The fifth was scarcely more than a boy. He hovered near the edge of the group and chewed his wet lip.

The stranger looked at them with a grave, hesitant courtesy, as if he had known they would be there to bar his way but had hoped for some twist of grace. The round dark one surged forward. He set his lacquered shoe against the man's cane and thrust his face close. He spoke low, but such was the stillness of the square that his words carried, distant and raging: 'No. No. Not here. Get out. We don't want you back. Any of you. Now get out.'

And the boy cried, 'No,' in a thin, angry whine.

The traveller bent a little to one side, as in a sudden rouse of wind. Close by a voice flat with rage said again, 'Get out. We don't want any part of you. Lucky for you you're a cripple. Not enough meat for a man on your carcass.'

He squinted against the high sun and remembered his bearings. He veered from the bristling shadows and started towards the street which led from the market square to the apple orchards on the western terrace of the cliffs. But even before he had entered the dark of the Rue de la Poissonnière, the boy had leaped past. He whirled, grinning with spite: 'I know where you are going. I will tell them. They'll stone you alive.' He spurted on and turned once more: 'Why don't you catch me, cripple?'

Tight-buttoned, the notary peered after the stranger. Then he spat between his lacquered toes and whistled. A large dog rose from under the meat stalls and ambled over. A leathery cur backed mournfully from a pile of fishgut oozing on the warm stones. Other dogs came off their haunches. The notary scratched his mongrel behind the ears and hissed at it, pointing towards the limping man. Then he flicked the dog across its snout with a lash of the wrist. The animal sprang away snarling. Monsieur Lurôt hissed again and the dog understood. He fanged the fleas from his raw neck and gave a queer yelp, cruel and lost. A retriever, who had been drowsing under the billiard table, tore out of the café. Now other men were flailing and whistling at the dogs and pointing to the Rue de la Poissonnière. The pack milled at the fountain snapping at each other, then hurtled towards the narrow street. In the van, Lurôt's mongrel let out a full-throated cry.

He heard them coming in a loud rush but they were at his heels before he could turn. They flew at him like crazed shadows, slobbering and snapping the air with woken fury. The man swayed off-balance as he swung his cane at the bellowing pack. He was able to stem his legs against a wall but the mongrel sprang at him, its eyes flaring with vacant malignity. The rancid scent of the dog enveloped him. He flung the animal from his face but felt a hot scratch raking his shoulder.

Beyond the reek and clamour of the charging dogs, like distant streamers on the wind, the lame man heard laughter from the market-place.

The animals were wearying of their sport. They stood off, baring their teeth. Only the retriever was still at him, circling and darting in, its head low. It evaded the man's cane with jagged leaps. Suddenly the bitch hurled herself at the stranger's inert leg. Her teeth locked on the leather heel. The man went down against the side of the house, clawing the air for support. The dog inched back, its tongue red over its bruised mouth. The cane snapped down on it with a single, murderous stroke. The animal subsided into a moaning heap; somewhere a bone had cracked and now its eyes spun.

The suitcase had fallen on the cobblestones. One of the hinges sprung and a small parcel tumbled out. It had shattered against the sharp rim of the pavement. Slivers of blue and ice-white china lay dispersed in the gutter. In the murky street they gathered points of light. The man dragged himself over and picked up what was left of the Meissen figurine. Only the base, with its frieze of pale cornflowers, and the slim, silk-hosed legs of the shepherd dancer were intact. Bereft of the arching body and dreaming visage, these legs, in their plum breeches and black pumps, retained the motion of the dance. The head had smashed into myriad pieces; only the hat could be made out, lying near the middle of the street, three-cornered and with a flash of plume.

The traveller lurched to his feet, picked up his suitcase and tightened the string over the broken corner. The dogs stood wary. Then the mongrel shuffled near and whined softly. The man passed his hand over its mangy ears. Lurôt's dog looked up with a wide, stupid stare. The pack did not follow the cripple as he moved away.

Before him the houses thinned out and the cliff towered into full view. The sea lay to the right, murmurous and hazy under the white sun. The salt wind dried the sweat from the man's face and body. But the yelp of the dogs had bitten into his marrow, and dim shocks of fear and tiredness passed through his limbs. In the sudden shade of the apple trees his skin prickled with cold. Now the path lifted again and the sea opened beneath him, glittering in the heat. Only the tideline moved, lapping the beach with a sullen vague rustle.

The way dipped into a hollow. Bees sang between the stubble and the grass had the dry savour of inland. Recollection came upon him vivid and exact. *Quis viridi fontes induceret umbra* – who shall veil the spring with shadow and leaf?

It was at this spot that the Latin tag had risen out of a schoolboy's harried forgetting. And its music had held through the mad clamour. He had hobbled his dawn round of the fortifications on the rim of the cliffs, inspecting the bunkers sunk into live rock, and peering through the rangefinder at the still haze on the Channel. He was returning to his quarters at the farm of La Hurlette. The path was staked between minefields, and high in the booming air he could hear planes moving down the valley of the Seine on their daily, mounting runs. Far away, on the river bluffs above Rouen, anti-aircraft guns were firing short bursts. The detonations thudded as from a distant quarry.

As he had limped into the dell, all sounds had receded. He had sat down to still the rack of his body. His wound was new, and he had suffered hideously in the field hospital near Kharkov and on the trains that wormed across Europe, furtively, with jolting detours over railbeds and bridges twisted by bombs. He had lain on a siding at the approaches to Breslau watching a bottle of morphine teeter on the shelf out of reach of his fingers. The orderlies were cowering in a ditch.

He had learned to live with his pain as one lives with a familiar yet treacherous animal. He conceived of it as a large cat which honed its claws, drawing them like slow fire from shoulder to heel, and then crouching down again in the dim and middle of his body. He had been posted to the Yvebecques sector of the Channel Wall as chief of military intelligence. It was a soft billet accorded in deference to his infirmity. As the pain slunk back to its lair, that line of Virgil had sung in his bruised thoughts. With it the gate of memory swung open and behind it drowsed the rust-green gables and slow canals of the north country.

Later that year the Channel haze had reddened into savage tumult. But through the hell that ensued, he carried the verse with him, and the image of this place, a hand cupped full of silence and water, guarded from the wind.

As he came out of the hollow, still grasping his suitcase, Falk's eyes lit. La Hurlette lay just beyond the next fold in the down, where the cliff subsided under green ridges and the valley of the Coutance opened out. He could see the stream, quick and chalk-pale between marsh grass. Now the farm was in sight and recognition beat at him like a wing stroke.

The pockmarks made by mortar shells were still visible under the eaves, but rounded by time, as if clams had dug their delicate houses in the stone. The byre shone with a new red roof but the outbuildings and the clumps of lilac and holly were exactly as he had last seen them, hurtling by in a motor cycle side-car, under wild, acid smoke, five summers ago.

Then he saw the ash tree to the left of the house and his spirit went molten. It stood in leaf, more grey now than silver. Through the foliage he could make out, unmistakable, the stab of the branch on which they had hanged Jean Terrenoire. The night the invasion had begun on the beaches to the west, a patrol had caught the boy perched near the summit of the cliff. He was signalling to the shadows at sea. They had carried him back to La Hurlette, his face beaten livid with their rifle butts. Falk sought to question him but he merely spat out his teeth. So they let the family out of the cellar for a moment to say goodbye and then dragged him to the ash tree. Falk had seen the thing done.

The tree had thickened but the branch retained its dragon motion and Falk could not take his eyes from it. As he started towards the house, he remembered suddenly that the Terrenoires would be waiting. The boy from the market-place had scurried before him to give warning. They would be at his throat before he could cross the threshold. Hatred lay across his path like an unsteady glare. Forcing back his shoulders, Falk glanced at the window of the corner room, his room, and saw the foxglove on the sill, as he had left it. Here had been his island in the ravening sea, here she had brought him the warm, grass-scented milk in a blue pitcher. He pressed on.

The door was loose on the latch and Falk stopped, nakedly afraid. He was momentarily blinded by the dark of the house but knew almost at once that nothing had been altered. The pots and warming-pans glowed on the wall like cuirasses of a ghostly troop. An odour of wax cloth and mouldering cheese hung over the room, and its subtle bite had stayed in his nostrils. The clock which he had bought during his convalescence in Dresden and which the Terrenoires had accepted when first he came, with neither thanks nor refusal, hammered softly on the mantelpiece.

Then he saw Blaise. He stood by the wall and in his fist Falk glimpsed the black fire iron. Blaise stared at him, his tight mouth wrenched with hatred and disbelief: 'Mother of God! The half-wit wasn't lying. It *is* you. You've dared come back. You've dared crawl out here. You stinking, murdering pile of shit!' He swayed nearer: 'So you've come back. *Ordure! Salaud!*' The mind's excrement of hate poured out of Blaise. He gasped for air as if rage held him by the windpipe. 'I'm going to kill you. You know that, don't you? I'm going to kill you.'

He reared back, his eyes crazy and hot, and lifted the iron. But old Terrenoire flung a chair at him, across the floor of the kitchen: 'Stop it! *Merde*. Who do you think runs this house?' He had gone grey and sere;

age had sanded down his beak nose. But the old, cunning mastery was still there, and Blaise winced as if the whip had caught him on the mouth. 'No one's going to do any killing around here unless I tell them to. Remember what I said. Don't drive the fox away if you want his pelt. Perhaps Monsieur Falk has something to say to us.' He looked at his guest with heavy, watchful scorn.

A low wail broke Blaise's clenched throat: 'I don't care what he says. I'll flay the hide off the stinking swine.' He crouched near the fireplace like a numbed adder, venomous but unmoving.

As Falk limped towards the bench in the opaque terror of a slow, familiar dream, he saw the woman and the two girls. Madame Terrenoire's ears stood out from beneath grey, wiry hair. There were tufts of white above her eyes. Nicole had kept her straight carriage but a spinsterish tautness lay about her thin neck. Falk saw that her hands were trembling.

Danielle had turned her back. Falk bore her image with him, inviolate and precise. But it was that of a twelve-year-old. She had large grey eyes and her hair shed the heavy light of hammered gold. She had not been beautiful, having her father's nose and angular shoulders. But she possessed a darting grace of life. They spoke together often, in a hushed, courtly manner. She brought him breakfast and stole to the corner of the room to watch his orderly wax his boots and mounted heel. She did not sit by him, but stood grave and malicious, as little girls do in front of old, broken men. Every morning Falk took coffee beans and a spoonful of sugar from his rations and set them at the rim of his tray. He knew she would carry these spoils of love to her father, racing noiselessly down the stairs.

On the day of the invasion, against the whine and roar of coastal batteries, Danielle had slipped into his room. Falk was putting on his helmet and greatcoat before going to the command car camouflaged under the oak trees a thousand yards from the house. She watched him warily, the floorboards shaking to the sound of the guns. As he turned to go, easing the strap of the automatic pistol over his shoulder, she touched his sleeve with a furtive, sensuous motion. Before he could say anything she was gone, and he heard the cellar door slam heavily behind her quick steps.

He had seen her once more that night. Through his torn lips Jean

Terrenoire said nothing to his family. He merely embraced each in turn while the corporal knotted the rope. Coming to Danielle, Jean knelt down and stroked her cheeks. She shivered wildly in his grasp. They hurried him into the garden. As Falk passed, the girl shrank from him and made a low, inhuman sound. It had stuck in his mind like a festering thorn. Now he hardly dared look at her. But he knew at a glance that she had grown tall and that her hair still burned like autumn.

Falk sagged to the low bench. He laid the cane on the floor, under the crook of his dead leg.

'You are right. There is something I want to say to you.' He looked at Blaise, coiled near him, murderous. 'I pray God you will give me the time.'

A black stillness was in the room. 'When I left you, I had orders to reach Cuverville and re-establish Brigade headquarters. But at daylight American fighters strafed us. They came in so close to the ground that haystacks scattered under their wings. On the second pass they got Bültner, my orderly. You remember Bültner. He was a fat man and ate the green apples where they fell in the orchard. I think he was secretly in love with you, Nicole. Anyway, he was so badly hit that we dared not move him, but left him under the hedgerow propped on a blanket. I hoped the ambulance would find him in time. But some of your people got to him fast. Later on we heard that they beat him to death with threshing flails.

'We could not stay in Cuverville and were dispatched to Rouen. I remember the two spires in the red smoke. An hour after we arrived, paratroopers came down in the middle of the city. Each day was the same; we moved east and there were fewer of us. In good weather the planes were at us incessantly, like a pack of wolves. We had respite only when the clouds came low. I grew to hate the sun as if it had the face of death.

'Each man has his own private surrender. At some point he knows inside himself that he is beaten. I knew when I saw what was left of Aachen. But we kept the knowledge from each other as if it was a secret malady. And we fought on. During our counter-attack in the winter I was in sight of Strasbourg. The next day my wound ripped open again. I was no further use to anyone and they shipped me back to a convalescent home, somewhere near Bonn, in a patch of wood. The windows had been blown to bits and we tacked army blankets across the frames to keep out the snow. We sat in that false dark hearing the big guns get closer. Then we heard tank treads on the road. That day the medical staff and the nurses vanished. The old doctor stayed. He said he was tired of running: had run all the way to Moscow and back. He had a bottle of brandy in front of him and would wait. He gave me my discharge papers. Some of our infantry set up a mortar in the courtyard of the house and the Americans had to use flame-throwers to get them out. I do not know what happened to the old man.'

Falk shifted his weight. The sun was moving west and the light slid across the window like a long red fox.

'I had to get to Hamburg. I wanted to see my home. There had been rumours about the fire-raids and I was anxious. I hardly remember how I managed to get on to a train, one of the last travelling north from Berlin. I had grown up in Hamburg and knew it like the lineaments of my own hand. What I saw when I crawled across the rubble of the station yard was unimaginable, but also terribly familiar. When I was a small boy, the teacher had tacked a greatly enlarged photograph of the moon on our classroom wall. I used to stare at it interminably, and the craters, striations and seas of dead ash were fixed in my brain. Now they lay before me. The whole city was on fire. There was no sunlight, no sky, only swirls of grey air, so hot it burned one's lips. The houses had settled into vast craters. They burned day and night homing the planes to their target. But there were no more targets; only a sea of flame spreading windward with each successive raid. And wherever the ruins grew hottest, gusts of air rushed in, poisonous with stench and ash.

'I must have started yelling or running about, for a shadow came at me out of the smoke and shook me hard. It was a one-armed man in a dented helmet. He told me to get down to a shelter before the next wave passed over. The sirens were wailing again but I could barely hear them above the noise of the flames. I did not know until then that fire makes that sound – a queer, hideous scratching, as if blood were seething in one's throat. The man pulled me by the sleeve; he was a warden in the police auxiliary; I was to obey him; he couldn't waste his time looking after damn fools who didn't take shelter.

'We scuttled down into a trench lined with sandbags and sheets of corrugated iron. It was full of smoke and rancid smells. I made out grey splotches in the dark. They were human faces. At first I thought they were wearing gas masks or goggles. But it was simply that they were black with soot and that the near flames had left livid streaks on their skin. Only their eyes were alive; they closed suddenly when the bombs fell. There was a small girl crouching near the open end of the trench. She was barefoot and had burn marks on her arms. She asked me for a cigarette, saying she was hungry. I had none but gave her a wafer of Dutch chocolate wrapped in silver foil. She broke it in two, thrusting one piece in her pocket and placing the other in her mouth. She sucked at it cautiously. It was still on her tongue when the all-clear sounded. She heard it before any of us, raced up the steps and disappeared into the stinging smoke. As I clambered from the trench, I saw her running beside a burning wall. She turned back and waved.

'I asked the warden how I might get to the Geiringerstrasse. He gave me a frightened, angry look. "Isn't that where the gas tanks are?" I remembered the two grimy tanks and the wire fence around them at the upper end of the street where the foundry works began. "The tanks are near there, yes." "That's what I thought. No use your going. It's all sealed off. The *Amis* have been after those gas tanks with incendiaries. They got them two days ago. No one has been allowed near the Geiringerstrasse since. Come along. We'll have a look at your papers and find you a shelter to sleep in." But I shook him loose and hastened for home.

'New fires had driven the smoke upwards and guided me like wildly swinging lamps. In the burning craters single houses or parts of houses still stood upright. The passage of flame had traced strange designs on the walls, as if a black ivy had sprung up. Often I had to step across the dead. Some had been burned alive trapped by curtains of fire; others had been blown to pieces or struck by shrapnel. But many lay outwardly unhurt, their mouths wide open. They had died of suffocation when the flames drank the air. I saw a young boy who must have died actually breathing fire; it had singed his mouth and leaped down his throat, blackening the flesh. Scorched into the asphalt next to him was the brown shadow of a cat.

'As I drew near what had been the Löwenplatz and the beginning of the Geiringerstrasse, a cordon of men barred my way. They were Gestapo and police. They had guns and were letting no one pass. Behind them the fires burned white with a fantastic glitter. Even here, at the end of the street, the heat and stench of gas were unbearable. The heat flogged one across the eyes and nose with nauseating strokes. I felt vomit in my mouth and grew hysterical. I pleaded with one of the Gestapo officers. I must get through. My family might be trapped in there. He shook his head and whispered at me; he was too tired to speak; he had had no sleep since three nights; since the gas tanks went up. No one was allowed through. His men were in there now seeing what could be done. At that moment I heard shots being fired somewhere in the street, behind the wall of flame. I began yelling and trying to wrestle my way through the cordon. One of the policemen took me by the collar: "Don't be an idiot. There's nothing more we can do. We've tried everything. We're putting them out of their misery. They're begging for a bullet." And now the burning wind brought voices, high-pitched, mad voices. The line of policemen flinched. Two Gestapo men shuffled out of the smoke and tore off their masks. They carried guns. One of them went over to a pile of rubble and fainted. The other stood in front of the officer swaying like a drunk: "I can't go on with it, Herr *Gruppenführer*, I can't." He shambled away in a sleepwalker's gait, dropping his gun. The officer turned to me with an odd look. "You say you have some of your people in there? All right. Take that pistol and come with me. Perhaps you *can* help." His eyes were like two red embers; there was no life in them, only smoke and fear. We put on masks and hunched through the searing wind. The Geiringerstrasse runs alongside a small canal. It was always full of oil and slag. As a boy I used to watch the sunlight break on the oil in blues and bright greens. Now, crawling forward under the blaze of the gas tanks, I saw the canal again. There were human beings in it, standing immersed up to their necks. They saw us coming and began waving their arms. But instantly they plunged their arms back into the water, screaming. The Gestapo officer lifted a corner of his mask and rasped at me: "Phosphorus." The Americans had dropped incendiaries made of phosphorus. Where it is in contact with air phosphorus burns unquenchably. Their clothes and bodies on fire, the people of the

Geiringerstrasse had died like living torches. But a few had managed to leap into the canal. There they stood for three days. Every time they tried to crawl out of the water their clothing flared up in a yellow flame. In the heart of the fire they were dying of cold and hunger. While the freezing water slid over them, their bodies shook with burns and mad spasms. Most had given up and gone under. But a few were still erect, yelling hoarsely for food and help. The Red Cross had fed them from the banks and put blankets around their heads. But on the third day, as the raids started again, everyone had been ordered out. Nothing could be done except to make death quicker and stop the inhuman screaming. So the Gestapo went in. Most of the faces were unrecognizable. Hair and eyebrows had been seared away. On the black water I saw a row of living skulls. The Gestapo officer had drawn his pistol and I heard him firing. One of the faces was staring at me. It was a girl, and on her scorched forehead the flames had left a tuft of hair, red like mine. Her lips were baked and swollen but she was trying to form words. I crept over to her and took off my mask. The heat and reek of phosphorus made me gag. But I was able to lean out over the canal and she drifted towards me, her eyes never leaving mine. Her tongue was a charred stump but I understood what she was saying. "Quickly. Please. Quickly." I slipped my arm behind her head and put my lips to hers. She leaned back and closed her eyes. Then I shot her. I can't be sure. The faces were too far gone. Yet I am sure it was my sister.'

The room was still as winter. In the gathered shadows the chime of the clock had grown remote and unreal. Suddenly Danielle spoke, without turning around, loud into the dark air: 'Good. Good. I am glad.'

Her voice sprang at Falk out of an ambush long dreaded but now intolerable. The hatred of it stunned him. It seemed to close over his head in a suffocating tide. The pain that had been lurking in his bent, immobile leg surged to a shrill pitch. It shot into his back and set his neck in a vice. The drag and harshness of the long day racked his will. Only the pain was real, like a red fist before his eyes, and it beat towards the ground. But even at the instant where something inside him, something of the quick of hope and bearing, was about to break, Danielle rose and moved swiftly past him. Her hand brushed against his sleeve in dim remembrance.

Falk raised his head to look after her and the pain grew bearable, ebbing into his hips, where it gnawed in sharp but familiar guise. Terrenoire got up and lit the lamp on the sideboard. It threw the shadow of his hooked nose against the wall like a child's drawing of a pirate. Madame Terrenoire and Nicole cleared the dishes, stacking the white and blue china. They did not look at the crippled man on the bench.

Blaise came off his haunches, his cat's eyes livid. He spat at Falk's clubfoot with derisive loathing and swore under his breath, "*Nom de Dieu.*" Then he picked up the milk pail in an easy motion and went out the door. Before it swung close, Falk caught a glimpse of the early stars.

He woke with a numb jolt. The sourness of broken sleep lay thick on his tongue. Momentarily he did not know where he was. Night was in the room and the events of the past few hours passed vaguely through his thoughts. Then he saw a shadow looming at him out of the stairwell. On guard, Falk groped for his cane. His fingers tightened on the grip, but nearly at once he recognized a familiar patch of white lace; Madame Terrenoire's nightcap, and beneath it the flat, coarse features of the ageing woman. She rustled towards him in her frayed houserobe, leaned against the stove and searched him out with her shallow eyes. Her scrutiny slid over him like a blind man's hand, neutral yet inquisitive.

Then she asked abruptly, 'Why have you come back here? Was it to tell us that vile story . . . *cette sale histoire*?'

'Yes,' said Falk.

'Is the story true?'

'Yes,' he said again, beyond outrage.

'You are lying,' she said, not in anger, but with malignity. 'You are lying. You didn't come here just to tell us what happened to you. Why should we care? You've come back to take something from us. I know your kind. That's all you're good for. To take and take and take.' The hands in her lap opened and closed rapaciously.

'You have so much to give,' said Falk.

She arched like an old cat: 'Not any more. You've taken it all. You took Jean and hanged him on that cursed tree. You took so many of our young men that Nicole has been left a spinster. Just look at her.

She'll soon be dry wood. Blaise is a ruffian. He was never meant to be an oldest son. When you killed Jean there was no one else for us to lean on. It's made him a brute. And what about me? I'm an old woman. There's hardly anyone left around here except the children and the old. You took the rest and hanged them on the trees. No, there's nothing more to take.' She closed her mouth hard, and to Falk she seemed like an astute fish snapping for air and then diving back into silence.

'Perhaps it's my turn to give. Giving and taking . . . *c'est parfois la même chose*. It's sometimes the same act.' She brushed the thought aside with a contemptuous flutter of her hand.

But Falk persisted: 'It was easy to take. Too easy. We must learn to receive from each other.' She gave no sign of comprehension. 'It may be that you are right, that I have come to take again. But what I can take from you this time is not life. It is some part of the death that lies between us. *Un peu de cette mort*.'

She countered relentlessly: 'I don't understand you. Taking is taking.'

'Even when it is love?' Falk asked awkwardly.

She gave a dry laugh: '*Vous êtes de beaux salauds*. You're a fine lot of swine. To speak of love in a house where you've murdered a child.'

'But this is exactly the house in which I must speak of it. Don't you see? After everything that's happened, where else can it have any meaning?'

Something in his vehemence stung her but she yielded no ground: 'You talk like a priest, but I know you for what you are. How could I forget? You killed Jean. Out there, on that ash tree.'

'None of us are what we were. Try me again.'

She shrugged him off: 'What for? Leave us alone. There's no place for your kind among us. We've seen you too often. You've been at our throats three times. *Ça suffit*.'

She turned from him with distaste as if she had expended too richly from her small hoard of words. But at the foot of the stairs she paused and after a spell turned with a queer jerk: 'That bench can't be much good for sleeping. You look as stiff as a dead mackerel. God knows why I'm letting you spend the night here.' Yet even as she said it, a note of pleased cunning stole into her hacking voice: 'There's a room at the top of the house, with a bed in it. I don't have to show *you* the way.'

Madame Terrenoire started up the wooden stairs. Falk hobbled across the kitchen. She waited for him to come near, looked back and said between her teeth: 'It was Jean's bed. See whether you can sleep in it, Captain.'

Having reached the musty room under the gables, Falk looked out the window and saw the moon in the orchard. Beyond the brittle noise of the crickets he caught the grating of the sea. He sat there for a long time, scarcely breathing the stale, warm air. When at last he fell back on the bedspread, the first glint of sunrise was visible on the eastern cliffs like a thread of copper in the morning grass.

The moment of pure, unthinking vengeance had passed. Werner Falk was endured at La Hurlette like one of those masterless dogs who forage at the edge of a farm. Hatred crackled under his feet in vicious spurts. Blaise was dark with outrage and the old woman looked on Falk with a patient contempt more insidious than fury. But they did not touch him when he passed in reach of the scythe or the heavy spade. The hideousness of his tale, the offering of it in exchange of grief, gave him sanctuary. Though they were only obscurely aware of it, the Terrenoires treated Falk as if there was on his skin the white shadow of leprosy.

Terrenoire himself said nothing. He observed Falk with gloomy complaisance; he discerned in his queer, unbidden arrival a hint of vantage. Nicole cast words at Falk now and again, and when they stood near each other a low flame lit in her sallow cheeks. She gazed after him when he trailed off to the steaming fields in the hot of the morning and threw him a nervous, irritated look when he returned at twilight from the cliffs. Only Danielle stayed outside the wary game. When they chanced to meet in the stairwell or across the neutral ground of the kitchen, her eyes narrowed with pain.

In the village voices rose and fell. Everyone knew that the German captain had returned to La Hurlette and that his presence there was being suffered in the very shade of the ash tree. Around Lurôt's table at the Café du Vieux Port anger and wonderment eddied. But the Terrenoires were regarded as deep ones. Drawing the pale white wine through his lips, Lurôt concluded that there was doubtless something to be reaped from Falk's visit. The Terrenoires were no fools; *ce ne sont pas des poires*. Vague, covetous suspicion hardened to belief: Falk had come to pay compensation for Jean's death. The Germans were rich now, filthy rich. What had he carried in his suitcase? Some of the banknotes and jewellery which the boches had looted from France. There would be a new thresher soon at La Hurlette.

So the villagers waited and pondered, like a herd of cattle, pawing the earth now and again in drowsy malevolence. They bore Falk's coming and going, though a sullen tremor ran under their skin as he passed. Soon they paid no heed and were hardly aware of the limping figure that emerged from the orchards to sit on the stone beach in the glitter of noon.

After three o'clock the tide receded nearly to the base of the cliff gate, leaving behind a green, shimmering expanse. Women and children swarmed out to harvest shrimp and mussels. Falk delighted in their scurrying progress and the swift fall of the nets. Often he hobbled a short distance into the unsteady ooze of stone and trapped sea.

A week after his arrival at La Hurlette he saw Nicole just ahead of him, her skirts tucked high. She turned and called under her breath: '*Venez donc*. Come on out.'

He followed precariously. Weed-covered and smoothed by the tides, the rocks were like glass. Between them lay brackish puddles. The afternoon sun played brokenly on the water, and rock and sand flickered like a mosaic. Falk slithered to his knees in the tangle of red weeds. Nicole stayed just in front of him, flinging words over her shoulder so that he had to strain after them.

'The others are wondering why you've come back. Blaise wanted to kill you on the spot. He still does. But I won't let him.' She turned for an instant, her face strangely flushed. 'I told *maman* you had no other place to go. All your people in Hamburg are dead. We're the closest thing you have to a home.' He caught the abrupt laugh in her voice: 'It sounds mad, doesn't it? But I'm sure it's true. You were happy at La Hurlette. We knew that. I think that's why Jean hated you so much. If only you had been unhappy among us or treated us badly, we could have borne it. But to see you come through the door in your grey coat as if it was really home to you, as if you were at peace, that was unendurable. You were terribly good-looking then. Do you know that? It made it worse.'

Falk slid grotesquely into a trough of bubbling sand but her arm swung back and held him. They stood beside each other on a rock at the edge of the flats. Before them the sea heaved in a drowsy swell. All around the herring gulls yawped and scoured for their prey. Nicole lifted her chin into the wind: 'We were all afraid of you. We had to be. But Jean hated you. Perhaps because he admired you so much; for being an officer and for the books you brought with you. He used to steal up to your room and read them while you were away. I wonder whether you knew.' Falk did not answer but bent close to catch her words amid the hiss of the returning sea. 'He tried to read the books of German poetry. And the thick one in the yellow wrapper. It was by a philosopher, wasn't it? With a long name. I don't remember. It drove Jean crazy to think you could have such books and treasure them. He wanted to kill you. It wouldn't have been so difficult either. The way you used to come down alone from the cliff at nightfall. But they wouldn't let him.'

'They?'

'The cell he belonged to, the *réseau* he took orders from in Le Havre. They didn't believe in acts of individual terrorism. Or so they claimed.'

'Who were they?'

'Surely you knew. Jean was in the Party.'

She faced him, her mouth drawn thin. 'He was a rabid Communist. We thought you had found out. That's why you hanged him, wasn't it?'

Falk shook his head and tried to keep his footing on the wet rock: 'No, we had no knowledge of that. We hanged your brother because he was signalling to the Canadian landing barges from the top of the cliff.'

'Ah. Was that the only reason? *Qu-importe?* He wanted to kill you and you killed him instead. That's war, isn't it?' She said it with indifference, as if it was a truth long buried. 'Father had no love for Jean. They fought like dogs. When he discovered that Jean was going around with Communists, he beat him half to death. But Jean grew to be stronger than *papa*. He didn't dare lay a hand on him later on. So they snarled at each other continually.'

'What about you, Nicole? Did you get on with Jean?'

'No,' she said. 'I'm not a hypocrite like the others. So I'll tell you. We never cared much for each other. I was the oldest but he showed me no regard. With his books and glib talk and stupid politics, you would have thought he was some kind of genius. But he wasn't. I'd say he was an arrogant puppy and that's the truth. No, there was no love lost between us. He knew I was plain-looking and used to joke about it with the other louts in the village. Said I was tall and bony as an old rake; that's what they whispered behind my back, *vieux râteau*. After you came I suddenly realized that Jean was nothing but a little boy, a clever little boy playing at war. I told him how good-looking you were and that you were a real soldier. It made him livid.' Nicole glanced away in vexed remembrance. 'When you killed him, I knew that I should feel bitter grief. But I felt nothing. Nothing at all. Danielle howled for days. We couldn't get her to eat or take her dirty clothes off. She adored Jean. She was the only one of us to whom he was gentle and they had all sorts of secrets. But I felt nothing. When the invasion came that morning, I had only one thought: perhaps I shall survive, perhaps there is going to be an end to this terrible time.'

'So that's why you've forgiven me,' said Falk.

'Forgiven? *Il n'est pas question de ça*. I'm no priest. I'm not interested in the past. I wish the past had never been. We must start living again. What have we to do with the dead? That's why you've come back, isn't it? You've come back to La Hurlette to show that the past need not matter, that we can salvage from it what was good and leave the rest behind like a bad dream, haven't you?' She flung the question at him with a sudden imperious surge, as if opening to the wind a hidden banner. Falk was startled by the intensity of life in her sharp features.

She bore in on him: 'That's what I've told them at home. Let him be. He's going to stay with us and make good for the past. Blaise and *papa* think you're going to pay them or make some kind of cosy deal. The fools. They must think you sell cider in Germany!' Her gaiety stung. 'But let them think that. It will give us time.' Her hand touched his in fierce, shy demand. Falk saw the waters rising and said nothing.

Nicole lashed out at his silence: 'Why don't you say something?' Her lips whitened and she drew nearer to him. 'Why don't you look me in the face?'

Her nakedness appalled him. He spoke her name softly and in fear,

166

as if it was an open wound: 'Nicole. You've understood many things which I've felt. You've said the things for which I found no right words. But I don't think there can be between us . . .' He stared at the moving sand, 'I don't think you and I, however close we must be to one another . . .'

Their faces were only inches apart. 'You don't think that you and I . . .' Nicole stared at him bewildered. 'Not you and I . . . Why then have you come back?' Falk reached towards her but she flinched away. 'What are you doing here? What kind of a foul trick are you playing on us?'

'I know,' said Falk, 'it doesn't make sense. I am like a sleepwalker looking for that which kept me alive in the daytime. Looking for the one door that opens out of night. Probably I shan't be allowed anywhere near it. It's madness, I know. But you will understand, Nicole. You must understand.'

She had already begun moving away. Her face had gone ashen. Only her eyes were alive and brimming with pain. Falk had once seen a gunner whip a horse across the eyes and he remembered the glare of anguish.

'Listen to me, Nicole, I beg you. I need your help. I need to know that you do not hate me. Without you I shall be hounded away from here. Just listen to me for a moment. Please.'

He called in vain. The girl was racing back towards the beach, skipping with grim agility from rock to rock. She glanced back at him only once, but across the gap of wind and spray he could see the fury in her. When he looked up again, he realized he was alone. The other fishermen were hastening landward. Over the entire flats and in the dark pools the water was seething in annunciation of the returning tide. The gulls were veering towards their nests in the high cliff and the sun glowed red on their wings. Falk saw that the sea was close upon him. He clambered towards the shore. But the tide was quicker. It sent sheets of foam flashing past him and the rocks grew vague under the charge and retreat of the surf. Crabs rose warily out of the quaking mud and scuttled away from his groping steps. He fell and slithered and drew himself up again, but the water sucked at his weight. Despite the chill wind, he was drenched with sweat. Soon his hands, grasping their way along the rock edges, were raw and torn.

The salt bit into his broken nails. In the failing light the beach grew distant and the roofs took on a remote, mocking blue. Labouring against the undertow, Falk remembered an ugly moment south of Smolensk. In pursuit of the Russians, his company had tumbled into a marsh. Unable to keep rank in the knife-edged grass, sickened by the flies and the stench of dead water, he and his men had crawled forward on their bellies, looking for steady ground. The enemy had turned on them with mortar fire. Wherever the shells dropped, stinking water sprayed over the wounded and the dead. Clawing his way through the lashing surf, his hands bloodied, Falk remembered the episode. The knowledge that he had got out alive screwed his will to a last, fierce effort. He lunged out of the flailing tide and on to the pebbles. On hands and knees he drew himself to a pile of nets drying in the late sun and looked back. The sea was yelping at the shore like a pack of foxes; its cold tongue darted at him still.

Nicole had raced blindly through the orchards. She met Danielle on the stairs and said in a strangled voice, 'It's you he's after. It's you. Make the best of it, *petite garçe.*' Danielle stared at her in bewildered protest and raised her hand as if to ward off a blow. But all she felt was Nicole's fingers brushing her forehead as if in dubious benediction.

The next morning Terrenoire broke his silence. Falk had watched him feeding a sow as she hammered her pink snout against the trough. Closing the wire fence behind him, Terrenoire asked, 'How long are you planning to stay with us, Monsieur Falk?' And before Falk could reply: 'Not that it bothers me. It's no skin off my back. I told Clotilde you would be paying for your room and board, and paying better than last time. But you seem to be stirring up the girls, just like you did when you first came. They're running about like crazy hens. *Et parbleu,* you must admit it's a strange place for you to choose for a holiday.'

'I'm not here for a holiday,' said Falk; 'it's more serious than that. In fact, it's the only completely serious thing I've ever tried to do.'

Terrenoire blinked peevishly at the implication of obscure, private motive.

'I grew up in a kind of very loud bad dream,' said Falk. 'I cannot remember a time when we were not marching or shouting and when there were no flags in the street. When I think of my childhood all I can remember distinctly are the drums and the uniform I wore as a young pioneer. And the great red flags with the white circle and the black hooked cross in the middle. They were constantly draped across our window. It seems to me I always saw the sun through a red curtain. And I remember the torches. One night my father woke me suddenly and tore me to the window. The whole street was full of men marching with torches like a great fiery worm. I must have yelled with fear or sleepiness and my father slapped me across the mouth. I don't remember much about him but he smelled of leather.

'School was worse. The drums beat louder and there were more flags. On the way home we played rabbit hunt and went after Jews. We made them run in the gutter carrying our books and if they dropped any we held them down and pissed in their faces. In the summer we were taught how to be men. They sat us on a log two by two. Every boy in turn would slap his partner as hard as he could. First one to duck was a coward. I passed out once but did not fall off the log. I never finished school. I suppose my final exam came in Lemberg when they told me to clean out a bunker with a flame-thrower. I had my graduation in Warsaw, marching with the victory parade. Now the drums never stopped. They were always pounding at us: in Norway; outside Utrecht, where I got my first wound; in Salonika, where we hanged the partisans on meat hooks; and at Kharkov, where this happened.' Falk's hand trailed absently along his leg.

'They never stopped, and in the hospital outside Dresden I thought they would drive me mad. I can't tell you much about it, Monsieur Terrenoire, because I hardly remember it myself. There were two of me. One night I came hobbling down the ward back from the latrine. There was no bed vacant. I must have hopped from bed to bed looking. Then I remembered that my fever chart had a number. I found it. There was another man in my bed. I saw the stain seeping along his bandaged leg and knew that this man was I. So I jumped on him and tried to get at his throat. After that they kept me under morphine.'

They had strayed into the orchard. Falk went on: 'Then I was sent here. How could I explain? In church they tell us that Lazarus rose from his stinking shroud having been four days dead. And they call *that* a miracle! I had been dead twenty years. I did not really know that there was such a thing as life. No one had told me. I first stumbled on that dangerous secret here, at La Hurlette. You probably don't even remember the first night I spent with you.'

Terrenoire looked at him guardedly: 'I can't say I do.'

Falk laughed, his voice exultant: 'Why should you? It was a night like many others. Officers had been billeted here before I came. To you it meant nothing: just another unwelcome stranger in the house. But for me it was the first hour of grace. I stood up there at the window under the gables, looked across the orchard and caught a flash of the sea. Danielle – do you remember how slight and small she was? – rapped at my door and brought me a pitcher of milk. It was a blue pitcher and the milk was warm. I know these are all perfectly ordinary things, a room with a low ceiling, a row of apple trees and a blue pitcher. But to me, at that moment, they were the gates of life. *Lazare, veni foras.* But that man had been dead only four days! In this house I rose from a death much longer and worse. That night, when Danielle set the pitcher down on the table, the drums stopped beating for the first time. I never heard them here. Oh, I know the war was everywhere around us, that there were mines at the end of the garden, and barbed wire on the cliffs. But it didn't seem to matter. I saw life sitting in your kitchen as if it was a brightness. Isn't that an absurd thought? But those who have grown up dead have such visions. And because the dreams had stopped, I began hearing myself. I had never really heard my own voice before. Only other men's shouts and the echo we had to give. That's all I had been taught to do, echo shout for shout and hatred for hatred. It sounds fantastic, I know, but watching you and your children, I realized that human beings don't always shout at each other. The silence in this house was like fresh water, I plunged my hands and face in it. And I discovered that men are not always either one's friends or one's enemies, but somewhere in between. They had forgotten to tell us that in the *Hitlerjugend* and the *Wehrmacht*.' Falk thrust his hand among the powdery blossoms. 'This is where I climbed out of the grave, Monsieur Terrenoire, in your house and among these trees.'

Terrenoire ground a cigarette under his mired boots: 'Perhaps you did, monsieur. I don't know about such things. You say you climbed out of a grave. But, *nom de Dieu*, it didn't stay empty. You put my son in it.' He glanced at Falk with a hint of satisfaction, like a player who has landed a difficult shot. He repeated the words savouring their astute propriety: '*Non, monsieur*, it didn't stay empty very long, that fine grave of yours.'

'I know,' said Falk, 'I killed your son in an act of futile reprisal, and in the hour of his victory. I found life in this house and brought death. You are right. Open graves gape until they are filled. That one should have had me in it.' He said it with harsh finality, as if it was a lesson learned long ago and implacably repeated. 'I don't deny that for a moment. How could I?' Terrenoire watched from under his lids. He had seen larks fling themselves about thus before yielding to the net. 'And I can't make it good to you, ever. There is no price on death.'

'To be sure,' said the old man, 'those are the very words I used to Clotilde. He can't make up for Jean's death. They've paid the Ronquiers for the trees they sawed down, and more than they were worth, believe me. But they don't pay for the sons they killed. So I said to her: Monsieur Falk must have something else in mind.' And again he blinked with an air of patient complicity.

'When I had to get out of here, the drums began all over again. I've told you what happened to me. But though I lived in hell and saw enough of horror each day to drive a man insane, it could no longer destroy me. Even at the worst, in Hamburg, after they dragged me away from the canal, and then in Leipzig when the Russians were on us, I could shut my eyes for an instant and imagine myself back at La Hurlette. I swore that if that blue pitcher went unbroken so would I. Before decamping with my men, I buried it under a mound of hay in your barn. It must be there still. I should know if anything had happened to it; something inside me would have a crack. Because I had lived here, I knew that outside the world of the mad and the dead there was something else, something that might survive the war intact. I swore I would come back one day and hear the silence.'

Terrenoire plucked a wet hair from the corner of his mouth: 'That's very moving, Monsieur Falk, though I don't pretend to understand all of it. *Mais c'est gentil*, and I can see that a place like this would seem better than *Wehrmacht* barracks or the Russian front. But now you've come back and had a good look. Just like the Americans who come here every summer to show their families the beaches and the cemeteries. But I don't see you packing your suitcase. On the contrary, you seem to be settling in. *À quoi bon?* What do you really want from us?'

'I wasn't sure until I came back,' said Falk. 'I knew inside me all the time, but didn't dare think it through. Now I know, beyond any doubt. I am in love with Danielle. I have been the whole time. I want to marry her.'

Terrenoire's face opened, startled and off-guard. 'You want to marry Danielle?' He was fending for time, like a clam burrowing.

'If she will have me.'

'If she will have you? *Parbleu*, she's not the only one concerned. *Non, monsieur*, things are not that simple around here.' He was on his own terrain now and confident. 'You've killed my eldest son and want to marry my youngest daughter. *Drôle d'idée*. You Germans are deep ones, I'll say that for you.' He laughed drily.

Falk made a tired, submissive gesture: 'Five years are gone since that happened. It's unredeemable, I know. But Danielle and I are alive, and there can be children and new life here.'

'No doubt,' countered Terrenoire, 'but there are many things to be thought of.' Falk passed his hand over the bark of a young tree: 'You are right, Monsieur Terrenoire. I don't even know whether Danielle will listen to me. I fear she will laugh in my face.'

'Haven't you spoken to her yet?' 'No,' said Falk. A glint of malice lit in Terrenoire's pupils: 'But you have spoken to Nicole?' Falk was silent. 'That was stupid of you, Monsieur Falk. You Germans have no finesse, for all your lofty ideas.' The two men had drifted to the edge of the sown field. The haystacks smoked lightly under the morning sun and to the left the ash tree cast its blue shadow. 'But perhaps you were right after all,' said Terrenoire. 'This matter really concerns Nicole.' He cracked his knuckles: '*Dans mon pays, monsieur*, we don't marry off our younger daughters before their older sisters are settled. *Et voilà.*'

Both the force and the irrelevance of the argument struck Falk. Even as he answered, pleading that there must be exceptions to such rules, his own words seemed to him feeble and wide of the mark. Terrenoire did not bother to refute him, but pressed forward: 'Nicole will make you a good wife. She's a little dry, *un peu sec*, like her mother, but a solid girl. She enjoys putting her nose in books, like you do, Monsieur

Falk. She won't give you any trouble.' He warmed to his theme: 'You may have got hold of something with all your fine talk. You can't replace Jean on the farm with that leg of yours, but you can make a proper home for Nicole and help us out a bit. That's some return for what we had to put up with.'

Falk intruded vehemently. There could be no question of marriage between himself and Mademoiselle Nicole, though he was fond and admiring of her. He was in love with Danielle. That she was the younger sister was awkward, he granted, but it couldn't be helped. If Danielle would not have him, he would leave at once and the Terrenoires would see no further trace of him. '*Merde*,' said the old man. 'Danielle is much too young for you. I won't allow it. She's too young.'

'I am ten years older than she is. But we're exactly the same age. We've seen and endured the same things. Outside Odessa we rounded up a group of partisans and made ready to hang them. Among them there was a Jewish boy. I couldn't believe that he was a day over fifteen. I asked him. He answered, "I am fifteen add a thousand. To get a Jew's proper age, you should always add a thousand." It's like that with the whole lot of us. For those who lived in the war, ten years' difference hardly matters. We carry the same mark.'

Terrenoire broke off. Words were like pips in his mouth; he spat them out and was done with them. Shuffling back to the farmyard, he kept aloof from Falk's urgent plea. He stopped for a moment at the pigpen and clucked his tongue, loud as a pistol shot. The sow shifted her haunches in lazy recognition. Nearly at the threshold, Terrenoire turned bitterly: 'Get one thing through your head, Monsieur Falk: if you marry Danielle, you won't get a penny out of me, *pas un liard*. I'll put her out like a beggar. With Nicole it might be different. I don't say I could give you much. You and your friends saw to that. But Nicole is the oldest. She wouldn't leave my house empty-handed.'

'I don't expect anything,' said Falk. 'That has never entered my mind. On the contrary.' Terrenoire looked up. 'I have put some money aside. I am an electrical engineer. I'm partner in a small business in Hannover. We are well on our feet. On the contrary, Monsieur Terrenoire, it is I . . .'

They entered the kitchen. Madame Terrenoire was scraping carrots over a cracked bowl. 'You'll never guess,' said Terrenoire with a watery smile. 'Monsieur Falk has not come back to buy apples or see the landscape. *Il est prétendant, parbleu*; he is a suitor.' She said nothing, but her hands ceased from their quick labour.

Falk found no immediate occasion to press his suit. Danielle had left for Harfleur, where her aunt kept a draper's shop. Falk remembered the little lady, hewn like a benevolent gargoyle out of a pink, brittle stone. Tante Amélie lived in implacable detestation of the English; she regarded them as cunning wolves who had sought to ruin France either by direct incursion or by entangling her in bloody wars for their own secret profit. Forced to leave her home when the old port had been turned into a German bastion, Amélie had gone to live with a bachelor cousin in Angers. She had passed through La Hurlette, giving away bales of cloth and her stock of ribbons lest they fall into English hands. She had welcomed Falk as an ally brought into France by harsh but provident destiny. When she chronicled for him the numerous occasions on which the English had sacked Harfleur, the antique conflagrations seemed to burn in her high cheeks.

Danielle often went over to Harfleur to spend a day in the musty shop, passing her fingers over the raw linen and crêpes de Chine. Nicole told Falk in a dead voice that her sister was coming home by the late-afternoon bus. He went to Yvebecques to meet her.

Watching Danielle step off the bus, Falk experienced a sense of painful unreality. He had rehearsed the scene too often in his imagination, first in the prisoner-of-war camp at Dortmund, and later in Hannover when trying to salvage life out of the rubble. Now the girl came towards him as in a warm, abstract remembrance. Even the excitement that rose in him was stale. And because he was numb and momentarily remote, Falk saw Danielle as she really was, not as he had obstinately dreamt her.

She had grown straight but her body had not filled out. It was full of hollows and awkward movement. Only her face had taken on a broad strength. The large grey eyes and steady mouth gave it an alert, nearly masculine beauty, but one could discern flat bones under the skin. Danielle would take after her mother, and Falk glimpsed, beneath the nearing girl, the later woman, secretive and perhaps a little coarse.

In an instant, however, he could no longer see her as someone apart from himself. Crossing the market-place and entering the Rue de la Poissonnière, she had passed completely into the troubled light of his desire.

Seeing Falk, Danielle gave a small, abrupt nod, as if to say, 'I knew you would be here. I have been thinking about it on the bus, all the way from Harfleur,' but neither spoke. She came near and suddenly put her hand out as adversaries do before a match. Unready, Falk did not meet her gesture and their hands fumbled. At this they laughed, the strain holding them close. She began walking beside him, slowing her step to his laboured progress.

They said nothing until the road started climbing away from the village. But Falk could not keep his glance from her hair. The blood ached in his temples. When Danielle spoke, it was as if their thoughts had already conversed in intimate dispute. 'Are there no girls left in Germany, Monsieur Falk?' He started. 'That's what I said to Tante Amélie. Poor Monsieur Falk. There are no girls left in Germany. *Pas une seule.* So he had to pack his suitcase and come all the way to Yvebecques to find one.'

'And what did your aunt say to that?'

'She told me not to worry my head about such matters but to thank *la bonne Vierge Marie* that you had come back. Tante Amélie is very taken with you, you know. You should visit her in Harfleur.'

'I hope to,' said Falk.

'Yes, she's still hoping that you will defeat the English. You've let her down badly.'

'I'm afraid we'll have to explain to her that it didn't work out that way.'

'It didn't, did it?' said Danielle lightly.

'No. But that's over and done with. It happened a long time ago.'

'A long time?' she echoed him as from a far dimness.

'Yes, longer than we need remember. Believe me, Danielle.'

'I thought so too. Until you walked back into our kitchen the other night. When I saw you again I heard the ash tree creaking. I had not heard it creak that way since the winter after you left. And when I ran past you I went into the garden. The bark is still worn where the rope was.'

'No. That's not true. The bark has renewed itself and the branch has grown.'

'That would be too simple,' said Danielle.

Falk blazed up as if she had touched the very nerve of him. 'Simple? On the contrary. It's much simpler to stiffen in silence or hate. Hate keeps warm. That's child's play. It would have been much simpler for me to die in Hamburg near the canal. Or to stay in Hannover and marry a widow with a pension and cast the image of you out of my mind. Do you think it's easy to come back here? In Germany we don't talk about the past. We all have amnesia or perhaps someone put an iron collar around our necks so that we can't look back. That's one way of doing it. Then there's the other, the unrelenting way. Steep yourself in the remembered horrors. Build them around you like a high safe wall. Is that any less easy or dishonest?'

She lashed out: 'God knows I wish the past didn't exist! I didn't ask for those memories, did I? You forced them down our throats, the whole savage pack of you! And now you come and tell us we should forget and live for the future. You're spitting on graves. The dead will start howling when you pass.'

She broke off; there were tears of rage in her voice. Had Falk not grasped her arm she would have darted ahead. But he held her rooted. 'Try to understand what I'm saying. I'm not asking you to forget anything. I want you to remember your brother, and, if you must, the burn of the rope on the branch. But remember Bültner also. Think of the apples he threw to you and think of him lying alive in the ditch when they came with their flails. And if you think of all the dead, of yours and of ours, it will become more bearable. I don't want you to forget. The stench of forgetting is so strong in Germany that I came back here to breathe real air. But that's only the beginning, the easy part, like learning to walk again. They taught me that in the hospital. It hurt so much I kept passing out. But it was really very simple. It's after you've learnt to walk that the terrible part begins. Suddenly you discover that you have to go some place.'

'I don't want to go. I want to be left alone.' And she drew away into the evening shadows.

When Falk caught up with her, lights were coming on in the village. On the horizon a tanker moved like a black thread across the molten wake of the sun. The air was still with the first touch of night.

Danielle turned to him: 'Nicole is in love with you.' She said it with the solemn malice of a child.

'Don't mock me.'

'No. It's true. We used to quarrel about you when we were girls. We knew how handsome you were but pretended you wore a mask and vied with one another in describing how fearful you would look without it. She said she couldn't stand you because you were nasty and conceited and gave yourself airs like an old rooster. I was silly in those days and believed her. But after you left she went grey inside. She never found anyone else. When she turned down Jacques Estève – his people own the dairy on the road to Fécamp – I ran after him and told him to chop off one of his legs. He thought I was mad. If *la Sainte Vierge* has brought you back here, it's for Nicole's sake. She will make you happy. *Elle sera bonne pour vous*. She's clever and serious. She knows ever so much more than I do. She can understand your books and the long words you use. And I would be your sister-in-law. Then we could sit by the chimney and talk about your children.'

Involuntarily, Falk took up her tone: 'And what about your children, *belle-soeur*?'

'Mine? Ah, the little horrors! Jean – he's the oldest one, you know – will always be in trouble. They'll send him home from school for putting girls' pigtails in the inkwell and for writing wicked things on the walls. So I shall have to be very angry with him. I shall pack him off to Germany to work in his uncle's factory. You will have a factory, won't you? And you will tell me how he's getting on and see to it that he writes his *maman*. And when he comes home I shall be proud of him, and he will have learned to be an engineer like you.'

In the pending darkness Danielle seemed to discern the shapes of her invention. She moved after them: 'And there will be many daughters. Four at least. They will have long red hair and blue eyes, not grey like mine. I shall have to go to Rouen and Le Havre to find husbands for them. They will be so pert that no one will want them.'

'And what will you do then?'

'I shall send them to you and ask you to put them in a nunnery deep in the Black Forest! Tell me, is it really black?'

'Yes.'

'They won't like that. They will drape their red hair out the window until someone rescues them and there will be a mighty scandal. So I shall have to bring them home and build them a house up on the *grande falaise*. There they will sit and stick their tongues out at passers-by and grow into spinsters like four tall candles.'

'Will you visit them?'

'From time to time. When the wind is high. And we will gather at the fire to talk about the past.'

'What will you tell them of the past?'

Danielle wavered and then bent near: 'That it was long ago.'

Falk found her clasped hands. He opened them gently. But beneath his soft motion she felt the surge of longing, watchful and implacable. It filled her with strange anguish, as if the entire weight of the night was upon her. She drew back rebellious: 'Look,' she cried out, 'look!'

Falk turned heavily. Banks of clouds had mounted in the northern sky. But here and there they were thinning out; behind them shimmered a vague white line. 'England,' she said. 'Those are the English cliffs.'

'I don't think so,' said Falk trying to keep the edge out of his voice. 'It's probably moonlight reflecting on the clouds. You rarely see the English coast from here. Even with our glasses it was difficult to tell whether we were seeing cliffs or a trick of light.'

'I remember your glasses,' said Danielle quickly, 'in their big leather case. Do you still have them?'

'No, I sold them to an American soldier for a tin of coffee. What else do you remember?'

'Everything. The smell of your coat and the loose strap on your helmet and the way you kept forgetting your furred gloves in the kitchen. And I remember the time after you left. I tried to hate you. With every nerve inside me, I kept my eyes tight shut so that I could see before me Jean's body and the bit of rope your men left on the ash tree. But I didn't succeed. That was what made me ill. I couldn't hate you. I didn't know how.' But even as she said it the weight of his presence enveloped her and she fought against it: 'You see, Monsieur Falk, I am a silly girl. I don't know much about hatred and I don't know about love. *Je suis bonne à rien.*' She laughed as if she had sprung free from his reach.

'Have you never been in love, Danielle?'

'Oh, many times!'

'Seriously?'

The hurt in his voice provoked her: 'Desperately. With Sicard at the florist's. With Monsieur Lurôt's cousin who lives in Rouen and owns two silk waistcoats. With Fridolin. He drives a green truck and takes me for rides in it.'

'And now?'

The lightness drained away; something urgent and wearing rose at her. She sought to force it down. She liked to tear green currants off the bush and put them between her teeth. It was the same bitter, exciting taste. Falk asked again, 'And now?'

'I don't know. I don't know.'

They had not taken the straight way to La Hurlette but had strayed on to a small path which led to the rim of the cliff. There it plunged sharply down the face, ending in a niche dug out of the rock. Just large enough for two men, the hollow had served as a machine-gun nest. Looming from the dirt parapet, the barrel had a cruel sweep of the bay. Below it the cliff fell sheer into the sea. Like a gannet's eyrie, the narrow platform hung suspended between the dark folds of the rock and the clamour of the water. Falk had often gone there to inspect the watch, to inhale the salt rush of night or peer at the red flashes on the English coast. One had to speak loud to make oneself heard above the seethe and bellow of the waves. During the March storms, spray had been known to leap skyward, sending a plume of cold white mist over the huddled gunners. But on summer nights, at the recession of the tide, there were moments of near silence, with the sea running far below, the foam driven on it like white leaves.

Falk held Danielle close: 'I love you, I love you.' The words seemed arrogant and trivial in the indifference of the night. But he went on heedless: 'I am not bringing you very much. This carcass of mine and half a wedding present. The other half is lying in the gutter in the Rue de la Poissonnière. Let's leave it there. Half may be enough. I don't want to ask for the whole of life any more. Only for you, and for time enough to quarrel and make children and grow old together. If I have to, I'll even take those four wicked daughters into the bargain. It's a bad bargain, Danielle, I know that. The merchandise has been damaged in transit. God knows, you could do better. There must be fine young men about, with fine legs. Of your own people. Not the enemy, not the *sale boche*. There may be some around who could love you more blindly than I do. They wouldn't notice that your nose has grown a little too long. They might even make you happier than I can. But I won't let them have you. I want you. Utterly for myself. You cannot conceive how selfish I have grown. I believe with all my soul that I will make you happy. But I don't know whether that counts most. All I do know, all I care for, is that you are life to me, all of it I can grasp or make sense of now. I was a dead man when I first saw you, when you walked into my room that night. I breathed you in like air and began living. The presence of you inside me has kept me alive since. I love you, Danielle, selfishly and desperately. I cannot take no for an answer.'

The vehemence of it held her rigid. But though she was afraid and uncertain, a bright malice flashed through her. 'Say it in German,' she demanded. 'Say it in German.'

'*Ich liebe dich*, Danielle.'

She shaped the words awkwardly for herself: '*Ich liebe dich*.' They stuck in her teeth like a bitter rind. 'It's not very beautiful that way. *Je vous aime* is better.' She felt the tightness and impatience in his grip. 'You are hurting me. Let go.'

He did, and she swayed against the sudden gulf of night. '*Ich liebe dich*.' She tried again and could not suppress an abrupt unreasoned gaiety. 'I would be Madame Falk. How strange. *Bonsoir, Madame Falk*.'

'Danielle, come back to me. Come into my room, as you always did, with the morning sun. Put your hand on my sleeve. Tell me that you know what I'm asking for. That you love me.'

She turned and took his head between her hands, staring at him for an instant as if he was a stranger; then she drew him down swiftly. They stood gathered to each other. Even now, unsteady with delight and a great tiredness, Falk urged once more: 'Tell me.' He heard the words from a sudden closeness: '*Je vous aime*.'

At the foot of the cliffs the sea was beginning to simmer. They drew in the roused air and the salt lay sharp on their tongues. Holding Danielle fast, Falk told her of the blue pitcher. At first she did not remember. And when he told her of how he had buried it in the barn and of what it signified to him during the last months of the war, rebellion stung her. He had planned it all. She had no existence of her own. She was part of a stubborn dream. She swerved back like a small angry flame: 'I can't understand why you make so much of it. It was a cheap little jug. We never used the good china for our guests.' She gave the word a fine edge of scorn.

But he seemed beyond her reach and she followed mutinous yet entranced as they clambered back up the cliff and struck out for La Hurlette.

'We must go to the barn, Danielle, and dig it up. I know we shall find it unbroken. I did not dare look before. Now I know. My love. My love.' And he clasped her tight as they hurried through the trees.

Joined to his lunging step, Danielle felt herself in Falk's power. It gave her insidious content, as if she had been a swimmer who stops thrashing and yields to the seaward drag of the tide. But she could not let go entirely. The precariousness of their condition was too vivid in her mind. Too much of what lay before them was unanswered.

'Falk.'

'Yes?'

'Even if it's true what we said back there, even if we are in love . . .'

'Yes, Danielle?'

'What can come of it, Falk? They won't let us marry.'

'Why not?'

'Because you're not one of us, and they look on me as a child. And it would do Nicole dreadful hurt.'

'None of that concerns us, Danielle. Not really. I know it's true, but it can't be helped, and does it matter?'

'I don't think I would like to come with you to Germany. No. I don't think I would want to leave here. You mustn't ask it of me.'

'Perhaps I will have to. And much more. Love is asking. All the time. For more than anyone ever dreamt of giving.'

'I don't have that much to give, Falk.'

'What there is I will take! Be warned.'

She caught the lightness in his tone but also the obstinate desire. In the dark of the hedgerows his step seemed surer than hers.

'I'm afraid, Falk. I'm afraid.'

'Of what?'

'I don't know. Of what they'll say in the village. Of your German friends. Of Jean. I fear his ghost. It will seek us out. It will harrow our lives. Don't laugh at me. It's God's truth. He will find us and damn us to hell.'

'I am not laughing, Danielle. Perhaps he will come. In some way I wish he would. It would make my happiness more bearable. If we receive him into our lives, he will forgive us. Ghosts are watchdogs and children must learn to live with them in the house. And learn the language. I have heard it. They speak like snow.'

'Father won't give us anything. If we leave here, I shall have to go as a beggar.' 'I know,' said Falk gaily, 'Monsieur Terrenoire made that quite plain. And here I came all the way from Hannover just to snatch your dowry. Think of it!' His laughter rang out.

'Be serious, Falk. There is so much against us. We are mad to carry on this way.'

'I love you, Danielle.' His voice left her naked. 'Don't you understand? I love you. Everything you say is true. We are surrounded by absurd and hateful things. It will be even more difficult than you or I can imagine. Perhaps they will want to hang me and shave your head.' She felt his fingers pass through her hair in rough solace. 'I don't know whether I must go back to Hannover or whether we can live in France. But does it matter? I love you. And if I said it over and over all night long, you wouldn't have heard the beginning of it!'

They moved in silence. Then Falk resumed. 'You have a beautiful name. I will often call you in our house, not because I shall need anything, but to say it. Danielle. It's like a cool bright stone that has lain in a mountain stream.'

'Please stop it, Falk. I can't bear it. I'm too afraid.'

They were nearly at La Hurlette. Falk entered the barn and advanced through the warm blackness with the surety of a blind man. Danielle saw him kneel in one of the old stalls now empty of horses. He scattered the crackling hay and the trodden dirt. Then he pried loose one of the floorboards and she heard the nails scrape. Suddenly he paused and she caught the tense pleasure in his voice. 'Danielle, come here!' Once again she felt as if she had become a shadow to his being. She stepped nearer. 'I have it. It's here. Exactly as I buried it.' The object tinkled faintly as if the lid was loose. Falk brushed the dirt away cradling the little pitcher against his body. Then he rose triumphant. 'It's unbroken, Danielle. It's been waiting for us all these years. My love, it's unbroken. Feel the edge. Not a chip. Take it. We shall drink from it in the mornings. Just as we used to.'

He was reaching towards her when the beam of light struck between them. The pitcher shone blue and abrupt shadows sprang up the wall. Blaise was standing in the doorway, the lamp held stiffly before him. Danielle grasped the pitcher and bent away. The cows shifted in the hot still air.

Blaise strode in, breathing heavily. He rapped the girl across the mouth with the back of his hand, not in fury but bewildered scorn: '*Petite putain.*'

Falk strained towards her but Blaise barred his way. He stood like a circus trainer, his powerful legs straddled: 'I'm fed up. *J'en ai marré.* You're getting out of here. Tonight. You've made enough trouble. You're going to leave us in peace. We don't want you around here. Never again. I'm warning you. Get out while you can.'

Falk flung out into the dark: 'Danielle, tell him we love each other. Tell him we're leaving together.'

'If she makes a move,' said Blaise, 'I'll beat the daylights out of her. But she won't move. She's just a stupid little goose. You may have turned her head with your fancy speeches. But she's coming to her senses. Look at her.' He swept the light across her inert face.

'Danielle, tell him the truth. Come with me.' She was staring at Falk but not seeing him. 'For God's sake, Danielle, rouse yourself! Remember all that we've said, all that's happened. If I go now without you, I can never return.' But she lifted her hands to her face and shrank from the light.

'Enough of this farce,' said Blaise. 'Get out of here. You can wait in the village. There's a bus to Rouen at daybreak. Get going, *mon capitaine.*'

'Let me through to her,' demanded Falk. 'She's frightened of you. You're an ugly brute. But she loves me. Do you hear? She loves me! And nothing you can do will change that.'

Blaise grinned. He knew his ground. When he turned to Danielle it was as if he had flicked a restive calf across the nose. 'Why don't you say something to the handsome gentleman? He's waiting.' He kept the lamp on her.

'Please,' she moaned, 'leave me alone. It's no good. They'll kill you if you stay. I told you it wouldn't do any good. You must go.'

'Come with me,' cried Falk.

'I can't. I don't dare. Perhaps I don't love you enough. Please let me be. Please.' She kept her hands before her eyes, against Falk's anguish and the unswerving light.

Falk raised his cane but Blaise tore it from his grasp easily: 'I could hammer your brains out right now. No one would care. But why bother? You're going to leave just like you came. Like a lame dog.' He snapped the cane across his leg and threw the pieces into a mound of hay.

As he hobbled out of the barn, his hands clutching for support, Falk caught a last glimpse of Danielle. She had turned to the wall.

When she set out in pursuit of Falk late the next morning, Danielle was like a creature possessed. Only moments after he had been driven from the barn, a sense of utter desolation assailed her. She had run through the courtyard calling Falk's name under her breath. But darkness had swallowed him. She knew with the blinding certainty of pain that she could not endure without him. Her love was not the unbewildered glory he had demanded, but though imperfect, it made up the sum of life. Having come moments too late, this knowledge mocked her. The remembrance of her evasion and of Falk's crippled departure under the derisive flourish of Blaise's lamp, made her skin tight and cold. It was like a palpable nightmare and she could not shake it off.

Loathing herself, she stood under the chill heavy rain which began towards midnight as if it could scour her clean. Danielle watched from the arcade of the market hall as the dawn bus left for Rouen, but there was no sign of Falk. She hastened along the top of the cliff and stared vaguely at the woken sea. Then back to La Hurlette. She put on dry clothes and started out again, brushing Nicole aside as if she were an intruder.

As she hurried back to the village, the whole landscape turned into bleak unreality. The thought of not seeing Falk again filled her with wild misery. Yet she was afraid of meeting him. He would not forgive her cowardice and giddiness of mind. He knew her now for a shallow girl. He had said he would never come back.

Danielle began whimpering like a child. When she had been very little, she had been banished to her room for snatching rowdily at a sweet bun. After a time her father had come to the door. She could have her brioche if only she would express remorse for her wicked manners. Fighting back tears, Danielle had refused. On his way downstairs, Terrenoire casually popped the bun into his own mouth. Seeing it vanish, Danielle had felt the world collapse. She had howled with rage and sorrow. Now the same feeling of absurd deprivation engulfed her. She had thrown away her life in frivolous unknowing.

Ferreting about in Yvebecques, she found news. Between gulps of coffee Pervienne told her that when crossing his field, just after daybreak, he had seen a man hobbling down the road. He was leaning on what looked like a large dead branch. After a while the man flagged down a truck and Pervienne had watched him clamber on to the back amid crates of lettuce and cabbage. Pervienne had an orderly mind. Wiping the last drop of coffee from the rim of the cup, he recalled that the truck bore the blue and yellow markings of the *Union agricole*. Doubtless it was on its way to Le Havre.

Only later, when the bus was actually entering the suburbs, did Danielle realize the futility of her search. The raids had torn great gashes in the city. Blocks of new, raw houses stood between stretches of vacant terrain. On the mounds of rubble the grass had a metallic sheen. The dust and clamour of construction lay thick in the air. As she hurried over upchurned roads, seeking out the garage of the *Union*, Danielle saw high cranes swing stiffly across the sky.

The garage was a cavernous hangar. Naked light-bulbs threw a cold glare. In the far recesses the trucks stood hunched and silent. The dispatcher and the drivers were lounging in a small shed. Danielle rapped several times on the murky panes before they took notice. When they opened the door she smelt kerosene and wet leather. She asked whether any of them had seen a lame man; one of their trucks had given him a lift from Yvebecques. He had been hobbling on a dead branch. Did anyone remember him, and where had they dropped him off in Le Havre?

The drivers looked at her and she drew her raincoat tighter. They told her to come in and get dry. The dispatcher rolled a cigarette and held it out. But she hung at the door asking obstinately. The man was very lame. He had red hair. Did no one remember? The drivers shrugged and glanced at each other. Finally one of them spoke up from the back of the shed. It was against company rules. But *merde*, the man could hardly walk and was worn out. So he had let him ride on the crates and when the rain had thickened had given him a sheet of burlap to burrow under. The dispatcher remarked sourly that the *Union agricole* was no bus line. Danielle asked: Where had the man been set down? 'I told him I could not be seen with a passenger near the garage,' answered the driver, 'so I dropped him off Boulevard Galliéni. There's a bakery on the corner. I saw him enter there.'

A young trucker with blotches on his chin called out to Danielle: 'Little lady, is he your lover?' 'Yes,' she said and hurried out of the garage.

One of the girls at the bakery remembered Falk. He had eaten several rolls standing at the counter. He had seemed ravenous and his clothes were sodden. He had left a puddle on the floor. The owner looked up from the apricot tarts and gave Danielle a sullen stare. Did anyone notice where he was heading? The girls giggled. Why should they?

During the ensuing hours Danielle wandered the city, now with directed intent, now in random circles, up and down the dust-blown boulevards, through the scarred streets, past the wharfs and corrugated-iron sheds, between warehouses and gantries, pausing in brief stupor on the freshly painted benches in the new playgrounds, and then hurrying on through the blind drifts of the afternoon crowd to the bus terminal and the railway station. She peered into brasseries, empty cafés and restaurants, treading the mill of the long day in a torment of loss and weariness.

A hundred times in the drag of hours Danielle saw Falk just ahead of her and ran towards him only to find a stranger in her path. His face and harried step seemed to leap at her out of the crowd; she saw it mirrored in the glass alembics in apothecary windows. Soon the city flickered in her sore eyes like the reels of a blurred film. Streets, building sites and quays revolved around her in a lazy, jeering motion, always the same, yet malignantly altered so that she could not be sure that she had already searched them out.

Looking up at the cranes, Danielle prayed for the miracle of momentary flight, imagining herself gyrating over the sea of roofs and streets, able to discern Falk and plummet upon him. Instead she plodded interminably and evening crowded at her with its delusive shadows.

She had tried to swallow a sandwich earlier in the day but it had gone stale in her mouth. Now a soft, sour nausea stirred in her throat. She sat on a fallen oil barrel and stared at the greying harbour. The rust flaked between her fingers, but she kept a stubborn grip and fought off dizziness. Suddenly she lowered her head and vomited. A great lightness overcame her and she felt a pang of hope.

Once again Danielle crossed the Boulevard Galliéni and circled the Place de la Libération. Hunger made her alert and quick. It rang in her head like a small chime. She began counting lamp-posts: 'At the sixteenth I shall find Falk.' And when the sixteenth had passed, she started over again with the same spurt of hope.

But after a time she stopped counting and began weeping helplessly. Despair stole on her as out of ambush. She had consumed the last of herself. The wine was spilt and she tasted the dregs and lees of her own being.

When she saw Falk she could no longer muster even joy. He was standing on a small wharf looking at the oil-flecked water. He was leaning on an umbrella. Despite its massive old-fashioned handle, it had already bent under his weight. Danielle called to him in a dead voice. It did not carry and she sickened at the thought that he would turn away. She called again and stretched her hands towards him. He looked about and grew white as if he had seen that which was crying out in the midst and secret of his being gather shape in the evening air.

As they left the wharf, neither spoke. Only their fingers touched. They drank coffee in silence and looked in bewilderment at their own image in the misted silver urn. They said nothing to each other as they followed the *portier* up the stairs of the hotel. Falk's umbrella tapped on the worn tiles.

The shutters were closed but from the streetlights jagged shapes fell across the brown wallpaper and enamel basin. They sat in the musty quiet hearing the noise of day ebb from the city. At last Falk wrenched open the wooden blinds.

Searchlights were sweeping across the harbour like blue dancers. As

Falk stepped back into the room Danielle rose. She guided his hands. Together they undid the buttons on her dress. The siren of a liner was singing westward. At first brazen and clear, then softly as if the sound had run into the sands of night.

The day of the wedding was unusually warm. The stone beach merged into banks of white haze. The first brown spots were appearing in the hedgerows, leaves burnt by the departing summer. The Terrenoires had assembled in the garden. Each had yielded in his own fashion. The old man had voiced muted approval: *Ce n'est pas une mauvaise affaire*. Madame Terrenoire had scarcely said anything. Events had come to pass as she foretold. She saw in the tumult and brusque conclusion of Falk's courtship proof of her divining powers. She kept the silence of an oracle and spent more time than she used to with Nicole. There was between them the unspoken discourse of conspirators. Both were old women now, gazing ahead to the bland pleasures of a common winter. To Danielle and Falk, Nicole had come handsomely, wishing them Godspeed and seeking to make her presence no attainder to their joy.

Only Blaise was absent. He had shrugged off Falk's attempt at conciliation and had thrust his hands in his pockets. The day before the wedding he took his bicycle from the shed and said tersely that he was off to the market at Coutance.

Tante Amélie had come over from Harfleur. She was whirring about like a drunken bee when smoke has routed it from its hive. She scattered loud delight and the hem of her mauve dress billowed along the ground. At every instant she would clasp either bride or bridegroom to the large cameo brooch on her bosom. Her warm cheeks were streaked with tears. The dreary war had not been in vain. All had come well in the end. Tante Amélie had stitched a pale yellow gown for Danielle and presented Falk with a plum-coloured waistcoat. Now she darted about dusting off everyone in a whirl of orders. Suddenly she peered at her pendant watch and sang out, '*Allons, enfants!*'

The party advanced through the orchard. They moved swiftly under the apple boughs, the women ample and flowery, the two men like sable penguins.

A few villagers were waiting in the silent chamber of the *mairie*. No one had taken the dust-cover from the chandelier. Monsieur Raymond, the mayor, was a spare, sallow man; but even he was perspiring. Having donned his tricolour sash, he read out the marriage service in a low, precise intonation. Danielle strained forward as if the grey words were of passionate interest. Falk's eyes wandered to the wall. From behind a dusty glass the General looked stonily on the proceedings. For a brief second Falk panicked. He could remember no French. But then he heard his own voice. Danielle assented in a whisper. Her lips were ash-dry, but as she embraced Falk, Tante Amélie vented a loud sob and Danielle began smiling.

Monsieur Raymond took off his glasses, wiped the moisture from the bridge of his nose and addressed the young couple. It was, he felt, an unusual, indeed, a portentous occasion. He would be doing less than his sworn duty if he did not call the attention of the newly-weds, of their family and friends, to the significance of the event. The Terrenoires had lived in Yvebecques longer than records showed. Monsieur Beltran, the clerk – *ce véritable savant* – affirmed that there were Terrenoires baptized and buried in the seventeenth century. Monsieur Falk belonged to another world. He had come (here the mayor paused) in a manner – how should one say? – not altogether natural or beneficial. But Yvebecques had proved stronger than tragic circumstances. Its style of life, its renowned natural beauties, had entered into Monsieur Falk's heart. He had come back 'over the hidden but unerring road of love'. The mayor allowed the sentence to unfurl in the hushed room and looked at the ceiling. Might there not be in this, he asked, a lesson for the weary and divided nations? Here, in the *mairie* of Yvebecques, *notre petit village*, two young people had achieved what the captains of the earth sought vainly. 'Yet, would Monsieur Falk forgive me if I add one further thought to this joyous hour? Even now and in this blessed moment, one should not forget the past. Like so many other families in the community, the Terrenoires bear witness in their bone and blood to the sufferings of France. *La patrie* had not wished for war, but thrice it assailed her. May this marriage be a portent of a more felicitous future. But may it also keep us in solemn remembrance of what has been endured.'

Amélie sobbed again and Monsieur Cavel, the aged clerk, blew his nose. The mayor congratulated the happy couple and everyone filed into the open air. But no breeze stirred. Passing the fountain, Falk shifted his new lacquered cane and dipped his fingers in the water. He touched Danielle's lips. She nibbled the cold drops and the flush of desire that spread through her limbs was so strong that she leaned heavily against Falk's arm. The wedding party entered the café.

When they started out again for La Hurlette, the awkward silences had melted. The small glasses of tart red wine and the aperitifs were busy in the blood. Joined by further guests, the procession straggled through the village and towards the cliff. The gentlemen loosened their collars and tilted their straw hats against the veiled, relentless sun. The ladies advanced slowly, prickly and pouting for air. They called to one another; in the heat their voices crackled like dry grass. Danielle and Falk moved a little to one side. She sucked the moisture from her lips and kept her eyes to the ground as if seeking coolness in her own scant shadow. Falk felt sweat pearling down his collar and back; it chilled him. Beating against the chalk cliff, the air simmered. The birds had fallen silent, but among the hedges and wilted stalks wasps sang with a hum of low flame.

'I've lived here sixty-four years,' panted Monsieur Cavel, 'and never been so hot.'

'It is unusual,' allowed the mayor, 'most unusual.'

'One might as well be in the Sahara,' said Siccard, combing back his flaxen hair. 'I've been there, and believe me, it was no hotter.'

'Ah, the Sahara,' said Monsieur Cavel.

Estève, who was now married and putting on weight, stopped and stared at the banks of haze drifting along the cliffs and over the soundless sea. '*Ça va barder*,' he announced, 'there's bound to be one devil of a storm before the day is out.'

'I hope so,' said Nicole, 'I'm stifling.'

But Fridolin, who was bringing up the rear in a white linen suit, muttered, 'Storms on a wedding night. A bad omen.'

'*They* won't hear it,' said Estève, trying to look roguish.

But no one responded or came fully to life until Tante Amélie called out, '*Courage, mes enfants*, we're nearly there.'

The orchard was not much cooler, as if the sun had seeped into the shadows. Madame Terrenoire paused to tug at her corset. The men wiped the sweat from their faces and Monsieur Raymond closed his collar button. Nicole bore in on the newly-weds: 'You must take the lead now.' The smile on her lips was taut as in a bad photograph. Falk led Danielle to the gate and the mayor began clapping. Others joined, but in the stifling air the sound fell flat.

Everyone hurried under the trees and Amélie came into the garden carrying jugs of cider frosted at the rim. Siccard bellowed with pleasure. He raised his glass to bride and bridegroom, emptying it at one draught; the iced cider stunned him and his eyes blinked stupidly. The ladies drank with quick, delicate sips and vanished into the house. Falk and Danielle drifted towards the shade of the barn. 'I love you, Danielle.' She did not answer but passed her fingers across her face in strangeness and wonder. They heard the clatter of dishes and the voices now more strident. Slowly they walked back to the long tables.

The food lay in garish heaps: bowls of dark blue mussels, steaming in milk; brick-red lobsters; fried mackerel bedded on ferns; plates of shrimp beside saucers of melted butter; larks, charred and spiky, cracking under one's teeth with a savour of game; two sides of beef sweating blood; tureens of fluffy white potatoes with warm napkins over them; watery endives; three cavernous bowls of dark green salad, shimmering with oil and nuggets of black pepper. Between the laden galleons, small boats and barks brimmed with spices, shelled walnuts and dried fruit. Long loaves were aligned on the sideboards next to squares of fresh butter, cold from the larder. There were wine and cider glasses before each plate, but soon the guests filled them indiscriminately.

A hot, ruttish wind blew across the tables. Terrenoire had scarcely tied the chequered napkin around his chin before thrusting his knife into a gamy pâté and spreading it thick on a slab of bread. Then he drew towards himself a mound of shrimp. What had survived of lust in him was gluttony. Everyone followed suit. Cavel stuffed a lark into his toothless mouth and spat out the fine bones amid a howl of laughter. Madame Estève, a flushed stout woman with yellow eyes, carried the mussels to her lips, sucking them loudly. Melted butter dribbled down the mayor's chin as he leaned across the table. Fridolin carved the beef with wide flourishes and licked the gravy off his fingers. Monsieur Beltran had followed the main party after setting his wax seal to the marriage certificate; now he shovelled food into his gullet like a squirrel. He was the first to undo his braces. Other gentlemen did likewise and Madame Estève squealed happily as Cavel unhooked her dress. Danielle and Falk ate little.

Legs rubbed drowsily under the table and the wine grew warm in the uncorked bottles. Nicole could hardly keep up with the empty glasses and her skin glistened. Fridolin wavered to his feet; the wine was toiling in his brain and he moved his hands before his face as if he had walked into a cobweb. He ambled to Danielle and bent low, staring down her dress. '*Mon poulet*, let me tell you a thing or two about marriage. I am an experienced man.' She felt his loud, liquorish breath at her ear. The mayor got slowly to his feet, sought to brush the crumbs and drippings from his rumpled shirt-front and proposed the health of Monsieur and Madame Falk.

The day was wilting, early shadows drifted through the vibrant air. Toast followed on toast. The surfeited guests roused themselves as Madame Terrenoire and Tante Amélie brought in platters of pancakes filled with raspberry jam. The black, sweet jam was full of seeds and Siccard spat them through his teeth, now at the mayor, now at Nicole. She set down small glasses on the crowded tables and the calvados went from hand to hand. Under the blazing rush of the liqueur nearly everyone stopped eating. Only Terrenoire persisted, using his fork to snatch cold leavings as Nicole began carrying the plates back to the kitchen. Above the chaos of voices and clinking glass, Monsieur Raymond called for a word from the groom.

Falk pushed the dishes away from in front of him and rose, bracing his arms stiffly on the table. He looked down at Danielle and was startled to see her so withdrawn. He expressed his delight at the festive occasion and thanked all the distinguished guests for their presence. He raised his glass to Madame Terrenoire, to Nicole and to Tante Amélie, who had laboured to provide this noble feast. Cavel fluttered his spoon against a decanter. But Falk could not sustain the mock ceremonious note. He turned to the mayor: 'Perhaps it would not be out of place, *Monsieur le Maire*, if I responded more particularly to your own eloquent words.' Monsieur Raymond, who was trying to scrape a clot of jam from his trousers, looked up blear-eyed.

'When I came back to Yvebecques, I was conscious of being a most unwelcome intruder. That is the burden we Germans must carry all over the world just now. And for a long time to come our children will have to carry it, though they had no part in our calamities. I have not tried to shed the load. I do not want to. But henceforth Danielle will help me to carry it and that is a kind of miracle.' His hand rested momentarily on her shoulder. 'I do not know yet where we shall make our home. But your village, Monsieur Raymond, will always be as close to me as it is to my wife.'

Ma femme: it was the first time he used the word. It made him light of heart as if in victory. 'Here in this garden,' he went on; 'here . . .'

'Under the ash tree, under the ash tree!' The voice stabbed at Falk exact and derisive. Blaise was hovering near the pigsty. With him were Lurôt and a coil of young men and women from the neighbouring farms. The voice sang out again like a javelin: 'Under the ash tree. That's where you want to make your home, isn't it, *Herr Kapitän*!'

Falk sat down heavily. But the guests neither understood nor cared. They thumped the tables and called raucously to the new arrivals. Estève staggered over to Blaise with a glass of calvados. He lurched into one of the farm girls and spilled it down her brown neck. The girl bleated like a goat as Estève wiped her off, his fingers inside her blouse. The guests lumbered to their feet and the music began. Blaise had brought the fiddlers and Lurôt blew his bagpipe. The sound skirled naked and hot through the descending twilight.

At first the revellers stomped awkwardly. Some dropped out. Cavel shuffled into the lilac bushes and was sick. Estève drew his wife towards the hayloft, tittering. But soon the music seized the dancers by the nape of the neck and flung them into motion. They moved in a fume of cider and sweat, their hobnailed shoes threshing the ground. Dogs who had been burrowing in the rank garbage turned and scurried between the dancers' feet. Flies swarmed out of the hedges.

Blaise danced with harsh abandon, lifting his partner from the earth and whirling her in jolting arcs. The girl's body lashed back and forth yieldingly in his grip and his face was set in cruel spite. The farmhands danced close, grinding their haunches into the flaring skirts. Now and again they strode back to the ravaged tables to pour cider down their parched mouths. Lurôt blew without halt. Driven by the acrid notes, starlings skimmed back and forth across the roof.

Beltran danced alone with the stilted precision of an old man. He brought his knees up sharply and held his hands above his head. The other dancers clapped to the beat of his mincing step. Faster and faster. He closed his eyes dizzily but kept whirling. Suddenly he faltered like a wearying top and stumbled sideways into Blaise. Blaise thrust him back to the hub of the circle. Out of control, the drunken clerk spun from hand to hand. He sagged towards the ground but they heaved him about. His mouth was open and gasping.

'Stop them,' said Danielle, 'stop them.'

Falk paid no heed. The scene filled him with loathing. Yet it was unreal, like a clamorous nightmare. He was afraid, but could not comprehend his own fear. A desire to escape from La Hurlette and even from Danielle beat strong inside him. But he sat riveted, leaning on his cane and letting the cold rise in his back.

Amid hoarse outcries the men put the cider on the floor and threw over the tables, clearing a wide space. The steaming air shook with their tread. Amélie's face appeared at the kitchen window. It was strangely white and she called out in protest, but her words were lost in the tumult.

'Let's go inside the house,' said Danielle.

'Soon,' said Falk. He scarcely knew what he meant. He was waiting for something to happen, something loathsome but of intimate concern to him. It was a feeling he had had once before, in those marshes near Smolensk. And he could not keep his eyes from the ash tree; its leaves seemed to grow thicker in the waning light.

The bounding couples had torn loose and all the dancers clasped hands in a single round. Glazed with drink and exertion, they swept on in wild orbit. Then the whiplash uncoiled. Before Falk could move, one of the young men had leaped over to Danielle, seized her by the wrist and whirled her into the circle. In the careering wheel her gown flashed like a scorched leaf. The blood ran heavy under Blaise's eyes and Nicole spun with her mouth agape.

The wind reared up without warning. It raked the farmyard with chill gusts. The haze scattered and the sky came down like lead. Large cold drops of rain splashed against the barn. The dancers wavered and one of the fiddlers began wiping his bow. Monsieur Raymond slipped away hurriedly. Falk rose with a surge of relief.

But Blaise yelled out, 'One more dance! A bridal dance for the captain and his lady!' He came to Falk breathing hard: 'Join our round. No man should let another dance with his bride. Not on your wedding night.'

Falk stared into his red eyes. 'I can't. You know that.'

'Just once. A man can do anything if he tries hard enough. You've killed my brother and now you're taking my sister to bed. What's a little dance to a man like you? For old times' sake!'

Falk called to Danielle, 'Let's go. You're getting drenched.'

But Nicole barred his way: 'Hold my hands. Come dance with me. You can't deny me that. It's so little to ask.' She hammered at him like an enraged child. 'I shall never beg anything of you again I promise.'

'Don't be crazy, Nicole, it's impossible for me to dance.' But hands tugged at him on every side and a voice shouted, *'Bravo, la Wehrmacht!'*

Nicole dragged him into the circle. Falk looked for Danielle, but those who surrounded him were strangers and had faces like vacant masks. Lurôt had drawn close; he seemed to be blowing a single screeching note. It cut to the bone like the cry of a broken bird.

Falk strove to keep his balance but Nicole pulled him after her and the dancers began treading their mad round. He attempted to lunge out of the circle but it hemmed him in. As it whirled past, Falk saw Danielle fling herself at the barrier of arms and thrashing legs. He laboured towards her and struck wildly with his cane, but the wall of bodies threw him back. He stumbled and Nicole's hand slid from his grasp. He called desperately, 'Help me, Nicole, help me!' But no one listened and Blaise's face spun around him, contorted with avid fury.

Falk started falling and heard Danielle scream. Her voice was coming closer and closer. He rose to meet it but the shoes kept smashing into his face. A wave gathered before him, higher and swifter than any he had ever imagined. It blacked out the whirling ash tree and Danielle's cry. Falk knew that the towering crest was about to break and engulf him. But beyond the green howl of water he glimpsed a trough of light. It was dim at first. Then it rushed upon him with a brightness he could not endure.

The dancers melted away under the downpour, bearing Danielle to the house.

After a time, Terrenoire shambled out to look at the dead man. He bent low gazing at his torn features. Blood was clotting in the fine red hair. He knelt as if to guard his guest from the rain, and spoke to him softly: 'You came back too soon, Monsieur Falk, too soon.'

Cake

War came to them hard. First, the Sunday cake grew smaller. Then the icing took on a grey, worn air, and crumbled under their teeth with a taste of ash. And now, on that first Sunday in March, rumour and unquietude sifted like fine dust through the parlour and corridors.

The guests of St Aubain gathered for tea in tight knots. They threw wary glances towards the kitchen door. Instead of the cake, on the habitual large tray with its riot of lacquered cockatoos, there appeared Dr de Veeld.

He was a small man with a high forehead and swift hands. He had the stoic verve of those who build proud, intricate sandcastles against a persistent tide. His reddened eyes took in the constrained group of men and women and he saw the edge of their expectation. He knew that their silence was rancour masked and ready to fly at him. Abruptly he smiled, in homage to the sharp-sighted malice of the adversary and in defence of his own failing.

'As you have observed, ladies and gentlemen, there is no cake.'

He explained that the staff at St Aubain, decimated as it was by flight and the demands of the military, had done their utmost to sustain the tone of the house, to provide, in the face of difficulties and chicaneries which he would not even care to describe, those comforts and graces of life which signified much to all present. But now was a time when the impossible could no longer be achieved. It would, he knew, come as a jolt to his guests (these being the kind of unpleasant facts he did not, as a rule, bring to their notice) that hunger was almost general outside the walls of the park.

At this the Owl interrupted in her hoarse, insistent voice: 'I know. It's no news to me. I know because the dogs don't bark any more at night.'

Dr de Veeld continued as if he had not heard. Up to now, it had been possible to scrape up enough margarine and sugar to manage cake on Sunday afternoon. It could no longer be done. What rations the *Kommandatur* in Liège allowed would barely suffice to cover the essential needs of staff and patients. As always, he bracketed the word with a momentary pause. Were it not for the arbour and vegetable garden, to which several of the ladies and gentlemen now gathered had shown admirable devotion, the situation would be even more drastic. With care and some sacrifice, St Aubain would be able to weather the coming months. No one could see further ahead. But he did not believe that the terrible events outside could last beyond the summer. After which it might again be possible to have cake and, indeed, other delicacies, on Sunday afternoons.

De Veeld walked back to his office and the kitchen-maid, an old woman with sallow skin, brought out the pale tea and the cups. She was deft at parcelling into each a wisp of coarse grey sugar. The milk was thin as smoke.

The patients lingered, many not drinking. They stared at the sideboard where the cake should have been and the sense of deprivation mounted in them, making their spirits acrid. One man stood by the window gripping the heavy black-out curtains, now drawn. The March light lay cold on the gravel walk. He began weeping loud and the tears stained his shivering wrist.

The Owl, a tall, spindly woman, whom the staff knew as Madame Alice, moved sharply among her friends: 'It's intolerable. We pay a great deal here. I know I do. There is always butter to be had somewhere. The farmers hide it, in the loft. But he's telling the truth about everyone being hungry out there. Remember what I said about the dogs. None of you would listen. But I don't sleep nights, so I know what's going on.'

The Grays, who inhabit the twilit zone of partial infirmity, and who at St Aubain, as in similar institutions, were of vital aid to the inadequate staff, finally drank their tea. But the boy with the thin hair tore the single crocus out of the vase on the mantelpiece and stamped on it. Then he began calling in an unwavering tone, 'Where is our cake? It's Sunday. It's Sunday.'

2

I knew nothing of all this when I was first brought to sanctuary, before daylight, a week after Dr de Veeld's announcement. I knew only the stench and smother of my fear. They held me closer than the strait-jacket or the injection which, though a mild dose, made my features so vacant that the German patrols, who twice stopped our gloomy progress to flash their lights under the canvas flaps of the small truck, flinched away in distaste.

I am an American. I found myself in Angers at the outbreak of war, writing a dissertation on the style and syntax of Garnier, the neoclassic tragedian of the sixteenth century. I say this without either embarrass-ment or that feline humility affected by minor scholars who burn, in their inmost, with a desire to be critics or poets. I have an exact mind and tenacity, but my reach is small. Yet if literature is the only true mirror held up to the condition and gist of our souls, then those who polish some minute blur on its radiant surface or mend a crack at its sharp edge, are not without merit. Some heat falls even in the shadow of a bright day.

I stayed on in France not only because there were decisive manuscripts unexamined (particularly with regard to Garnier's knowledge of Italian Senecan drama), but because the homeward tug was faint. Neither the house I had inherited in Rockport, nor the vague expectation that I would enter my uncle's insurance firm, seemed real beside the task in hand and the muted charm of Angers and the Loire. I have private means.

At first the war seemed remote, and even when the occupation came, in June 1940, my life scarcely altered. The authorities behaved with propriety and allowed me to travel to Paris quite often to work in the rare-book room at the Bibliothèque Sainte-Geneviève. I have always loved that room for the leap of afternoon light through its high, veiled windows.

But one evening, the unheated, blacked-out train in which I was returning to Angers, halted suddenly in a small wood. An SS patrol combed it from end to end, irrupting into each compartment. Across from me sat an old man and a girl. As the searchers stomped nearer, sweat trickled down his lips and hands. The officer handed back my American passport with a slight flick of the head. He scrutinized the old man's papers for several minutes, and the old man's body gave off a sharp smell. Then the guards thrust him out of his seat, not in rage, but with venomous pleasure. They pushed him down the steps of the railway car and he stumbled to his knees by the side of the track. They struck him with unhurried blows, let him lurch to his feet and kicked him to the ground again.

The girl raced out of the compartment and lunged at them. They held her down and rubbed cinders in her face till it was black and raw. Then the train began moving. I do not recall what happened in the next few instants, but I found myself in the latrine vomiting.

Yet the image gripped me. It dimmed my mirror when I shaved in the brown-upholstered room at the Pension du Roy Henri, and it lay, like a flickering stain, on the pages of the Garnier manuscript. I saw them rubbing the cinders into her hair and mouth, and though I had lost them from sight as the train began rolling, I felt certain I had seen them pull off her coat. I knew that something bestial and slow had come to pass in that leafless wood. The remembrance sickened me, but it also brought a queer warmth and drew my skin tight.

Each time I travelled to Paris after that, I waited for the train to reach the stand of ash and scrub-oak where we had stopped. As it entered the wood, my excitement mounted. The blood raced in my ears and I had to leave my seat and stride up and down the corridor. Pressing my fist against my closed lids, I would see the night group with utter sharpness, the old man being thrashed and the officer picking up cinders and gravel in his gloved hand.

When I returned to my seat and sought to resume work on the texts or glossaries I carried in my Harvard bag, the letters danced before my eyes. I must have looked strange for everyone stared at me. But I anticipated each journey with obscure thirst. I could have finished the chapter on Garnier and the theme of vengeance, but kept it incomplete. The American Consulate wrote me that it was advising all nationals to return home; the letter gathered dust in my bureau drawer. It seemed as irrelevant as my memories of the three elms and the yellow awning in the backyard of my mother's house in Belmont. But the cinders burned my skin and I woke nights shivering with an unclean sweetness.

I was afraid. But more than that, I was envious: of the old man and the girl by the side of the track, of the torments being wrought on them. Of what I supposed had been done to them once they had been dragged to the SS barracks, and then afterwards. Not supposed – knew. For by the late summer of 1941, and in the fall, the correctness of our hosts had worn thin. Even in the stillness of Angers there could be no doubt. Those who had been taken from their houses at night turned up in the rushes of the Loire, their faces and bodies torn. One had to be deaf not to hear the wolves in the wind.

But my envy grew like a cancer. It made my very soul itch. Looking back on that time (and nothing in my life has been more vivid), I can hardly give a sane account of my feelings. I was living an unsavoury dream. I wanted to be that man. I cried out in my prim solitude for those heavy blows. Imagining the rake of cinders on my face. I grew dizzy and had to grasp the edge of my enamel wash-basin. With a scholar's ferreting nose, I scanned all I could glean from the censored newspapers of hostages, deportations and the rising ferocity of German reprisals. The military were beginning to put up placards with the names and pictures of those executed. I stood before them in mournful lust. I memorized their features and relived, in the privacy of my room, what I could conceive of the obscene torment of their several deaths. I envied them crazily. Yet at the same time, I sweated fear.

For I have always been a physical coward. My childhood was marred by cowardice, by my inability to climb walls, by the panic that held me rigid at the edge of a diving-board. I tried fiercely to be as bold and easy as other boys. I forced myself up rock spurs in the New Hampshire hills and rode my mother's large, unsteady mare. But she caught the scent of my fear and threw me. So I grew sly and scuttled like a lizard to my books and the refuge of our garden when my cousins went out to steal apples or dared each other to skate the loosening ice on Mattackwa pond.

Physical pain was a nightmare and I was afraid of the holidays because I knew my mother would take me to the dentist. By some insidious betrayal, my mind seemed capable of storing up past hurts; they ached and stung in remembrance. In school, they jeered at me and called me Killer.

Reading reports of the Maquis and of what happened to those who fell into Gestapo hands, I twitched with fear. Somewhere I had heard, or perhaps imagined, that they made prisoners insert their fingers in the jamb of a door and then slammed the door shut. The wild tear of pain, the bone splintering, infected my dreams. I often woke moaning and wet.

But envy was shriller than my fears. I wanted to be one of those men. It seemed to me a deprivation, the omission of a rare chance, that I should not have visited on my own flesh and nerve the hideous contrivances they had experienced. We live at the airy top of the spiral staircase of our inward; only the great fears and pains can force us to the long descent. Yet who has not been in the well of his being, in the foul lightless place, has taken no journey. Not to know how you will behave when you are strung on the bench and they walk towards you with their gloves, is to know little. It is to live with yourself as spinsters do, in the brittle familiarity of mere acquaintance.

The dramas of Garnier are blood-red. Now there was a bridge between the antique matter of my labours and what was actually happening around me, in the prison camps and in the cellars of the Rue de Lorraine. How could I apprehend the cry of the blinded and the torn, as it rose from the still page, unless I had heard it in my own throat?

But these were hypocrisies. I was riveted to a puerile, mad fancy. I could not keep my mind from the thought of how marvellous it must be to have endured. Already there were legends of couriers and *maquisards* who had kept silent under torture, who had spat in the face of their tormentors and then locked their teeth. Some had survived or even been released, too broken to be of use. To be one of these, to have walked the entire length of the tunnel and to have come out into the light, seemed to me consummation prouder than any dreamt of by lover or poet. After that there would be no more fear; the furies would no longer threaten but walk by one's side like old watchdogs.

I detest club dinners and college reunions. But during that late summer in Angers, I spun a fantasy so intense and detailed that it became the centre of my existence. I saw myself at a Harvard commencement, joining the other members of my class behind Widener Library for the alumni procession. It would be one of those hot, still days when the light dapples the elm leaves and straw hats in Harvard Yard with flecks of green and gold. The class marshal would lead us past the great flight of steps. Some around me had wilted and grown stout; others preserved their greyhound air. But all kept a gentle, wary pace so as not to hurry my progress. They knew how heavily I leaned on my cane and what austere panache I showed in being with them at all.

As we paraded under the blue shadow of the spire, women turned their heads slightly and stole a glance at me and whispered. For I had borne the worst that can be flayed and charred on a man's body, borne it eleven days unyielding. On the last day, the SS major had lifted his hand towards the rim of his cap in covert salute. I had been on the other side of the gate; my sinews were rent beyond repair, but all dread had been cleansed from me. Hearing the quick hush of voices wherever I went, in my mother's drawing-room on Thursday afternoons, when the committee of the Fairfield Club met, among the clerks in my uncle's office, or in the rare-book room at Houghton, where I was putting final touches to my definitive edition of Garnier, I kept a shy mien – but my soul sang loud in its depths.

I rehearsed this vision, I revelled in its every detail. It furnished my dank room at the pension and warmed me when I walked along the deserted banks of the Loire. It became the thing worth living for. At any cost. So I spent my days between fear and desire, between hysterical imaginings of pain, and a secret longing. If it is granted us to live on earth some stretch of our damnation, I must, in those months, have won remission of hell.

The trap closed softly. As if I had taken a Sunday stroll into the Gobi desert.

There was hardly any paraffin left for the small stove in the reading-room. To keep warm I took quick turns around the *Cour de la Mairie* with its ornate sundial and bust of Ronsard. One afternoon an elderly woman followed me. I recognized her for she had come several times to sit in the chair next to mine at the library. She had a green cardigan and chafed, wavering hands. She asked me whether it was true that I was an American, and without pausing for an answer: 'Will you help?'

Others had asked, but they sought something banal: a note commending them to the consulate in Marseille, or the chance to barter an old book or engraving (I was known to covet such things), for the cigarettes and cooking-fat I occasionally received in half-ransacked parcels. Here was something else, finer-edged.

Would I take a volume of poems to Paris? They were oddly underlined. A man would meet me at the number forty-eight bus station outside the Gare d'Orléans and ask me whether I liked the white wines of the Loire valley. I was to hand him the book and take another in exchange. This she would collect from me, under the library arcade, the following Tuesday.

Though the device seemed to me stale, as in an old film, I felt a jab of fear and excitement. She saw me hesitate and asked again. There was a harried pride in her manner. They did not like to entangle outsiders in their affairs. But help was badly needed. I would be running little risk. An American, carrying scholarly books, would pass the gauntlet of French militia and German guards unquestioned. We were neutrals. She flushed, as if the statement was itself an indecency.

That is how I became a courier for one of the numerous networks of amateurs and trained agents which were then being formed, in spurts of roused hatred and mutual distrust, throughout France. Our *réseau* consisted mainly of radical or marginal Catholics. Several of our most valuable informants were men of the lower clergy. They acted their part with the zest of schoolboys who have slipped over the seminary wall into the sun. Threading through the hedge country on their bicycles, they brought warning and solace. We were supposed to be in disciplined touch with a larger organization to the south, and ultimately with London. But I doubt whether the web was that strong-woven.

I was content. My dreams were proud and did not wake me.

My first three journeys were placid. But one late afternoon in November, at Châteaudun, a girl entered my compartment (I always travelled first class to make the unruffled ease of my American status more apparent). She was shivering and her legs were scratched raw, as if she had been caught on wire or climbed a sharp paling. She asked me whether the first snow had fallen in Boston. That was the signal prescribed in our somewhat romantic code. Then she bent forward as if to brush the dirt off her shoes, and told me that we would have to jump off the train when it slowed down in the marshalling yard, before entering Paris. The Germans had wind of our coming.

She must have seen how afraid I was and said there was nothing to worry about. The train moved at a crawl when rounding the last curve and it was not much of a drop. She had done it often. She said it without mockery, but seeing my hands shake she looked away embarrassed.

I fell stiffly and tore a muscle. She helped me over the maze of tracks and in the rain and darkness we passed unobserved. We spent the night in an empty apartment in the *banlieu*. Sitting on the mattress, she told me that the easy times were over. The hunters were getting cleverer and more savage. A number of clandestine groups such as ours had been infiltrated and destroyed. She went to the lightless window, her back to me: 'You've done more than we had a right to ask. Perhaps it's time for you to go home, to your own people. I am sure the first snow *has* fallen in Boston.' I was grateful, but hated her cool voice.

And, of course, it was too late. They routed me out of bed before daylight on 8 December and took me into hiding. When the police called at the pension, they found only my soiled linen and a summer suit. I left my notes and the two completed chapters of the Garnier study with the landlady. She stashed them in the attic, beside a red rocking-horse. I shaved my small beard and was given a set of false papers. Staring at my naked lips in the mirror, I found their expression sly and feeble. I loathed my assumed identity. I had slipped into an alien skin and it rubbed my nerves. When I saw the girl again, at a farm on the outskirts of Angers, she said, 'You are one of us now.' But I wasn't, and because she knew it her tone was irritable. They grudged me what claims I had to their anguish.

This time, I travelled to Paris on a farmer's truck. We carried potatoes which were frozen and smelled of rain. The *réseau* found work for me in an antique shop. I was to prepare inventories and catalogues for appraisal or auction. But the hours were empty and I lived in dread of the night when there were tracts to be distributed or messages to carry.

Why did I not break my tenuous, amateurish link with the underground? Paris is an inland sea with deep, brackish pools. Keep your head down and you're safe. I might have slipped into southern France or even tried to buy my way across the Spanish border. What drove me to take chances for which I had neither sufficient nerve nor blindness?

The girl played a part. Her solicitude enraged me. But the cause of my feverish inertia lay deeper. I must have believed, in the secret place of vanity, that the game could be won unscathed, that it would not exact its price.

The warren of the city gave odds to the hunted. The Germans stabbed out after us, but we slid between their fingers like dry sand. Every time I went to distribute a clandestine tract or help move parts of our transmitter from one loft to another, in that humped sea of grey roofs, I caressed the image of my heroics. I whispered to myself that this was the last hazard, that I could withdraw at will into the warming light of remembered danger. In the vacant shadows of the warehouse, where I dusted and catalogued the seven-branched candelabra of the deported and the dead, I fancied the high grace of my return. Though Paris was dark that winter, I saw, from the corner of my eye, the tawny gold of the elms on Brattle Street. And I heard the voices: 'You stayed on in France after we entered the war, didn't you? Is it true that you were in the underground? That *is* a rosette in your buttonhole.' And the women asking, 'Is it true they did things to you, terrible things?' I practised a shy nod, and gestures of diffident avowal.

The nearness of my obsession fascinated me. We never spoke of torture. Allusions to what had happened to friends or contacts taken in the net and brought to the Gestapo cellars were harshly suppressed. In the Rue de la Pompe and the Avenue Jean Jaurès, parents sat by their children at night and put cotton in their ears. Men had been known to scream for twelve hours; their voices cracked through the pavement like thorns. But we said nothing to each other. Every man acted as if he had held a talisman or bond of fate. The thing would not happen to him. Yet the thought hovered in one's mind constantly and seeped like marsh gas into our brave, clipped words. Often, in the midst of a briefing, or when we scattered on our night errands, the image of torture, the stifled conviction that it lay in near ambush, made the room prickly and cold, as if a lamp had dimmed. Then we saw each other naked.

Soon my excitement, my modish display of nerve, gave out. Nightmares won't let themselves be fondled; they lurch into reality like huge stinking cats. Fear shrilled in me. I lay at night dreaming the lash and rose in the morning with the grit of panic in my mouth. I could think of nothing else. I lost weight and my urine darkened.

I was afraid. I was hideously afraid. To keep a hold, I sought to convince myself that the pain would be endurable, that the rumours which filtered through to us were exaggerated. If the things rumoured were true, and not the mere brain-fever of a period sick and damned, a man would pass out quickly. What was the use of that if you wanted information from him? I do not smoke, but scrounged for cigarettes so I could touch my hands and stomachs with their glowing tips. I passed a nail file over my teeth till I shook with nausea. But my fear only grew worse: it lived in me like a stench.

On 26 February, the Gestapo seized our transmitter. Two men and the girl were in the attic when they smashed down the door. One man threw himself out the window, but they manacled .the two others before they could move. They dragged the girl down four flights of steps head-first.

When I heard the news, my nerve broke. I realized that my fantasies of heroism were a fraud, that I was contagious with fear and betrayal. I knew with certainty that I would howl at the first blow. I would whine and creep before them and kiss their hands and boots. I would tell them everything they wanted to know, every name, every contact, every location. There would be no need to tie me to the bench. I would yell out everything at once. They would stare down at me in derision, kick me in the belly as if I was a dead, bloated marmot, and let me go.

It is not easy for me to remember that week or set it down in words. Is it possible that the hysterical creature who scurried from one member of the *réseau* to the next, begging for safety, for release, for a drug with which to glide into painless death, was I? Did I try to hang myself on the night of the 27th (when we believed that the man had yielded under the torments and that our names were out) and merely fell from the chair losing control of my bowels? God's image may dwell in each of us, but it has precarious lodging.

The next morning they pounced on one of our couriers. Foolishly, the man had contacted his concierge in order to recover from his apartment, now a mousetrap, his winter coat. We were ordered into immediate hiding. Together with an old typesetter, who had done most of our illegal printing, I was sent to Lille. We spent five days burrowed in the back room of a grotesquely ornate garden house. At every footfall obscure shocks went through me and my stomach turned. I sweated in the cold.

We crossed the frontier with false papers and were harboured in a convent in Charleroi. A group of *maquisards* was active in the gorges and thick woods of the Ardennes. We were invited to join them. But I was burnt out. I though that in some moment of unbearable fear I might run into the street and throw myself at the mercy of the first German patrol. I had grown loathsome to myself and dangerous to the hounded remnants of our group.

A man they called Sambre came to see me. He said that he too had been at a university, working on early Flemish art. In the far background of the paintings of Christ's agony there were always blue mountains, or meadows tranquil under the morning star. He felt these were important.

We walked in the cloister and looked at the wet snow. He was not angry, only tired. He said there were casualties of every kind; some could be infectious. He had been in touch with a rest home. It was a good hiding-place and they had used it before to guard British airmen on their run to the coast. Dr de Veeld could be trusted; he had been one of the first to conspire against German rule. I could lie hidden until war's end or until the Gestapo called off the chase. All I need do is to feign idiocy for a few hours, while they brought me to Liège. They would give me a drug. I tried to tell the man of my shame, but he left abruptly.

Two sisters of the Order of the Sacred Heart conveyed me. Lying in the truck, confined and numbed, I gazed on their starched coiffs. I dreamt vaguely of the Irish king borne westward by white gulls. Perhaps I have a pompous imagination.

That is how I came to St Aubain.

3

'Don't you understand? He *has* butter. And there are packets of sugar in the bottom drawer of his dresser. Under a cambric handkerchief. Good God, I've seen them. Why doesn't he let us have any? He keeps it locked. He's sly as an eel. But I swear to you I've seen them.'

She drilled the words at me.

'It made the week go by. I couldn't have stood it otherwise. On Saturday morning they stirred the batter. And they baked in the afternoon or sometimes in the evening, when they thought I was asleep. But I don't sleep. Heaven knows how much they licked from the bowl before putting it in the oven. It smelled like summer. Knowing it would be there, on that sideboard on Sunday afternoon, made the week go by.'

She combed the rust-grey hair from her ears: 'How dare he treat us this way? I want you to know I pay a great deal here. I could not bring the dresses. But you should see me in the bronze chiffon. And in the organdie. They are in the tallboy in my bedroom in Bruges. Oh, I knew I should have brought them. I hoped I would be among refined people. I could no longer endure the things that came by in the canals. I watched at night. I saw what they were doing in the streets. So they came to demand my house. Did they take yours? But I mustn't think of those dresses and the Persian shawl. Dr de Veeld has forbidden me to think of those things. I have heart-flutters. I tell you that because you are a refined person. What right has he to treat us so abominably! Don't you understand? There are squares of butter under his cambric handkerchief. We must help each other.'

Madame Alice turned away. Then she flapped back at me with a hoarse moan: 'I'm hungry. Don't you understand? I'm hungry.'

Sudden safety unnerves. During my first days at St Aubain, I moved in a furry half-sleep. On the railway to Boston, Route 120 is the last stop before South Station where the chauffeur would be waiting for me in the old, gleaming Dodge. I knew he would be there, brushing the snow off my mother's plaid blanket. And the Christmas holiday lay before me; an immensity of ten days in my own bed, with its stiff, fresh sheets, and the nutmeg grater, and the toboggan rides down Concord hill.

When the train pulled away from Route 120, I shut my eyes tight and pretended that we were going the *other* way, that my mother had seen me off, crumpling the wet handkerchief into her glove, and that I was heading back to Choalten. I hate the school with a hatred that still leaves me shaken. Thinking that the holiday was over, that I would, in a few hours, be back in purgatory, with its reek of sawdust and wet bath-towels, I drove myself to the verge of tears. In that instant, the conductor would sing out, 'South Station'. I opened my eyes and could see Oscar, silvery and smiling, lifting his cap. Before I knew it, I would be wrapped in the Shetland blanket, speeding home. The game made me limp with delight.

I played it now, in the stripped arbour and behind the kitchens. I imagined that the Gestapo was at my heels, that I was trapped in my room at Angers. I could hear the grating breath of their dogs. But when I took my hands from my face, there was only a garden and a gravel walk, or Dr de Veeld looking past me from the window of his office. And far off, the widows' voices of the bells at curfew.

A man with florid cheeks tugged at me: 'The Owl has been croaking to you. You believe her, don't you?' He stared with heavy scorn. 'The woman's sick. She never had a house in Bruges. It's all lies. She worked in a hotel kitchen. Yet she acts as if she had rights around here.'

A thin trickle slid from his full, jeering lips. He could not retain it and his chin twitched: 'But she's telling the truth about the cake. Sometimes they made mocha icing, with candied flowers. In every second flower they put a walnut. Those of us who have some decency had worked it out. Whoever had a slice with a walnut one Sunday would take one without the week after. But not the Owl! She cheated like a scullion. She popped the thing in her rotten mouth before anyone knew what had happened. It made me ill. I wanted her to choke on it. I wanted it to stick in that scrawny gullet of hers. But why have they taken it away from us?'

He put his wet lips to my ear: 'Speak to de Veeld. You're new. He'll listen. Why is he hoarding the butter and the sugar and the walnuts?' He gripped my arm. 'I can't forget the smell; it was all warm.' He gave a flustered laugh, but would not let go till his knuckles grew white.

4

De Veeld knew, of course. He had made my rescue possible. But he treated me with so scrupulous a composure that I sometimes winced. I realized that the mask had to be worn while others were about. Yet I longed for some private signal of our complicity. Whenever we crossed, in the parlour or dining-room, I tried to draw from his polite mien an intimate wink, an admission of the bleak privilege of my status. I wanted this man to signify plainly, even if only between ourselves, that I was not mad.

After a week I lost patience. I waited outside his consulting-room and asked point-blank whether he did not wish to see me. He looked up, surprised, and said, 'No.'

Like the milder cases, I was assigned odd jobs around the house and in the garden. Our rations had thinned and I too was hungry. The ghostly remembrance of a cake I had never eaten made my mouth water.

One afternoon I was weeding among the pale rhubarb and the radish beds by the wall. A thin fog lay in the branches. The work was light, but a sour queasiness heaved inside me. My skin was wet and my legs fluttered like an old man's.

The birds had been at the grape bushes. A girl was coaxing the scraggly vine back to the trellis. She glanced over and took a sliver of bark from her pocket: 'Put this in your mouth and chew on it. You'll feel better.' It had a wry taste. 'It's hard at the beginning. Until you're used to being hungry, I mean. But soon it'll stop gnawing. It just leaves one feeling a little cold, even in the sun.'

I remember her as I shall remember nothing else in my life. She was slight of stature, and her features were fine-drawn, as if the brusque agony of late events had set on them a steady shadow. She had high, delicate cheek-bones. Her eyes were large and deep-set. They had in them a glint of wary malice, like the eyes of a fox when the light is grey. The shock of her tense grace passed through me. Only her hair was strange. In its natural darkness lay crude strands of bleach.

She saw my eyes on it and turned away amused: 'My father emptied the whole bottle on my head before they came for me. When I arrived here it was like burnt flax. But it doesn't last.' She pushed the heavy black curls from her temple and laughed in a remembrance so private as to shut me out entirely. Later that low, guarded laugh often came between us. Hearing it the first time, I felt a sharp longing and pressed my fingers against the wall. I must have looked as if I was about to be sick for she stepped nearer: 'Is anything wrong? Do you want to sit down?'

'It's you.'

'I?'

'You're very beautiful. I think you're the most beautiful person I've ever seen.'

She brushed her hands down her skirt. 'Not here. Please. There are enough mad people about.'

Her flat tone jolted me. I realized suddenly that she too was an outsider, that we both stood above the tideline. The dead, green smell of the undertow hung close, but we were miraculously on shore.

'You're not . . .' The word was like grit.

'Insane? No. No more than you.' And she turned back to the torn fruit. Her gestures were exact and contained. But every few moments there pierced in them a surge of pure, bounding life. She carried her small, swift body as against a hidden wind. Everything in me seemed to break open at the sight of her, at the low, clear chime of her voice. I was happy. In that pitiful garden, amid the hungry and the mad, I was happy as noon.

'Don't stare at me.' She said it smiling.

'I can't help it. To find somebody like you here. . . '

She lowered her head: 'Perhaps I was pretty. People said so. I don't know. But I don't want to be any longer. I don't even know whether it's right that I should be alive here, like a scared rabbit in a hole. Not when all the others . . .' She stabbed at the vine and looked away: 'Don't pay attention to me. I talk too much. I didn't mean that you're hiding because you're afraid. I am thinking of myself. You see, they've taken father and Jacob. And now there's no news from mother or from David. He's my younger brother. He's the baby.'

Her eyes stared wide and unseeing: 'Surely they wouldn't take

David. He's only fourteen. My God, they wouldn't take him, would they?'

Hearing her was like holding a live coal in my hand. I looked down helpless. I said that I didn't know, that I had run away because I couldn't bear the thought of physical pain.

'But David's only a child. Why are they taking the children? Oh God, why are they taking the children?' Her body shook with angry desolation, and I stooped low over the frozen weeds.

'I'm sorry I wailed at you. I don't usually. But seeing someone from the outside. Someone who knows. That's the awful thing about being here. Most of them don't realize what's happening on the other side of the wall. No more cake on Sunday. That's all it means to them. What right have they to be at peace? They're taking the children now, aren't they? I can read it in your face. And here everyone walks around in a greater stillness, not knowing. When I was a little girl and caught cold, they gave me a syrup. It was so warm and sweet you could taste the sleep coming with it. It must feel like that when the mind sleeps, all warm and dark. You see, I talk too much. And I get mixed up in my own words. But soon you'll know what I mean. Being here is like running around in a nightmare. You know there's something hideous just behind you. You shout at people and shake them; but they just walk by in their own dreams, smiling.'

'How did you know about me?'

'Sometimes Dr de Veeld tells me things. He's taking terrible risks. The Germans have been told once already; they came with their dogs. I was working in the kitchen and one of them patted my fine blonde hair: *echt Flemisch.*'

'You admire Dr de Veeld very much, don't you?'

She heard the scratch in my tone and looked puzzled. 'Of course. Who wouldn't? He came for me only a few hours before father was taken away. I didn't want to go. I fought and bit in the car. I tried to jump out. Later I was horribly ashamed. But he's never mentioned it.' She was again beautifully in control of herself: 'Of course I admire him.'

My new, absurd jealousy must have shown.

'Don't make a face like that. Now you really look ill.'

'What does our eminent doctor say?'

'That you have a minor infection. Outside the walls it might be contagious. But not here.'

I hacked the ground. After a few moments she said she had work to do in the main building. We would meet again in the refectory. Moving through the mist, she seemed a far-off personage in a silk landscape.

I called out in pure desire, 'Wait. What's your name?'

She hesitated, as if I had touched her: 'My name is Rahel.'

5

We were together that evening, our shadows close in the falling light. The high, rich note of her being held me utterly. The tale was a horror, but in those days common.

The Jakobsens had lived in a large house in the suburbs of Brussels. It had a garden with laburnum and dark tulips. Inside were a Bechstein and a music-stand with Chopin études. There were two Chagall still lifes, early, sinuous watercolours on the walls, and books in many languages. There were servants downstairs and festive candles. Monsieur Jakobsen often took the wheel with the chauffeur beside him when driving to the Bourse in the morning. There were uncles from Frankfurt and sleigh-rides and long summers on the beach at Le Zoote.

Samuel Haagen, Madame Jakobsen's brother, came from Antwerp and would show Rahel and David small uncut diamonds in silk paper. Sometimes he had spoors of glittering dust on his thick waistcoat. Rahel had a childhood friend, Annie Landau. Their intimacy was full of fierce secrets. Holding hands, they prowled the verge of the golf-course at Waterloo and whispered. At Christmas the families raided each other's houses and built a snowman in the garden, placing on his mad moon-face, amid shrieks of annual delight, the large-brimmed hat Monsieur Landau had worn as a boy in Odessa. The Landaus and the Jakobsens still went to the synagogue once or twice a year, but in black English Homburgs.

When Uncle Joseph and Aunt Ruth had to leave Frankfurt, they stopped at the house on their way to America. They had been allowed only one suitcase. Aunt Ruth came down to dinner in her high-laced walking-shoes. The new maid stared at them. Rahel flew at her in a rage and ran to her room. She lay on the wide, soft bed, with its pattern of strawberries, and wept uncontrollably. Her father sat by her, held her cramped fingers and told her not to be afraid. There had been bad times before. That summer there was barbed wire at the end of the beach, and Annie Landau's cousin – with whom Annie was grievously in love – emigrated to Brazil.

It all came quickly as if a break in the power line had plunged the house, with its rich weave and legacy of life, into blackness. Soon Rahel was kept home from school. They sat in her mother's room, driven from the chill, dust-gathering spaciousness of their former ways. Monsieur Jakobsen was much with them and taught the boys their lessons. Rahel could not take her eyes from his hands. They had been her pride and she envied the bleached manicurist at the Hotel Métropole where her father had gone every Friday afternoon. Now there was hair on the knuckles and the nails were broken. The servants left and the cook marched off with one of her mother's furs threatening obscurely. Instead of milk bottles, they found small parcels of excrement on the doorstep.

One evening Madame Jakobsen told the children to lay their coats and jackets on her bed. She took her sewing-box, with its gold-leaf monogram, threaded the needle, and emptied on her lap a bundle of yellow stars. Later Annie came over; she too was wearing a star, where the emblem had been on her school blazer. The two girls held each other and stood in the rank garden sobbing. That was the last time they met.

In January a man came to see her father. He had an unkempt beard and said that the end of the community was imminent. The lists of those to be deported were ready at the Brussels *Kommandatur*. It was the time foretold, the time of the wolves which is night. It had been like that during the pogroms. God's will was strange; but Akibah of ever-blessed memory and other learned Masters have said that so long as we cannot fathom His inscrutable purpose, we may strive. The children must be saved. Some were being taken in by Christian families, others might be smuggled into convent schools. The man gave them the name of Dr de Veeld. Only two weeks later, Monsieur Jakobsen and his eldest son were summoned to the Gestapo for the customary chat.

When de Veeld appeared, Rahel knew she would not see her father again. But the worst agony was his refusal to look at her. He held her in a smothering embrace. She felt the spasms racking his body and his tears covered her face. But he kept his head averted. Now she was no longer certain she could remember the colour of his eyes. Only that he had said her name over and over, Rahel, Rahel, in a voice not his own.

'But why me? Why not David? It's he that matters. I don't know whether I believe in God. Not any more. But we used to light the candles and say the prayers for the dead. Only a man is allowed to lead those prayers, to intone them in God's house. Even if I live and have children, they cannot carry my father's name. It will be death all over again. Why not hide David? If only you knew him; he's like my father.'

I urged that her mother and the boy might be safe; he was too young to be alone. She pressed her hands to her temples, as if she were trying to see in the wide darkness.

'If de Veeld had asked mother, it *would* have been David. I'm sure of that. But my father cared for me more than for either of my brothers. It's a queer, ugly thing to say. But he made no secret of it. He had a wild temper. Sometimes he shouted at Jacob so loud that the glass decanter shook in the dining-room cupboard. And when David sulked, father hit him. He never touched me. I used to scream in my crib at bedtime. He would swoop down and bundle me off to his study before mother or my governess could interfere. If Jacob or David ruffled the papers on his desk, he would glare and scold. But he let me rummage where I wanted and gave me his cigar-box to open. When I failed algebra, mother wanted me to stay in Brussels and work with a tutor during the summer holidays. But father absconded with me on a business trip to London; he bought me a red handbag and we took a boat-ride down the Thames. He sent me away because he loved me best.'

We had come to the high gate with its chain lock. She gripped the staves and her body was stiff with protest. Then she leaned forward, hardly breathing. She seemed to hear, in the blacked-out landscape, a distant, terrible sound. It cut through her like an unseen shaft and she let go: 'Now they are taking the children. They are going to send David to those places. I hate God. I hate God.'

I had intruded on an ancient, pitiless dialogue. All prayer is indictment.

216

Her body went slack and she allowed me to put my arms around her. A great lightness whipped through my nerves. Purge me with hyssop, and I shall be clean. It was a verse we heard often during morning chapel at Choalten (the fifty-first Psalm being a favourite text). I did not know what hyssop was. I imagined it to be a leaf tasting like holly. It was a secret herb to burn out fear and the things in us that are muddied.

Gathered to me, that slight, mutinous form, and the liveness of her hair against my hand, were like a sudden harvest. It was not I who had scurried for cover like a wet rat or dirtied myself in fright. Holding her in that tawdry strip of garden, I broke from my own shadow.

I blurted out to her brazen assurances of life. If the Germans won, which I thought likely, there would be peace; they would allow us to go home. If not, they would have neither the strength nor occasion to carry out their plans. Our panic was breeding insane fancies. Germany was the land of Schiller and Beethoven; it spoke the language of Rilke: 'Remember what was imputed to the Germans here, in Belgium, during the First World War. It turned out to be a grisly fable. They did *not* go around cutting off people's hands. We must get a hold of ourselves. Your mother and David are probably safe. You shall see your whole family again. You will live to recall these things like an evil dream. They pass.'

She pulled away from me, denying: 'They're dead. I know they're dead. I can't bear to know it. But I do.'

'You'll make yourself mad, Rahel. You're imagining hideous things that may never happen. Your father had warning; he must have sent your mother and the little boy into hiding. The Germans can't be everywhere. You and I are alive and safe.'

We act love in a worn similitude. I wanted to find a way of my own. Instead I drew her near and laboured to enmesh her hand. I said the old words, hating those who had used them before. To me, who had never spoken them, they were new as morning. Even that is a cliché.

'If I had not met you only a few hours ago, I would say I am in love with you. I know that I will say it very soon. And that it changes everything. For both of us, if you will allow it. If you will not laugh or explain that we have empty stomachs and are light-headed. Don't say that this is happening because there's no one else we can look to in this lost hole. I would have found you anywhere.'

Rahel considered me with an odd, ironic sweetness: 'Yes, I think you will live. I want you to. You must promise to stay hidden or to make them let you go.'

Even in that instant, with her lips pressed to mine, I sensed that the core of her yielding was hard and watchful. But nothing mattered. I exulted. I groped my way to my room, as agile and sharp-honed as a man part-drunk. As I sat down on the bed, my hand brushed against a piece of paper, folded into a minute square. I opened it and pried loose a corner of the drapes to let in the grey dim of the night. The lettering was spiky and ceremonious: 'I pray you, *cher ami*, do not get involved with that little person. I don't sleep. I have been concerned over you. Probably you do not know. Indeed, I feel certain you don't. Her hair is not really blonde. It never was. She is merely a dirty little Jewess.'

6

The next afternoon I found the note in my pocket. I took an enraged step. I thought I had torn up the vile scribble. But it clung like a burr.

Naturally I knew. That was the point of her being at St Aubain. From it sprang the marvel, the sheer marvel, of her presence. But being a part of the story she so urgently told and of circumstances I could not separate from her vivid charm, Rahel's Jewishness had seemed to me no less impalpable or exotic than the diamond dust on Samuel Haagen's lapel.

Now that it confronted me in the malignant awareness of an outsider, the fact took on a more unpleasing savour. It obtruded with the subtle rawness of a fever sore.

My contact with Jews had been sparse. The Fairfield Club had no Jewish members. There were, I believe, five or six at Choalten, but the only one in my field of vision was a wet, pudgy boy. He was rumoured to be under analysis. I did not know what this signified, but inevitably the word and his appearance conjured up the thought of indelicate bottles on a hospital trolley. The lore of my crowd at Harvard held that Jewish girls were both easy and difficult. Easy, because they took a 'mature' view; difficult, because they made of it what we called, scornfully, a 'production'. I acquired no direct evidence on the matter.

Yet as a group, bristling and coherent, the Jews did force themselves on my consciousness. No one can engage in literary studies without being made cognizant of their seducer's gift for language and their ironic devotion to the abstract. The Jew makes of language a place. He is not really at home in it (how could he be, lacking that tenebrous, immemorial complicity with the stone, leaf and ash of a land which gave to speech its precedent, unspoken meaning?). But he masters it with the nonchalant adroitness of a privileged guest; he chucks it knowingly under the chin.

In my Renaissance seminar there was one of these gipsy conquistadors. He was a heavy young man with an actor's mouth. At one instant he was all edge; in the next, humility hung on him like a banner. He had been educated in half a dozen countries ('Herr Hitler, you know') and spoke English with flair; but he retained a sugary intonation, part-French, part-German. I detested the fluent acrobatics of his mind. He made a vaunt of being a freelance, a bird of passage skimming from centre to centre. But he loved Harvard with covert design and hoped to be kept on. When last I heard of him, he was pursuing a vague career in journalism and writing his academic patrons arrogant, melancholy letters.

Like most people, I found that Jews left me uncomfortable; I parted from them as from a stiff chair. When I began working on my edition of Garnier's *La Juive*, I recognized in the soaring lament of Israel, in the desolation of those whom the Assyrian had ravaged and blinded, the crux of my discomfort. By their unending misery, the Jews have put mankind in the wrong. Their presence is reproach.

That I should have fallen in love with Rahel Jakobsen was part of the logic of bad dreams which harried me since Angers. But the fact was unassailable. It braced like hope and the flash of rain on a summer's night.

Light of heart, I provoked occasions of sentiment. I tried to pierce the Saturn's ring of quiet and miasma behind which the deranged and the obsessed travel their blind orbit. One of the senior inhabitants of St Aubain was a small, bulky personage with a grey lion's mane. Ordinarily, he was housed in sour repose. But twice or three times a day, he leaped out of his seat into a prize-fighter's stance and weaved and jabbed in a close bout with the air or his own shadow. I met him in the parlour, his guard up and his left hook slashing. I countered his posture and we sparred. Into his eyes came a sudden focus of reason and delight. He nicked me smartly on the nose. My own jabs went wide; through the drowse of his mind, the body remembered its cunning. But the blaze of nerve passed from him as abruptly as it came. In the instant in which his arms fell, I landed a blow on his chest. He stared, uncomprehending. He retained no glint of awareness of our game, but swore at me with loud, recondite obscenity.

Madame Alice had stolen upon us. She gave a frosty laugh and pulled me away.

'You do make a fool of yourself, don't you, *cher ami*? How can someone of your breeding humour this scruffy old beggar? He never bathes.'

I rubbed my nose.

'You have a kind, genteel spirit. I knew that when I first laid eyes on you. But you are indiscriminate. One must guard oneself and keep up proprieties. Particularly in a place like this. There is so little tone here. I say it for your own good.'

Her hand fluttered on my sleeve.

I was too buoyant for astuteness: 'I got your note, Madame Alice.'

The Owl took a distant air: 'My note?'

'I am new here and I value your interest. Believe me. But it was not kindly put. As you say, these are thin times. We must show to one another grace of heart.' The phrase had come to me during the night's content; I took pride in it: 'Grace of heart, Madame. It's the only way.'

She regarded me with mournful hauteur: 'I require no lessons in grace. I wonder whether you would have been of our circle in Bruges. I fear not. You could not see my garden for dahlias, and in the autumn there were fresh chrysanthemums on my table each morning. No, Monsieur, you are indelicate.'

The reproof was acid but her fingers tightened on my arm. And when she spoke again, her voice had a cracked, anxious note: 'I told you we must stick together. Are you blind? Don't you realize that this place is thick with Jews? They're holding us as hostages, to deceive the Germans. They're weaving behind our backs, like spiders. I suppose you think de Veeld is one of us?' She grinned harshly: 'He's not. His real name is Grünfeld. He was an abortionist in Liège. I can tell the chosen people a mile off. It's the way they walk.' She instructed me in a fervent whisper: 'They lean forward on their toes. They belong nowhere so the ground is hot under their feet.'

I was startled; it was an observation I had made in my own casual experience.

The Owl sensed her vantage: 'You know I'm right, *mon cher*. You and I are in their net. But we shall turn the tables. I have friends in high places. I have told them about you. There is no need for you to know who I am. Perhaps you have guessed.' Her breath was on my cheek: 'Promise, my dear, promise you will stay away from that little slut. She's not your kind. Promise me.'

I disengaged gently. The fact that Rahel and I were linked, even in so withered a mind, made my passion less fragile, less premature. From Madame Alice's galled reproach it took substance. I was grateful.

'You must bear with my follies.' And I kissed her parchment hand.

'Ah. You won't promise. That baggage has seduced you. Your tastes are vulgar, Monsieur. I shall have the organdie dress sent home.'

'Let's be friends, Madame Alice. I know I shall need your help and counsel.'

But she ruffled away in anger and I felt too much heart's ease to care. Had I been cooler and less involved in the novel wealth of my feelings, I might have thought twice about the proposal Dr de Veeld made to us that night, in his terse, indifferent manner. He remarked that those who felt inclined might contrive a sketch, or a few scenes from a play for the staff and guests: 'It will take our minds off our stomachs.' Rahel clapped her hands at the idea. But I still wonder at the impertinence which made us choose *Le Misanthrope*. The play and its inevitable casting fixed the constellation of enmity.

To our frayed circumstance, rehearsals brought a tang of the old, free habits. We gave of ourselves with spendthrift urgency. The realness of our stage, with its three chairs and spread of canvas in a corner of the refectory, created in St Aubain that unbarred skylight by which prisoners reckon their chances. For a few hours each day we lived our masks.

Dr de Veeld's assistant played Alceste. An insurgent liver had yellowed his skin and kept him out of war and conscript labour. He had a heavy Flemish temper and entered the role with admirable gloom. I, of course, was Philinte. Rahel cast me for the part the first evening we met to read the play. She saw in me the sweet reason of the trimmer. I winced at the aptness of her choice. Madame Alice accepted the guise of Arsinoé with such lofty calm that I wondered whether she had previously reconnoitred the piece.

Rahel took Célimène in glittering tow. She lavished on our meagre enterprise the prodigality and quicksilver of her being. She hoisted sail and pennon and rode before our petty wind as if all the west were open. In contempt of anguish, of what she knew of her family and foresaw, unblinking, of her end, the girl assumed, during the hours of our mime, the pert, flickering lightness of Molière's lady. But because our actual condition hovered close, revoking us to fear like a muster on a prison morning, Rahel found in the marquise what I take to be the secret key. Under the sparkling insolence, amid the fusillade of whimsy, ran a current of feverish alarm. When she moved, even in minuet, it was like a leaf driven.

In our nervous, exhilarating game, we crossed the line between acting and daylight. The marquise says in rhymed couplets, 'Be my confidant,' and I took Rahel at her word. But the trust she gave me, the intimacy in which I shared her thin hopes and nightmare dread, had its purpose. At first I was too unguardedly happy to notice. As we knelt near each other, daubing white paint on our canvas backdrop, the Owl leaned over to hiss lugubrious warning: '*Mon pauvre ami*, don't you realize she's using you?' That Madame Alice should be jealous, and I the object of her wilted ardours, seemed doubly appropriate – to her imaginings and to the play. I evaded gently: 'Ah, Madame, you are right. But how may I resist the charms of the marquise? She is using us all.'

But the force of her suggestion grew. In those March days, liberated from the gritty shyness which had so often severed me from other human beings, I gathered, as with arms outflung, Rahel's presence, her touch, her evening welcome. Late winter has its sudden gold. But I also discovered her tenacious design. Perhaps that is too cool a word. She obeyed desperate impulse.

Rahel carried inside her, like still water, the brooding of death. A grain of tender malice persuaded her that I would survive. She never doubted that I would be released from St Aubain and come home to America. She resolved to store in me her only possession. I was to remember. That was her unspoken, vehement demand. I was to remember every detail: the house, Uncle Samuel's diamonds, the last holiday at Le Zoote, the Chinese mirror in the foyer, Aunt Ruth's arrival in her ominous shoes, the Friday manicure at the Métropole, the high-flown loves of Annie Landau. Everything. Every detail.

No repetition was superfluous; no insistence too blunt. Each conversation, between cues or when we met at work in the kitchen garden, narrowed to a hawk's circle; after a few moments, Rahel would descend on a stretch of memory and pin me to familiar ground. She made of my listening a sanctuary. In it, she and her family were to have their only survivance. There would be no other trace. She used me, with utter intent, against the monstrous oblivion unleashed on her kind. Outside St Aubain were those who had sworn that no one would even recall the names of the dead, that their sum would be ash. The Jakobsens, the Haagens, the Landaus would have neither graves nor the fitful resurrection men are allowed in their remembrance of their children. Dust had more future.

Against this enormity Rahel set her will, as if the flare of a match could rebuke night. The Jakobsens would have their ghostly life in our house in Belmont, in cousin Peyton's library on Mt Auburn Street, in the Somerset Club. She did not realize that living Jews have small welcome in these places. But for the span of my recollection, Rahel and those near her would escape the obscene silence of massacre. One by one she lit in me the candles for her dead.

Proud scruple compelled her to offer an exchange. In retrospect, it seems obvious. At the time, I had only obscure, painful intimations. In lucid moments, I hated myself for cajoling from her tragic need a hint of recompense. I knew the bargain was contemptible. But Rahel had jarred me into blind want. I whispered to her that we were safe, that there lay before us a spacious chance of life. I lied to myself about her motive and took the pressing, unashamed gift of her past as if it was a spray of lilac tendered in flirtation.

I listened closely. I exhibited the virtuoso precision of a scholar. I repeated what she told me and echoed her merest allusion. I did not make a single error in recalling the tangled lineage of her Galician uncles. When she forgot the name of Annie Landau's governess, I reminded her. Rahel was grateful and left her hand in mine.

7

Only the violent did not attend. Guests and staff crowded the hall. Excitement simmered during the afternoon and at supper there had been spurts of sultry impatience. The tow-headed boy let loose his unsteady rein and charged about the tables telling nasty jokes. He climbed on a chair and grimaced till the tears came. De Veeld had difficulty calming him. But now he perched on the crowded bench, his face pale with delight. The florid gentleman wore the defiant remnants of evening dress and stared at the curtain, as if to exclude from his urbane content the maimed and bewildered who sat beside him. The cook and the two serving-maids had come from their lair. They commandeered the sofa and whispered loudly. The gaunt creature who rationed out tea looked around like a queen of cards, her eye unblinking; she knew that everyone in the room depended on her cold grace. The gardener leaned at the rear; he had put on a clean collar and moved his neck in irked pride. Now and again he winked – not at anyone in particular – but at the entire company, gathered in the curtained, steaming room in the complicity of common magic.

An armchair had been reserved in the front row. De Veeld reclined as if the blade of his ironic alertness had snapped closed. He drew in small puffs on one of the Player's from his dwindled store.

Our means were ragged. A Bunsen burner, masked with red paper, served for a flambeau. The kitchen table wobbled under imagined brocade. We had patched our costumes of what eccentric or reversible clothing lay at hand and must have looked like a shabby-genteel family driven out of its house by a night fire. The sole object of unfeigned grandeur was a Victorian inkstand. On it, a mother-of-pearl Psyche spread desolate arms over an enamelled Eros. Madame Alice had brought it to St Aubain from some improbable corner of her past. She added it to our scarecrow furnishings with high disdain. It proclaimed a world inaccessible to our vulgarities.

But despite our starved props, the play held. In St Aubain no one thought it absurd that a man should find society a bruising riddle, that he would try to lash its cobwebs from his face and strive for exit. The rage of Alceste played on the raw, broken nerves of our audience like intimate memories. When I spoke my worldly sermon, warning the Misanthrope that total sincerity could shade into madness, a heavy, electric wave broke over the benches. Behind my stiff make-up and the hiss of the burner, I could hear the boy breathing hard.

But it was the scene between Célimène and Arsinoé, the flash of feather and claw in Act III, which brought our performance to a pitch, and made disaster inevitable.

Madame Alice rustled on to the stage in a froth of black. She had pinned to her grey, unruly hair a cone of tissue paper. Her silhouette stole before her like a smooth bat, its wings mantled.

She opened on a note of syrupy venom: 'Madame, I am here as a friend. I have come because friendship has its duties.' She dropped the word *friendship* from the edge of her lips, giving it the acid whisper of steam. Recounting to Célimène the censorious gossip of the town, each item a small crystal of venom, Madame Alice seemed to uncoil. Her shadow bulked over the marquise in thick, happy gloom: 'Ah, my dear, how firmly I laboured to defend your honour, your reputation and good name. But there are things one *cannot* overlook!' She ended her tirade on a cracked chime, and the lust of condescension shone on her rouged cheeks.

Rahel soared against her. She shook from the ruffles of her light, coquet dress the brown stench of the night bird. She riposted fiercely, but in the easy vein of a duellist sure of his ground. She repeated in exact, mocking counterpoint Arsinoé's pledge of amity, of unblemished kindness, and pirouetted into an irreverent curtsy.

The elegant gentleman began applauding, but held back in the nervous silence.

Madame Alice stood rigid; the blaze of virtuous reproof mounted in her bones. She grew with anger, and her features took on a weird, beaked sharpness: 'You make a vaunt of your years! Am I so much the older of us two? Am I so ancient and despised?'

The arc of hatred flared between them. Rahel carried her youth unsheathed. Madame Alice sought to parry its cruel strokes. But under the menacing pavane with which she circled the stage pierced the fallen nakedness of the old.

She cried out in envy, 'Is it your virtue, Madame, which doth draw such admiration from the town?'

But Rahel kept at her throat, gay and sharp-toothed as a lynx:

> I pray you, Madame, let the gallants court,
> And we shall note what charms in you are sought.

Arsinoé gripped the inkstand. A gust of violence went through her. In a second she would hurl the murderous thing. De Veeld sat upright, and the boxer half-sprang from his place. I was paralysed by the near leap of madness.

But Madame Alice pulled herself tight. Her heavy lids closed. She cast a spell of silence, and the air went flat and stifling as in the still centre of a tropical storm. When she spoke, a breath of anguished but restored consciousness passed over the hall. Her tone was soft and deadly: 'No more. We go too far. I should already have taken leave, were it not that my carriage has been slow.'

I shall never forget how that haggard, outraged woman pronounced *carriage*. She made it glitter with the lights of pride. It bore her away, past the box-hedges of a rococo garden, four Spanish pacers prancing.

As Rahel glided from the stage, in uneasy triumph, the audience rose at us. The boy screeched and the cook stamped her drowsy legs. De Veeld turned to his patients and waved them down, but the excited murmurs continued. Nothing in the rest of the play came near the savage glitter of that moment.

When the curtain fell, Rahel stood behind the canvas flap. She passed her hands over her face in a puzzled gesture, as if to wipe away the stain of Madame Alice's fury. When I touched her, she said, 'I'm afraid.'

De Veeld beckoned and padded ahead, conspiratorial. We trailed behind, still in our costumes. There were cups around the blue-shaded lamp and he had laid out a fresh cigarette on his blotter. He poured coffee, sour-thin and only a demitasse, and said it had been a fine performance. Did we realize how racked a man must be to invent such laughter? And because the thought was trite, he puckered into a shy smile. At that moment the kitchen-harpy entered, her mien torn between pride and remonstrance. She set down a covered dish. De Veeld made a large gesture over it, half-sacrament, half-conjuror's flourish. He whisked off the napkin. Cake.

Small, flattened at the edges, and with only one almond in its inviolate centre; but cake. De Veeld's assistant belched gently and bent forward. I was shamed by my own avid delight. 'Our last egg powder,' murmured the magician. 'A silly waste,' said the kitchen-maid. But I saw crumbs and a glint of icing on her fingers.

De Veeld plucked the almond and presented it to Rahel: 'Madame la Marquise . . .' I could taste its burnt brown. Then he divided and was unfair only to himself. I tried small, lingering bites, but was suddenly ravenous. I was scouring the plate before I realized that everyone else had stopped eating. Madame Alice had risen, gaunt and armoured: 'Thank you for this charming feast, *mon cher* de Veeld. But I am a little fatigued. You will excuse me, I know. As Mademoiselle here has so eloquently pointed out, I am an old woman. Bedtime for me. Though God knows, I don't sleep.'

'But Madame Alice, your cake . . . you haven't touched it!'

We were out of our depths.

'Ah, the cake. How kind of you. But I don't care very much for sweets. A few pralines now and again, for the children, you know, and a *boule Mozart*, oh, ever so rarely, when we used to go to Vienna. But otherwise, no.'

The corners of her lips were moist, and she spoke in a frail tone, as if to obscure an indelicate hurt. She looked at the untouched slice, savouring the bitter edge of conquest: 'I know it will not be left over.' We drank gall and stared at our plates. Then she turned and slid away, dropping a general 'goodnight', like an ironic, twilit fanfare over a won field.

I followed Rahel to her room and ached to find it so bare.

'No pictures?'

'We had very few. Father hated being photographed. He said that those who make a portrait of us steal a tiny piece of our souls. I don't really know what he meant.'

'I think I do.'

'But there is this.' She took from her night-table a tall menu with Gothic lettering: *Le Duc de Bourgogne*, Bruges. From the *pâté du chef* down to the brandied cherries wound a garland of signatures. Her father at the top, in a heavy surge: Nathanael Emil Jakobsen. Then her brother. Near the bottom came Annie Landau, the A round and wavy.

'We lunched there on my seventeenth birthday. There were fifteen of us. Look at the way David signs, with that kite-tail at the end. Do you know the *Duc de Bourgogne*?'

'Yes. It's the only place where the chocolate mousse is really black.'

We sat on the bed.

'It's the first time for me.'

'For me too.'

'I don't believe you.'

'I don't mean it in the same way. But it's true. This is the first time that matters.'

'Have there been many?'

'No.'

'Were they beautiful? I'm sure they were prettier than I.'

'No.'

'You won't hurt me, will you?'

'Not for the world.'

She rose and stretched her hands towards me. I held them fast. Did she say, 'Remember'? I think not. Her purpose was desperate but not gross.

'Please don't look. It's such a silly costume. I made this of cardboard and one of de Veeld's handkerchiefs.' She undid her bodice. 'I wish I was wearing something beautiful. Mother has a slip bordered with dark blue lace. She said I could wear it at my wedding.'

Her breasts were small and high. The dizziness of the wood came on me. For a moment, I was certain it was Rahel, that it was into her skin they had rubbed the cinders. Then my mind cleared. I saw her supple, guarded body.

'Please hold me. I'm cold.'

My hands were on her back. We shivered like the gently drunk. Then she closed her eyes.

Much later, nearly at the grey of morning, she began laughing. I lifted her warm cheek. 'It's Annie. She said the first time was like a saddle-sore. She had read it in a book. It isn't.' And she laughed till I drew the blanket over us.

8

They came four days later. The bark of the dogs woke me, and going down to breakfast I saw the two black cars in the yard.

They made us sit in the parlour in a wide, still circle. One of them leaned against the door. There was no savagery in his face; he had a puffed skin and swollen lids, like a factory-worker at mid-afternoon, when the light tires and there is precise, tedious labour in hand. I had seen such faces in my cousin's foundry in Waltham.

He did not shout at us, but announced that if anyone wished to leave the room and use the toilet down the hall, they would have to ask permission. At this we grew obeisant as children. Each one seemed to fold inward, attending, in embarrassed isolation, to the sting of his bowels. The gentleman gave a stifled sigh; even at this early hour, and at sudden alarm, he had inserted a handkerchief in the breast-pocket of his pyjamas.

After a spell, one of the elderly women got up; holding her green houserobe she shuffled to the guard. She whispered. He made her repeat her request out loud and shook his head. She retreated to her seat, bewildered, and kept her eyes on the man's face in abject alertness. Then he nodded and she hurried past. Later he summoned the Boxer: 'Stop flailing about. You may go and relieve yourself.' The old prowler flushed: 'But I don't need to.' 'I think you do,' said the guard patiently.

We did not dare look at each other, but sat utterly divided, each cowering in his own sweat. When the officer came, they made us get up and sit down again. But the boy had wet his trousers and the leather chair, so they stood him in the corner with his forehead to the wall. The officer expressed regret at our inconvenience; he hoped we were being looked after. If everyone behaved sensibly, we would soon be allowed to go back to our rest. He pronounced the word with nostalgic malice, as if it came from a child's primer. It was really up to us. They had thought for some time that the home was being used to shelter Jews and subversives. They had been very patient, but now the matter had to be cleared up. It was for our own benefit. He only hoped

Dr de Veeld would take a reasonable view. If not . . .

In the corner the boy sagged; another faint trickle ran over his shoe. The guard stole up behind him, gripped his flaxen hair and thrust him against the wall, twice, not very hard. When the boy sat down, his teeth chattered.

Without lifting my head, I caught a glimpse of Rahel. April was in the garden and she was staring out. Against the lit window, her features were delicately drawn and calm. She was fully dressed, as if she had been ready before us. I cried to her with every nerve, but she did not hear.

It seemed to me as if a day had come and gone under the glass bell. My mouth was hot. But perhaps it was less than an hour. Then the other sound. From somewhere in the covert of the house, a thin, blurred cry, a cellar murmur, and the cry again. Rahel shut her eyes and the woman in the houserobe scraped her hands convulsively on the arm of the sofa. The guard yelled at her, 'Quiet. Stop that stupid noise.' But he himself was whistling and banging his heel against the door. I realized that the dogs had stopped barking.

They dragged de Veeld through the room, slowly, forcing us to look. His mouth was a dark hole, and his right hand hung from his sleeve, the nails bleeding. As they slid him by the arms, down the corridor and towards the stairs, one of his sandals came loose. De Veeld always wore sandals; he said his feet were rheumatic.

This time the officer's tone grated. His tie was twisted and there were stains on his silver-edged lapel. He disliked having to do this kind of thing. It was no pleasure; he hoped we realized that. But de Veeld had been stubborn and a liar. It was a doctor's job to care for the sick, not to hide runaways and Jews. The *Kommandatur* had allowed St Aubain special rations. None of the buildings had been requisitioned: 'We have treated you like a hospital. We shall know better in future.' He hoped the patients would prove more reasonable than the doctor. The guard laughed. The officer said he would wait in de Veeld's office for anything we chose to tell him. But he was a busy man. He would wait fifteen minutes. If no one came forward, if those who were hiding under false colours did not have the decency to give themselves up, he would clear the house. And in the garden were the dogs.

I do not remember how many minutes passed. I knew her prim step so well there was no need to look up. I could have acted – sprung from my chair and throttled her, or gone to the officer myself to warn him that Madame Alice was a hysteric, that everything she said was a crazy lie. I could have convinced him that it was I they were looking for, that there was no one else. All the resolute, sane gestures of daydreams or remorse are possible; but they hover on the edge of an instant. I sat paralysed. In the second before the needle enters or the mask comes down, the brain races through a vile litany: let it happen to someone else, to anyone, even to someone close to me. But not to me. So the reel unwound, hideous and expected.

The officer returned and examined our huddled group. He called, not loud, 'Rahel Jakobsen.' She rose. 'Get your things. *Sie kommen mit uns.*'

He left and she began moving towards the door. Then she looked me full in the face.

Theology tells of a moment, intolerable to reason, when Judgement will be over and the gate of hell will close on the final damned, not for unnumbered millions of years, but for motionless eternity. As the light fades upwards, the damned will look at God's back in terrible forgiveness.

I tried to read in her still face a shadow of fear or of relief. But there was only this terrible mercy. Then she was gone, and soon the cars drove out of the yard.

I flung myself into her naked room. The menu was on the bed. I knew there would be a message, a word of parting or of hope. I scanned the signatures wildly, turned it over and searched the corners. There was nothing. Nothing whatever.

9

I have been back to St Aubain.

It was a very hot day and my mother stared with irritation at the sweat-blisters on the chauffeur's neck. He was encased in his grey uniform, and though the front seat was large, his elbow brushed continuously against the three-tiered package which towered beside him.

We crossed new bridges and the houses were freshly painted. My mother shifted on the leather armrest and tapped her alligator travelling-case. She regarded the venture with prickly scorn; it was the kind of complication she associated with the infrequent appearance in Belmont of unemployed French Canadians or refugee doctors from central Europe. She had allowed the excursion only because it fell easily between the Memlings of Bruges and the tulips of Delft.

Mother's first cousin was in the State Department. Through his influence and the good offices of the Swedish Red Cross, I had been extricated from St Aubain before the war ended. 'Why do you want to go back to that place, Bunny? We had enough trouble getting you out.' Europe was an old enemy; Uncle Winslow, her younger brother, had gone there in the thirties. After idling in Paris and Dublin, he had come home to a hasty marriage. As we crossed the canal, mother said, 'I do wish the chauffeur wouldn't perspire so.'

The home had been enlarged. There were white roses in the hedge, and parasols and croquet mallets on the lawn. Where the kitchen garden had been, they had added a solarium. Behind the screened windows, I saw shadows at ping-pong. 'This is more pleasant than I expected,' allowed my mother, 'but then you do exaggerate.'

The senior psychiatrist received us in his office. He frowned thoughtfully when I asked about de Veeld. He had died in a camp. It was a wretched business. But he had never quite understood why de Veeld had dabbled in clandestine politics. A doctor's prime duty lay with his patients. Though it had no red cross painted on its roof, a mental home was precisely like any other hospital, neutral ground. So far as he knew, the Germans had been scrupulously correct. It was de Veeld who brought on the difficulties. 'I myself happened to be in Switzerland during the war, working in Dr Jung's clinic.' He pointed to a signed photograph on his large desk. No, he had no record of what had befallen most of the patients. In 1944, the Germans used St Aubain as a field-hospital. Then the Americans took over. 'It was in dilapidated shape when I first came. But we feel we've done quite well. We're planning a separate wing for electrotherapy.'

Dr Brunel was so pink and serene that I grew flustered. I tried to explain what it had been like and why our chauffeur had carried in, and unwrapped on the hall table, a large cake. Mother had insisted on a frosting of stars and lilies, but I wanted him to know why it was a mocha layer-cake and why the walnuts were so important. I tangled in my own words.

'You're getting all flushed, Bunny. Please relax. I'm sure the doctor isn't interested in the unfortunate details. What we want to do is get the cake to a cool place.'

Dr Brunel dimpled and said it was a charming gift. Of course, most of the patients were on a low-calorie diet: 'In the old days, psychiatrists were careless about that. We know now how vital slimness is to the ego. In a way, rationing was a blessing in disguise.' But the cake and the thought behind it would be fully appreciated. If we had a moment to spare, he would be happy to show us around: 'When the Americans left, they presented us with a bowling-alley. It's in the basement. Let's start there.'

I excused myself. There were a few places I wanted to revisit on my own. Dr Brunel winked: 'You are a sentimentalist, I see.' 'He gets overwrought,' said mother. But I slipped away.

There were muslin drapes in the parlour and the old sofa was gone. A young woman in a starched white uniform was arranging flowers and putting lotto cards on the tables.

I went upstairs, sick with loneliness and desire. I prayed, in absurd hope, that she would be in her room, that I would hear her voice once more, and touch my face to her dark hair. She would turn from the window as I entered and laugh low to see me so wild and happy. I would cry out to her that since she had left me, my life was zero.

I walked towards her room and stopped. The corridor was unchanged except for the new, beige wallpaper. But I no longer remembered which door it was. I hurried up and down the hall; I counted. But it was no use; I simply did not remember. The doors stared at me vacant. I heard myself whimper like a lost dog. Then panic and wretchedness swept over me. I gripped the radiator pipes and tried to call. But bile came up in my throat. I vomited and stood over my dirt helpless. Luncheon music sounded from the garden.

I came down the stairs, still dizzy. The cake had been cut and was being handed out on flowered plates. My mother was deep in conversation, her hand on another lady's arm. She turned to me, the small lines around her chin crinkling with pleasure: 'Come over here,

Bunny. I've met someone who remembers all about you. She's told me the sweetest things. What a small boy you still were.'

I stood rooted. Madame Alice had grown plump and there was a blue sheen in her hair. She set down her plate and billowed towards me in a profuse print dress: '*Cher ami!* How lovely to see you! How perfectly lovely. I knew you would come back one day to visit me. I said it to Dr Brunel. He never contradicts; he's a dear. And why did you never tell me about your *maman*? *Elle est charmante!* Come here, you wicked young man. I've got something for you.'

She held before her a parcel festooned with ribbon. Through the cellophane, I saw the inkstand, and desperate Psyche, her wings outflung in never-ending sorrow.

'It's for you, *mon petit*, in remembrance.'

Perhaps I uttered a cry. Everyone in the room suddenly looked up and mother called my name sharply. Then I began running.

Sweet Mars

1

The amorist loves London in June. Your true lover is a November man. When the air is grey to the breath. And the armada of houses tugs at its mooring, as if the winter gust of the sea were in the streets, and the salt spray in the stripped gardens. Nowhere else in the world, in the smoke-light of a winter evening, does the harvest lie so close-packed, of the past, of the present hurry of mind and footstep. The rain draws its curtain in Talbot Close; the undersea lights go on in Cheyne Walk; and the wind carries the savour of the Smithfield stalls across the dark of St Bartholomew's. At the quick edge of night, the gulls pass indifferent from the spars of the ships riding off Limehouse quay to the inland masts of the steeples. The trains run empty between White-chapel and Holborn, and the City is left to its bells. If you want to hear silence breathe, stop in Princess and Poultry Yard after the last jobber has gone home.

Or to his club. London is a city against women. Full of burrows down which foxes vanish. But there are chinks in the curtains on Brook Street and St James's, and on a November evening the lights make a dim, golden stain in the wet fog, as if someone had spilled a Barsac on to a grey rug. Which simile begins our story.

A Barsac would have been unlikely at the C. Rather a hock for eight shillings. It had once been a club of some lustre. New members were shown Palmerston's chair and a brace of silver-mounted shoe-brushes presented by Kipling. But the C. had been damaged in the blitz and funds were lacking to rebuild the top floor or replace the cut-glass chandeliers in the smoking-room. Dust had bitten deep, and the lift had moods. Older members, reluctant to affront the stairs, along whose worn banister Swinburne was said to have rubbed his cat's paw, had to be extricated fairly regularly by means of a stepladder kept in the porter's glass cage.

To stay afloat, the C. had opened its doors widely at the end of the war. Men were taken in who would not normally have been considered. It sufficed to have held a commission in an acceptable branch of the service (and the net was cast wide to include the Royal Catering Corps), and to be able to pay the admission fee of twenty-five guineas. Thinking they would want to stay in touch, that they might want a place in which to drink in the old way – bottoms up, chin-chin, here's to you, boy – a crowd of younger men had joined. They wore their suits like tunics and whistled in the urinals. Frequently the bar ran out of whisky, and the Library Committee had to remind junior members that the *Church Times* was not intended primarily for sanitary uses.

In 1949, the C. had enough of a surplus to replace the charred wainscoting in the billiard room with a pastel motif. But strangely, a smell of ash and burnt plaster lingered in odd corners of the house.

Soon the younger men drifted out of war and into the morass of life, to Croydon, to Sevenoaks, to the modern flat and the children come too soon. The club sank back into its torpor, and on most winter evenings, when he would gaze from his perch in the chill entrance foyer towards the darting shimmer of the sitting-room fire, Pritchard, the head-porter, would know, unthinking, whose legs protruded out of the hollow of the chairs. F., a colonel from the *other* war, the real war, DSO at Mons, and a collector of Arthur Symons first editions; T. Raisley (*not* Nicholas, his younger brother, whom Pritchard had seen as a boy, in the summer before Passchendaele); S.R., a City man, a Jew, but who had captained the Brigade of Guards golf team; Geoffrey Carr, who had done the first north face on the Pico Verde, and then lost his right leg in a car smash; and Ted Hobhouse, a sodden, unkempt brute of a man, a novelist botched, now a critic who wrote with a broken bottle – twice asked to resign from the club for having insulted other members and relieved himself in the umbrella stand, but readmitted for the growl of his wit. And Pritchard would set his feet delicately against the guard of his small electric fire, and doze off to the chime of the clock, far off in the dim of the stairs.

But not on the third Tuesday of the month. Having attached the notice in its copperplate script, *Reserved for Private Party*, to the knob of the smoking-room door, Pritchard would return to his perch, alert, or relieve the Desert Fathers of their duffle-coats and scarves as they came in out of the cold. Ten or a dozen ex-officers who had known each other during the war. Who gathered, once a month between October and May, to dine with mock ceremony and drink a toast to the accompaniment of a private limerick. Sometimes they sang, loud or embarrassed behind the muffling door. When they left, suddenly distant from each other, to flag a taxi or catch the last tube at Green Park, Pritchard would see them out. If there was glass broken, there might be a pound note from Major Reeve.

Reeve was secretary and master spirit. Pritchard had always supposed that the Desert Fathers were his invention. But Reeve denied it. ('This was Gerald Maune's idea; Gerald thought of it. I'm only the sod who collects the dues and worries about breakage. Maune likes to talk about the war, you know. Misses it.') Reeve was a tall man with spare, exact motions. He wore his hair long, flung back, and his face had a carved elegance, the shadows in the right place, the mouth agile. He had tawny eyes and the habit of looking away, into private laughter, when challenged. There seemed to be between him and Maune a companionship so intense, so joined at the root, that Pritchard could hardly imagine the one without the other.

It had been that way at school. Maune had come to Brackens terrified. He was strong and easy at games, but small of stature. He was found out as having three older sisters who giggled and a commanding mother, who appeared at unpredictable intervals and walked up and down the courtyard talking to the housemaster in a fierce whisper. For some occult reason – Gerald never forgot the fact, but its tangled, sadistic motive escaped him – he came to be called Chloë. When the pack was after him, it would shout, 'Chloë, Chloë,' in a wild treble which would still make him sweat when he thought of it.

Reeve was house-prefect and unpopular for his abrupt, jeering manner. He was thought too clever by half, but played rugger with nervy grace. Maune marvelled at his serenity and worshipped. One morning, after a night's fracas, someone having strung all the chamber-pots to a clothes-line and pulled them past the Master's bedroom window, the lower school was marshalled on the rugger field and made to run the cinder track in shorts. Maune had a toothache and had lain hot and shivering much of the night. It was drizzling and the sudden cold stung his bowels. He tried to put on a brisk canter but started falling behind. He was nauseated to the bone. A prefect came behind the small boys riding hard on a bicycle. It was Reeve. Maune looked back, sickened and out of breath. For an instant, he saw Reeve's face come alight with a strange, covert tenderness, and the eyes were fixed on his as if to hold him steady. Then he stumbled and passed out.

Reeve had come to see him in the infirmary. He had enclosed Maune's wrist in his supple fingers and left a small book, with a dark blue cover and gilt spine. 'You will find some jolly stuff in there.' It was an edition of Macaulay's *Lays*, and Maune had it with him still, fifteen years later, in his kit in the Libyan desert.

The story of how Captain Maune lost and recovered that kit under the fire of German mortars during the evacuation of Tobruk was known to all the Desert Fathers. When drunk or coaxed, Gerald would retell it with increasing embellishment. Half a mile out of the burning city, he discovered he had left his bed-roll behind. Though mines were going up with an evil thud, he threaded his way back to the cellar where he had been quartered. He extricated the bulky roll from dust and fallen girders. He was only part-way across open ground when a German patrol nosed out of the blazing rubble. He lunged into a desperate, crouching sprint. At that moment the roll of toilet paper jammed in his kit came loose and trailed behind. Instead of shooting, the Germans doubled over with laughter and shouted encouragement. The company of Greenjackets who were covering the retreat looked up from their gunsights to see what was going on. They too began laughing. It was only when he lurched, choking and exhausted, into a fox-hole, that Gerald saw fluttering behind him, like a chevalier's pennon defiant to the wind, the long trail of paper. That night, in the shelter of the half-tracks at Wadi Haraph, he unpacked his kit and made certain the Macaulay was safe.

After his release from the school infirmary, Maune sought out Reeve. They grew inseparable. Reeve's parents had parted under circumstances the boy depicted as mysterious and sordid. Soon he spent most of his holidays at Maune's house in Richmond. The three girls pecked around him like demure herons, and Mrs Maune was enchanted that her 'nervous little man' had made so handsome a friend. One August they went sailing off the Norfolk coast. Their sloop ran on to a sand-bar and the sea hammered at it in an ugly, yellow froth. Maune never forgot how Reeve turned to him and said, clear into the wind, 'If we drown here they'll never find our bodies,' or the pulse of delight that rose in him when he heard the words. Reeve won an exhibition to Magdalen, and Gerald followed a year later. One October night, in 1938, they stood together in the garden, looking back at the still tower, its blackness heavier than the night air. Unthinking, they clasped hands and swore they would take life at the full. And Reeve said, 'C'est le partage de minuit.'

But that pressure of the real, which Gerald strove for, came crass and unbidden.

He had gone hiking in the Cotswolds and came to a pub near Long Compton drenched. The girl who worked at the bar took him upstairs and told him to strip off his clothes so she could hang them by the kitchen grate. Her voice had a warm edge and Gerald felt his skin prickle. After a few minutes she came back into the room, dark and loud with the lash of rain. She was carrying a pot of tea and a jigger of rum. Gerald huddled on the bed, wrapped in a towel and sweater. She asked him whether he had caught a chill and poured the tea. The abrupt heat made him shiver. 'It's a rub you'll be needing.' Her hands passed over him like her voice, heavy and near. She found the nerve of him and the darkness of the room hammered at his throat. He turned and touched her breast. 'You're a quick one, aren't you? There. There now. Don't be mussing my hair. It's your first time, isn't it?' And she had laughed with a low, queer warmth, seeing him so wild.

They had not met the next morning and when the letter came, two months later, Gerald stared at the signature perplexed. 'You've got me into a spot of trouble. Bad trouble. I'll meet you in front of the Lamb and Flag tomorrow at six. I hope you're keeping well. Very sincerely. Ina.'

She was waiting, her mouth sullen. She was damned sorry. But there it was. More than a month gone. No, there could be no mistake. She had been to see a doctor in Birmingham. She had told her aunt. He would like her aunt. She was a real sport. She had said to Ina, 'Don't fret so, duck, he'll do the right and true thing by you.'

They were walking through the Parks in the dead smell of early winter. 'You will do the right thing, won't you love?' She slipped her arm into his. 'I'm not a tart, you know.' He was choking with fear and misery. She taunted softly: 'You were a bit livelier that night, weren't you love?' Oh, she knew all about what the nice young ladies at Oxford did when accidents happened. Had it taken care of in London or abroad. Have an abortion? Not bloody likely. It made her retch to think of it. Let some filthy brute of a Jew-doctor put his hands on her? There'd be none of that, Mr Maune. Yes, she had seen his name (a sweet name she thought it was) and college when he registered at the pub. The sooner they got settled the better. He didn't want everyone to know she was in a family way, did he? She'd have to hurry along now. 'I'll meet you here again next Friday. It's my afternoon off. And we can have a spot of dinner together. Take me to the George, won't you. I hear they do a smashing dinner. Be a sweet, won't you love?' At the gate of the Parks she kissed his cheek and breathed in his ear: 'Maybe we'll go somewhere. Afterwards. It doesn't matter. Not now, love. Ina Maune. I think it sounds super.' He tore away, appalled.

The next days were a nightmare. His whole world lay splintered. The years of school, the proud hopes, the compact with life made under Magdalen tower, all gone to nothing, to this hideous, vulgar trap. The thought of thrusting such a creature on his mother was unbearable. He loathed the sight of her, the rough, wet smell of her hair, the dabs of rouge on her chafed skin. He could kill himself. He would settle his account at Blackwell's, write his tutor a note suggesting he found university work too stiff, and do away with himself. The notion of living with the woman and her child in some rathole was far worse.

After taking his decision, Gerald felt at peace. It was morning and he walked through Christ Church meadows strangely elated. The sky was immensely high and the ground sang with frost. A white mist came off the river, and the early sun pierced through. A thrush stood in the wet grass and rose away from Gerald in a slow arc. He exulted at the silence and the mounting fire of the light. Then he strode home and fell into an utter sleep.

But when he woke, the foul stupidity of the thing closed on him. Every nerve cried out that there must be a way, an escape. He would simply leave, drop out of life, change his name, hover about in hiding until the whole sordid affair had blown over. He would go far away. The name Valparaiso trotted through his brain in an absurd jig. Other men had got women pregnant and not had their lives smashed. It was hideously unfair. Other men slept with girls as if they were cracking nuts. It had been his first time. Why had he stopped at the place, why had he let her come into the room when he was naked and feverish? Maune turned desperately in his cage. Then he went to Merton chapel, knelt and touched the altar rail. Sixteen times. The number was his talisman. After the sixteenth time he would wake, and the whole thing would pass from him like a vile dream. He performed the rite with furtive passion. But he came into the light helpless.

Friday came inexorable, and he hurried to see Reeve. Reeve glanced up when he burst into the room: 'Crikey. Do you have malaria? You look like the mother of death. Have a drink.' Gerald poured out his misery; even to himself he stank of fear and lack of sleep. His legs were shaking. Reeve surged out of his cavernous chair and stood over him: 'You nit! You little nit! You've really gone and buggered yourself, haven't you. Jesus, how could you be so bloody stupid! Just look at you.' Gerald remembered a whipping he had had in school. Reeve's contempt made his eyes water. Then, as quickly as it had blazed, Reeve's charring anger dropped. He spoke very quietly: 'You're not going to see the girl. You're not to go anywhere near her. Do you hear me? I will. She's probably lying. She's trying to put a bite on you. Crummy tart. I'll give her five pounds and tell her we'll call the police if she shows her face again.'

'What if she's telling the truth?'

'Just leave it to me, boy. I know where she can get fixed up.'

An obscure, bewildering pain stirred in Gerald. But he was too grateful, too burnt out to say anything. Reeve left him crumpled on the sofa, asleep.

When he awoke, the shilling had dropped in the gas meter and the air was bitter cold. But Gerald's body was full of sweat, and hearing the tower bell strike seven across the dark, chill quad, he cried out in the empty room. The minutes crept over his skin and he shivered till he thought he would break. Loud as his own pulse he heard Reeve's footsteps, across the echoing flagstones and up the unlit stairs. For a maddening instant, Reeve seemed to pause on the landing, then he entered. Gerald rose at him, his teeth on edge.

'You gave me a start. I thought you'd gone home. You look a fearful mess. And there's no need to stare at me like a lunatic. You can get off your knees now. She's gone. Lost and gone for ever.' And he hummed the tune under his breath.

Gerald was choking for air: 'What happened? What did she say? For God's sake, tell me.'

Reeve crouched by the gate and brought the flame to a slow, exact hiss: 'I tell you, everything's all right. Forget about it.'

'But I want to know. Is she going to have something done to her? Did she want to see me?'

Reeve turned, breaking the used match between his nails: 'You worry too much. That's your trouble, Maune. You worry too much.' And he came near: 'You asked me to take care of it, didn't you? You came in here shaking so bad I thought you were going to puke your guts out all over the bloody rug. You were on your knees for help. Well it's over and done with. No fuss no muss no babies born. Fair enough? Now leave off, boy, I'm telling you, just leave off.'

Gerald caught a queer note in Reeve's voice, as of envy. Then relief welled up in him, uncontrollable: 'My God, Reeve. I'm so grateful.' He grasped Reeve's hand: 'You don't know what this was doing to me. You can't know. I was going to kill myself.' He gave a loud, sad laugh. 'I was going to kill myself. I'd got a note ready for old Tyson. And one for you. You don't believe me, do you? But I swear it's true. I couldn't face it. Kill myself. Can you imagine? But I'm never going to be such an idiot again, never.' He began dancing through the room. 'Let's get pissed. Let's get so bloody pissed they'll have to float us home!'

'You're on,' said Reeve.

They sat at the Trout, dangling their feet over the parapet. They had had six pints and it was near closing time. Reeve blew the foam from the rim of his glass. He was outwardly sober, but curiously alert, as if there were voices in the river. Gerald was swaying in a soft stupor; happiness had loosened his nerves. Between draughts, he gulped the cold taste of the night and the rank scent of river-grass. Part of him was drifting into thick sleep, but still he laughed to find the gates of life open again.

Then he heard Reeve asking, as from far off, 'Do you know there's going to be a war? You believe that guff about Munich, do you? There's going to be a war, Maune, and I'm going down to London to see about a commission.'

'Are you?' said Gerald, and then with bleary tenderness, 'Are you really? I say. That's rather grand.'

Reeve shook him by the shoulder: 'You're blind as a newt. You're absolutely stinko. We'd better get a move on.'

Gerald laboured to his feet and saw the world was on a tilt: 'Is there really going to be a war? I think you're just trying to confuse me. That's what you're trying to do. Confuse me.' He stumbled gently against the table.

Above the churn of the weir, the peacocks shrilled their naked cry. Reeve was standing on top of the parapet and calling to the loud tumble of water, 'I tell you, boy, there's going to be a war. Any day now. And mark my word: it's going to be the biggest and best war ever!'

2

It was. The finest hour. Full of the ceremony of death. But also a high holiday for the living. Away from school and spinach. A time in the half-light, when one's flabby shadow took on the airs of a hawk, and one mattered. All of a sudden, to oneself and to others in the complicity of the mad game. When women said yes, in covert places, because men carried about them, like a sweet, unnerving scent, the claims of death. Because pity makes one's bowels hot. A time when strangers locked arms and sang in a common sweat. When chartered accountants grew sunburnt and grocery clerks looked tersely at the moon. A vacation from paper towels and blocked drains, from Sunday afternoons at Woking, and the office party. Some met Dante on a roof-top in Russell Square, coming out of the voice of the smoke; others saw the glow of a cigarette in the shadow of a hangar, and a girl in a tunic saying, 'Keep well.' A time when a man found himself asked and able to do things he had never dreamed of, in intricate, murderous machines, behind antennae and code-books, under the white hammer of the Libyan sun, or in the cockpit of the sea. A time when he could do them in bed, and found a friend in the mirror. Sweet Mars. It was not like the one before, with its rats, and gas-stench, and eternity of mud. If you weren't a civilian blitzed or shovelled into the camps, if you could stay out of Burma or the Murmansk convoys, it was a good war. And hard to come home from.

Major Duncan Reeve had a distinguished record in Intelligence, first in the Mediterranean, later as a liaison specialist in France. He was awarded the DSO in 1944. War's end found him in Hamburg. He tried to settle in England, but drifted about loathing its grey virtue. In 1946, he decamped to America on the strength of a vague contract as publisher's reader and the chance of writing as a stringer for the *Yorkshire Post* (he had met editors and correspondents in the corps, and they had told him there was always an opening for a man with a quick eye).

He bought a third-hand Pontiac, a typewriter in a red plastic case, and *The Leaves of Grass*. Then he set out across America. In the evenings, and off the road during the heat of the day, under a sky flung wide and wasteful as it never is over England, Reeve wrote a novel. About the war and the comely dead. He was uncertain whether it should be acrid or mournful; but racing down the green canyon to Salt Lake City, he hit on a title: *Chariot over Jordan*. He scrawled it across page one of the manuscript and blew smoke into the air, exultant. Sometimes he said it to himself out loud.

It was in a dinette, on the South Side of Chicago, that the girl heard him and turned smiling. She had wide, pale features, sumptuous black eyes, and wore the honeycomb of her hair cut close like a boy. She was dressed in a man's shirt and tailored slacks. The heavy Mexican brooch at her throat caught the light, and Reeve laughed at her cigarette holder, with its long lacquered stem. She was like something out of an Aztec version of the flappers.

'I am Vivianne,' (she insisted on the French spelling, though she came from the East Side of New York), 'who are you?'

They went to the Beehive and ate pizza, sauntered through Lincoln Park under the yellow eyes of the cops, and stood by the lake shore watching the red pulse of light over the steel mills in Gary.

She made her eyes wide: 'I don't like the name Duncan. It tastes like a crunchy-bar. I want you to be called Siegfried Sassoon.' She sang it out across the lake: 'Siegfried. Siegfried. Isn't it a gorgeous name? It makes me all cold inside. *Ici*.'

'I entirely agree,' said Duncan. 'I can't understand why I haven't changed before.'

'But you are a hero, aren't you?'

'I certainly am. All Sassoons are heroes. Come home and I'll show you my citations.'

'Kiss me before we go.'

'No, not here.' It was their first quarrel.

She said she was an art student and had done modelling. She was writing a poem in heroic couplets entitled 'The Lesbian's Lament' and recited Baudelaire at breakfast. Maman came from an old French family, but had married a bum who had drunk himself to death in Scranton, Pennsylvania. Duncan listened to her tales with complete disbelief and total trust. Whatever Vivianne said, had in it the truth of the moment. Her imagination could not lie; she wore it naked.

They drove westward and he finished the novel in a motel near Lake Tahoe. She dared him to go in the icy water and stood on the bank, suddenly frightened, as the cold knocked the wind out of him. Then back east to make the round of the publishers and pick up some money lecturing about the war. Sometimes they would drive the night through and spend the whole day in a hotel room. Vivianne registered as Siegfried and Siegmund Sassoon, or as Mr and Mrs John Katz, of St Agnes, Hampstead. ('I am sure that was his real name. Who ever heard of anyone called Keats?') When Reeve lectured – his best performance dealt with Arnhem: 'Was it Espionage that Betrayed our Gallant Force?' – Vivianne sat in the last row, behind the gorgon ladies with their blue-tinted hair, waited for moments of high pathos, and made ribald faces. 'You are a fraud, aren't you, *chéri*? I hope you didn't put that crap in the novel.'

They got married the day *Chariot over Jordan* was accepted. They drove across the bridge to Hudson County and Vivianne insisted on paying the Judge of the Peace an extra ten dollars so they could take along his rubber plant.

'Did you see what was embroidered on the antimacassar?' asked Vivianne. ' "May Jesus bless Your first caress And make each kiss A fount of bliss." Isn't it beautiful? Isn't it just beautiful?'

Reeve laughed, but she was crying, and when he bent close to stroke her golden boy's hair, she gave him a startled, remote look. He felt suddenly very tired, and instead of pushing on to open country, they decided to spend the night in Trenton.

The hotel had a sour smell and the neon signs slashed through the venetian blinds. Chewing the soggy toast in the cafeteria, Duncan thought with abrupt hunger, 'I must get back to Europe and a piece of real bread.' Vivianne said she wanted to go upstairs, 'but give me half an hour. And don't put on that silly, supercilious smile. This is our wedding night. It's different. Or hadn't you noticed?'

She was sitting on the bed in a thing lacy and ephemeral.

'Let's have a drink,' said Reeve, 'I'll ring the bellhop and tell him to bring us some whisky and a bucket of ice.'

'No. I don't want anyone else to come into the room. Not tonight. Please.'

For a long time, he stood by the window.

'Won't you come to bed?'

The flashes of neon cut across the dank wallpaper.

'Look, Vi, don't be mad at me. It's just no good here. The place is too god-damned ugly. Just look at it. Just look out the window. I've never seen anything so bloody awful. Look at those signs. They keep the bloody things on all night. "Serutan. Spells nature's backwards." It does. Nature's backwards. My God, it does! I'm sorry, sweet, but I'm going to have that drink if it's the last thing I do.'

She was very still until the bellhop came. Then she leaped up on the bed, kicked her heels at the ceiling and cried out, 'May Jesus bless Your first caress And make each kiss A fount of bliss.' Louder and louder.

'Stop it, Vi, stop it! This isn't a god-damned whore-house. It just smells like one. Now stop it!'

But she wouldn't, and after the Negro boy retreated, with a frightened grin, Reeve slapped her hard.

They took an apartment in Greenwich Village. When the basement laundromat started up, the floor shook and Vivianne declaimed Empson on earthquakes. Reeve taught French in night-school, tried to sell articles about his travels in America, and hammered at a second novel. But even as he wrote, he knew the thing was strangely inert. The edge of feeling had gone out of his work; it wore thin over the exits and alarms of his daily life.

A year passed.

His marriage seemed to move from quarrel to quarrel like an electric arc. But the reconciliations were worse, great gusts of pardon and intimacy which left him hollow. Vivianne had gone back to modelling and came home frayed and restless from the long hours of tense poise under the lights. The good times came before dawn, in the unsteady silence of the Square, when they perched on the rim of the fountain, too drowsy to play on each other's nerves.

Chariot over Jordan was published in the fall. For the first ten days, Reeve bought all the newspapers and magazines unashamed. There was no mention of the book. He and Vivianne circled each other in silence. She knew his hurt and it made her raw, as if he were sitting in the room with no clothes on. A week later she came quickly up the stairs: 'There's a notice in the *Village Voice*.'

'Have you read it?'

She lied: 'No,' and handed him the paper. He took it and turned to the window. He read it to himself, then aloud, in a dead tone: 'This first novel, by an English author now living in the Village, sets out with high intentions. Using the war in the desert as an allegory of the larger struggle between reality and dreams, between the quest for solitude and the demands of love, Duncan Reeve asks that we judge his work by high standards. Unfortunately, he has bitten off more than he can chew. There are patches of lyric prose which betray the obvious influence of Malcolm Lowry, and a few flashes of sardonic wit. But as a whole, the book is pretentious and lifeless. It gives the impression of being the work of an old man, gone sour, rather than of a first novel by a young writer who still has everything to learn about his trade.'

For a time Reeve said nothing, but stared at the paper as if it were a living thing. Then, folding it carefully and throwing it away, he remarked, as to himself, 'I haven't read Malcolm Lowry.'

She watched him pour the drinks and started towards the light-switch.

'No. I don't want any light. Not just yet.'

So they sat in the heavy dark and drank.

'Poor sweet. Perhaps you are an old man. Perhaps that's what's happened to us. They've found us out. The chariot isn't swinging low. It's left the station. *Pauvre vieux*.'

It was her own voice, but she did not remember saying it. He got up and she thought she could hear his fists close. He picked up the pages of manuscript on his desk and tore the sheet that was in the typewriter. Then he went to the bathroom. She heard the toilet flush and gurgle mournfully, and flush again. His misery made her spine cold. When he came into the room, she said in a stage whisper, 'I'm Hedda Gabler. I've destroyed my child.' Reeve bent over her, his breath stale with whisky: 'You're not Hedda Gabler. You're just a bitch.'

A few weeks later, Reeve asked Vivianne to come home with him to England. When she said, 'No,' he knew she was right. Being modern, they decided to part friends. Vivianne was keeping the apartment and Reeve asked her to forward the mail. They went for a cup of coffee in the corner drugstore.

'I hope things work out for you, Duncan. You know that's true, don't you?'

He nodded.

'And you'll think of me sometimes. I wasn't a bitch all the time, was I? You remember when you said I was your golden boy. "But golden lads and girls all must Like chimney-sweepers, come to dust." Those are marvellous lines, aren't they? They're so marvellous I don't think I can bear it. Who wrote them?'

'Siegfried Sassoon.'

He stared down at his knuckles. He felt her hand on his shoulder.

'Look Vi, shouldn't we give it one more chance? Just one. I mean . . .'

Then she was gone.

Reeve stood at the railing as the liner entered Southampton Water in the grey of a March evening. He was chilled to the bone, and wondered why England was the coldest place on earth, colder than Labrador or Queen Maud Land in the white Antarctic, cold with a thousand years of damp. The ship moved slowly between the anti-submarine booms, the radar-towers and camouflaged caissons. Reeve could see the broad gashes burnt by the raids in the Southampton waterfront. The houses stood small and huddled against the cold green of the hills. A plume of soot drifted over the water and across the pale bar of twilight. Reeve felt trapped. Why is the place so ugly, so cowed, like a cat gone rotten in the teeth? What am I doing here? Panic swept over him, and the impulse to return to America at once, as soon as he could beg or pilfer the passage money. Three years since the war ended. And you'd think the place had been blitzed last night. My God, we love our wounds.

Reeve flinched at the bored, clipped tones of the customs officials in the wet gloom of the shed. He went out in the street, with its charred walls and rain-puddles, aching for a drink. He had forgotten about licensing hours and found the pubs closed. He took refuge from the downpour in the parlour of a small hotel. An odour of floor-wax and gas-burners, of aspidistra and bacon rind enveloped him. Reeve asked whether he could have a meal. The girl's voice was triumphant with denials: 'I'm very sorry, Sir, but we don't do suppers. Not at *this* hour.' 'Do you know of any other place around here?' 'I'm sure I don't.' She waited in austere scorn. 'How about a pot of tea?' 'I'll see if the kettle's on. We don't usually do teas, not after supper, you know.' 'My God,' said Reeve under his breath, and stared with utmost concentration at the framed lithograph of King George V, *Our Sailor King*. The bearded personage behind whom vague dreadnoughts were firing at a vacant sea, stared back. 'And a pack of Player's, if you would Miss.' Now Reeve remembered that matches had to be extracted from a box marked *Dr Barnardo's Homes. Thank You*. He fumbled in his pocket and found nothing but an American dime. The girl's stony eye watched him as he turned away and crushed the unlit cigarette in his palm.

The need to hear a living voice rose in him like a dizzy spell. He had lost touch with Maune. They had met in Alexandria during the war, and Reeve recalled, with distaste, Gerald's unguarded enchantment, the candid, nearly vulgar pleasure he seemed to take of life and the new intimacies war had brought. They had drifted apart. But now Reeve experienced an intense longing for their old trust. A childish relief went through him when he found the name in the directory: Gerald Maune, 12 Hillcrest Lane, London, SE19. He remembered to push Button A, but was utterly, absurdly taken aback to hear a woman's voice. 'Mrs Maune speaking. Who is it? Who is it, please?'

Reeve said his name and the voice took on a brisk cheeriness. 'How lovely to hear from you! What a surprise this will be for Gerald. He speaks of you often. I feel I know a lot about you. I'm Sheila Maune. Yes, we've been married two years. Let me see, more actually, twenty-six months. We did send you an announcement. I know we did. Didn't it catch up with you?'

Now Reeve remembered, vaguely, the little envelope and rustle of silk paper which he had glanced at, amid a pile of letters and circulars, when driving through Phoenix, Arizona, or was it at the San Francisco post office?

'Where are you? When will you be in London? How marvellous! You must come and look us up right away. Gerald is out, but I know how anxious he'll be to see you. How about Monday night? No, wait half a second. Make it Tuesday, could you? Do you know how to get out here? It isn't too bad once you get on the right tube. It's going to be grand meeting you after hearing so much about you. Just wait till I tell Gerald.'

Reeve had a few minutes to spare before the London train. He walked out of the station to look at the harbour. He could see nothing, only the black downpour, and far away, the blink of a lighthouse. He buttoned his collar, but the cold lurked inside.

3

The Maune flat was brisk Scandinavian. Two Braque prints on the living-room wall. A Danish travel-poster showing a family of improbable ducklings halting traffic in a crowded street, Vivaldi's *Four Seasons* on the record player, and the Penguins on the bookshelf. Momentarily, Reeve toyed with the idea that he was back in the Village, or visiting friends on Morningside Heights. But as Sheila set down the sherry and tired biscuits, he knew he was home.

She was small in stature but strong-boned, with rather heavy features. He was struck by a low, rough-edged quality in her voice. Gerald had gotten heavier, and the years in the desert seemed to have reddened his skin. He had a boisterous laugh which Reeve had not known before, and a trick of drumming on the table with his knuckles.

He was delighted to find Reeve again, and they stood clasping hands like victorious schoolboys.

'We'd given you up for lost, you know. Gone for a Burton.'

'Only America.'

'Same thing, I imagine. Gone for ever. It's grand having you back. You *are* back for good now, aren't you? You won't run out on the old place again, will you?'

'I don't know. I've just come back. Give a chap a breather. I've lost touch.'

'A fair number of people are thinking of going to America,' said Sheila, 'more of a chance all around. It must be odd coming back. Don't you find things drab here, and a bit mildewed? You know what I mean, as if they'd been in the wash too often and had never had a proper airing.'

'One does feel that a bit. I keep looking for lights to switch on. As if the whole place were having a power cut. It's grey.'

Gerald laughed and turned on a large Chinese lamp in the corner.

'We got it at Primavera's,' said Sheila, 'one of our first splurges.' She poured more sherry: 'Don't you think you'll miss it? America, I mean. We're terribly run down. It's beginning to smell like a rooming-house we used to go to in Eastbourne. They'd never let daylight in. Not since Prince Albert passed by. It was a funny smell, lavender and cabbage.'

'You do exaggerate,' said Gerald, looking at her with plump ease.

'There *are* things I'm going to miss. Fiercely. The size. I don't see how you can put it in words really. But America is so big. There's enough sky for everybody. We had a spot of sun this morning, you remember? I was walking in Green Park and looked up. Suddenly I had the queerest feeling, that I shouldn't look too long, that I was taking more than my fair share. As if they'd rationed the whole place. A shilling's worth of sun, a coupon's worth of lawn, half a pint of sea air from Ramsgate, and oranges for the kiddies. And no cheating. Coming up from Southampton, I kept staring at the houses. They'd all shrunk. There's so much room in America. Here I'd worry about gunning the car; I might go right over the edge.' He sipped the flat sherry, and memory came on him with ironic force: 'I was driving north from Boston last October. The sky was so blue it made your eyes blink, and I turned into a stretch of wood. The maple-leaves were red;

not rust-red, but deep flame-red. The air had a tang of wood and sea in it as if the world had just begun. Every time I took a breath it was like neat whisky. I had to stop the car. It made my bones sing. And the way American women walk. You know, as if they had a wind at their back.'

'We have thick ankles,' said Sheila, 'it keeps us steady when the deck rolls. Seriously, what made you come back? It all sounds too marvellous.'

Reeve knew she was jabbing: 'Oh, lots of reasons. I don't really know, I suppose. But it isn't all peaches and cream. There are things you can't have in America.'

'Draught Bass,' said Gerald.

They laughed, but Sheila kept alert, trying to mark the real drift. When Reeve began telling them, she leaned forward immensely interested.

'You see, I got married over there. And it didn't work out.' He told them the story, or parts of it. In an odd way, he found it fascinating. He hadn't, in fact, heard it before. His voice gave it a peculiar distance. 'I dare say that's the real reason I came home.'

After due silence, Gerald said, 'Have another drink.' He said it a little too loud, and flushed.

Sheila vanished. Then they heard her call, 'Supper's on.' As Reeve passed into the small dining-room, Gerald went over to the lamp and switched it off.

'I've done all the talking. What about you?' Reeve listened intently. Failure had left him raw. But already, as he set them in the apology and composure of the past tense, America and the ruin of his marriage seemed to grow less urgent. Listening to Gerald and cutting the potatoes which Sheila served from a bone-china tureen, Reeve felt ground under his feet. Gerald's words, which meant either more or less than was actually being said, were deeply familiar. He recognized their exact pitch. He had found the flat candour of American speech marvellously exciting; but he settled back, as after a hard run, into the old semitones.

'I work on *The Real Estate Chronicle*. We're the biggest in the trade, you know. We've got a new press in south London that can turn out colour stuff as good as any in France. I write for the paper on and off. But my job's the research department. Looking into the history of

252

properties, trying to forecast trends, advising clients about local regulations and county councils. I'm on the road a good deal. As much, in fact, as I'm in the office. That's how I met Sheila. There was a block of freeholds up for auction on the edge of the New Forest, and I went down to have a look. Sheila was on holiday in Lyndhurst.'

'Cursing myself, the rain, and the treacle. Gerald came into the hotel bar and dropped his papers all over the floor. He looked so stuffy and angry that I couldn't help laughing. He was down on all fours and looked up as if he was going to bite my head off. Then he came over and we met.'

Gerald poured the wine. 'God bless,' said Reeve. It was tame claret but made him feel easy.

'It's not a line of work I've ever thought about. I don't suppose I ever thought about anything very practical while the war was on. I happened to be in Tunis when the show ended, trying to get a mob of prisoners sorted out. Chap I knew in the Quartermaster's office – older man – asked me what I was going to do after I got out of the army. I told him I hadn't made any plans. I must have imagined the old war would never end. Go on until they put me on retirement pay. He told me to look him up when I got back to London. I didn't at first. I couldn't get used to things. You know, ordinary things.'

Reeve noticed Sheila's hand poised, very still, on the stem of her glass.

'I tried to get a rest at home, but Mother drove me crazy. Every time I tried to tell her anything, about how it had been and why I was all wound up and bashed inside, she looked at me with an air of frantic interest, and I knew she wasn't listening to a word. There was no one I could talk to. And I had all sorts of wild dreams.'

'What about?' Sheila had gone to the kitchen, and had turned on the water with a loud spurt.

'You know, things I'd seen or heard chaps talking about. One in particular. It kept coming back. It must have been a few miles outside Benghazi. An eighty-eight had hit one of our tanks full-on, and the bloody thing caught fire. I don't suppose I was more than a hundred yards away. I heard the man in charge – I knew who it was, Welshman with blue eyes that didn't quite match – telling the crew, very steadily, not to panic, that they'd climb out of the turret. But the shell must have bent or fused the hinges. They couldn't get it open, and the rear port-hole was full of burning oil. So he called for help, saying please, all calm. We tried to get near, but the sand was going black under the heat, and the plates were buckling. So they began screaming. Like men trying to scream to other men. They were roasting alive by inches. Then their voices changed. They sounded like a pack of little boys. You remember, Reeve, when they used to yell at me, "Chloë, Chloë!" Something like that. All high and crazy. But it wasn't the worst. Near the very end, when they were burning alive in there, knowing we were just outside and couldn't help, their voices stopped being human. It was like hearing a bird, when it's on the ground crippled, and the fox is near. Just an insane whine. And in the middle of it, the Welsh chap saying please, gentle-like, as if he didn't mean to inconvenience. I kept dreaming about those voices, and hearing them in odd places. When the tea-kettle started up or a train whistled.'

Even across the table and the steamy smell of greens, Reeve caught the edge of fear and sweat. But Maune took up, relaxed, as if a precarious rite had been performed.

'I larked about for a bit. Dropped in on chaps I'd known in the regiment. I sailed on the Broads for a week with a bloke from Bomber Command. Mad as a hatter. Wanted me to go into business with him, running a special kind of holiday tour for Yanks: "Come and see the ruins of Coventry. Weekend in Rotterdam. Look at what you've been missing." Then I got tired of drifting, and went to see the man in London. He turned out to be rather a big fish, and got me a berth on the *Chronicle*. I met Sheila on one of my first trips out of the office. I was lucky. I don't think it would have worked without her. I was still pretty jumpy. We had our ups and downs, I can tell you.'

'He almost didn't show up at the wedding.'

'I would have dragged him there,' said Reeve.

'God knows where you were! You never wrote a line. Not even condolences.'

Reeve lied: 'The announcement must have gone astray. Pony Express once you get past Chicago.'

'No matter,' said Gerald, 'it's good to have you back. I've missed you, you old devil.'

Sheila bustled: 'Why don't you both make yourselves useful and get out of here. I hate men hanging around when I do the dishes. Anyway, if Gerald doesn't put in an appearance at the Queen's Arms, they'll start worrying. He goes there every night.'

'Sheila, you know that's a lie!'

They bantered, and Gerald surged into the kitchen. Reeve heard Sheila catch her breath, and then a warm, smothered laugh.

The Queen's Arms was a Victorian pub, with cut-glass mirrors and stained panelling. Gerald ordered stout. He drank fast and the words spilled: 'It's going to be all right, you know. On the paper, I mean. The flat was a bit of a strain, I can tell you. I'm into the bank rather more than feels comfortable. But we're starting to put aside a little. So far as taxes allow. You'll find out soon enough; they can sweat blood out of a stone. I don't suppose it's anywhere near as bad in the States. But still, we're keeping the old head out of water. Have to. Sheila wants children. She wants them very much.'

'And you?'

'Oh, I don't know. Yes, I suppose I do. It'd be rather nice in a way.' He laughed and shook himself like a wet hen. 'But what I really want now is chaps I can talk to. Sheila's a poppet, and I don't need to tell you how fond we are of each other. You have eyes. But I often feel as if I was carrying a bloody big suitcase everywhere I go, and couldn't put it down. It's got the things inside it that made me the way I am. The things I remember happening in the war. There's no use telling anyone who hasn't been in it. They listen, all right, but they just don't hear. Not even Sheila. Am I talking rot?'

'No. I often felt that in America. They've had a war. But it's theirs. Not like ours at all.'

Gerald's voice thickened: 'That's exactly it, chum. And if everyone is going to act as if it hadn't happened, as if we'd dreamed it up on a bad stomach, I'm going to start believing them. But it's a lie. A lot of spivs who don't know what it was like and don't have any use for us.' His arm was on Reeve's shoulder: 'Mustn't let the buggers steal a man's shadow. Look silly without it.'

'Time, gentlemen, time.'

'Nice thing about American bars, they don't kick you out into the rain at ten-thirty.'

'Fuck 'em,' offered Gerald with glad rage.

'Last round. Time, gentlemen, please.'

In the cold of the street, Gerald's tone cleared: 'Sheila doesn't know this. But those dreams.'

'What about them?'

'They're back. On and off, for a while now. And you know, Reeve, a funny thing. I had the one, about the bloody tank burning, the night you rang from Southampton. Sheila told me when I came home. I was more pleased than I'd ever admit, you old bastard. But I woke in the middle of the night shaking. I could hear those screams as if they were in the room.'

'Home with you now,' said Reeve, and as he gripped Gerald by the arm he thought of the evening at the Trout, and of the golden treachery of that last summer.

4

Of Gerald's need, and of Reeve's discovery that divorce had left him lonely – it was a feeling he had never experienced before, and it jarred him – grew the Desert Fathers. Gerald had a schoolboy's pertinacity in keeping track of chums, of their whereabouts and private lives. The ease with which he conjured up out of the anonymous vast bustle of London, a dozen friends or acquaintances happy to meet once a month and share with each other memories and contempts that were becoming unreal or embarrassing to those around them, convinced Reeve that Gerald had been a remarkably competent, popular soldier. Plainly, he had been the kind of officer who hurried leave papers and covered other men's failings of exactitude or nerve. He had found the decent word in the ugly moment and made quite the best of the crude, stylized intimacies of men at war.

At first, the Tuesday nights had an uneasy casualness, everyone acting as if they had dropped in by mere chance and had to be quickly on their way. But men who have been to public schools or spent time in an officer's mess have an instinct for ceremony. Put them together, and they will, with an unspoken self-amused art, contrive rites and forms. No one seemed to remember who first ordained that evenings should end with a toast to the 'Young lady from Cairo Who always carried a Biro', or the rule of the sconce, whereby whoever missed two Tuesdays in a row had to buy port for the whole table and contribute five bob to the Limbless Ex-Service Men's Association. Pranks or habits of speech, which are puerile to an outsider, can bind. Hearing the smothered echo of Quinton Moore's delivery of 'Lili Marlene' (with new and unofficial lyrics), Pritchard would shift happily in his seat. No women, no civilians, all was well in the world.

Nearly all the members had served in the Middle East and the desert. Several had been in Gerald's mess. Reeve, who had found work in a small publishing firm, renewed acquaintance with two former colleagues in Intelligence. Each had gone his private way; but they shared a deep, unsettling awareness of the force of memories, a covert suspicion that the ballast of their lives had shifted to the past, and that they might not find again a like tautness and intensity of being. It made them nervous like a buzz in the ear.

Brian Smith had a phrase for it: 'They've gated us. They told us to go out and have a whopping rag on the town. Now they've shut us in. Welcome to the coop, chum.' His own was narrow. He had married a dry, vehement girl who did modern sculpture; now there were two spiky children. Smith had joined the reserves, and had an annual fortnight's training with the Territorials. His usual air of mournful cunning brightened at the approach of summer.

Brownlee had served in the cavalry. Nothing in his elegant, soft features and prematurely silvered hair indicated that he had taken a patrol of armoured cars through the El-Quatarah depression, that they had been cut off by sandstorms and pinned down without water, and that he had led them out, half-crazed with thirst, but without loss of a man or vehicle. Just before the war, he had married a girl somewhat older than himself and of means. He had come back to find a woman sour about the years lost and the gnawings of middle age. She strove to make up for the nights apart, but after two miscarriages there fell between the elegant, reserved man and the accusing woman a large silence. When Brownlee left the club, it was not always for home.

Moore was the only member to have been in the Brigade of Guards. Small, raffish, but gifted with a fine tenor voice and Irish lilt, he still recalled with cheery disapproval the time when he and his platoon had perched on the back of American Sherman tanks during the assault on Tunis, and had listened, appalled, to the querulous informality of exchanges between officers and enlisted men. In the Guards, a man asks leave to address an officer. But Moore was no fool. He glimpsed the merits of the other code. During the scrap in Sicily, an American company on his left had been surrounded. The ranking survivor was a Negro cook-corporal. Moore had got through to him on the wire: 'Listen to me closely, corporal, and don't panic. Are you presently in contact with the enemy? Repeat: in contact?' Back came the chocolate tones: 'In contact boss? Why, we's eyeball to eyeball!' Moore told the story with delight, against himself. He had an Irishman's lust for chaos and found peace drab. 'I feel overweight.' He was in advertising. 'It's a trade for tarts and ponces. Any advertising man would sell you his mother. In my firm they'd deliver.' Now his main pleasure was to collect wines. His need of women was furtive and occasional.

Parkins had been parachuted behind the German lines after the breakthrough at Monte Cassino. The partisan group with which he was to establish liaison had been rounded up. He himself was captured a few hours after coming down. At the Waffen-SS post, they put his head into a large vat of urine, over and over. Each time he passed out, they kicked him back alive. When he no longer stirred, they left him for dead. He had come out of the affair with a DSO and a vagueness in his eyes. He was a barrister of some note, and would have thought it intolerable to make of his experience emotional or professional capital. When his growing son proclaimed that middle-aged men who reminisced about the war were retarded Boy Scouts, Parkins said nothing. But his memories kept their cancerous hold. He found a great calm in being, from time to time, among men who could, out of their own lives, gauge the truth and quality of his hurt. Who knew that such things had happened, and that they had had some order of logic or necessity. He was senior in the club (Father of the House), and in charge of the annual dinner.

The second took place in the winter of 1951. Inevitably, the long table, with its decanters, its silver cigar- and snuff-boxes and candle-sticks, evoked a full-dress night in a regimental mess. Parkins had come early to see that all was in place. The drapes had been drawn in front of the high windows, but he could hear the brush of wet snow against the panes. He worried the black tie in his slightly frayed wing-collar, and peered again at the printed menu (engraving had been voted too costly). The Desert Fathers. Second Annual Dinner. 16 November 1951. The health of the Society to be proposed by the Father of the House: Lt. Col. R. Parkins, DSO. Mr Gerald Maune, President, will reply. *Vegetable cutlets Kiev. Boeuf braisé à l'Irelandaise* (rationing cast its shadow). But Moore had picked the wines. Couched in its silver basket, the Château Talbot reflected the tipsy flicker of the candles.

'Evening, Smith. Come in, man, you look frozen. There's Brownlee. Close the door like a good chap, will you. Let's get started on the Fino. Hullo, Simpson. I say, that's a handsome dinner jacket. I hear they're wearing them in neon-blue in America. Do join us. Or do you prefer the very dry?' Parkins poured sherry and had a last quick look at the place cards.

Moore lifted the claret out of its repose and held it fondly to the light: 'This is the real thing. Wasted on you chaps. Utterly wasted.'

Reeve came in rubbing the chill from his knuckles, followed at once by Gerald T. Wilson, Royal Artillery, late. 'As usual,' said Simpson. 'Shall we sit down?' 'Give the blighter half a minute.' Wilson barged in apologetic. He had stepped too near a land-mine in Tobruk and carried a cane. 'Awfully sorry. Came as fast as I could. Work, you know.' General groan of disbelief. 'Some of us do have to work for a living, you know. Don't see how the rest of you manage.' He was a partner in a small brokerage firm in the City: 'Fearful jam in the Tube. Gets worse every winter.'

They sank into their places and the club steward began serving.

It was Brian Smith who arrested the general tide of voices, clinked glass and china.

'Do you mean that, Smith?' It was Wilson, startled.

'I'm afraid so. I don't honestly suppose I'll be with you chaps a year from now.'

Simpson, his knife suspended: 'Hullo, what's all this about?'

'I'm getting out. Taking the family to Australia.'

'Why?' Brownlee leaned forward.

'Fed up. That's all. Just plain fed up. Bloody pipes frozen. Coal shortage. Another winter like this? Not if I can help it. I'd like to live in a place where you can get really warm, through to the bone. I caught a whiff of my children the other day. I tell you, they're going mouldy.'

'Come on, Smith, be serious.'

'I am, Brownlee. We were sitting home last week, wondering whether we had enough shillings for the meter, trying to figure out whether there'd be anything at all, one bloody farthing, left after taxes, and all at once Claire and I looked at each other and had the same thought. Why hang on? Geoff might have an outside chance to get into a decent grammar school. Jimmy's a nice little devil, but not long on brains. Won't get near it. I don't know what's happened, but everywhere you go now, there are a million people queuing for the same spot or trying to scramble ahead of you. Haven't you noticed? You go to a restaurant, and you queue out the door. You drive to what used to be an empty stretch of beach in Devon, and you can't park within a mile of it for all the caravans and comfort stations. I tried to put Geoff's name down at Charlton. My uncle is an Old Carltoonian and it looks a decent sort of place. They're booked solid till 1965. The whole island is like a boat with too many people jammed in it. One of these days some bastard will pull out the plug, and it'll sink.'

Voices cut in, nervous and aggrieved.

'We've had a bad patch of it, I'll admit that,' said Wilson, 'but from where I sit, it looks as if we'd turned the corner.'

'Until the next balls-up. We're awfully good at crises and girding our loins. Look at this flan. I shouldn't have thought it had come anywhere near a fresh egg. Why, the Krauts are eating better than we. And getting more of it. Right now. After the whole place was smashed into a shambles. We have a real talent for being dreary and pretending it's good for us. The old loin has been girt once too often.'

'There's something in what you say. But I couldn't imagine living anywhere else. Not among foreigners. And I rather like the flan!' Simpson chewed with obstinate flourish.

Voices were still loud and at cross-purpose when Gerald tapped his glass. Silence gathered, then a scrape and shuffle of feet.

'Gentlemen. I give you His Majesty.'

'His Majesty,' and Parkins, under his breath, 'God bless him.'

'Gentlemen, you may smoke now.'

Some edged their chairs back from the table, stretching. Others strolled in the room lighting cigars. The steward put more coal on the fire, took away the wine glasses, and set down brandy snifters and small glasses for port. Moore took a pinch of snuff and let the tawny flakes lie on the back of his hand.

Gerald went to the wash-room. He had a grey, absent mien, as if he was in secret pain. Reeve had followed him.

'Anything wrong?'

'No, not really.' He moistened the corner of a towel and sponged his face. It shone with small beads of perspiration.

'You sure you're all right?'

'Perfectly. I had rather a set-to with Sheila. And a poor night. I'm feeling a bit flogged. That's all. We'd better get back.'

Maune in the chair: 'The Honourable Secretary will now read the minutes of the last meeting.'

Reeve did so, with customary embellishments. Resolution that Wilson be sconced passed by acclamation. His assertion that he had missed two meetings because of a business trip to America was rejected as implausible. He had been observed with a lady, not his wife, behind a potted palm in Brighton.

Wilson: 'Mr President, Sir, I protest.'

Protest not allowed. The port started around the table.

Reeve went on: 'Proposed assessment for the present dinner: seventeen and six per head.'

Ritual cries of 'Shame!'

'Far too expensive. How much of a profit does the honourable member make on these inferior clarets?' Simpson's question was ruled out of order. Further protests, and Moore, mock-outraged: 'I take a loss. A cruel loss.'

'If no other honourable member has any point he wishes to raise, I will sign the minutes.' Reeve placed the blotter on the page and closed the leather tome.

As Parkins got to his feet, the room grew so silent that the Desert Fathers could hear Pritchard's winter cough reverberating bleakly in the club foyer. Parkins stubbed his cigar, carefully, into the silver ashtray by his plate; there was a nervous glow in his pale cheek: 'Mr President, Sir, I am no public speaker.'

Soft denials: 'Rubbish.'

'Ask anyone at the Bar. That's why I settle all my cases out of court. I used to fancy myself a regular orator. Lost too many clients that way. When I got up to speak, the Judge began brushing his black cap.' (*Laughter.*) 'So I can promise you, Sir, this will be brief. I don't know about other honourable members, but for myself I can say that I am very pleased that every month has a third Tuesday.'

'Hear, hear,' and rapping of glasses.

'I don't know that we're a frightfully bright lot . . . '

'Point of order,' hissed Moore, joyously.

'. . . or that we accomplish very much beyond helping Moore lay down his cellar,' (*laughter*) 'but I know how greatly I value the chance to be with a group of men – how should I put it?' (He seemed to cast about for his meaning, his fingers searching, and in the absence of his voice the rain was loud.) '. . . With a group of friends – I do feel the word is in order . . .'

'Hear, hear.'

'. . . who don't need to have things explained to them. The things that matter. Because at a time when each of us learned what certain words meant – the old-fashioned words, the ones we had read in books but not felt in the cold of our own backs – we were in the same boat. Hanging on for dear life. But not only for that. And no one pulled the plug out, though I dare say we all wanted to more than once. And may I say, Smith, that I hope you'll be with us, not only a year hence, but for many years to come. Because I just don't believe we're finished. Not yet. Not when I look around this table.' (*Loud approval*) 'Sir, I take great pleasure in offering the health of the Society.'

'The Society.' Then fists hammering till the glasses danced and Brownlee, with a connoisseur's nod: 'Nicely put, Colonel, very nicely put.'

Gerald got up. His eyes sought the opposite wall, as if trying to focus on some point in the shadows. He took from his pocket, and unfolded, smoothing the ruffled edge, a front page of *The Times*. He began low, and Wilson, at the far end, cupped his ear.

'Honourable members are no doubt familiar with this object. It is the cover page of *The Times*. The only page on which there is any news.' (*Laughter.*) 'Known to all men who served in HM's forces for diverse other properties. Particularly when on airmail paper.' (*Loud amusement.*) 'There is no end of wonder to be found on this page. Miss Doris

Moufflon: colonic irrigation; opens and relaxes.' (*General mirth; Simpson doubled over.*) 'Betty: letter lost; please write. Your Tooty. Or: Am eighteen. Anything legal considered. Also other possibilities.'

A happy roar. Gerald read on: 'Entrancing black chihuahua bitch. Fearless. A real charmer. Rabies serum available.'

Moore pounded the table, his eyes watery. It was the hour of port and smouldering cigar ash, when laughter is a conspiracy, doubly warm because it is withheld from the poor buggers who do not share the code and are slogging by in the rain outside. Only Reeve noticed the clenched whiteness in Gerald's face.

'But I wonder whether honourable members ever look to the left of the page. Bottom left, or top of the second column. Depends on how many there are. Every day of the year. Unfailing. Even Christmas Eve. Never a single day without them. Rather a lot this morning.'

Brownlee had come alert; the others were leaning back, drowsy and smoke-wreathed. Gerald read slowly, as if there was a desperate shrillness poised, ready to tear his voice at the root:

'Colmer – in memory of Jack. Lt. J. N. Colmer. Killed in action. 16 November 1942. He gave all. Per ardua. Mum and Joan.

'Forbes – In proud and loving memory of Harry Forbes. Captain, 9th Durham Light Infantry, killed near Mareth. 16 November 1941. With firmness in the right. Anne.

'Greggson – In treasured memory of our beloved only son, Pilot Officer Lawrence Greggson, Eton and King's, 12th Bomber Squadron, RAF. Did not return from a flight over Germany. 16 November 1944. We shall not see his like again. Mum and Priscilla.

'Hoskins – In constant remembrance of Nick. Lt. N. Hoskins, MC, the East Yorkshire Regiment, killed near St Fleury, 16 November 1915, aged 19. For your tomorrow he gave his today.'

Simpson had ducked for his brandy. Moore kept his taut smile, but had his eyes to the ceiling, as if tracing an obscure, menacing fault. 'Look here, Maune, you've made your point. Carry on old chap, will you. Don't hammer it into the ground.'

It was Brownlee, softly but distinct. A shiver of embarrassment passed around the table. Gerald seemed not to hear: 'Rather a special one, this:

'Londsdale – In never-dying memory of Major T. F. C. Londsdale,

King's Shropshire Light Infantry, killed at the head of his battalion near Corvin, 16 November 1917. Of his son, Johnny. Lt. J. Londsdale, 5th Battalion, York and Lancaster Regiment, killed in the landings on the Normandy beaches, 6 June 1944. And of Susan, nurse at St Mary's Royal Infirmary, Singapore, who died in enemy hands as a result of maltreatment. 11 February 1943. Why am I thus alone. B. L.

'Pitt-Neame – Raymond Pitt-Neame, Captain 3rd Fife and Forfar Yeomanry, RAC, reported lost in the sinking of the troopship HMS *Niger* in the Indian Ocean, 16 November 1943, aged twenty-three. May God give us to see the right. Billy. Peter. Dad.'

The ash on Parkins's cigar had gone cold: '*We* know. No need to tell *us*. There but for God's grace were you and I. Don't make a production of it. No one *here's* going to forget. Bless them all.'

'Quite right,' Wilson spoke loud, 'I think the whole thing's in damn poor taste. Morbid, if you ask me. Downright morbid.' Then to the entire table, in a busy sweep: 'Do you think Pritchard can turn up some whisky? Shall I ask?'

'I second that.'

They were all talking fast and shrugging off the dark. Smith stabbed the fire-iron into the grate and a shower of red embers scattered. Gerald's voice came sharp as a cracked bell:

'In treasured memory of George Walker, DFC, reported missing after a raid on Aachen, 16 November 1944. We miss you so. Mummy. David. Lizbeth.'

This time, Brownlee pushed his chair back: 'I don't know what you think you're doing, Maune, but I've had my fill. I hope you'll excuse me, but I must get on home. It's late.' Smith spun the stem of his glass between his palms, and made dim noises of reproof. Parkins crossed to the window: 'I say, snow's stopped. Turning to rain.' Reeve leaned over from his seat to touch Gerald's arm, but he felt curiously exhilarated.

Then Gerald spoke again, haltingly, into an abrupt, rebellious silence: 'I won't go on. Though it doesn't seem fair. There are other names. Chap with a Y. Polish, I suppose. But there's something I wanted to say. About the lot of them. Every day of the year. All this stuff about how young they were. What rotten luck it was for them to die. Never-fading memory. Well I'm not sure. Maybe *they*'re alive.

Maybe *they*'re the ones that are really living. That's what I'm trying to say. Don't look at me as if my fly were open, Brownlee. Give me half a minute, and I'll try to explain. It's something I've been thinking about a lot lately. Maybe we have it all wrong, and it's *we* who are dead. We don't smell dead, but we are. And they're having a laugh on us. A bloody great laugh.'

Reeve tugged at his sleeve: 'Stop it, Gerald.'

'We're the ones they should have in *The Times*. Don't you see? We, the living dead. In loving memory of Colonel Parkins. He was a hero, but who's got any use for heroes? They take up so much room around the house. In never-fading remembrance of Gerald Maune, Captain, 2nd Battalion, the Royal Norfolk Regiment. Looks alive. But isn't. Stone dead. Ask his wife.'

His lips were still moving, but the scrape of chairs and the tangle of voices cut him off.

'Disgusting!' Simpson said it twice, fiercely. 'Can't hold his liquor.'

'Goodnight, ladies, goodnight, ladies, we're sorry to see you go,' hummed Wilson, 'time for the old sack.'

'She was waiting by the lamp-post,' Moore's tenor capped the angry, embarrassed noise.

Brownlee left quickly, and outside the door, now ajar, Pritchard hovered torn between curiosity and reserve. Parkins gave Gerald a shy tap on the shoulder: 'Don't worry about it, Maune, I mean the way things have gone tonight. I am not sure, but I think I know what you meant, at least part of it. And take care of yourself, old man, will you? You look as if you could do with a bit of sun. Beastly winter. Goodnight, Reeve.'

The room emptied in loud eddies: 'Goodnight. Can I give you chaps a lift? Night, Reeve.'

The candles burned with a low, writhing flame. Only the red ash on the grate glowed against the silver and the cold stain of darkness. Gerald filled his glass and raised it to the guttering light: 'Gentlemen, I offer a toast. To the memory of the living. May they find deliverance.' He emptied it at one draught.

Reeve watched from the blackness of the window. He saw the tears, and the face of a man haunted.

5

When he received Sheila's note, couched in a feminine casual imperative, and asking when and where he might be free to lunch with her, Reeve felt a needling under the skin. He had been expecting this to happen, and had the nagging sensation of having been cast for a part in a banal yet cunning script.

Edging between the tables in a small restaurant near Covent Garden, one of the few where he would not, at every moment, be nodding to other publishers, Reeve saw that Mrs Maune was waiting. She looked compact and fairly tarnished, her hands tight on her lap. She had no small talk that day; nearly at once her queries ached at him.

'I don't suppose you knew, but Gerald has not been well, on and off now, for almost two years. Oh, I know he looks well enough, for months at a time, but then he'll have a sudden break, as if something inside him splintered, deep down, and drove a lot of sharp bits into his nerves. I know when it happens. He starts flinching all over, wherever you touch.'

She was perfunctory over the menu.

'It started when we'd only been married a few months. We were moving into our flat and were pretty hard up. They'd asked Gerald to take on a new job in the firm. He'd been doing awfully well, and they wanted him to take charge of part of the research department, to do more of the editing and look after staff. I don't remember the details. But it meant a raise, and I thought it a grand chance. Gerald hadn't been doing it a fortnight when he came down with something queer. Couldn't sleep or keep his food. The doctor found nothing actually wrong with him. Thought it might be a touch of jaundice, or something he'd picked up in Egypt. He told him to have a rest. Well, it went away the day Gerald took back his old job.'

She dotted a crossed, nervous pattern on the tablecloth with the prongs of her fork.

'I don't really know Gerald very well. Odd, isn't it? But it's true. I don't mean that twaddle about human beings never getting to know one another. But because all of him that matters, deep down, that makes him stand or back away when he does, happened before we ever met. I don't know how it is in America,' she looked up momentarily with a flick of malice, 'but here at home, when you marry a man of Gerald's class, it's as if you were being asked to move into a house that's all furnished, that's got suits hanging in the wardrobe and cigarette-boxes, and jokes you laugh at but don't quite understand. And often the phone rings, and you hear voices which sound muzzy, as if the line were bad, but they've called before, before you were ever there to listen.'

The waiter interposed, but Sheila scarcely glanced at the plate.

'It's all been put together and furnished, the curtains hung and the walls stained, before a woman gets near. In school. Does anything ever happen to you after? Really happen? And at Oxford. And then in the battalion and at war. I imagine that's like being back in school, with prefects and outdoor games, and nurses in the infirmary.

'Before I met Gerald, there was only half of me. I may have looked all of one piece, but honest to God, I was only half alive. I thought that's how it would be for him. That it took two to make a whole, that it was something one built from the ground up, together. Oh, I knew everyone had their past. I suppose even I did in a small way. But I thought one would pool that and make it new, that everything you remembered would be different because you now remembered together, or decided to forget lest it hurt. I think every woman wants to make her husband a gift of certain memories, so that he can throw them away for her.

'But it doesn't work that way with men like Gerald. They invite you into their lives, as a kind of staying-guest. I've been doing quite well alone, thank you, but do come along for the ride. There's room for two. Mind now, don't bump into anything.'

Her tone had sharpened, and she checked herself, putting her fish-knife to the fillet of sole and the tinned peas, with their bright false sheen.

'I sleep with Gerald,' she gave the phrase a flat stress, 'but there must be half a dozen men who know him better than I do, or ever shall. Who knew him at Brackens, or up at Magdalen, or in the war. the ones you drink with at the club. You've seen him cry when he was beaten and laugh when he won. You've heard him say the things men

267

say, when they are afraid and trying not to lie. You'd know what's wrong with him, what's cutting him to ribbons inside. He wouldn't have to tell you, because you wouldn't need to ask. It's the words and things you have between you, which you won't share. Not with me. Not with any woman.'

She jerked out of control.

'Why don't you marry your college scouts, or the porter at the club? They'd know better than I how brown you want your toast, how to mend your cuffs and keep the place tidy. And they wouldn't nag you at night!'

He heard the crack in her voice, but before he could see the shimmer of tears, Sheila was on her feet and had brushed past him.

She came back after a few moments and drank her Sauternes.

'I'm not going to apologize,' she said it smiling and both laughed. For a spell, they chatted intently of odds and ends, of Reeve's authors and the latest Rossellini film. Then she looked down and blushed.

'Duncan, please try to answer what I'm going to ask. You know Gerald better than anyone. So much better than I do. You were always together. Try to remember. Has he ever had a child? Has he ever made another woman . . . ?'

She stopped, her mouth thin, and her eyes on the plate.

'I have no idea, Sheila. I'm sorry, but I haven't a clue.'

Even as he lied, the lie having come more swiftly, more easily than the will to deceive, Reeve felt a wave of affection break through him, of tenderness for the flat-boned young woman sitting across the table, now staring at her empty wineglass. With the lie came a strange, happy remorse. He wanted to lean over and touch her, to pass his hand along her cheeks and the shallow dip of her throat. He was dizzy with gentleness.

'Why did you ask, Sheila?'

'I'm not sure I know myself.'

The fight had drained out of her. She pecked idly at the food.

'I thought it might be important. That it would help me understand where things have gone wrong.'

'Does Gerald want children?'

'I do. I always have. Somehow I can't imagine being without them. Later on. And Gerald says he does. But so far . . .'

She paused, off-balance: 'I'm not as modern as I pretend to be. I mean there are things I find it difficult to talk about. Even to someone as close to Gerald as you are.'

Reeve touched her hand lightly: 'Quite. I'm not very modern that way either. Vivianne used to laugh at me and say I was a prude. There are things I don't know how to listen to.'

She took the plunge, with a faint, nervous twist of her shoulders: 'I won't go into details. I wouldn't know how. But things haven't been very good. Along *that* line. You know what I mean. Of late, they've been pretty awful.'

She dabbed a finger across her dry lips, and again Reeve felt a surge of solicitude. It made him warm and inventive. He wanted to touch the bruise in her: 'You don't need to tell me, Sheila, I've gone through hell that way.' And with the astute shyness of a man talking sex to a woman he pities, Reeve began telling of Vi and himself, of the raw and sudden void between them, of how she had flung from the room one night in a dance of rage, her naked feet barely touching the ground.

But Sheila wasn't listening. Her own need was too blunt.

'I've said to Gerald, why don't we adopt a child? Maybe it's an old wives' tale, but they do say after you've adopted you often find you can have your own.'

'And Gerald?'

'At first he didn't pay much attention. But when I pressed him, he went into a black mood. He said if anything was wrong, I was the one to blame. He could prove it. It wasn't any of my concern, but there had been something at Oxford which made him certain. Nothing like this had ever happened to him before.' She was darkly flushed, but drove ahead, the cry for help loud inside her. 'We had a frightful row. As if he was trying to slam the door between us. He hit me. It was the first time. Then he cried like a little boy. When he calmed down, he wanted me to . . .' She broke off with a shiver of distaste: 'No, there's really nothing else to tell. When he said Oxford, I thought you might know. I'm sorry. Now I've gone and spilled it all over. Perhaps I shouldn't have. I hate little girl talk. And I don't suppose these things are as rare or as awful as they seem at the time. But it helps to have someone listen.' Her voice had the sour ring of tears.

Reeve pounced: 'Tell me, Sheila, did that row take place just before the annual dinner?'

She nodded.

'Ah, that's it. That's why he made such a morbid ass of himself.'

'So I gathered. But I've never managed to take your little table-rappings very seriously. Maybe you can explain. Why do perfectly reasonable, grown men, who publish books or assess real estate during the day, scurry off to play charades in the evening and get fearfully soused doing it?'

'Come off it, Sheila, you don't need me to tell you. All the chaps in there are hiding from their wives. Night off. There's candlery in heaven, all the husbands are put out!'

She didn't laugh: 'I dare say.'

Reeve parried: 'You know it isn't that simple. You remember when you said a woman wanted to give her husband a parcel of memories, so he could tear them up for her and throw them away unopened? Well, with men it's different. We need to take our memories out from time to time, and make sure there are no moths in them, that they haven't gone rotten on us. We like to know that they're as real and gilt-edge as we thought them. Take them away, tell us they've depreciated, that there's no market for them, and we're left bare.'

Sheila focused: 'Ah, that does help. I'm glad you've told me. Those things I don't know about and can't share with him. They're probably in a kind of safe, inside Gerald.'

'Quite. And he has to take them out now and again. To give them an airing.'

'Once a week,' said Sheila.

Reeve looked puzzled.

'Why yes, or didn't you know? With A.G. up in Hampstead.'

'A.G.?'

'Dr Arthur Goldman. Gerald's being psychoanalysed. Weekly sessions. We'll soon be selling the furniture to pay for them. Surely you must have known. He tells you everything.'

Reeve's ignorance and startled mien were an obscure triumph. She savoured it briefly and wondered.

'When did it start?'

'Just about the time you came back from America. The old dreams were coming on, so he couldn't sleep properly. The doctor wouldn't let him have any more pills and he suggested he should see Goldman. Just to have a chat, you know. I suppose that's how they began. I couldn't imagine that Gerald hadn't told you. Is that why you look so angry?'

Reeve drew a long breath: 'I'm not angry. Why should I be? Gerald's a big boy now. He's got to decide for himself. And if he thinks it'll help . . .'

'Don't you?'

'That's a pretty large subject, Sheila.' He tried to say it lightly, but she saw him tense. 'I wish I could go into it now' (he glanced busily at his watch) 'but I can't. Back to the mines, I'm afraid.'

They had coffee and said little, parting into their own thoughts. At the door of the restaurant, Reeve pulled himself erect.

'I'm awfully glad you've told me. You and Gerald mean the world to me. You know that, Sheila, don't you. There's really no one else I feel as close to. I'll do all I can to help, if I can. Let's see each other again soon. And keep the old chin up.'

They shook hands warmly, as strangers do.

But instead of turning towards Great Russell Street, Reeve found himself hurrying west, his thoughts turbulent. He loathed psycho-analysis. The very word stung him to a cold passion. It had been the first shadow to fall between him and Vivianne. It was intimately a part of her world and speech. She moved in a circle in America where nearly everyone was in the game, where they gossiped of their analysis in a cunning chatter, of its blocs and transfers, of the analyst's sour breath or twitches. The first time he heard it, at a party in San Francisco, Reeve had understood: they were masturbating in public. And he had shouted it at them. Vi had turned, and warbled at him across her cigarette-holder: 'Why, of course, you sweet dodo. Don't you think we know? But isn't that what you did in the little boys' room at Eton? And isn't it better than doing it alone?' They had laughed at him and told him to go read Reich on orgasm.

Reeve wasn't sure about God. On balance, he thought, probably not. But he could see that a man, in agony of spirit, might pour out to a priest the bile and refuse of himself. The priest being there as a mere cipher of the other presence, as a promise of God's ear. But to strip oneself naked before some Jewish twerp with cigarette stains on his cuff, to give him money every week so that one could empty into his lap one's garbage, the private parts, the privy in each of us – it made Reeve want to vomit. To pretend the old goat wasn't excited, that his own sex didn't rise when you told him of your itches and wet dreams! The whole thing was a dirty farce.

Reeve had known men tortured and starved hollow by the Germans, men who had their fingernails torn out, one a day, and their balls smashed. And they hadn't broken. They'd held. Because being a human being was something fantastically strong, something it had taken unimaginable luck and decency to achieve. He had known women who came home to Stepney at the end of the night-shift to find their home burnt off the face of the earth and their children ash. And after they'd screamed, they'd kept proud, and not asked anyone else to carry their pack of misery. But the ones that uncoiled on the couches, or sat in the warm mud-bath of group therapy, what had they done, what had they endured, what Belsen, what desert? Bitches. Real bitches. Little girls in toreador pants and cashmere. Doing a weekly striptease. And paying a man to watch them. Reeve knew there were blokes who wanted to take off their trousers in public parks, and wave the thing at passers-by. Obscurely, he could feel the force of the impulse. But he found it resistible. Otherwise, what was the use of trying to be a human being? Why not give up, and become a dog pissing and fornicating in the sun?

Reeve tore along William IV Street. He knew, with jarring conviction, that he wasn't being truthful. Not all the way. It was more than his revulsion at analysis, more than a whiplash of abstract disgust. It had grown like a razor-edged cactus between him and Vi. Now it was taking Gerald away. Who was that quack in Hampstead? Who was he to barge in where Reeve had been the only, and the closest? What were his fingers prying for in the secret places which Reeve had shared, and of which he bore the key? He felt a tug of nausea, as if he had come home tired, and discovered the sheets in his bed faintly soiled. Why had Gerald not told him? Was Goldman's authority that great, that intimate already?

Reeve checked his stride and looked up. He found himself on the steps of St Martin-in-the-Fields, in a cry of pigeons. The truth came over him, blinding – he had had one divorce, he could not endure a second.

6

After that, Reeve lay in ambush. He had not long to wait. Gerald's requiem for the living dead had offended. The Desert Fathers met as before, but Brownlee wore an air of fastidious malaise, and some went home early. Pritchard could hardly conceal from himself that he found the singing less buoyant.

Two months after his lunch with Sheila Maune, Reeve had a call from Gerald: 'We haven't had a real talk in a hell of a long time. There's something I want to ask you. Why don't we have a drink at the club before the dinner starts next Tuesday. Say we make it half past six.'

Posted by the high window in the smoking-room, Reeve saw Gerald turn the corner of Londsdale Terrace. For a brief instant, he had the hallucination that he was looking at the wrong man. Maune had gotten paunchy, and in the sharp gust which swept the street his gait was imprecise. Reeve tautened his muscles, and noted with content that he himself had kept lean, that he would still be able, without shortness of wind, to follow the beagles over hedgerow and muddy ground, as he had done at Magdalen fifteen years before. But it was Maune's face – Reeve peered at it with the closeness of imperfect recognition – that arrested. It was a young face gone indecently old, without the buttress of intervening years. The hair was still flaxen at the temple and the chin unsteady; but the eyes were set deep and tired, and the skin was finely cracked. Like a new house, hurriedly plastered, and already flaking to dust.

They ordered drinks (the barman knew that Gerald took a double with only a wisp of tonic) and arched their legs against the fire-guard. Their talk strayed here and there, of taxes, of an acquaintance gone to New Zealand, of a libel action to which Reeve's firm was party. The old, easy cadence seemed between them.

Gerald went to fetch a second round. Bending over the back of Reeve's chair, the glasses poised in his hand, he asked with a casual drag in his voice, 'I say, old man, you wouldn't happen to remember Ina? That girl I got involved with at Oxford?'

Reeve blinked at the fire and half-turned his supple neck: 'Ina? I'm not sure I do.'

Gerald stirred heavily: 'But you must. Don't you remember the funk I got myself into? I sat in your room and sweated like a frightened hog. Then you went and saw her.'

'I do have a vague memory of the thing, now that you mention it. But she didn't make the same impression on me, old boy, as she obviously had on you.'

Gerald coloured: 'No. Of course she wouldn't. I was just wondering . . .' He faltered.

Reeve spun out the bogus silence: 'You were wondering about what?'

'At the time I must have been too damn scared to ask. About what happened. Now I'd like to know. Whether she got herself taken care of,' he winced saying it, 'or whether she was going to have the baby.'

'How should I know? I wouldn't have the foggiest notion.'

'But surely you must. You went and talked to her. Don't you remember? She was to meet me in front of the Lamb and Flag. You were going to tell her what to do. She must have said something.' The words had a dry, fuzzy taste in his mouth, like a blotter.

'I imagine I gave the little tart five quid and told her I'd call the police if she ever showed her face around Oxford again. But maybe it was only three. Yes, that's it. I gave her three pounds and she went off snivelling.'

Gerald hunched forward, uneasy in his weight: 'Look here, Flash,' (it was a nickname Reeve hadn't heard since he ran for his house at Brackens, and it set his teeth on edge like a hint of blackmail), 'I'm sure you know whether or not she was lying. I mean she *was* pregnant, wasn't she? And so there might have been a child.'

Reeve leaned back in the dun mantle of his chair and spread his palms wide. He was amused to note how near to his mood were the stale postures of Victorian villainy: 'How would I know?' He made reasonableness knife-sharp: 'You *are* a nit! I'd almost forgotten the whole balls-up until you reminded me just now. How the devil should I know?'

'Because you weren't going to give her a farthing if she was lying. She wouldn't have stood a dog's chance with you, Flash. You liked things neat. And you were a great one for finding out.'

Reeve mimed amazement: 'Are you blaming me now? No, don't shake your head that way. I'm asking. Did I set asunder whom God had joined? You were going to kiss my hand when I came back to tell you it was all right. You were going to get down on your bloody knees, lad, and kiss my hand. Or don't you remember?'

'Come off it. You know damn well how grateful I was. And still am. It's just that I wanted to know about the baby.'

'Why? What's all this about?'

Gerald made an odd gesture, as of a broken wing: 'There are some things I've been trying to straighten out in my own mind. And I want to know. Very much.'

A shard of live coal had tumbled from the grate; Reeve darted at it with his shoe.

'The whole thing's a blur. I don't even remember what the slut looked like. I've never given it another thought. But if it's any comfort to you, and you're making your peace with the Lord, thanks to St Jude for favours received and all that, well I'll tell you, boy, she wasn't any more pregnant than my Aunt Sally! So stand easy. No one's going to turn up at the funeral and shout 'daddy'. You *are* a queer one.'

Reeve came out of his chair making a face like a gargoyle, his long fingers to his chin and his face convulsed into an air of impish lechery. It was one of his best turns. But Gerald didn't laugh.

'You're sure of that?'

'Absolutely. She played you for a patsy. She saw what a soft touch you were and tried to pull a fast one. Pregnant? Don't make me laugh.' He exhaled with mock finality.

'You're lying,' said Gerald. 'I don't know how I can be so sure,' (the knowledge had sprung upon him, with a jarring, sickening impact), 'but I know it. You're lying.'

And in the moment he said it, all changed. The contour of the room, the bite of smoke and cold in the air, the yellow of the lamp, the rub of the tweed suit against his wrist. All changed utterly. A huge, dim shape had passed across the light making his heart hammer and be still.

He said it once more: 'You're lying to me.' Not in hatred, but in amazement before the breadth and simplicity of his ruin. The shrill of the lie had sounded out of the depths of Reeve, and Gerald had heard it resonant in the room, derisive. There need never be a second. The scratch was unalterable in the voice. To hear a lie in a friend, and Reeve had been the sharer and strong shadow of him, was to hear the soft start of death. It changes all.

Reeve did not know whether he was lying; perhaps the falsehood lay only in the easy stress he had put on his denial. But Maune's outrage, and what he dimly perceived of withdrawal and contempt, goaded him like the sight of an open wound. He would not let silence pass judgement: 'Look here, old boy, I've had a hard day. I don't know what you're after, or why you should think I'm lying. I've never been in such a bloody silly argument in my whole life. OK. Have it your way. She was going to have twins. I could hear them saying, "Where's poppa? Where's old man Maune?" We decided to name them Jeremy and Egbert and put them down for Eton. Now be a good chap and get me a drink, will you. Christ. You'd think I'd knocked her up.'

'Forget it. I don't care to talk about it any more.'

Gerald stood quite near, but Reeve had difficulty hearing him, as if a sudden turbulence had cut between. A sour spasm gripped him, and his skin went hot: 'I don't know what the hell's biting you. But don't take it out on me. I'm telling you, boy. Don't you take it out on me!'

'Keep your shirt on, old man. I'm not saying anything.'

'I'm fed up sitting here and having you look at me as if I'd stolen money off a blind man. Who the hell are you calling a liar? It's time you grew up, Maune. I'm telling you for your own good.'

'Why are you getting so excited? I said, forget it.'

He spoke it kindly, there being room for kindness and tact in the new emptiness. Reeve heard the note. It made his nerves leap, and he lunged out like a runner stumbling: 'Are you patronizing me? Well, *are* you?'

Gerald looked away, and made a vague motion towards the bar.

But Reeve pulled him close: 'Look Maune, *I'm* not your analyst.'

Being in a new world, where touch and voice betrayed, Gerald was not startled.

'Ah. So you know. Of course. Sheila must have told you. She's cut up about it. She thinks it'll ruin us. Probably true.'

'That's not the reason, and you know it. She can't bear the thought of you making an ass of yourself. Of your doing something so utterly bogus.'

Reeve felt back in the saddle. He poured out his derision of psychoanalysis, his intimate, contemptuous knowledge of the havoc it created among his American acquaintances. His arguments flashed bright and crowded as from a Roman candle: 'You're having a rough patch with Sheila. All right, I don't want to know the details. None of my business. Nor anybody else's. I don't suppose there's a marriage going that doesn't have its bad stretches. Right from the start, and when I was most involved, there were days when I looked at Vi and had grit in my mouth. Fair enough. That's the old snake's apple in our throats. Thou shalt sow thy seed in stony furrows and sweat thy balls off doing it. But you're a big boy now. You're the only one who can make a go of it. You and Sheila. And you know damn well there's nothing I wouldn't do to help, if you want me to. So why open your fly and wave the bloody thing at some Hebe in Hampstead, and pay the old goat for leering?'

Gerald listened, but found it hard to place the man who was addressing him with such insistent flourish. The voice was familiar, but somehow off-pitch, as if it had passed through a fret of static.

'You've got to stand on your feet, lad. To stop leaning. There was always someone, wasn't there? At home, it was mum. And crikey, she was a strong one. At school, it was me. You remember the day you passed out in the yard? You held on to me as if I were the Lamb of God. I don't know who it was in Cairo, but you looked as if you had a pair of golden crutches. Someone was carrying you. Right on top of the bloody wave. Well it's time you got out of the old womb.'

'I suppose it's true. I've never been as clever as you, or as sure of myself. Perhaps I always *have* needed someone to prop me up. I won't deny it. But if you think that's what Goldman does, you couldn't be more wrong. When I'm with him, I have to walk alone. Farther than I ever wanted to or thought my legs could carry me. You remember that obstacle course they made us slog through, with the bloody sergeant-major bellowing and waving a stick at you. There was a mound of earth you had to run up and jump from, into a lot of murk and water. They made us do it at night. I'll never forget that. I was so scared I nearly wet myself. Falling into a black hole, and the air hitting you. Well, it's hard to explain. But it's rather like that. He kicks you off the edge, and you come down all shivery and not wanting to move. But you pick yourself up and start crawling in the dark. Somehow. And I'd never have believed you could be so alone with someone else sitting right behind you in the same room.'

His face lit with an expression of wry love.

'You look like a bobby-soxer swooning,' taunted Reeve.

Gerald smiled, out of reach: 'It's terribly difficult trying to explain to anyone who hasn't gone through it. Who's outside. There are times when I feel it's the reallest thing that's ever happened to me, and the only thing that will help. Other days, I loathe the whole business and want to chuck it. Once, I remember wanting to take Goldman by the neck and strangle the voice out of him. It was like a dentist's drill.'

Again he smiled, in a recollection so rich and private that it jarred on Reeve like a door closed against him.

'But don't you see the whole thing's a fraud, an utter fraud? That he's just a quack sniffing at a lot of garbage? Jesus, boy, you don't have to have a nanny any more to wipe your bottom when you've been to the toilet. That's all he's doing. Don't you understand?'

'I've always thought you were the cleverest chap I knew. I never dared argue with you. But right now you sound stupid. My fault. I'm sorry I ever bothered you with all this. Let's just forget it. Anyhow, time to go.'

He said it easily, looking up at the clock, but it had an undercurrent, drawing the present occasion towards a dim, cold finality.

'I'm warning you. If you don't stop seeing that charlatan, and making a show of yourself like you did here the other night, you'll lose Sheila. And you're not a one to go alone. I'm telling you, Maune, not alone!'

'Sorry, old man, but as you say, I've been leaning too much. I've got to decide this one for myself.'

'You've got to listen to me. I can prove the thing's a bloody racket. That you're being taken for a ride. I can *prove* it!'

Beneath the angry mask of Reeve's face and his darting finger, Gerald heard the wail of jealousy. It threw him off-balance.

'I wonder what Goldman would say hearing you. Why does it matter to you so dreadfully? Why do you hate it so? You should look at yourself in the mirror. You're all white. Perhaps I'm not the one who needs it most.'

'Meaning what?'

Gerald sought to break clear, but it was too late. Their intimacy had gone overripe. Now it burst, and a rancid venom spilled. 'Meaning that you haven't done so well either, Flash.' The nickname mocked. 'I was only saying to Sheila the other day: Duncan hasn't gotten over it, has he? Walks around like a ghost. Don't we know anyone we could introduce him to? A nice girl with a bit of money and a garden.'

Being full of their new hatred, and savouring its cool, bracing fumes, they both calmed down. Drink left Reeve's intelligence armed and ungoverned.

'Look here, Maune, make you a bet. Give me three weeks and I'll prove to you that Dr Goldman's a fraud. That the whole thing is utterly bogus.'

Gerald listened, as to a bright, dangerous child.

'He asks you about your dreams, doesn't he?'

'Yes, that's the most important thing. It starts you off. Pushes you off the jump.'

'And the dream is supposed to take the old letch right inside you, down to the balls of your soul.'

'I wouldn't put it that way.'

'But that's the whole point, isn't it?'

'I suppose so. It opens the door. Like going down a staircase inside yourself.'

'And no one else's dreams would do? I mean dreams people told you, or you'd read in a book?'

'Of course not. What a stupid idea. Like showing an X-ray of your Aunt Tilly when you wanted to find out about your own lungs.'

'Exactly. And if a doctor couldn't tell which was which you'd know him for a ponce, wouldn't you?'

'Look, old man, time's a-passing. Hadn't we better go in now?'

But Reeve pulled him down, his knuckles aching.

'I told you I can prove it. How often do you go there? Twice a week, is it? All right. Give me three weeks. I'll make up some dreams for you.

A whole packet of them. And you'll learn them by heart. They'll be short enough, I can tell you. And you'll spew them out for old Siegmund Fraud exactly as if they were your own, as if *you*'d dreamed them. And he won't catch on. He'll put his nose to them just as if they *were* your own. And you'll crawl down the shaft together. But it won't be you. It won't be you at all!'

'That's absurd! You *are* a silly ass. Why should I waste my time lying to him?'

'Because you'd see with your own eyes that the thing stinks. That it's as fake as card tricks. Because you'd realize that he's making a sucker of you. That you're getting the finger right up you, boy, right where the old Yid can smell the money.'

Reeve pitched back in his chair, quivering and hoarse with delight.

'You make me sick,' said Gerald, but he said it with a dull uncertainty.

Reeve crowded in, the lash of the harpoon whistling in his tone: 'Three weeks. I'm not asking for much. Maybe he'll see through it. But you don't really believe that, do you, Maune? You're afraid. You're all shaking inside, aren't you?'

'Leave off, will you. Just leave off.'

'One hundred pounds. I'm betting you one hundred pounds. And I'm in your hands. One wink, one giggle and he'll smell a rat. But I trust you. You're going to repeat those dreams just as if you'd dreamed them the night before, as if they'd made you wet the bed. I trust you like I wouldn't trust anyone else in the world.' He said it with acid relish. 'One hundred pounds to back up your new god. It's cheap, boy, it's cheap.'

Gerald was on his feet. He felt that if he struck out with his fist, accurately, the crazy wasp of a voice would stop whirring. Gin had made him heavy, but he sensed that he must rivet his attention, that the instant was like a top spinning, and could fall into an evil shambles. Still the wasp sang and stung.

'One hundred pounds.' He said it to himself. And saw, at the same moment, that they were not alone.

Brian Smith had come over from the bar, all ears: 'I say, are you chaps making a bet?'

'We are,' said Reeve.

'What about?'

'That I can dream his own dreams for him, and no one the wiser.'

'You're a fool, Reeve. Why should I do it?' He said it without conviction. The thing was dragging him down, away from the light. He had crossed the imperceptible shadow-line, leaving behind the feel of his own will.

'I'll be dashed if I understand a word you're saying. But one hundred pounds! I say.' And Smith glowed with excitement. He turned to the barman: 'Timms, will you hand me the betting-book. There's a good chap.'

He opened the clasp and turned the yellowed pages, the high note and rebuke of ancient wagers faded to a wraith-like scrawl. 'Anyone know the date?'

Timms read off the calendar.

'Rightio. D. Reeve bets Gerald Maune that he can . . .' He faltered, perplexed. '. . . I say, how did you put it? . . . dream his dreams for him and no one the wiser. For the sum of £100.'

Smith stared at what he had written, but a beautiful stupidity carried him before the wind. Gerald signed as if it was a tortuous joke, having nothing to do with him. Nothing real. He would wake from it as from the hammering dullness in his brain.

'Witness: Brian Smith. I'll be dashed. A hundred quid. Crikey.' He hurried out brimful.

Through the open door, Gerald saw the Desert Fathers gathered and waiting. He drove his hand through his dampened hair and turned to go. But Reeve caught him smartly by the elbow.

'I'll send you the first tomorrow.'

'The first what?'

'Why your first dream, old boy, your first dream.'

And as he followed Gerald, Reeve's body seemed, for an instant, in the grip of a wild, secret dance.

7

'*Gerald Maune*. GM. George Medal. Grand Marnier. G. M. Trevelyan. If I had got that Trinity Fellowship. All the difference. Walnuts and port in the Combination Room the first night you're made a Fellow. Read about it in Hardy. *Jus primae noctis*. The Jews of the first night. Trevelyan striding up and down that long room on the afternoon war broke out. Crying. Why don't you say it? Why don't you tell me that I've been an utter fool about Mr Hitler. *Mr* Hitler. The Fellows silent. Listening to their own bowels. Old frauds. But I wanted it. God, how I wanted it. Lukes got it. Tall, pimply sadist. Voice like a cracked flute. But Eton. And fathers and grandfathers prebendaries of where was it? Chichester. Or St Asaph. Best thing I ever wrote. *Hume on Causation in the Light of the New Psychology*. Craven meeting me in Great Court. Decent buzzard. Voted for you, Goldman. But no good. Sorry. Bit of advice, old chap. Bad thing in England to be clever; unforgivable to show it. Lights in the Combination Room that night. Knew Lukes was in there. Went to my room and masturbated into the wash-basin. Hadn't done *that* for a long time. All the difference. Wouldn't be here in Hampstead. Four patients a day. Not bad actually. But oh, the *meschugene* crap. Nearly always the same. More or less. And Irving coming up to my room the next morning, seeing the closed trunk. Cheer up, *mensch*. Did you really think they'd elect you to the College of Heralds?'

From the labyrinth of his resentment, still acid, came sudden laughter.

'I might not have met Hannah. First time we did it, on the floor, by the electric fire in her bed-sitter off Belsize Park. Does she still have those slacks? Green velvet. Probably not. Big in the hips now. But that time on the floor. Like the trumpets of Jericho. And the landlady sniffing at us as we went out. Now Aaron. I love him. Yea more than the apple of mine eye. Queer expression. *Augenapfel*. But I don't like him much. Soft, and where he hardens, a kind of cunning. Not like Hannah or me at all. Moves like Uncle Reuben. Same trick of the shoulder. But Judith. Does one really want to fornicate with one's daughter? And if she fell for a *goy*? Indiscretion. A stranger reading the family letters. Because that's where the memories are. In the black box. The old memories between the legs. Childe Roland to the dark tower came. Browning knew. Poets always know. No one to listen. We live off dead poets. Friend Oedipus. Good title. Must tell Rudi. Tennyson at Trinity the night of the feast. All the Fellows lined up, white tie and scarlet. The candle-sheen on the dark wood. How I wanted it. Each stepping forward to meet the Great Man. Oscar Browning, small and fat. I'm Browning. Tennyson, after long silence. No, Sir, you're not.'

This time, Dr Goldman laughed loud, and pulled out a corner of his handkerchief to wipe his misted spectacles. *Gerald Maune.* The dossier was on the blotter, thick and untidy at the edge. He stooped his back to harness.

'Where did I lose control? When did it go wrong? Too easy at the start. When McIvers sent him to me. Decent of McIvers. Doesn't really believe in analysis. Scrapped like dogs when we were both at the Maudsley. Doesn't like Jews either. In that special British way. Thinks history has given us such a raw time, that we've all got bad breath. *Suspected jaundice. Symptoms of hepatitis or possible anaemia. Biopsy negative.* Re-examination after three months. Complaints of insomnia and compulsive dreaming. Loss of appetite but steady increase of weight. Consumption of alcohol probably greater than patient admits or is fully aware of. Obvious even to McIvers where the roots lie. Charcot to Freud: *les vraies causes sont dans l'alcôve.* One of the great moments of history. No bells. And for S.F. no Nobel. Why does the brain pun more when it's tired?

'Came to me 11 April. Two years ago. Nightmares. Of men burning and their voices turning to birds. Birds, *vögeln* = to fuck. The birds diving down with their beaks, tearing. In the beginning was the pun. After the dreams, nights when he couldn't. Complete fiasco. Mrs M. trying to help. Probably more intelligent than he. Sudden erections during the day. Embarrassing. These things had never happened before. Lying, of course. They all lie during the first months. Lying on the couch. The lie of the lay. The lay of the lie. *Lorelei.* Ballad of our craft. Clear that it had never really been satisfactory between them. *Coitus interruptus* at the start. Then the decision to have children. Premature ejaculation. When at all. Blames her. Savage on this.

'19 June. First time I felt ground. Strange feeling that. Like coming out of muddy water. Meaningless. Then, all of a sudden, solid ground. Something in the voice, or a twist of speech. A real word under the cliché. The darkness visible. We and the poets. Blind to hear better.'

Dr Goldman brushed cigarette ash from a page of notes. He wrote on foolscap in a small, crowded hand.

19 June: The first dream that spoke loud. A woman undoubtedly his wife. But in profile. And legs like a man. M. trying to reach her. Digging. Wet sand sliding across his hands. She is not buried in the sand, but on top or to one side of it. Nevertheless, fierce compulsion to dig. She turns the other way. M. calls as loud as he can, but is not certain she can hear. Wakes, with the name Cold Harbour distinct in his conscious memory.

They had quarrelled two days before. Leaving a dinner party, Mrs M. had said that he drank too much. No one else at the table had taken three glasses of port. *Port* and *harbour*. M. recalled at once that it was a bottle of Sandeman's port. *Sandman*, the bringer of sleep, or the place of thirst, of dunes that shift and choke. *Cold* because, as he had remarked to Mrs M., the J's never served any of their wines at a proper temperature.

So far, only surface. M. himself makes the verbal connections. 'Like a double-acrostic.' We talk of Torquemada, the pen-name of the contriver of the most difficult acrostics. M. has read somewhere that Torquemada is, in real life, a schoolmaster. 'A man who can dream up those fiendish things every week must be a terror with the old cane.'

25 June: M. is in a large hall with mullion windows. He is to one side, but when he cranes his neck, he can make out a high gallery, and in the shadows, men watching. In the hall, there are clothes-racks, most of them bare. Someone – *this part of the dream is unclear* – is saying that he has come too late. Most of the clothes are sold. He sees another rack hung with belts and braces. Starts choosing. The person selling them is Mrs M. Whatever item he picks, she drops awkwardly to the floor. M. is very angry: 'This is a job for someone older. You're too young to do it properly.' The personage – he is no longer quite sure it is Mrs M. – starts laughing. The figures in the gallery laugh also. The echoes reverberate, and M. is suddenly in a swimming-bath. He is wearing gloves.

A number of strands are obvious. Torquemada, head of the Inquisition: hence the word *rack* (clothes-rack). Fear or desire of nakedness. (M. is himself aware of the implications of, *'You've come too late. Most of the clothes are sold.'*) The hall suggests the school refectory, and the swimming-bath, with its splashing echoes, is the one at Brackens. M. recalls that the boys swam naked, and how uncomfortable that made him at the start.

Why the gloves? M. apparently does not know that *mullein* (*mullion* windows) is the common name of a species of flowers known in America as fox-*glove*. Tries to evade my insistence on the point. Finally provides his own explanation. M. often passes through a street behind Charing Cross on his way to work. Store with surgical appliances, rubber goods, trusses, and usual books on sex-hygiene and perversion. Two have caught his eye: *A History of Flogging* (cover shows a man stripped to the waist, *braces* hanging loose, being flogged against a kind of wooden crossbar), and *Records of the Holy Inquisition* (a monk bending over a blurred female figure, nude and tied to a *rack*). Just underneath the books, a display of rubber gloves, one of them on a stand, erect, long-fingered. M. is disturbed and excited at the idea of such gloves being used *ad anum*. He realized that the dream signifies far more than appears, that these surface recognitions are only the outworks. But he refuses to look deeper.

3 August. A month lost. Two appointments not kept. One cut to twenty minutes: 'Sorry, I have had no dreams this week. I must be getting well.' M. obstructing, and conscious that he is doing so. Today the dam broke.

He asked me to draw the shades: 'I have a touch of migraine.'

Could he see the notes I had taken on *that* dream? I read him his own version of it without comment. 'I suppose there's something you should know, if you don't already.' M. explains that the failure of *coitus* is due to his wife's passiveness, to the time it takes to get her stimulated. ('It's like digging through sand.') She expects foreplay but gives nothing in return. M. has often hinted that he would like 'to try something new', to explore. But she is indifferent or queasy.

He came home from the pub one night. ('I won't deny I was a bit liquored up.') Always hangs his belt or braces across a chair near the bed when undressing. *Ejaculatio praecox*. M. annoyed and embarrassed. Determined to provoke second erection. Hands Mrs M. his belt and lies on the bed face-down. She gives him a light tap. Then starts laughing (same sound as in the dream). She can't do it. If he needs 'that kind of thing', he'll have to find it elsewhere. Later that night, the dream and involuntary pollution.

M. is bitter and talkative: 'I know it's a queer thing to ask. But I was drunk, and there are things they want us to do to them. Pretty nauseating, if you ask me. But part of the game, I suppose.' He voices the conviction that English women are notoriously passive, that they want sex 'served up like tea, with a dash of sugar and cream, and thank you, James, you may go now'. Ask them for a touch of invention, for 'something a bit special', and they look at you 'as if you'd been caught buggering the vicar's goldfish'. Lewd as cats in their own way, but not letting on. 'Make you feel like a slave or a ruddy sex-maniac.' He had met a girl in France. 'She went all white when she touched me. And used the words for the things she wanted us to do. Sheila wouldn't be caught dead saying those words. She doesn't say anything. Like making love to a mute.'

M. claims to know a lot of men who feel as he does: 'You'd be surprised whom you'll find in Soho on a weekday afternoon. Businessmen, dons, chaps from the bank. Going into the little doorways on Frith Street. French model, second floor. *Correction. Special massage.* I don't fancy that kind of place myself. But I can see where a perfectly decent chap might be driven to it. We had it better, over there, in the war. I suppose that's the root of it.'

Pours out stories of what he had come in the way of, or heard about, in Egypt, Naples, France: 'Bloke in my battalion had two sisters doing it to him in a house just outside Naples. Kept them naked, right from breakfast on. Girls who meant it. Not just doing you a bloody favour. Or setting their jaws as if they were playing hockey for Roedean.'

I let him talk and thrash about until he himself didn't believe it. Until he could hear himself lying.

Why the *gallery*?

M. looked at his watch and apologized for running beyond the hour. I told him it was important. He didn't have a clue. He offered to go and try to remember before the next time. I said we might be near the beginning of a coherent pattern, that if we didn't break through now the defence mechanisms would grow more tenacious, and the track more difficult to follow. Why the *gallery*?

Moment of truth. It always comes in analysis. Sometimes after six months or a year; sometimes when it is too late. The crack in the voice. Unmistakable. Half-fear, half-bravado. Even in the *Angst*, the unbreakable little core of vanity. The patient to himself: I *am* an interesting case. Otherwise the old bird wouldn't be listening so intently, he wouldn't be prying so hard.

'There was a gallery like that in the Upper School library. The library was where the prefects met, and you were called up for your beating. I wasn't caned often, mark you. I was rather mousey and kept low. But some nasty little rotter put ink in the shoe-polish, and when I did the house-captain's shoes, they came out a fearful mess. So I got six. And I can tell you Frank March had a powerful wrist. Played lacrosse for Sandhurst later on.'

Did he remember anything else about the occasion?

'Yes, now that you mention it. I wet my bed that night. Not in the way you might think. The *other* way. It was the first time. I was frightened out of my wits, but wanted it to happen again. Kept my eyes shut, waiting. Odd, isn't it? But they do say there's nothing like a beating to make a man of you.'

Goldman leaned back, his vision bleary. Though he had come across exactly this same pattern, this rusted trap, in numerous cases, it still stirred him to a dull rage. The black idiocy of it. He often wondered what resilience or bluntness of nerve kept the general run of ex-public-school men out of mental homes. In Soho, the rate was said to be one pound a stroke. Clearly an upper-class trade. Mrs M. must have understood. She was too alert not to. But she had wanted no part of it. Goldman had never met Sheila Maune, but he knew that women could make of their poise and sufficiency a weapon against a man's need.

He recalled how that hour (it was, in fact, nearer two hours) had ended. After a complete silence, Gerald came off the couch like a switch-blade closing: 'I know what's in your mind, Doctor. I know exactly. You think I'm a queer. That deep down I'm queer! That I'm a masochist or something. That's what you call it, isn't it? Well, isn't it?'

Goldman had expected him to shout. But not so loud.

'You think you're on to it, don't you? That you've got the living gut out of me. That I'm some kind of crazy queer who needs to be beaten!

God almighty, you make me sick. You're no better than the others. You don't even want to understand.'

He had controlled himself, but in a false way, like an actor poised for exit. He had taken the money out of his bill-fold and dropped it on Goldman's desk: 'That *is* what I owe you, I believe.'

Goldman caught a faint savour from somewhere in the house. It lit on his tongue. Pot roast, with heavy, dark gravy and garlic. Hannah must be in the kitchen. He stirred in his chair, his attention cast wide and downstream. Then he reeled in, hunching his mind. He pulled out the next page in the file and turned on the desk lamp.

There had been no word until 1 September. *Memorandum*: 'Call from McIvers, himself rather shaken. On the night of the 24.8., Mrs M. had asked him to come. M. in excruciating pain. Unable to lie down or straighten fully. Insomnia and accelerated consumption of spirits during previous fortnight. *Examination for kidney-stones negative.* Provisional diagnosis: slipped disc and inflammation of the nervous tissue. Aetiology obviously psychosomatic. M. both depressed and obsessively anxious about the prospect of resuming analysis. McIvers calling on his behalf. I concurred immediately, and predicted that pain would subside rapidly.

'First appointment, 5 September. M. shows signs of physical fatigue, but is anxious to please, to "play fair" and "give it a real chance".'

The next weeks, however, had been unsatisfactory. Maune talked in a compulsive stream, but the associations and snatches of dream-imagery which he offered were logically contrived. He was striving to win Goldman's approval. During the process of transference, even patients of mediocre intelligence marshal an extraordinary cunning. They tender to the analyst, as a gift trimly ordered, the skein and clues he has privately unravelled. He must guard himself against the seduction of their hope. It was, Goldman recalled, a bizarre duel.

Now he leafed slowly through the notes and memoranda covering the subsequent months. On the corner of one page, he had doodled a rough graph of the case, with its characteristic curve – small rises followed by sharp drops, monotonous plateaux and moments of recoil or backlash when all the work accomplished seemed like blank waste.

You thrash away from the wreck, somehow, blindly. The suction pulls you under, into the drag of black water and black oil. Your lungs burst with the cold filth pouring in. Each time you flail to the surface, the downdrag gets stronger. So does the temptation to let go, to swallow the muck and have done. But the whirlpool vomits you to the light, and you find yourself swimming. There is someone swimming just to one side and a little behind you, and at first the shore looks near, say half a year off, like an unwavering line between the trough of the waves. But it comes no closer. When you crane your neck, with enormous effort, to see beyond the grey heave of water, the line has vanished or changed direction. You are kept going by the stroke of the swimmer behind you. It has the beat of sane purpose, it seems to know where you're going. But it doesn't hold you up, or very little. And you come to loathe the drive of it with a spent hatred. Sometimes, with immense luck, you reach shore. Usually, it's only a spit of brackish sand, with more seas on the other side. There is no certain end to an analysis, no warm and promised earth for the soul to drowse on unguarded. At best, you will learn to swim with the cold and treasons of the current, rather than against, and you will dive into the deep not for oblivion, but for its secret, nocturnal roots which, when we touch them with salutation and reserve, yield us what power we have to endure on the mutinous waves.

It was the antique allegory of the mind's harassed voyage. Goldman had learnt the force of it during his own training analysis. With each case, he felt its truth renewed.

Maune started out bravely. If this evil thing lurked inside him, he would come to know it full-face. But he could not believe that it *was* evil. On the contrary. The probe had touched a central nerve. Hence the gust of rage and the flight from the net. The intimacy with Reeve wove its skein around the core of his own life. Nothing in that life had been finer, richer of meaning, than the brief companionship of Jan K. in Cairo, in 1942. Now the strong place had been broken open and pillaged, the last of his possessions strewn in a hard light. Maune felt as if he had taken a hammer to his own skull.

In December, Goldman had sent down a summary of the case, a contour of work in progress. It was written in a code of brevity, of wilful simplification, and as he read it now, his lips miming, irony assailed him.

'Classical preconditions for sexual ambivalence: early death of father; the mother a dominant force; a house full of sisters. In school, the development of the libido was inevitably associated with latent homosexual patterns. M. is himself aware of the coincidence between corporal punishment and erotic stimulation. Coincidence looms large in his onanistic fantasies. In R. he found a substitute father-figure, one who judges, punishes and protects.

'The affair at Oxford, with its accidental pregnancy (?), confirmed the pattern of ambivalence. M. was apparently seduced by a woman who exhibited initiative and specific masculine traits (he recalls her *rough voice* and *broad hands*). By sending R. in his place, he subconsciously denied his own sexual responsibility. The fear and humiliation were traumatic. Yet, at the same time, M. buttressed his ego with the conviction that he had proved his virility, that he had performed the part of the man and the father.

'Then came the war, with its re-enactment of school fantasies and rituals. The pack mauling and yelling in the field, body to body, only more naked than rugger. The latent homosexual impulses hover near. In the amorous sweat of groundcrews waiting for their pilots to come home. The kilted boys play the pipes, and the officers stride into combat behind them, carrying their canes. Many of the women met were brown or olive. They did not speak proper English. Hence they were outside the rules. One could ask them or pay them to *do the things* middle-aged men and boys have fantasies about when they masturbate.

'For Maune, the war meant separation from R. But it brought the chumminess of the ward room and the affair with Jan K.'

(At this point, Goldman had doodled a question mark, and it had spiralled into a chaotic serpent. He began to skip intervening pages.)

'M.'s motives for wanting a child are complex. Compulsive desire to prove to himself and his wife that he is *normal*, that he can have children like any other man. At the same time, he has an acute, neurotic insight into the fact that a child keeps a woman busy, that it compensates for a certain diminution of sexual activity. It takes off the pressure. The idea of adoption was intolerable precisely because it leaves open the question of personal sexual adequacy. In many English middle-class families, children are not necessarily a proof of sustained sexual interest; they may represent evasion from it, or compensation. Complicated subject; needs to be clarified.

'With R.'s return from America, M.'s dormant homosexuality, and the associated masochistic fantasies, were intensely activated. The neurosis declared itself (symptoms of jaundice, spells of insomnia, heavy drinking, the severe back pains in August). The rebellion against the super-ego, with its heterosexual demands and standards, assumed drastic forms. The danger of a manic-depressive cycle, or of complete nervous collapse, cannot be ruled out. M. himself seems aware of this, and the analysis is showing progress.'

He pushed the file away, and a shrug passed through his stooped shoulders. A glass, or a knife clicking against a plate, sounded from somewhere in the house. G minor, thought Goldman, the key of evening.

All very neat, like a case in the textbooks or the *Traumdeutung*. The Sphinx lay on her back purring. But what relation did it have to the vital disorder, to the singularity of a man's ruin? No more than had the mite of tissue, mounted on a slide, to the multitudinous weave and cunning of organic life.

Exasperation rose in him, like bile. *What should he have done?*

'I am not God, though there are moments in analysis when the analyst takes on a queer authority, when he pities or torments as God does His creatures. "Give the patient's ego *freedom* to choose one way or the other." The italics are the Master's. But that's arrogance and self-deception. How can he choose, how can we ask him to, in a society whose laws and expectations are outside our control? We do not live in a vacuum where all rational possibilities could, in fact, be explored. Suppose I had said to Maune: "Stop this bitter, suicidal process of repression. Let the energies and drives of the id penetrate your ego instead of undermining it. Your present mode of emotional and sexual life is a legal fiction, built on the needs others have felt for you, not on your own. This obsessive desire to conceive a child is a mask. If the homosexual compulsion asserts itself – and it is probably less frequent or exclusive than you unconsciously fear – don't choke it down at the price of your health and sanity. If you need to be slapped on the buttocks once in a while in order to live at peace with the energies of your psyche, with its receptive and creative powers, don't make a production of it. Go to it, as a man might do when he has to relieve himself against a hedge. The psyche can burn as sharply as the bladder. There is hardly a human being alive in our crazy warren who doesn't have a poisonous itch under the skin. You're luckier than most, because you've seen yours, not for a dragon, but for what it is – a cumbersome, ugly, but by no means rare housepest. Don't pretend it isn't there. Live with it. Easier to let it have dog-biscuit than raven on your own flesh."

'But what right have I to say that if I can't, at the same time, reorganize our whole *meschugene* society? If I can't cry from the roof-tops that half the marriages I know about among men of that type and class are a sham? I'm neither God nor the Archbishop of Canterbury. What should I have done? And if our culture were to change, to change radically, who would need psychiatry?'

Goldman yielded to a familiar vertigo. Unawares, his hands sketched an immemorial gesture of ironic defeat, palms raised and outspread.

'I didn't even try to say those things. I did nothing to subvert M.'s belief that he could work "*this garbage*" out of his system. And the crust of illusion was beginning to harden and take life when those other dreams came.'

Goldman sought to make hindsight scrupulous. He *had* known. Not exactly, but as in the hot doze of a fever, when we know that we are not ourselves, not only. Just out of reach, another presence loomed. It was in the room during those three weeks, and he had waited for it to spring. It crouched in Gerald's voice, in his meticulous, absorbed apartness, the man listening to himself, rigid and dizzy, like someone bending from a great height. Goldman *had* realized – he was not consoling himself now, after the fact – that Gerald's words were not directed at him, or only obliquely, that he was overhearing a dialogue, as of wrestlers careening in the room, their teeth clenched.

These dreams were compact and luminous, like a spray of poison-berries. With gashes of bright colour, where M.'s preceding reveries had been invariably dun.

Ash trees calling, coughing in the wind, and when the dreamer lunged out of the house, naked, the branches shearing loose like birds, and burying him with reeking droppings. Dreams that showed a puerile, sadistic wit. M. in an empty house, the phone ringing. Water rising from the floor. M. compulsively anxious to find the receiver. Feels himself drowning. Woken, inside the dream, by a man saying, 'I wanted to give you a toot on the blower.' M. sees the man turning to the wall and hears a drilling sound. Wakes with the nursery-twister – peck of pickles – on his tongue. The *blower*, the *pecker*, the rise of water, all beautifully ravelled. The repressed fantasies of the libido seemed to have torn loose. They were stomping through the psyche in a crude devil's dance. Too crude. Goldman had sensed it. Same feeling if he had observed Maune entering the consulting-room unwashed.

Alien splinters in Maune's usual speech. Like the Americanism in the nightmare turning on the ambiguity of *deck* (a *deck* of cards, the *deck* of a boat).

That lewd fragment: a beggar unscrewing his leg, urinating on a chessboard full of pawns, and saying to M. that he had to hurry back to his shop. When Goldman had drawn attention to the coil of meaning (beggar-peddlar-piddler-*pédale*, the common French slang for homosexual; the obvious castration gesture, and the connotations of *screw*; the old, randy joke about meeting at the *pawnshop* to kiss under the balls), Gerald had shown no disgust, only an uncanny, tense fascination.

The suspicion that some game was being played, that Maune was compounding these strident dreams out of a manual of psychopathology, had crossed Goldman's mind. Gerald would not have been the first. At moments when the ego lay fallow or gagged, other patients had filched dreams out of novels and even the works of Freud, either to trick the analyst, or not to come empty-handed.

Why had he not challenged him straight out? Simply because these dreams had a gross but intimate relevance. They were a brutal mimicry of the covert, tentative shadowplay of repression and censorship, but they followed closely the contours of Maune's neurosis. In one of the notes he took during the second week, Goldman had scribbled the word *schizophrenia*? But he had crossed it out. It did not fit the case. Some part of M. appeared to have broken out of the grip of identity. Goldman recalled the strange passage in Aquinas which defines ghosts as shreds of our psyche, momentarily transmitted into pure force. Listening to those dreams, he had felt the

dim feverishness of the ghost brushing his skin. But he had not wanted
to arrest what might be a dangerous, yet ultimately healing trick of the
subconscious.

That was why he had not responded to Maune's provocation: 'Is
there nothing *you* want to say, Dr Goldman, nothing you want to tell
me?' Nor had been unduly perturbed when Gerald announced that he
was off on a business trip for a couple of weeks, that he was planning
'to use up the expense account'.

Once more, Goldman raked over in his mind every detail of that
Friday afternoon. He felt certain – or almost – that the shock of a secret
need had passed through him. That he was on the point of calling
Maune back from the door to ask – where are those dreams from?
What vulgar devil is running your life just now? But, in fact, he had
said no more than: 'Very well, I'll be waiting to hear from you when
you're back.' Now he had heard.

Again, the drowsy scent of Hannah's cooking warmed the air. When
Goldman straightened, the weight in his spine and shoulders shifted
painfully. He was bone-tired. But he dug his elbows into the table and
began rereading the letter, for the third time. Twelve pages, neatly
pinned, and covered to the very edge with an urgent, exact hand. The
paper itself was grey. It was emblazoned at the top: *Hotel de France*,
Cracow, and the *w* ended in a baroque flourish which rejoined the crest
of the *C*.

Even as he strained to keep his attention unwavering, to hold in
abeyance the impulse of anger and blame, Goldman remembered
Aaron's loud pleasure at the Polish stamps.

8

Dear Dr Goldman,
Early on, you warned me against writing letters. A patient who writes
his analyst is evading. I know. But this time it's different. I have to
write because I won't be seeing you again. And I'm not running away.
I'm coming clean. Now that's a queer one. One never *comes* clean. You
know, in the other sense. Here am I starting to play the game, to find
things *inside* words. It hasn't been a waste. I've learned a lot from you.

Don't think I'm ungrateful. Only ashamed. About that last bit.

Those were not *my* dreams. Not the last three weeks. I kept hoping you'd guess. Then I didn't want you to. I realized that it wasn't fair, that I was playing a nasty trick. But it is odd that you didn't smell a rat (I lost £100 betting that you *would*). Perhaps you did and weren't letting on. You said once that a patient can't lie, not really, because his lies are often the loudest part of the truth. So you listened, as if those dreams had been my own, and helped me spin the filth and cunning out of them. On the last day, I was damn near to telling you. But I couldn't face up to it. And it didn't seem to matter any more. Because those fake dreams made me see myself as I am. More than anything else that has ever happened to me, or that you've said. Now that I think of it, you never did say very much. I suppose that's the art of it. Make the patient scour the wall until it turns to a mirror. Make *him* do it, or he won't get a sharp look at himself. I have. Right inside those counterfeit dreams. After that, I knew whom I wanted to see before I packed up. That's why I left to come here.

Is that what Reeve wanted? He wrote those dreams out on small sheets of blue notepaper, and sent them twice a week, registered. I had promised to learn them by heart and try them on you. It makes my skin crawl to write this. I know what you'll think of me. I'm sorry. Please believe that. He said he would show you up for a fraud, so I would have to stand on my own feet. In a way, I'm sorry you didn't guess (I couldn't really afford that hundred quid). But I don't see that it proves anything about analysis. Either way. We don't close down the National Gallery just because it's bought a fake picture. And I don't think that's what Reeve was after. Not really. He hates the whole business, a man pouring his vomit into another man's lap. That's how he put it. I dare say there's something in that. Like a chap in the mess not able to keep down his liquor and puking all over his orderly. And Reeve got a dose of it in America. To listen to him, you'd think it was the national sport over there. But there was something *else*.

In the old days we were very close. I could tell the mood he was in by the sound of his step halfway down the stairs. He used to finish my sentences for me. We had words we shared with no one else. Reeve was faster than I, and much, much cleverer. But I had more weight. When the gale caught us, that time off the Broads, he said he'd pitch me overboard and use me for an anchor. But during the war we lost touch. And for me there was someone else. I don't know how to put this without making it sound crazy. But I wonder whether it was *you* Reeve was after, whether it was really the analysis that enraged him. He doesn't know about Jan. He couldn't. But a pointer will sniff a man and know if he's been with another dog. Reeve has a nose. He can smell the soul in you.

I didn't realize how alone he was when he came back from the States, how sick at the edges. I thought I needed him to keep those nightmares off. But they got worse. I must have been afraid that he'd get on to the scent, that he'd try to put his hand on something I wouldn't let him touch. Him or anyone. Not Sheila. Not you. So he went after it. Like a thief hunting for a hidden room in a house, tearing up the floorboards, making a shambles. Reeve lied about Ina. To keep me off-balance, to make certain of my need. I don't have to lie to myself any more. Ever. She *was* going to have a child, and if I hadn't acted like vermin, if I'd gone to her and taken my chance, the whole of my life might have turned right.

But Reeve wouldn't have me free or out of his reach. He knew better than to worry about Sheila. It wasn't she who had stepped between us, who made him alone when we were together. I'm not saying he thought it all out, or planned it down to the last detail. I don't imagine that's how it happens. But the dreams he sent were devilish clever. *You* must have known for a long time where the real trouble lay. But I wasn't going to admit it to myself. Reeve ground my face in the truth till it flayed my skin and nearly gouged my eyes out. He must have hoped that that would drive me back to him, that I would come all broken and reach out for him. We could hobble together, picking up the pieces of our lives, and stick close, as if there was only one wretched shadow for the two of us.

I know it sounds mad, but Reeve wanted the quick of me, the last secret place of the living spirit. So that he would never be alone, never again. That must be the sin they don't talk about, the one that can't be forgiven. To put your grip on another man's self, to filch it for your own use.

I promise you, I'm not off my head. I know that Reeve wouldn't understand half of what I'm saying (I can see the face he'd make reading this). But because of what's happened these last days, and because I know the end, I can look at things plain. As if an enormous cold light had switched on.

I imagine Reeve is pretty well damned for what he did, for trying to flush the soul out of me with those dreams. He'll walk the floors of Hell blazing. And won't even feel it.

Not that it matters very much now. I've seen Jan, and that's what I have to tell you about. But first, there was the boy.

I had forty-eight hours' leave in Cairo. We knew there was a big push on. Every time I thought of what I was going back to, my insides did a flip. So I kept on the move, buying a lot of fancy trash and crowding it in a room, a hidden place of my own, in a jumble of mud-houses and garden down by the river. Carved fly-swatters, a stuffed cat with yellow glass eyes – Hamid swore by his mother's sacred tits that they were topaz – a Turkish musket, a grand thing all chased in silver. To make the room so absurdly and secretly my own, that I would have to come back to it, dead or alive.

On the second day, I did the bazaars. You have to dive deep holding your breath. The usual pack was at my heels, and all around me, feeling my clothes and shrilling. If you haven't seen it, the living filth and misery of wog children is something no one can make you believe. There were the things one reads about: the open sores, the worms they squeeze out of themselves in the street, the flies hanging in bunches from the mouths and eyelids of the blind. But what I hadn't known about was that smell – a yellowish smell that came at you from their breath and skin – the smell of hunger. I took what change I had and bought a bagful of candied fruit, great sticky globs. It was like tossing crumbs in the sea, gone in a minute, and the little devils pawing and whining at me worse than before.

Then the boy came. He was a head taller than the rest, and had marvellous white teeth. He kicked and flung about till the pack trailed off. Then he asked whether he could carry my purchases: 'I shall not steal. By Allah, I shall not steal.'

He walked just behind me, soft as a young wolf. It was hot; hotter than I'd ever known it, even in Cairo. More than likely, I had a touch of sun and fever. Everything around me seemed to flap. The fly-curtains, the awnings and tin shutters, the air like a stinking bat whirring and flapping around my head. We threaded our way home through those back alleys, the sewers running with filth. I thought I'd go mad if I didn't get to a cool place and a shower. I felt the boy at my heels. He had a high, dainty step, as if no dirt could touch him.

On a day like that, a room in which the shutters have been closed, or which gets a breath of wind off the river, is like a cold-box. I heard his teeth click as he put down the birdcage – it had brass foliage and little bells, and must have been lifted from one of the old French whorehouses – and a cane I'd haggled for, with an ivory handle. He slipped around the room, looking at my gear, passing his hand over my towels and bedsheets. The flapping was in my brain, and I was anxious to get rid of him. I dug in my pockets for a bill, when I saw him pick up my flashlight. It had a blue plastic finish and a switch to cut the beam high or low. You can get it at any Woolworth, but I could tell he'd never seen anything like it. He switched it on and played it against the wall. He was so excited that he'd stopped breathing.

'I want this. Please give it to me. Please, gracious Sir.'

'Why should I? What will you do for it?' I meant nothing saying it.

'I'll do anything, Effendi, anything.'

It was the word *anything*. It must have unhinged me; I could hear the nerves inside me going strange. I don't think I uttered a word. But he looked at me grinning. He was only wearing shorts and a rag around his neck. When I put my forehead against his naked skin, it was all burning and cool. Then I must have lost control. I turned him around and pushed him on to the bed. Even if I wanted to, I couldn't tell you what happened. I don't remember. Only his laugh when he slid out the door.

After a while, I came around and saw he had taken the flashlight, my plastic raincoat, a pack of Player's and two tins of dried milk.

When I was a child and had been wicked – 'played with myself' or cribbed – I was sure I'd perish the next day, in some hideous accident. Unless I could do certain laborious magic rites, hammer my head against the floor when saying my prayers, or flip a knife into the ground off the back of my hand, nine times in a row. Even then, I knew something would go wrong, that I'd be punished.

After the boy, I expected that I'd be killed the moment I got back in the show. I even wrote the usual letter: 'To be sent in case of . . .' I was literally waiting for the bullet to plough through me. Actually, it was a piece of shrapnel, two nights later, on a forward patrol near Sidi Meraa. I remember lying there wondering why it took so long to die, and why it didn't hurt more. I tried to think of the boy, and found I couldn't remember his face. Then they picked me up.

The base hospital was overcrowded and there were holes in the fly-netting. That can be torture, with the sand-flies going at your bandages and the heat coming down on you like a foul blanket. There wasn't enough of anything to go around except English ladies from Cairo, elderly ladies mostly, with cool dresses, asking whether they could write letters for you or read to you from the Good Book. Most of the chaps were browned off, and made fun of them behind their backs. But I thought them rather sporting, and so did Jan.

He was in the bed next to mine. He had a Polish accent and courtly manners. When one of the old girls had read to him, he would stick his head out from under the netting and kiss her hand, saying, 'Thank you, Madam, I am your debtor.' The other men found it a huge joke. But Jan had a trick of staring you down. His eyes were night-blue; I'd never seen anything like them. He had pitch-black hair, and despite the desert his skin had stayed pale. He was small, but all wire. The rest of us shuffled in those shapeless grey slippers they handed out; he moved down the ward like a fencer, his heel barely touching.

The medical chaps were a bit afraid of him. When he said, 'I shall be out of here in ten days from *now*, and I want no misunderstanding about that,' they smiled feebly and went to the next bed. Soon he announced to Matron, in a tone of implacable sweetness, that there were only four days to go. Would she be so gracious as to see that his kit was ready? She tried her bark, but before she could get a sentence out, Jan had bounded from his cot, bowed low, and proffered a small bouquet of violets (God knows how or where he had managed to get them; they were dark as velvet). The old sea-cow burbled into complete submission: 'Oh, Lieutenant Jan. Oh.' No one ever tried his full name.

He served as liaison between our brigade and the Second Polish Army. His motor cycle had triggered a mine. The driver was blown to shreds, but the side-car came down on top of Jan and he had only flesh-wounds.

He had seen his family – his father, mother, and two sisters, one aged twelve – herded into a barn by the SS. Then they had set the barn alight. Cowering under a pile of dung and wet leaves, Jan had watched the flames and heard the screams in the fire. Somehow, he had escaped and got across the Baltic. The Danes put him in a foster-home. It was a barrack and smelt of tar-soap. When the Germans came, he smuggled his way on to a herring trawler. They were blown off-course and had no water to drink the last forty-eight hours. They reached harbour, somewhere in East Anglia, and the authorities were gravely perturbed because Jan had no papers. He still laughed under his breath when he recalled their embarrassed mien, or how they'd said, 'There'll be tea served in a moment,' when he asked for water.

At eighteen, he had joined the Polish forces in London. Now he was in the desert, 'running errands and killing Germans'. He was the first man I met who thought of it in that way, who had a personal war. He said that whenever he could, he shot low, so that they would feel themselves die. Once he had surprised a three-man German patrol dead-asleep near their weapons-carrier. He stole in barefoot and slit the throats of two of them, leaving the poor bugger in the middle to wake between them. 'I don't want to survive this war, Maune. It would be a jolly bad thing if I did. They'd have to put me in a cage.' But mostly he spoke of books or music. And when the pains came on (I had a splinter of the bloody thing in my kidney), Jan would bend over from his cot, hold my wrist, and whistle like a thrush.

We took our convalescent leave together. Jan bought a victrola with a large, antique horn, and set it in the midst of my loot. He rifled the bazaar for old records. I had never known much about music. It wasn't the sort of thing you did at school. Now we lay in the dark listening, Italian opera mostly, and those hot, cracked voices pouring out gusts of life. The cicadas in the garden rose to the sound. Often we were too lazy or entranced to get up; the record went on hissing under the needle, and behind it came the wailings from the river. There was one tune Jan played over and over. I don't suppose I've got the name right. 'Nessun dorma': 'No one sleeps in the city tonight'. And the voice made a wild, soaring curve. We didn't sleep either. It was too hot; the air was so heavy you could push it with your hand. And there was so little time. Our chit only ran to a week.

It's the only time in my life I've been completely happy. At peace. He liked to lie on the floor, his blue eyes open, like embers. Watching Jan, I knew what it meant to be in love with another human being. To say anything you wanted, even if it was new or confused, without having to talk. As if one's body, and the mere fact of being near, had voice. It sounds like pretentious rubbish, and I don't imagine I can make you see it. I've told you how close I was to Reeve, and I've been fond of Sheila. More than that. I've loved her in my own way, and wanted her. It's excited me to know she was in the house, to hear her moving about. But when I compare that to what I felt for Jan, it's as if I was talking another language. It's the only time I've stopped being *me*, that I've got out! Skin, my castle, my cell. But not with Jan. As if you could melt into another person, not to pillage, not to master, but to lie at rest in.

I thought we would both be killed soon. That made it all clear and right. It was the marvellous trick death had in store. The schedule had gone awry and we were being allowed a taste of it while we were still in the sun, and could hear each other turn in sleep.

I told him about the boy. Jan made a flute of his cupped hands and blew a long note, like the blind man in the café. Then he laughed and said that the English were voluptuaries of remorse. He repeated it in Polish and it came out like dry wood cracking. He believed there was *no* experience one should forgo, not with death our neighbour. He was certain that the soul was immortal only through the power of its memories, that the strong grass over graves came from recollections thrown like seed into the rushing dark. One must not go empty-handed, but with such store of particular remembrance that eternity would seem too hasty. It was not Plato or Aquinas had proved the soul immortal, but Proust. I had never heard of Proust. Jan drummed on the wall and said I was a barbarian. And a hypocrite; for having bribed the boy: 'Love bought is like old fish. It leaves a smell.'

You remember that time I flew into a black rage. Because you were making me out to be a queer. I wouldn't have it. Not then, or at any time. This was something else. Utterly. I suppose I lied to you when I said Jan and I had not touched. But not really. The lie is in you and in anyone stupid enough to think that the words meant anything of what happened between us, that they tell even an inch of the truth. The words are beastly. And meaningless. As if you were trying to make a man see the sun by the dark of its leaving.

I've known something – I dare say it was only a minute – which most human beings – oh, the lot of them – never get a glimpse of, not in their wildest dreams. We touched. Hardly that. Mostly, we only lay near each other. But I can swear by God's face that the stuff in the poems is true, about the stars coming down on top of a living man. I know because it happened. In that room – and the blackness outside holding its breath, going dead still.

I won't reread this letter. I'd be afraid to. It must sound like drivel. But why should I care? I'd cry it from the roof-tops if I could. This *has* happened to me. I've heard my own soul dance. If you don't believe me, it's because it's never happened to you. Don't you see? I've had all the luck.

And am doomed for it, I suppose. Because I've gone around comparing everything else in my life to that week – to those two or three nights out of time. It's made all the rest ash in my mouth.

I tried to forget about it. You know how hard I tried, all the games I played with myself. But just as Jan said, forgetting is the death of you. The real living death. You walk about and act as if you're alive, but you're stone dead inside. I was honest about Sheila. I pitched my heart into it. But it was never as good. Not like that bit of flame. Right in the marrow.

That's the whole truth. I'm not going to try to tell you any more. I'm rich. I'm taking it with me. You can close your file (how I hated that brown cover!) and put at the end: *repressed homosexual*. I don't care, because it's gibberish. Like a monkey spewing words. It means nothing. Not to *me*.

Perhaps it would to Jan. Perhaps it would put him in a fury. I don't know. Because he's different now. I had to go and see him once more. After Reeve tried to cheat the living daylight out of me. I had to see Jan, to make sure that he remembered, that there was someone else in the world who knew the truth, who could tell me that I hadn't dreamt miracles. I *have* seen him. These last few days. As I say, he's different.

I could tell the moment I saw him. He sat encased in a square-cut tunic, and a great laugh was coming out of him, raucous, out of the

302

belly. He rose at me, arms flung wide, calling my name, but not looking at me, not straight. We hugged and panted at each other like circus bears. He had told me to meet him in a kind of tavern, in the Old City, down a flight of stone steps. They're rebuilding that part of Warsaw, brick by brick, to get it exactly as it was, the same doorknockers, the same window-boxes. To prove you can't make oblivion, even with dynamite, and so memories will have a place to lean on. Rather like what you're doing, isn't it? Brick by brick. Clearing the rubble with a fine-tooth comb.

There was a mob, but Jan barged through. Two women were sitting at our table. They flurried about me, kissed me, and dabbed their faces. One was his wife, the other her cousin or best friend. I couldn't make it out. They spoke very little English and kept saying my name as if they had a sweet at the end of their tongues. Jan shouted for the waiter, and we drank a gulp of something that went down like raw flame. It nearly spun me out of my chair, but the women pounded my back and said, 'Hallo, Gerald, hallo, Gerald.' My eyes were tearing and Jan looked bulky and far away. They heaped our table with small dishes, all hot and full of seed, and paraded around us carrying burning things on spits. The other woman – a tall girl with flat shoulders and pale, sandy hair – kept putting little dabs and bites on her spoon and passing them to me. I didn't know what I was eating. It made me steamy inside, so I poured that iced blazing stuff down my throat. Each time we emptied a bottle, they stuck a candle in it, and soon there was a lit crown in the middle. I could see Jan's face through a hot mist; it ran sweat.

We danced. There were so many people packed in that stifling cellar, that all you had to do was clutch tight and turn on your heels. The girl pressed her hands in the small of my back, and I could taste the wine on her breath. Jan kept lurching into us, or giving me a happy jab with his boot. I don't suppose they've seen many Englishmen in Warsaw, and Jan sang out at the top of his voice about how we'd fought together in the desert and eaten Jerries alive. So men and women crowded close, perfect strangers, all gaping and excited, carrying fruit-brandy or vodka, and demanding that I drink with them. Then the band played 'Tipperary' (would you believe it? 'Tipperary' – in this day and age!), and the girl laid her cheek to mine. It was full of tears.

We slogged our way back to the table. It was again heaped with food and sweet wine. As we sat down, the girl caught my hand and set it on her knee. My head was hammering, and I could see the whole room taking a slow turn. But I felt her running my palm up and down her stocking, all the way under her dress, right to the skin. When I drew away, she swayed after me and dropped her head on my shoulder. Jan and his wife winked and made noises, like children at a party. Then the two women went off to the powder-room, their arms around each other.

Jan and I locked elbows and drank, the way he'd taught me in Cairo. He said I looked puffy and out of sorts – 'like salt-haddock'. Poland would put life in me. Yes, he'd stayed in the army. Killing was the only thing he'd ever been trained for properly. He was too dangerous to be let out of the zoo. So he was in the cage, but at the lion's end. He was a colonel now. Colonel Jan. I tried to ask more, but he cut me off. 'No serious talk tonight.' There'd be plenty of time for that. I ducked and some of the brandy dribbled on to my collar, but Jan got it down me anyway, and the women were back saying we should dance.

The fiddles came at us and the band tapped their red lacquered boots on the floor. I was in the middle and felt the girl's hold go soft and spin away. People were clapping hands and shouting at me to do a reel. I must have looked a damned fool. But the clapping came quicker, as if blackbirds were at my head, and I could hear glass breaking. Then the ceiling took a sickening dive and I shut my eyes.

Jan caught me and trotted me up the stairs in a rush. We were in a black, wet yard. The air was ice. It belted me in the stomach and I threw up. Jan held my head, laughing: 'You're out of practice, Gerald! You remember the night at the mess, when you made me drink Black Velvet till it came out of my ears!' I cleaned up in the washroom and tried to drink from the tap. It came out rusty, and Jan brought a bottle of mineral water. I felt better, just a little chill and light in the head. Jan was telling me about the girl. Her fiancé had been shot down in the rising. Two Russians had found her crouching in a sewer. They'd taken their time with her. Now she had a taste for men. But she was a fine girl and would show me the sights. I wanted to find out about Jan's wife, about what he'd been up to. But he talked in a loud, flailing torrent, and I couldn't stop him.

It must have been three in the morning before we shambled out of the place and into Jan's jeep. There are few cars in Warsaw and he's madly proud of his. The girl and I bundled in the back seat and he yelled at us to hold tight. He made wild, clucking sounds at the ignition as if it was a horse. Then he jammed the accelerator to the floor and we swung out of the cobbled square in a screech. There are hardly any lights, and the roads are makeshift tracks between craters and piles of rubble. Suddenly you're in a maze of high walls, with window-frames hanging loose, or bits of bath-tub swaying in the empty air, then back in the charred waste, up to the mud-guards in yellow water.

Jan whipped the car in and out of those smashed streets as if we had been on the Le Mans circuit. We were shouting, but when he turned or slammed the brakes, it knocked the wind out of us. All the time, he was damning or coaxing the jeep in a high-pitched call.

We careened through a foul pit, with an old coil of barbed wire lashing the wheel, and over a mound of debris on the other side, when the whistles started behind us. Jan pulled the jeep to a sudden halt; the girl fell all over me, gasping. Jan grinned at us like a small, devilish boy: 'That'll be the militia. They hate the army, and they hate anyone who can run their own car. They've got a little Russian job. Pure junk. I can beat them blindfold. And they know it. Now watch!'

He caressed the wheel and we ripped away. Down a tunnel of broken walls and mudholes. There were no street lamps and Jan kept his own lights low. Shadows and solid edges flew at us, and I kept my head down in complete panic. The whistles were closing in, and I could hear Jan sing between his teeth. The militia had us in their headlights when he threw the jeep into a mad turn, two wheels off the ground, shot over a wooden trestle, and through a gate into sudden calm. The militiamen whistled and shouted, but had stopped outside. Jan tilted his head back and let out a happy roar: 'Military zone! Off-bounds. They can't follow us here. It's about the only place where the weasels can't get at you.' I made out a dim hulk of barracks and saw a sentinel – he wasn't more than a boy – give a startled salute.

The women sat up and rubbed the jolt out of their ribs. Their breath came short and excited. Jan said he and his wife had a fine room in the officers' compound. That was a feat. Rooms were hard to come by.

Why didn't we go up now and get a bit of sleep, the four of us. The girl gave a tense giggle and pressed against my thigh. Jan said there was room to spare. We would make coffee – real coffee – and get out of our clothes. He too was excited and looked straight into the dark.

I said no; that I'd rather go back to my hotel and meet him the next day. He turned and gave me an odd stare. Then he explained to the two women, with heavy gaiety, that in England it was customary for ladies and gentlemen to separate after dinner. *Ladies* and *gentlemen*; he repeated the words with hollow emphasis. We shook hands and embraced, and the two women trailed off across open ground. I climbed into the front seat and Jan started the motor.

He drove carefully now, without pleasure. We crossed a moon landscape of ruin, and came to the edge of the river. Jan halted. We watched the first streak of dawn stain the high bluffs on the eastern bank.

'That's where the Red Army stood and waited during the rising. They didn't even let their artillery open fire on the Germans. We sent couriers swimming across, desperate for help. But they waited. Till the *Wehrmacht* had wiped us out and killed the best.'

He said it without hate or insurgence, nearly in admiration of a tactic so far-reaching, so tenacious in nerveless cunning.

'What they liberated was a desert full of women and starved children. The women were so shell-shocked that many of them didn't utter a sound when the Kazakhs grabbed them. But now Ivan's our ally, and we get to love him better each time you ship a tank or gun to Adenauer. What fools you are. To trust Germans. To buy the tiger a new set of teeth.'

Light was beginning to move on the water. I told Jan I had not come to argue politics, but to talk about the past, about the strong remembrance that kept us from the dark. What had happened to our room in Cairo? Who used it now? And did Jan remember the elephant-foot umbrella stand? I had to make sure that my poor devil of a soul hadn't fed on lies.

He lit a cigarette and blew a smoke-ring, and watched it unwreathe in the cold air.

'What is there to talk about? Does it worry you? It's something that happens to boys, in the school lavatory, or when they're out together in the woods. In the green woods. We were both a little slow growing up. That's all. Why churn up your guts about it?'

I cried out. His voice was like pain inside me. He couldn't mean what he'd just said. It was too stupid, too vulgar. It left me nothing.

Jan heard. I knew because the lines of his face had gone sharp. But he wasn't listening.

Instead: 'Why were you so awkward back there? Acting like a wet hen. You should have gone with us. That's a nice girl. You've hurt her feelings.'

I couldn't get the words right. Like treacle in my mouth. But I tried. God, how I tried! To make him see why I'd come. How it was the world to me. I tried to tell him about Reeve and those dreams. About the voices in the fire (I know *now* whose voices they were). How they burned and hammered in my skull. I won't repeat to you what I said. I couldn't bear to. I was skinning myself alive. Right there sitting in that car. Every layer of me. Till I could smell myself, down deep. I swear to you it made me sick.

And all the time he was smoking and looking at the river. No one could have stood it long without going wild. To be so alone right next to him, to cry into the wind and get nothing back. It was God-awful. He just sat there, all blank and armoured, and kept his sleeve from brushing against mine.

He let me talk until my mouth went dry. Then he turned the ignition and looked straight at me. It was the first time that night.

'Ah, you English. You voluptuaries of remorse.'

He didn't remember that he had said it before. I know he didn't remember. But because the words were the same, exactly, because they came out with that same cracked sound, time went weird. For a moment we were back in our room in Cairo. I swear we were. Jan's eyes had that hot, blue point in them. It made me go soft and a bit crazy with remembrance. I must have leaned towards him or looked out of hand. Because he hit me, oh, not hard, but enough to knock me out.

I woke in my hotel room, sick as a dog. I sat on my bed retching, and felt so sorry for myself I bawled.

After a while, I found Jan's note. He had torn a page from my diary where it had fallen on the floor when he carried me in.

He said we had drunk too much. We were old men now and shouldn't have got so pissed. He was sorry. He didn't really remember the things I had referred to. In any case, he was sure they weren't worth raking up. He couldn't imagine life without Rada, and hoped that I too would soon get married. He misspelt *married*.

That's all there is to tell. I left for Cracow the next morning. To be someplace else. This is a handsome town, and I've had time to get things untangled.

I don't care about anything any more. Or *anyone*. That's the best time to decamp, isn't it?

I'm sorry about all the trouble, and about lying to you. But that's under the bridge now. I know you'll give Sheila what help you can. She's a level-headed girl, and she'll be all right. Life owes her another turn. I'd like to have told Reeve that he was too clever by half. Right to his hound's face. And to see the ash on him. Because he's going to burn. Believe me. He's going to burn.

But it doesn't matter now. Nothing does. It's a strange, grand feeling, like the time I flopped into the Dead Sea and it carried me so easy I could sleep on the water.

I imagine this is quite the longest letter you've ever had. I feel rather posh taking it to the post office. But I'd best get on with it.

Wars kill a long time after, don't they? Thanks for everything.

Yours very sincerely,

GERALD MAUNE

For a long time, Goldman kept staring at the neatly pinned bundle of paper, helpless. As soon as he had read the letter, he had alerted Mrs Maune and Reeve, and cabled the embassy in Warsaw.

Now he was waiting for news. But not really. Simply for the ring of the bell or the voice at the door which would confirm what he knew already. A man does not need to draw the curtain when it has been snowing the night through, he hears the dead quiet in the morning air.

Goldman rubbed his palms against the blotter. They were numb. A mortal tiredness bent him. In a corner of his mind he was aware that Hannah had called to dinner, that she had knocked twice at the door of his study. But moments passed before he could turn his head and answer.

9

Gerald Maune left the post office feeling beautifully easy. It was a mood he could place. The last Friday of term, in the afternoon, when the trunks stood ready and the clothes-boxes tightly roped, when the sheets had been stripped from the beds, leaving only the neat square of blankets. There were always twenty minutes or half an hour in hand before the bus loaded, taking the boys to the station and the start of the journey home. Gerald would stroll in the garden, by the long wall, and watch Brackens go silent, the cries and rush of feet passing from it, like a covey of loud birds receding.

After the rubble and crude renascence of Warsaw, Cracow intact was balm. Gerald set out for the castle, but was soon enmeshed in a hive of cobbled streets. The contour of bastions and turrets, which rode high over the city, had vanished behind the near gables and chimney-pots. He sought to retrace his steps and looked up at the street-signs with their spiky consonants, so many dragons mute. A girl stopped and asked whether she could be of help. Her English was brave but short of breath. She had plain, broad features and wore glasses. In her brown mackintosh and cork-soled shoes, she looked old and a little charred. She said she was an art-student and would be happy to show him the way. She didn't have much chance to practise her English. Again, Gerald was struck by a quickness of encounter he had found everywhere in these last few days, as if the crowd of the dead – you caught the dry whisper of their feet even here, in the unbroken streets – had drawn the living close.

They leaned over the parapet in a blaze of sky, watching the river swing its loop around the city. Then she showed him the baroque *palais*, the improbable pleasure-house of cream and gold, carved by Italian craftsmen, far from home, into the gloom of the citadel. There was a ramp broad enough for horsemen to ascend and enter the dining-hall mounted. Gerald strode up it and the girl looked after him, smiling. They threaded their way down bent lanes and worn flights of stairs, to the market square and the Trumpeter's Tower.

Gerald asked the girl to have tea with him. She peered at her watch, tugged the sleeve back over her wrist, and said she would be pleased. The small pastry shop was crowded with people who had a harried air but seemed in no particular haste. They found a corner of a table and Gerald brought a plate of cakes. They tasted of chalk, faintly sweetened. The girl made apologetic motions. It was all very difficult. Too many people swarming into the towns, and grain being left to mildew because there were not the lorries to carry it or the bins to store it in. But tea came in a steaming glass and Gerald said it tasted fine.

She was writing a doctoral dissertation on 'Botticelli and his Use of Medieval Motifs'. Had Gerald been to Italy?

He told her he had had his fill of it during the war.

She asked about the Mantegnas and the Medici chapel. Had he seen Urbino and St Ambrose in Milan?

Gerald ransacked his memory for details of pictures vaguely wondered at, of basilicas hurried past in the tumult and boredom of troop movements. As he spoke, the focus sharpened, and he found himself hauling to the light clear-edged shards of knowledge, fragments crystallized into bright certainty, and far more vivid than he thought he possessed. She drew him on hungrily, and he recounted a visit to Torcello, in a captured German barge, smoke still hanging on the brackish waste of the lagoon. The island stood unkempt, the grass rank, and burnt or bloated things drifted between the rotted palings. He had climbed the campanile, as up a tower of silence, and looked back on the silhouette of Venice, bone-white on the winter sea.

The girl was crying, with loud sniffles. Gerald flushed, but no one else seemed to take notice. She apologized, blowing her nose and wiping her glasses against the hem of her dress. She had read of all these marvels, ah interminably, seeking the strong light of their wonder on the dead page or browned photograph. She had told the rosary of their names – Volterra, San Gimignano, Masaccio – till the beads had worn lucent in her mind. Now she was lavishing heartache and years – years unrecapturable and that would leave her dry – trying to write of the strange master and his shapes of flame. But she would never see those towers or piazzas; never pass her fingers over the living stone. 'I am a blind man gossiping about colours!'

But why? Why should she not go?

She blew her nose again and tried to smile at the innocence of

Gerald's challenge. It came from another world. Very few were allowed to travel. And then, only the scientists.

Things would change. They were improving all the time.

Not for her. She had not been adroit about 'politics and such matters'. She had cried out of envy, out of naked desire. Because Gerald was so unutterably free. To go where he pleased. Because he could see Aracoeli again, on its high throne of stairs.

Gerald said he didn't think he would do much travelling after this. In the West, too, there were bends and sharp corners for the heart to bruise against.

She pressed her hand on his arm; she didn't want to hear about those. It would only make it more difficult.

Gerald saw an ink-stain on her fingers and felt a keen impulse to rub it off, to grasp her ungainly, chafed hand in his. But that would have meant a temptation of disorder, a crease in the blanket, so he smoothed the thought away.

Outside the tea-shop, he said he was sorry he had upset her. It was stupid of him. But she bent close with denial, and her face shone. He had made her very happy. She would remember everything he had told her, every detail. Did he know how lucky he was? And as she walked away, still pressing her wet handkerchief, she turned and waved.

Gerald went back to his hotel and asked for the bill. He explained that he might be leaving very early the next morning. The clerk demurred. There was no early train to Warsaw, and he added, piqued, that there would always be someone at the desk. Monsieur was in a first-class hotel. Gerald insisted. The clerk took the money with displeasure and muttered dimly that there might be extras at breakfast. If Monsieur had eggs. A flash of rage passed through Gerald, a desire to cry out the titles and ceremonies of death. But he checked himself and went quickly to his room.

Looking for the bottle of pills, small mauve capsules under a tuft of cotton, he found a clean shirt, the laundry-wrapper still on it. It filled him with a sense of waste, of means unspent or sown to the wind. He wanted to take out the pins, to wear the shirt and soil it in some abrupt extravagance of gesture. Then he laid it back in his travelling-case, and said out loud, not knowing why, 'To the church of the Laodiceans, To the church of the Laodiceans,' twice.

A little later, he started out of a cold, dragging sleep. Through the glass of the bottle, now empty, he could see the window. It had been wrenched open and the sky was spilling into the room. He was choking under its bright, towering mass and wondered, brokenly, how air could strangle. He knew that he must reach the window and close it fast against the racing tide.

Gerald Maune tried to get to his feet. But suddenly there was no need. A perfect stillness was in the room, and when he held out his hand, he touched it.

Proofs

1

Now the burn seemed to smart behind his eyes.

Thirty years and more a master of his craft. The quickest, most accurate of proof-readers and correctors in the whole city, perhaps in the province. Working every night, and throughout the night. So that the legal records, deeds of sale, notifications of public finance, contracts, quotations on the bourse, would appear in the morning, flawless, exact to the decimal point. He had no rival in the arts of scruple. They gave him the smallest print to check, the longest columns of figures to justify, the interminable catalogues of lost and found objects to be auctioned for the post office and public transport. His proof-readings of the bi-annual telephone directory, of electoral and census rolls, of municipal minutes, were legend. Printing works, the public-record office, the courts of law vied for his labours.

But now the sensation of burning, just behind his eyes, felt sharper.

A lifetime inhaling the tang of fresh ink, of lead warm to the touch. The linoleum in his cubicle, his sanctum of the unerring, shook to the beat of the presses. Rotogravure, Linotype, electronic type-casting, photo-engaving – he had seen them all. He had outwitted the imperfection, the recursive bugs, the clotted snarls and gremlin upsets of each technique. He knew the provenance, weight, watermark, fibre-content, resistance to ink-roller and hot metal of diverse papers by the antennae in his thumb. As he knew the impatient awe of the sub-editor, stock-market messenger, auctioneer, bank-clerk, notary public poised at the door of his cell, waiting for the discreet, singular check-mark, his as famous as the colophon of a renowned designer or the signature of a great artist. The incision of his pencil or ballpoint at the extreme right-hand bottom corner of the page signifying: *nihil obstat*, this text is ready, error-free, sanctified by precision. Let it be printed, published, franked, mailed to reader or taxpayer, to client or dealer, to litigant or advocate. There to order the world as only print can. Codex, pandect, register, the pamphlet or the tome. Now check-marked. His mark, sometimes before the ink was entirely dry. Legendary as is all perfection.

And with the burn, like a thread of smoke, a blur.

He who had never known the weariness of other proof-readers. Their migraines. Their losses of concentration and trembling fingers. The law students and unemployed lawyers who read proofs for libel in the late evening or early morning stared at him blear-eyed and envious. The firm in charge of printing lists of shareholders for market flotations had, in irked humour, offered a prize for anyone who could spot an error, be it a false initial, in his work. The bottle of champagne remained uncollected. He had heard a tale of proof-readers in another country, men no more schooled than he was, who had corrected the formal arguments in an august work of mathematical logic simply because they observed irregularities in the prescribed system of symbolic and algebraic notations. The story filled him with pride. Once an antique dealer, waiting for his catalogue of manuscripts, autographs and curiosa to be proof-read, had recounted a strange story of a printing error that transmuted the lines of a paltry Elizabethan poet into inviolate gold. Some vagabond had written banalities of a lady whose hair was greying, from whose hair a former brightness had fallen – of which cliché a hurried printer had made the words 'a brightness falls from the air'. To those for whom the language lives, the poetaster was now immortal. He both cherished and hated that anecdote. It made him feel strangely ill like the smell of sex in his younger years. Any erratum is a final untruth.

He rubbed his eyes. The forbidden, hitherto unnecessary gesture. The savour of ink and cigarette ash on the back of his hands was, momentarily, pungent. Behind and below him the presses were hammering.

It was the instant he loved best, almost childishly. At the ebb of night when he restored the finely sharpened pencils to their case, the frayed one in which his father had kept his straight-edged razors, and replaced the congeries of erasers, corrector-fluids and masking-tape in the right-hand drawer, then switched off the light. After which he locked the door to his cubicle and touched his cap, in discreet valediction, to the printers, messengers and packers on the loud floor below. Next he emerged through the small heavy door into first light. Into the first breath of the coming day. The thermos under his arm was now empty. Also the sandwich-bag, unless the cadence of the night's deadlines had been too pressing. If empty, he dropped it in the bin at the corner. He hated litter. Waste paper struck him as the very waste of waste. A devastation. At times, if the winds blew a piece towards his feet, he would pick it up, smooth it, read closely and make any correction needed. Then he would deposit it in the garbage receptacle, feeling obscurely rewarded and saddened. Any witness to this rite would have thought him deranged. But he did not cut a conspicuous figure.

He stood, waiting for morning to print shadows on the warehouse roof. There paper was stacked in leviathan rolls, waiting for the delivery trucks and messengers' mopeds to bark into life. He felt the cool of dawn on his skin. The sheer mad wonder of sunrise, even when it was veiled or rain-swept. Even when it was little more than a lost sheen behind the frequent fogs. He turned slightly eastward, to the native place of morning. Then down the metal steps, towards the square and the tram which would take him home.

2

He was thoroughly familiar to the tram-drivers and ticket-inspectors on their milk-run. Among themselves they called him Owl. Not only because of his night-job and of the ruffled, blinking mien with which he mounted the streetcar platform, but for the way in which, his frayed pea-green muffler wound around his thin neck, he perched immediately behind the conductor, closely observant. Exact craft fascinated and consoled him. He took renewed pleasure each morning in the driver's measured touch on the starting-lever, in the flick he gave the brake-handle, in the fine gauging which seemed to guide the exact speed at which he took the tight clanging curve that led into Via

Grande. In the late afternoon or early evening, in turn, when journeying back to work, he savoured the adjustments conductors made to balance their cars when they were thronged, when more and more passengers, homeward bound, elbowed their way through the automatic doors. Eyes shut, he could, according to the lurch of the tram and the particular sound of the grinding gears and overhead wires, tell unerringly where he was, and at which of the eleven stops between Santa Lucia and the printing works the car was whining to a halt. Sometimes he and the inspector exchanged views. But he was not spendthrift of words. There had been too many through the night; there would be too many more during the night ahead, minuscule, tightly aligned, prodigal of mistakes.

Why converse when he could scan the city as it passed? He knew his transit by heart. Façade by façade, street-corner by street-corner, each junction inwardly mapped. He knew the cobblestones which led down an alley from Piazza Borromeo to the glass-blowing manufacture in which his father had had his lungs shredded by searing dust (compensation had been refused). As the tram rattled on, he could peruse the house-fronts, the names over the shops. At the merest glance. The texts changed. Buildings were torn down and remade. He had seen small archipelagos of green tarred over and flower-beds uprooted. A garage now stood where there had been the malodorous, choked Fountain of the Three Masks. To be noted most alertly was the coming and going of placards, billboards, national, regional and civic notices, graffiti, which his eyes had taken in untiringly as the tram slowed or accelerated.

The memory of the marmoreal and Augustan placards of triumph, that man on his white horse, his chins mountainous, remained heavy inside him. He could visualize still the letters in flame-red on the call-up notices, on the decrees of rejoicing or retribution. Unforgettable were the ochre and black – the brazen typeface of the roll of hostages executed in vengeance. After the liberation came the plethora of election posters with their sheaves of grain, Phrygian caps, roosters crowing to azure skies, hammers and sickles, and laurelled women with bounding children at their heels. A flaking, perpetually changing palimpsest which he had to leaf through at speed as the tram churned by. With the raucous years, posters had been glued on posters, promise on promise, edicts of fiscal reform preceding edicts, each in turn scissored by the winds that came from the nearby mountains in the blue of late September, then discoloured and made soggy refuse by the winter rains.

Now the placards and inscriptions were different. They proclaimed lagoons, platinum beaches, palmy cruises on the never-never. Overnight deities of pop beckoned. Hamburgers house-high, softly ebullient with the blood-tide of ketchup. There flashed past the leather twist of the horror film. Everywhere bodies shone bronzed yet ethereal. A world so neon-lit, so thrustingly on offer that it demanded to be viewed through those sunglasses, harlequinned and dolphin-tailed. The fonts, the leading, the designs sickened him. Brutal machine-work. He seemed to hear the pulping of silent forests being pounded to dust so as to produce the lettering used on lavatory tiles. Nevertheless, he could not turn away. On each tram journey he read on, mesmerized.

As he neared home, the shops were opening. His needs were few and pedantically habitual. He drank his coffee under the arcades on Liberation Square. Then bought his bread in one of the very few small bakeries left in the district. He had weaknesses: for sardines lightly grilled, for anchovies from the Balearic Islands (the western Mediterranean having become, as headlines proclaimed, a 'cesspit'). He chose his cheeses with deliberation. The narrow, cavernous shop stayed cool even in the weeks of white heat. He favoured goat-cheese and, especially, a gritty variety from the interior of Sardinia. On occasion, he lingered over the fruit and vegetable stalls. They had been grey and fibrous at the end of the war and for some time after. Now they beckoned, chromatic and opulent as a Persian carpet. Offering plump asparagus, pink grapefruit, blood-oranges, egg-plant, broccoli in profusion. He palped the peppers gently, letting his thumb luxuriate in their clefts. He bought eggs, ground coffee, two bars of soap (there was a sale on), washing-powder, and proceeded up the stairs to his two-room apartment, now called 'studio' even in this undistinguished quarter.

Having put the shopping-bag at his feet he unlocked the double lock. Break-ins were everyday. He had gone up the four flights breathing easily. Having put away his purchases and slipped out of his scarf and jacket, he tested. He opened the window and looked steadily in the direction of the dome of the basilica of the Blessed Martyrs. It rose westward, in a direct line across the morning-lit sea of roofs. Testing. He knew that the dolphin rampant on the ancient weather-vane wore a coronet with four fleurons. He noted three. Then five. He covered one eye with his hand which smelled faintly of cheese. Then the other. He stood for a spell. Then lowered the blinds, drew the curtains against the spreading light, undressed, and set the alarm for three in the afternoon. There was, he remembered, a meeting.

3

Meetings. How many had he attended in a lifetime? Even his martinet memory could not marshal the lot.

The first, to be sure, remained unforgettable. It took place during the bestial civil war between the Fascist legionnaires, still nesting in their barracks and scouring the blacked-out streets for the partisans, democrats, deserters, fugitives. It had been a clandestine meeting, in the boiler-room of the municipal baths, the building itself having been almost flattened by liberating bombs. He remembered the prickling odour of chlorine and burnt plaster, his father's hacking cough amid the muted voices, and going to bed hungry. His very first political meeting, and his father's defiant pride as they stole home by circuitous alleys and waste ground to the accompaniment of scattered gunfire out of the thick dark.

Meetings innumerable during his time of probation as messenger and sweeper on the shop-floor: syndical organization, wage protests, strikes, meetings to hear shop stewards and more elevated union officials. There stayed with him the brusque silence of the presses and the drone of oratory by city voices raw with tobacco and lack of sleep. Some time thereafter (he knew the date and hour), baptism: when Tullio took him along to hear a lecture on surplus-value in Marxist and Leninist theory. It was delivered by a sweating doctoral student, behind thick glasses whose reflections darted oddly around the brown and green stucco in the packed room. His very first Party meeting. *In memoria*, inviolate, as was also in that same wild month – the bells had been proclaiming freedom and chewing-gum – his first serious experience of sex. More meetings and yet more before he was admitted into that freemasonry of hope. The handshake all around, the austere fever of enlistment, the Party card thrust, with affected calm, into the pocket of his overalls and Tullio's joy at brotherhood within brotherhood.

After that, meetings were legion. Lessons on Marxist social theory, on the heritage of Gramsci, industrialization, the tactics of proletarian protest, the place of women, of the media, of sport, of the arts and sciences, primary and secondary education in a classless state. Films on life in the Soviet Union and analyses of its vanguard destiny. Meetings, obligatory, on Party funding, on the recruitment of new members, on electoral propaganda and discipline, on deviance and fractionalism. Sessions devoted to the composition and dissemination of tracts and posters (he was to be made secretary for information and publication). He could remember heated gatherings at the time of the great anti-imperialist, anti-Nato riots and general strikes. Meetings to gather money for comrades with cracked skulls, for the locked-out and the blacklisted. How well he could recall the commemoration, airless, opaquely vibrant as in a sealed chamber, of Stalin's death. They had become orphans huddled in sombre bewilderment. Tullio in tears. A few months later, there had been his only encounter with Palmiro Togliatti, when he had travelled, with other local delegates and committee members, to the rally and plenary assembly in beflagged, red-draped Bologna. He remembered the leader's sharp smile and the thunder of concordant voices. Meetings at the level of the cell, of the district, of the Party's regional executive so frequent and repetitive that he could no longer distinguish them.

Until the command performance, in the derelict cinema rented for signal occasions, during which he, so frugal of words – for only a written statement can be checked, made intractable to error and false memory – had spoken at length about the evident potential for a Fascist resurgence and CIA-financed coup from inside the Hungarian uprising, about the notorious Jew-hatreds of the Cardinal and his White Guard acolytes, about the tragic but unquestionable need (the phrase he actually used was 'dialectical logic') for Soviet intervention.

Short of breath but pressing on. The imperialist and plutocratic powers were only waiting for just the tragic, yes, tragic misprision and macabre accident represented by events in Budapest. Witness their actions over the Suez canal. The motion of total solidarity must, therefore, be passed, the complete adherence of the local Party branch to Central Committee resolutions in Rome must be made manifest.

The pitch of his own voice during that long afternoon and evening stayed with him. As did Tullio's look of desolate love, of a man flayed alive at the moment when his exclusion, together with that of seven other revisionist saboteurs and crypto-Trotskyites, was carried unanimously. Eerily he could hear, as from some archive of echoes within himself, the thud of the baize door as the seven men and the one woman, who was Maura, left the hall.

He had not attended his own ostracism, which came after Prague. Given his intervention during the session called to approve of the Soviet invasion, that ostracism was now as foregone as death itself. Had he not cited Lenin's suppressed testament which revealed the menace posed by Stalinist bureaucracy? Had he not adverted to the penitential verities of the Twentieth Party Congress revelations of corruption and the cult of personality? Had he not alluded, transparently though without naming him, to Trotsky's model of spontaneous and permanent revolution of the kind, he treacherously inferred, they had witnessed during the Prague Spring? Automatically, the next meeting would be his last. The summons had reached him. Together with the agenda on which his refusal of adequate self-criticism, his violation of Party democracy and discipline, figured amid matters arising.

During what he knew to be the relevant hour he had sat in his room, motionless, made stone. He had sat like a paralytic, his temples pounding as in a cold fever. Knowing that he was being read out of the scroll of the saved, of the elect to hope and meaning. The loneliness of that hour branded him irreparably. It was more solitary than death. He dragged himself to the staircase, intent on going to work, but found himself incapable of useful motion. His legs shook and the nausea made the stairwell spin. He took sick-leave and immured himself in his leprosy. Till Tullio hammered at his door, insistent.

The Circle for Marxist Revolutionary Theory and Praxis numbered less than twenty active members, but met almost as regularly as the Party sections.

And now, as he entered, the props and smells in the schoolroom (made available at nominal cost by the grace of one of the faithful, a primary schoolteacher), were not much different from those which he had known during his long stay in the belly of the whale.

4

'Tullio.'

'*Professore.*'

The old, heart-warming joke. Consecrating with that fictive title one whose schooling had been rudimentary but whose physique, with its gaunt concavities, was indeed a touch professorial. More emphatically, that greeting did label a man whose obsessive scruple in respect of the minutiae of print, whose bristling distaste in the face of the approximate and the loosely mistaken, were magisterial and pedantic to a degree.

They shook hands with that hint of mock ceremony which intimate friendship fosters. Handshakes all around, in an aura reassuringly familiar and low-key. Chalk-powder, the odours of scuffed linoleum, the light-bulb slightly fugged under its ripped shade. Why, he wondered, were the light-bulbs at all such meetings inevitably both grimed with dirt and aggressive, dispensing a yellow, sick-room sheen? Why were the flowers on the desk or podium, even when exalted characters from the regional or national roster came to speak, so waxen? Idle thoughts, when he wanted to concentrate on Anna B.'s report. Comrade Anna. Why his notice of the down, slightly moist, on her upper lip, that hint of a moustache to come?

He tautened and focused on what she was saying.

But the word 'laundromat' kept recurring in so desultory a manner as to make his attention veer. Anna was seeking to analyse the lacunae in classical Marxist social theory revealed by the 'horizontal solidarities' which had developed and coalesced 'spontaneously' – a perilous, crucial adverb – in the working-class high-rise apartment buildings and estates at the new rim of the city. In these solidarities, in

321

the crèches and launderettes, inherited lines of class loyalty and militant activism (Anna's tone was momentarily vibrant), traditional demarcations such as that, for example, between clerk and heavy-goods transporter, were being blurred or frankly eroded.

The dartings to and fro across natural divides of class interest and ideology were, in the main – and Comrade Anna paused slightly – the result of women's clusters. It was the unplanned conviviality of women around the laundromat and the coffee dispenser which wove new alliances and political–social impulses.

The speaker glanced up from her notes. Had anyone, she challenged almost reproachfully, bothered to investigate the radical differences in social infrastructure and peer-group communication as between coffee drawn from, and consumed near, a mechanical dispenser and that brewed in one's own kitchen and poured into one's own cups for a neighbour specifically welcomed and hosted? The new impulses, she reported, were of an essentially consumer-oriented category. This was natural enough and, in its own way, to be welcomed. But the inherent contradictions, the dialectically negative feedback, needed to be understood and fought against. The class struggle in which husbands were inevitably engaged, the combat for better wages, shorter hours and improved safety in the factory were of a kind with which the women, the wives and mothers, found it increasingly difficult to identify. A significant portion of the men and indeed of the women living in the industrial estates were now white-collar, though, to be sure, the percentage among women remained small. These transitional phenomena were, as yet, ill-understood. (Too often in his hearing, in his participation in discussions across the long years, had 'ill-understood' been the saving phrase, that which made the suspect or tenebrous visage of the future bearable and the frank insight worth shelving.)

Anna B. went on. There were checkers, counter-personnel, assistant managers at the trucking depot who acted, exactly as Marxist analysis postulated, as parasites on exploited labour. But as their wives mingled with those of the true proletariat on terms of easy intimacy and 'collusive desires' – Anna let this phrase echo, as if in troubled evocation of her own privileged employment as a statistician in the psychiatric social service of the General Clinic – as their daily contacts grew more cohesive, the very concept of the political tended to fade away. What had Marxist and Gramscian sociology to contribute to a better understanding of these 'gender-bonded and gender-oriented socializations'? Had Kautsky or C. Wright Mills said anything to the point?

A certain gloom hung over the Comrade's closing queries. A gloom thickened by the acknowledgement that her untiring efforts to attract even a single potential recruit from the teeming warrens east of the river to the Circle's discussion-evenings had failed. Not a single one. He had managed to listen closely. But had he, at a point of especial gravity, caught the imp in Maura's eyes? Was it her bench, that worn school-bench incised to the grain with initials, sobriquets, minor obscenities and arrowed hearts, which had creaked in such irreverent accompaniment to Comrade Anna's report? 'It is necessary to dream' (Lenin, 1902). But not, he reminded himself severely, to day-dream. And at that very moment, Anna having been duly thanked and her most valuable paper having been earmarked for detailed discussion at a later occasion, the members present, ten or eleven in all, turned to him, to the *Professore*, for what had come to be known, in affectionate irony, as the 'homily'. At successive meetings, it was he who glossed the news of the preceding two or three weeks, as culled from *their* newspapers and from *ours* – though no actual newspaper or even review, save a cyclostyled and infrequently distributed bulletin, genuinely reflected the views of the Circle. His commentary drew on eminent foreign papers as well, which his schooled eye sped across in the reading-room of the public library in his *quartiere*, that of St Jerome-in-the-Marsh.

What could, what should he say tonight? What must he say if he was to deserve the trust of those now turning towards him (by instinct he always took a seat at the rear)? If Tullio and Maura were to continue being his? He caught himself staring at the wall-map of the nation, as displayed in every schoolroom. He was trying to isolate, among its four colours and infinitely familiar contours, the location of the escarped valley in Sardinia from which came his preferred cheese, the one he had bought and eaten that very day. The island shape was plain enough, as was its capital city in heavy type. But the detail, the recess in which that valley shone, swam before his eyes.

5

News from Prague and the German Democratic Republic, he observed, clearing his throat and bending forward slightly, was indeed difficult to interpret. The facts looked to be undeniable, though dramatized and cheapened by the western media. Thousands were storming embassies, camping at rail-heads and streaming towards the borders. Surface motives were plain enough. The socialist and Marxist regimes had been overtaken by ferocious exasperation, by a break-down of elementary trust between government and governed. It was worth recalling (he felt the sadness in his bones as he said it) that Gramsci had warned of just such a contingency, of the corrosive fatality of 'family quarrels' in the wake of the Milan and Bologna strikes in the 1920s. But it was the task of the Circle to probe deeper, to lay bare the true nerve of history. The phrase was pompous; he knew it as he heard it out of his own mouth. Could it be that, once again, and in grim similitude to what historians told of the Dark Ages, migrations were thrusting westward out of a deprived, turbulent and inchoate east?

'What about the cars?'

Cesare Lombardi's interruption arrested his train of thought.

'Cars?'

'They are abandoning their cars. Thousands of them. They are dumping them at the frontiers or giving them away. I've seen it on television. Men and women kicking their cars and leaving them in the ditch.'

Friend Lombardi did have a gift for angular queries. He launched his circuitous darts from a stooped posture, eyes downcast, perspiring behind his tortoiseshell glasses.

'I know that.' (Patiently.)

Lombardi breathed heavily. He chain-smoked, as if the hunger which he had traversed during the last years of the war, when he crawled from lair to lair in fear of denunciation as a half-Jew and known anarchist, had never left him.

'Their cars are miserable. It is said you can smell their exhaust for miles. But imagine abandoning them. Just like that!'

He warmed to his theme, gathering it in like a faintly repulsive quarry.

'I ask you: why do they have all those foul machines in the first place? Polluting, wasting raw materials, consuming fossil fuels. It's pure lunacy. As bad as capitalism. Worse. When we know that bicycles will do for ninety per cent of our actual daily needs. That bicycles are clean and silent. And that a proper public-transport system can provide for the rest. Those herds of stinking cars by the roadside. Don't you see what that really means? It makes no difference whether we live over here or over there. Even the worst of those automobiles,' (the epithet which Lombardi appended was an old-fashioned, eroded obscenity), 'is totally beyond the reach of the Third World. Imagine what a doctor in Angola or Peru or China would give for even one of those Trabants. For the energy they consume, a useless dream, I know,' (the point of his cigarette drew an angry arc), 'but one which hundreds of millions of human beings in Africa, Asia and Latin America would pray for. Every bloody and killing day of their wretched existence. Can you imagine what these men and women feel when they see those pictures of junked, abandoned cars and homes and jobs? There can be no life worth living on this pillaged earth, no justice worth having so long as . . . '

Lombardi paused to draw breath.

'Your analyses make me ill. Don't you see? We must learn to make do. Each and every one of us. With essentials. Using our legs to walk or pedal. Baking one decent sort of bread and not ten cellophane kinds. Our forests are going to pulp because there are a hundred – or is it more? – girlie magazines on the kiosks. We fly half-empty jumbos to cities already served by a dozen other airlines. Now cars are being littered by the side of the road like used Kleenex. To each according to his needs. Blessed Karl Marx! Does no one remember what real needs are? How few. How richly they could be satisfied? Superfluity enslaves. We have gone mad with superfluity. In the shanty-towns of Rio or Soweto – have you seen those television pictures? – families try to stay alive under bits of corrugated tin and rubber, next to open cesspits. Every one of those tossed-away Trabants could shelter . . . '

His incensed delivery failed him. Being corpulent, addicted to nicotine, a tireless collector of vintage jazz records and memorabilia,

Cesare Lombardi, telephone engineer by profession, harboured a burning predilection for images of asceticism, for ideals of saintly privation. He dreamed of the Desert Fathers, of the Stylites, naked to the winds on their pillars of denial.

Father Carlo Tessone, sitting at an angle to him, knew this. Father Carlo, their only comrade from the Church, though his status had been, for some time, marginal. He, evidently, was a man who did not find it difficult to make do, to stay thin, to walk the city in his one-patched garb and mended, high-laced boots. A self-denier with amused eyes and a touch of courtliness in his spare gestures.

Now Father Carlo spoke softly.

'Lombardi, to hear you one might think that Marxism must arrive at deprivation. That a just, proletarian distribution of resources and of the means of production is, after all, a sort of monasticism in the barrens. A clerisy of abstinence.'

Father Carlo let this elegant phrase fall with a hint of embarrassment. He had, he knew, a weakness for eloquence. No abnegation there but the old schooling at the seminary in rotundity and rhetoric.

The *Professore* realized he must take the reins.

'Yes. This is one of the charges brought against us. Against all Marxist models. That ours are the politics and institutions of backwardness. I remind those present here of the debates on this very issue in Plekhanov and Veblen. Is Marxism at bottom a strategy for survival in underdeveloped or stagnant economies? Is it inherently alien to material progress and consumer-oriented social structures? When it is, so manifestly, a product, an analytic science, a discovery of historical laws, sprung of the industrial revolution and of the expansion of planetary resources?'

Tullio interjected. His tone was oddly neutral, which made his question the more ominous.

'*Professore*: those East German Trabants. Why should they be so undesirable? Why can a Marxist economy, in a country with a history of industrial strength and a skilled work-force, not produce a satisfactory internal combustion engine and chassis? Isn't that the real question?'

Further voices chimed in. The discussion eddied. It was inconclusive and, at times, ill-tempered.

He had to get to work. Outside the unwashed windows, the bells had sounded vespers. It was agreed that the questions raised would be further argued as events unfolded in the East. Leaving – renewed handshakes and the shuffling on of raincoats – he noted Maura's nod. It was, he judged, imperceptible to anyone else. It signalled Sunday.

6

Weather permitting, they met at the end-station of the tramline in Via Alba. Then took the rackety train which looped the hill towns and villages to the north of the city. Maura brought the sandwiches and the fruit. The coffee thermos and bottle of wine were his responsibility. Sometimes he felt lavish and added cheese or a jar of olives. Without any particular destination in mind, they would alight at one or another of the small stations, punch the gravel with their walking-sticks and head upward. In the past, Tullio had quite often come along; once or twice Lombardi had puffed in their wake. Even Anna B. had been of the party, blushing at her hobnailed, sensible boots and tight trousers. But not of late. Maura and he had become, so distinctly, a couple.

The air was soft with October's end but had in it the uncertain light of the coming rains. Crossing the village, they passed the door, left ajar, of the church, and heard the muffled echoes of Mass. Soon the cracked voice of the single bell would chime briefly to the hills. They took the goat-track which meandered skyward through the laurel, the thorn-bushes and the fallow strips of stubble, scratched as if with bare hands and blackened nails out of the jumble of rocks.

The valley fell away quickly. Turning back he and Maura could see, even of a Sunday, the dun scarf of pollution unwound across the city and the new industrial zones. But here, above the dozen rust-tinted roofs of Verzani (they had noted the name on the station-master's hut), the folds of air shook softly as the last of the summer winds sang past, bound southward, he fancied, to nest and noise in the broken barns, in the almost spectral, bleached hamlets from which migrant labour was now pressing north. And as in rebound to his thought, a train-whistle shrilled in the valley, on the main line, with its second-class carriages ferrying the uprooted and the bewildered to the slums of the cities.

He drew a long breath, saw Maura's lithe back rounding a turn in the trail just above him, and inhaled a faint trace of thyme. Soon now the sun would top the ridge and Maura would pause to strip off her jumper, knotting it around her hips under the rucksack. Her motion made his heart loud.

It was she, roughly ten yards ahead of him, who, shading her smoke-grey eyes, pointed to a hollow in the overhanging screed. The very-recent first autumn rains and gusts of colder wind had splayed the bushes. Something whitish and shaped shone in the little dell. They cut to the left through barbed grass. His metal-tipped cane struck a fallen, flat piece of stone paving. The impact rang bright. Other stone fragments lay near under the overhang of rock and tufa. Barely visible in the tangle of heather and striated chalk stood a small column, its fluting encrusted with lichen. Maura gave a low, cheery cry. The carved stone was cracked and at an angle, but her fingers could trace remnants of lettering. They knelt side by side. The air was still and warm in that hollow place. Minutely, he began brushing the mud and the lighter shards of rubble and crystallized rock from the graven lines. Maura turned to him enquiringly. He caught the nearness of her cheek and the embers in her hair. She was not, he supposed, beautiful. Only so much more than that.

They had, he proposed, chanced on one of the numerous miniature shrines or modest family memorials which dotted these hills. He added, with a pedantry which at once amused and embarrassed him, that these dated from the palaeo-Christian period, at the ebb-tide of the decomposing Roman Empire, when Christendom flourished in the silent places. This site must, he ruled, be marked on the fifty-metre-scale archaeological survey in the *Museo municipale*.

Now he extracted the large old-style handkerchief from his pocket (Maura always smiled at the gesture) and began cleaning the incisions. He blew neatly at the detritus and cleared the thin branches that had made their bed of the antique marble. Maura's shoulder warmed his arched back.

The text was fractured and eroded nearly beyond supposition. It ran between shallow double-borders and a motif, perfunctorily carved, which might, he guessed, be acanthus leaf. In one of the whorls a snail had left its indelible mark. Hurried labour, he reflected, the work of unskilled or hunted hands using, almost certainly, an earlier pagan site and votive stone for their urgent purpose.

'How can you be so sure that this is a Christian marker or inscription?'

Instinct. He might be wrong. But his fingers read the chiselling, the style of the letters as fourth century, late third at the earliest. And although he could not be confident of making out correctly the roughened, largely effaced emblem, he could swear it was that of a fish, crudely drawn, between two stars. The symbol of the Son of God, the contours of resurrection so common in early Christian lapidaries and cult objects.

'*M*,' said Maura.

'And *N*. I can't make out the letter in between.'

His fingers passed and repassed delicately over the lost braille.

'*E* and *T*.' He spelled out the two letters with assurance.

'*MANET*.' And in this buried spot, the sun now full above them, his voice boomed. For he was certain of his reading.

The words, following only edges and the remembrance of scoured angles and curves which worked stone retains across time, could only be guessed at. But he had little doubt. The rotundity of the *O* was live to his thumb. No hand or eye acquainted with the serration characteristic of the stem of the capital *R* in the early Christian or late Roman stone-carver's alphabet could mistake the word or, more precisely, its certain shadow.

'*AMOR*.' He spoke the four letters with gentle triumph.

'*MANET AMOR*.' Love remains. Love endures.

'You are making it up,' whispered Maura, but repeated the Latin.

'The name must have been on the upper half of the tablet. A child's name, I think. Given the size of the stone. A child gone. Here, in these hills. When the family was under way, perhaps. Fleeing, or just crossing the col to join another community. A Lavinia, a Drusilla, of whom love remains.'

'It could just as well have been a little boy,' objected Maura.

He nodded, and his heart drummed.

She asked: 'Ought we to have uncovered it?'

'The rains did that. And the winds.'

'They did not read the words. If we found a letter fallen on the road, would we read it?'

'This letter, Maura, was meant for us.'

He felt awkward at the sound of his own intensity, hearing in that banality the hunger. But she nodded lightly and smiled. They rose to their feet. She peeled off her sweater and looked about for a moment. They propped their sacks and sticks against the warming stone. Again, he tasted a touch of thyme in the air and the secret scent of lavender late in the parting year. He half-closed his eyes so as to take in fully the brush of her clothes as she slipped out of her jersey and hiking pants. She glided her arms behind her back and he could hear the hooks open. The ground was strange under his feet. When he stretched beside her, she was naked.

7

He had given television a wide berth. After the night's proof-reading it was sensible to allow his eyes all possible rest. The afternoon programmes, which he could have switched on, were, he knew, trash: housewives' striptease, family quiz shows and morose comedians out of the *hinterland*. Maura's insistence that they should install themselves in front of the little screen on that late November Sunday evening had irritated and disturbed him. Now he sat mesmerized.

Father Carlo had joined them. There was no television in the broom-closet of a room which he occupied fitfully at the hostel. He had brought a bag of macaroons of which the *Professore* was inordinately fond. The grit of almonds and burnt sugar clung happily to one's teeth. The padre too was spellbound, hunched forward on the kitchen stool, so compact in his observance of the screen that his weight and occasional shuffle seemed shadowy.

The titles, credits and presenter's overture had been breathless. Pictures, action sequences, interviews, exclusive documentary footage would be shown over the next two hours to mark 'the greatest wave of revolution, the greatest blossoming of freedom history had ever known'. There would be expert commentaries from Minister X,

Professor Y and novelist Z. They would, in turn, join a panel assembling further luminaries of the political spectrum and of sociology. As the celebrated compère spoke, his mouth an almost perfect *o* of bounteous excitement, bursts of Beethoven deployed their great wings on the soundtrack, and the chorale of the Ninth rose towards the fiercely spotlit Brandenburg Gate.

First came the Berlin saga and the crumbling of the Wall. Once again, the screen showed a wave of humanity pouring through jagged rents, climbing over wire. Border guards grinned vacantly and reached for cigarettes as do the bears in a bankrupt circus. Shots of teenagers from the east tumbling into West Berlin supermarkets, rocking in wonder before the shelves, emptying them in a sleepwalker's sweep. Bright-tinted toothpaste, lacquer for toenails, soft toilet-paper in the hues of the rainbow, deodorants, tights finely meshed and stippled, jeans bleached or mended. Sunglasses for the night, amplifiers, cassettes, coffee-beans from Brazil being whipped off the shelves and display cases. The reporter's lens and microphone homed in on a bounding, guffawing troupe, their carrier-bags piled high with video cassettes and sun-bright plastic rainwear. One of the lads mouthed his message straight into the bobbing mike: 'Horror films, man. Porno. Hot lips, man.' And the girls in his wake screeched with joy and did a twist on the pavement. The camera swung back to the Wall itself and to the idle bulk of the Gate. Politicians embraced. A film star (minor) signed autographs on the platform of a watchtower. At every instant, the throng grew larger and more torrential.

Cut, and over to 'our colleague in Prague'. The bells pealing across unkempt gables. Havel on the balcony. 'Freedom . . . nation . . . democracy.' Eyes misted, the whirlpools of sudden laughter and tears in the crowd, the voices echoing from group to group, from parade to parade, the multitude at once empowered and set free. Newsreel shots of Soviet tanks in 1968, on the exact same street-corners where the Czechs now stood in recollection and soft drunkenness as if the very wind, clanging with bells, were alcohol.

The ads rolled on. Then Warsaw and Gdansk. A gross memorial to the Soviet liberators of 1944–45 being toppled into a cloud of brown dust. Brief collages of the death-ditches at Katyn, of Stalinist edifices against a sullen sky. Then the early images of Solidarity, of that walrus-man with the obstinate eyes and slow triumphs. An interview with a foreman outside a steel-mill: 'We have nothing left. We must begin again at zero. They stole everything. Communist bandits. Filth.' Close-up of his bony face, of hands sandpapered like those of the unfed in some African drought.

The first of the pundits, in a professorial study. Yes. He agreed entirely. 'An earthquake. Promethean. The liberation of the human spirit from the shackles of Marxist–Leninist folly and despotism. May I emphasize "Leninist"? You will be so good as to recall, *cara* Valeria,' (the interviewer nodded supportively), 'the book in which I pointed out, many years ago, oh, the clairvoyance and confidence of one's youth, that so-called "Stalinism" is nothing more than an ineluctable development, I stress "ineluctable", my dear friends, of the homicidal Leninist, indeed Marxist, blueprint.' At which pronouncement, the camera glided tastefully behind the sage's brow to show a panorama of the Milan skyline.

Now back to the action. To a meeting of the Hungarian Democratic Centre. Demands for the immediate withdrawal of Soviet forces. Immediate. Pictures of the walled-in barracks on the outskirts of Budapest, of women and children shaking their fists at Red Army sentries, teenagers with glazed faces and cheap plastic gun-belts. A capsule-chat with the new Minister of the Interior. 'We do have the infrastructure here in Budapest. Remember our illustrious economists. But help is needed. Urgently. Investment, *Signore*, and more invest-ment. As I told my friend Andreotti, democracy costs money. In this whole building there is hardly a phone left that works. Not a single fax-machine at my disposal!' Arms outflung in quixotic despair and resolution.

'We are taking you to Sofia. Exclusive.' The presenter's vibrato rose. 'Pictures not seen before. A people on the march.' Fields. A file of men, women and children in embroidered blouses following a flower-decked tractor. A village hall. Editorial apologies for the quality of the sound. A large man, his braces sweated through, yelling into a small loud-hailer. Something about the price of oats and those Bolshevik locusts in Sofia. The assembly in responsion: 'Down with the Communists. Zhivkov to the lantern.'

A second break for ads. Motor-scooters circling a house-high jeroboam of alcohol-free champagne. 'Safety bubbles,' crooned the young woman, her Adam's apple pulsing ecstatically.

The round table, which was to crown the programme, had harvested politicians, more professors, the winner of this season's stellar prize for fiction (was the man lightly rouged?).

'Oh, there could be no doubt. No shadow of a doubt. History had turned on its hinges. The nightmare of state socialism was lifting. It was plain as daylight: Marxism had led to the Gulag and the massacres at Timisoara. To the extermination and enslavement of millions. To those cunning falsehoods which had suborned and infected western sensibility.' ('Sensibility' dropped subtly from the novelist's pursed lips and was taken up in caressing counterpoint by the eminent psychologist.)

Communism? *Finis.* Only Cuba, North Korea and Albania – but Albania for how much longer? – left in red on the world map. 'An unholy trinity, dear colleagues and treasured spectators.' Decorous mirth around the tinkling water-bottles. The evident problem was Russia itself. How long before it broke into pieces, its deprived millions trudging westward? How long before the Baltic republics, the vast Ukraine, Armenia, Georgia, Uzbekistan, little Moldavia, Siberia itself (who could foretell?) declared their independence from the impotent centre?

The bald historian urged caution: 'These seismic movements take time. Russian patriotism . . . the hydrogen bomb and space programme. After all . . . '

But the syndicated columnist tugged impatiently at his bow-tie and offered wagers to all participants: 'The USSR will collapse within eighteen months. There will be anarchy when the soldiers come home. Pogroms. Bread riots. Yeltsin is ready to make his move. I have it on highest authority. From the horse's mouth, believe me! Within a year and a half. Perhaps less. *Kaputt.*' And he passed his hand across his windpipe, the heavy signet ring glinting.

The moderator turned brusquely to Comrade Gabrieli of the Central Committee in Rome. 'Well, *Dottore*?'

A final bouquet of ads. To maintain suspense. To prepare the audience for revelation.

Why was Gabrieli ill-shaven? The idiotic thought pressed on Maura.

'We are, as you know, committed to a multi-party democracy. We have been for a long time. Even Togliatti . . . This present crisis . . . how shall I put it?'

He lunged at the television and stabbed at the switch. Neither Father Carlo nor Maura moved. The sofa, the bookshelves, the stool brought in from the kitchen, lay in darkness. He glanced at the plants in the window-box. Their leaves hung motionless. Rubbery. Maura turned on the table-lamp (it had been his first gift to her) and brought coffee. Father Carlo stretched and massaged his thin back.

Leaving, the *Professore* almost tripped over the door-sill.

Maura caught his elbow: 'You must see the eye-doctor. You *must*.'

She had urged it under her breath, but Carlo, who had preceded him down the murky stairs, turned and looked back.

8

'Not for this!'

He heard himself repeating the phrase. The pink and yellow flashes from the window display of the all-night video-rental shop made his cheeks clown-like and his eyes blink.

Father Carlo grinned at him.

'Careful, *Professore*. That's been *our* line. Not for *this* world. Not for the filth and lucre and beatings of this life. There must be something better. Since that day when they drove the nails into his hands and feet. There just had to be something beyond bread and circuses.'

Father Carlo's cadence seemed to mime and tease his own.

'It would be unbearable if it had all been only for this. As you say, old friend. All that pain, the dirt up to our eyeballs. If this turned out to be the be-all and end-all, the sum total, we would do best to hang ourselves on the next lamp-post. On the next meat hook. When the great white dawn didn't come and set Galilee or Samaria alight, there were those who did hang themselves or pitch themselves head-first into wells. They had seen the black sun on his dead eyes, on his torn flesh. All for nothing. So they did away with themselves. Many did it again when the year one thousand came and went, with the usual rain and the customary plagues and the ordinary famines. And they'll do it again, on the first common morning of the year two thousand. Shouting: "Not for this! It's been too long. How can it all have been only for this? The promise and the desolation."'

Father Carlo continued:

'That's where we came in. The Mother Church. With the aspirin. Gently now, good children. Don't swallow too fast. Let it melt in your mouths. Wrap it in a wafer. Wash it down with a sip of wine. Gently. For it is his body and watery blood. Spilled for you, and now within you. The pain-killer. So that you can endure. Till Sunday week. In your garbage lives, in your hunger and lice, in the incontinence of the geriatric ward or that of the new-born cretins. Just another little week to crawl through. Till the next medication. Let the promise fill your empty bellies. His kingdom will come. Not quite yet, not here in any real sense, but without fail: in the tomorrow after tomorrow's tomorrow.

'Observe our mercies. Do not rage at injustice, at the wealth flung in your face, at the torture of the innocent and the helpless. Do not lament your own misery. Do not flash your broken teeth against your children's hunger. These are but passing trials. Bear them meekly. Give the slaughter-house men a smile, bow to the rich, cast down your eyes when the depraved roar past. Theirs may be the rewards here and now. Yours are yet to come. Acknowledge the cunning of my text. Order and obeisance in this vale of sorrows, compensation over there. Around the next corner of time.'

He had listened, his chin against the raised collar of his coat: 'Do you know what socialism is, reverend Father? Do you know what it really is?'

Father Carlo turned to him lightly: 'What is it, my friend? What is it really?'

'It is impatience. Impatience. That's what socialism is. A rage for now.'

And the spurt in his voice made him sound hoarse.

Father Carlo nodded: 'So it was in early Christianity. Exactly so. Impatience ran wild in Jesus. When he cursed the pitiful fig-tree, or when he said that he had come bearing a sword. When he bade the dead bury their dead or when he rushed into Jerusalem unprepared and ran riot in the Temple yard. His impatience may well have been more terrible than that suffered by any other living being. He was so impatient to enter into the mystery of his own beginning and become what he was. And what did Christ leave his little mafia? A treasure of impatience. They panted for the end of time like dogs dying of thirst. For the last sunset. They believed it to be imminent, a week away, a month at most. They smelt the huge rank smell of the end. They thought they saw the seals breaking on the book of life. But it didn't come to pass, did it? Or it came and went like snow at midnight, unnoticed. History had not pulled down the shutters. And we were back on the treadmill. Whereupon the Church ordered patience and more patience, and handed out tranquillizers.'

He laughed almost joyously: 'But you see there have been quite a few among us who never learned the arts of waiting. Heresy also is impatience. The heretic takes short cuts. We too have had our dreamers of tomorrow. Justice for everyman, as Jesus wanted. Peace upon earth. No more swollen bellies and to each according to his dignity and aspirations. Tomorrow at daybreak. Or, at the very latest, Monday next.

'How effectively the Church has dealt with the impatient ones. The millenarians, the mendicants, the Anabaptists, the Adamites, the Brethren of True Love, all the crazed preachers of a new Jerusalem! How it has scourged and erased them from history. Not a single text left of the Cathars, who taught perfection here and now. There is nothing Rome has dreaded more than impatience. His kingdom is not of this world. Has there ever been a more adroit political manifesto? Tell me, *Professore*.'

The two walkers found themselves looking at each other and so nearly in step.

'It is not only you socialists who have been impatient. Some of us have been pretty well mad with impatience, *mio caro*. For so long. But what earthly use has it been?'

Father Carlo stumbled over his own word. He took it up a second time with a chuckle.

'Earthly. That's the whole point, isn't it? Of what use has it been here *on earth*? How impatient Jesus must have been in that tomb. Three days can be a very long time. A small eternity. For us it's been longer.'

They had left the Corso. Unnoticing, they headed towards the river.

336

'Much longer.'

They crossed puddles of thicker blackness where the high, nailed-over portals of condemned palaces and tenements cast their night shadows.

Father Carlo was humming. A vacant, up-down tune. The hum of the Psalmist or of the half-woken monk in the chill of matins.

They caught the scent of the river. Tar and wisps of diesel.

'We did take that impatience from you. I know that, Carlo. But you were not the first. The hunger is much older. The rage was in Moses. The commandments of justice were his and the abstentions. Those endless inventories of what it is we must do without. Moses knew he couldn't enter the promised land. It would be too small for his fury.

'Have you read Amos, *reverendissime*? Only Communists now read the Bible. Amos was out of his mind with anger. At the greed which parades through the cities, at the empty eyes of the child beggars. All our impatience since seems to me like an echo of his voice. He knew. He knew the world in which grain is burned or rat-poisoned so that prices do not fall on the commodities exchange and in which children are sold on the night streets or set to labour in carpet factories and bead shops, fourteen hours at a stretch, till they go blind and tubercular. Amos had seen it all. He had heard the giggle of money and stepped in its vomit. And Jesus after him, I agree. "There shall come a time when men will exchange love for love, justice for justice." Not lucre for lucre. Was it an Evangelist? Was it St Francis or Mother Theresa? Tell me, Father Carlo, who prophesied thus? Marx did. In 1844. When he was writing to and for himself. Putting impatience to paper. Not strategy or analysis or polemic. But prophecy and promise out of a great rage. The very beard of that man was angry.'

They had come on to the bridge.

Carlo's move: 'Moses and the Prophets. The man from Nazareth. Marx. Just as the Nazis said. Communism is Judaism writ large, the virus of Bolshevism is the Jew-virus.'

They were leaning over the wrought-iron balustrade, enamelled with pigeon droppings. His nails scraped idly at the stuff. Would Father Carlo, he wondered, perform the stock gesture out of morose

French movies. Father Carlo did. The match flared and arched from his fingers into the slow current below.

'I don't know much about Jews. I was young when it was done to them. But I have my own theory. That business about being a chosen people, the covenant with history. I believe in it. But not in the way they tell it, Father Carlo: it is the wretched who are chosen. It is those who are born into hunger, into AIDS. It is the congenitally deformed and the deaf-mutes. It is almost the whole cursed lot of us. The numberless tribe of the losers. God chose us to be those who wait. Till our waiting will grow so unendurable that justice and brotherhood must explode out of us. Have you ever looked closely at those waiting for the soup-kitchens to open, for the blankets they hand out in the doss-house? They only *seem* like the dead. Look closer. Behind their eyes, a long dark way behind, the embers are alive. The thorn-bush is burning inside them. They are the chosen people of despair. But also of hope, Carlo.'

He had veered towards him, full-face: 'What the hell can a rich man hope for? Why bother with hope when your belly is full? That's what makes every victim a Jew, a real Jew. The truly chosen do not descend from Abraham, who was a millionaire. We do not come from Job, who doubled his holdings. We are the children of Hagar. We have fed on stones, and wasps have sung for us. There can be no Communist, no real socialist who is not, at bottom, a Jew.'

A string of barges, their lights reddish, passed underneath. The arches of the bridge resounded to the coughing motors.

As he stared at the receding lights, conviction quite overcame him: 'Do listen to me, Carlo. It sounds silly. But here is how I see it. When a man or woman is made an outcast, when they humiliate and spit at us, whoever we are, wherever we may be, we become Jews. In that instant.'

'A dark syllogism, *Professore*. Look where it led.'

'But that's the whole point. Don't you see? The Jews refused to take the promissory note. To swallow what you call aspirin. They saw that nothing had changed after Jesus. Men ate men, just as before. Beggars remained beggars. So he could not be the Messiah, could he? Not the one worth waiting for, whose true coming would make a lit place of the world. Now and for ever.'

Father Carlo let a second match flare in his cupped hand and watched its descending glow, but said nothing.

'It does make sense, surely you see that? There were Jews who saw deeper and understood that the Messiah would never come. Never. Or rather, that the Messiah was man himself. That the revelation and the great winds to come were those of our own history. That ordinary men and women had not even begun to *be themselves.*'

He exulted at the obviousness of it.

'Men and women, creatures of reason, custodians of this earth: yes, there is a Messiah and a Jerusalem but not after one's funeral and not out of pink clouds. And there are laws, but not ones spewed out of some volcano in Sinai. There are laws of history, and science, and supply and demand. And if you need miracles, look around you! At the irrigation of a desert, at the finding of penicillin, at the invention of braille, at the ability of simple algebra to fix the exact location of a star a hundred million light years away. So many miracles that it's embarrassing. Why turn water into wine – any village conjuror can do that – when you can turn rags into paper and lead into print?'

He was talking too much. Orating. Pontificating as if in some third-rate allegoric novel. He flushed at the heat of his own voice. When he knew that talk came cheap, that his only true craft was that of silent print, which could be corrected, checked and checked again. Chattering away like one on the threshold of drunkenness.

They fell into step and crossed to the eastern quarters of the city. These had their own night hum. When Father Carlo turned to him they were on a flight of damp steps from the embankment to the tramlines and to one of the tunnel-dark alleys which led from the river to Piazza San Severo.

'Miracles?'

Father Carlo had made the word sound sadder than any other in the language, and grimier.

'The miracles of reason and the laws of history? I don't know about you, *Professore*, but I can just about picture to myself, say, a thousand people. In a hall. Or, vaguely, a few thousand in a stadium. A figure like one million means nothing to me. I can't get any purchase on it. *Twenty-five million.* That we are told was the number of men, women and children Stalin starved, froze, tortured to death. Twenty-five. I can say the number but can grasp nothing of its reality, of its concrete meaning. So I focus on one single human being. On a nun they arrested for counter-revolutionary attitudes and sabotage some time in 1937. They transported her to Kolyma, to the Arctic Circle. In the hold that took prisoners from Vladivostok to the mines, on one of those hell barges, she begged and screamed for water. They pissed in her mouth, asked her whether it was as tasty as communion wine, and raped her. She was then told to make neat mounds of the earth and stones being hauled out of the shafts. The women had only a kind of raw shift to wear. In the summer many went mad, literally mad, with mosquito bites and swamp fever. Sister Evgenia lived into the winter. One day there was so little light on the tundra that she piled the stones without due care. They toppled over. She was beaten, on and off, for ten hours. Then she was sent back to pile them up again. No sleep allowed her. When she passed out, they poured ice water over her and made her stand to attention in the puddle. Her feet froze to the ground. Burning more horribly than in fire. Sister Evgenia stood there through the whole day. We have eye-witnesses. First she said out loud, "May God forgive you." Over and over. Then she crooned prayers and begged the Holy Mother to intercede for those who had beaten her. That evening the other women in the labour-squad had to chop down her body with an axe. Her eyes were still open.

'So I do my best to make Sister Evgenia stand for 24,999,999 other human beings done to hopeless death by your miracles! By your proud winds of history and scientific laws of social progress. I can't manage it. No brain can comprehend what your fine freedom did to man on this planet. There is not, just now, dear friend, a day when they are not digging up mass graves in the forests of the Ukraine, skulls by the ten thousands, each with a neat little bullet-hole in its back, skeletons, their wrists bound with wire so that the pain would grow worse till the moment of execution. That's what came of your Messiah for man. A savagery beyond understanding. Mass murder which makes the soul sick when one even tries to think of it. Arise ye prisoners of starvation. Oh yes: so that we can push you into the lime-pits. Break your chains. So we can flog you to death with them. Red dawn in the east. Light by which to kill and maim and reduce to cringing terror the millions of coolies from Beijing to Prague, from Kolyma to the Turkistan desert. As you say: they did irrigate those deserts. With blood. And there was penicillin: for the killers and court-jesters. Why, indeed, turn water into wine? A paltry trick, I agree. When you can turn human blood and human sweat into gold and iron-ore.'

Father Carlo flung the question at him as out of some huge distance though they had kept the same pace. The narrow alley, with its rare, stove-in lamps hooked to the tenement walls, rang with their voices.

'Stalin was trained in a seminary. He was taught damnation and the blessed necessity of Hell and had behind him a thousand years of anathema, of church despotism and censorship. Who has massacred more consistently than the churches?'

Carlo interrupted, flaring: 'For pity's sake. Not that old saw again. The Inquisition and Galileo. Even a novice dialectician could do better than that! Do you honestly believe that I don't know what suffering, what destruction the churches have caused? Do you imagine there is a day when I don't remember that Jew-hatred and the hounding of the so-called heretic sprang from the very first roots of Christianity, and feel sick to my soul? Can you believe that I would be with you tonight, *mio caro*, or be one of the faithful in our pitiful Marxist coven if I didn't know all that and worse?'

At the word 'coven' they both laughed loud and loosened. They had entered the trim square with its fountain. Undersized obelisks encircling nymphs and sea-horses rotund and decrepit in their immemorial thirst. Odd, he reflected, how the ring and plash of a fountain is different at night-time. More subterranean, somehow. A chill blew from the plumes of water and he tightened his scarf.

'But there is a difference.'

The emeritus priest said it calmly: 'A cardinal difference, if you will allow the term. The crimes of the churches have been committed in the name of a revealed, transcendent verity. The fires were no less hot or the censorship less suffocating. I know that. On that level, there can be no apologia. But those who did these hideous things were labouring to save souls. They were betting on eternity. They held themselves, poor cruel imbeciles, to be God's agents. The stakes were so high, so pure and free of earthly benefit, that any sin would be a crime, an uncaring without end. But at the heart of Communism there is a demeaning of man and woman worse than the tyrannies and depravities in Christendom, foul as these are.'

Father Carlo stopped, fixed for an instant in his own perception: 'At the heart of Communism is the lie. The central, axiomatic lie: a kingdom of justice, a classless brotherhood, a release from servitude here and now. In this world. That's the great lie. The systematic bribing and betraying of human hope. The perversion is monstrous. To turn war into the word "peace", a continent of slave-labour into the motherland of socialist freedom. For seventy measureless years that perversion made human beings tremble in their rooms like trapped animals, rewrote history according to the lunatic whims of the despot, rubbed out the names of the executed and the banished so that memory itself – memory, *Professore* – would be emptied of truth, like a garbage-bin. So that the names could not be made a prayer. Sister Evgenia. Sister Evgenia of the frozen feet. Just speak it with me this once. She will hear us. She and the erased ghosts butchered not in the name of grace everlasting, but so that gangsters and hangmen and bureaucrats could fatten. Corruption without end. The lie in every nerve. What your scientific state-socialism produced was not even Satan's realm as the apocalyptics and the inquisitors foresaw it. It was something smaller, tawdrier, more inhuman. Like a world ruled by poisonous lice. Your earthly messiahs turned out to be nothing but hypocritical hoodlums. Lords of lice.'

At the corner of the wider street was an all-night café, harshly lit. The steamed urns with their crowned tops and silvery sheen reminded Father Carlo of Torah scrolls he had seen in an exhibition of Jewish remnants. The thump of the juke-box could be heard even in the street, but as if muted by the dead hour. Its tired cadence blended with the beat of the fountain as it receded behind them. Sugary crumbs and rolls gone hard (the bakeries would open in about an hour) clung to the glass bells on the formica table-tops. But the coffee was hot and they cradled it in their hands. Father Carlo went back to the counter and bought two glasses of *Strega*. He set them down cautiously, brimful. From across the room, under the calendar of the *Mundial*, now sacred history, a woman flashed the two men a companionable leer.

And fluttered her hands in some heraldic sign of complicity before slipping back and inward into the spongy deeps of her aloneness. Her hair must, he thought, have been at some point lustrous and even softer than Maura's.

'But now, Carlo? What now?'

'*What then shall we do?* A fine title. Lenin's most honest book. Written when he was powerless. An exile. What you would call "a Jew".'

'Consider the source of our error. Of that great lie. And mark you, I don't accept that it was. Or that there were only venal butchers at the top. Consider.'

Momentarily, he held the coffee in his mouth. It was good coffee, but as he swallowed and let the dusky heat seep through him, a greater tiredness seemed to follow.

'Marxism did man supreme honour. The Moses and Jesus and Marx vision of the just earth, of a neighbour's love, of human universality, the abolition of barriers between lands, classes, races, the abolition of tribal hatreds: *that* vision was – we've agreed, haven't we? – a huge impatience. But it was more. It was an overestimate of man. A possibly fatal, possibly deranged but none the less magnificent, jubilant overestimate of man. The highest compliment ever paid him. The Church has held man in doleful contempt. He is a fallen creature, doomed to sweat out his life-sentence. Dust to dust. Marxism has taken him to be almost boundless in his capacities, limitless in his horizons, in the leaps of his spirit. A reacher to the stars. Not mired in original sin, but himself original. Our history is nothing but a savage prologue.

'A true Bolshevik, Carlo, owns nothing but the clothes on his back. No home. No family. No forgiveness if he breaches discipline or makes a mistake. Listen to me carefully: *he does not even have hope.* Not in your sense. No lilies and incense to come. No Mass said for his dead soul. He has something more unyielding than hope, more worthy of man's unmapped intellect and gut. The right words are hard to find. He has *insight.*'

He said it twice over.

'He understands his own condition and necessary suffering. He knows what defeat tastes like and even passing despair. There are 40,000 Communards, men, women, twelve-year-old boys, buried in mass graves under the shopping streets of Paris. The hopes of a Communist are a way of seeing with absolute clarity. Exactly as through a radio-telescope which brings us the facts about a universe infinitely older than the human race and which will evolve long after our extinction. Such seeing is clearer than hope. It honours man beyond every honour. That's where we went wrong.

'And never forget, *padre*, that there *have been* men and women, and more than just a handful, who lived up to the expectation of Marxism, who have *lived up*! Rosa Luxemburg when they clubbed her to death or the volunteers in the International Brigade or Gramsci, here, among us or the Communist partisans silent under torture. All deceived. But were they deceived? Who gave what medical aid they could in the starving villages, and kept faith in the Gulag, as your nun did, and died praising Stalin, knowing even in their own insane misery that it was he who had made Russia capable of withstanding the Fascist onslaught. Mankind is not made up of saints and martyrs. It is not made up of those drunk with justice and possessed by reason. Yes, we got it wrong. Hideously wrong, as you say. But the big error, the overestimate of man from which the mistake came, is the single most noble motion of the human spirit in our awful history. To me, to so many before me, it has compensated for our failings. It has made of that drunken slut over there something without limits. Every beggar is a prince of possibility.'

Father Carlo saluted the formula: 'You *are* a dialectician, old friend. Your health!'

The *Strega* went down like brown flame.

They took a second glass, and his hand shook a little as he brushed Carlo's sleeve.

'Capitalism never made this mistake. Don't you see? The free market takes man at his mean average. And *mean* is the word. It invests in his animal greed. It makes a balance sheet of his egotism and his petty interests. It caresses his appetites for goods and comforts and mechanical toys and holidays in the sun. Tickling his belly so that he rolls over and begs for more. Which keeps consumerism going. Capitalism has not left man where it found him, it has lessened him. We are become a pack snarling for luxuries, grunting at the trough.

That second car. A larger refrigerator. We are indeed possessed, more so than any of the crazed and the demonic in your manuals of witchcraft. By possessions possessed. By unnecessary, idiotic wants. To the pitch of mutual savagery and stupor. That's it, Father Carlo, I have it now . . . A kind of savage stupor or supineness. On the couch. In front of the television. Have you read about American children, aged five and less? Twenty-seven hours a week in front of the screen.'

He gestured towards the calendar on the café wall.

'A billion and a quarter viewers for the *Mundial*. What is your sacramental aspirin compared to television? Compared to the way in which men's dreams are packaged by advertisement. We make love according to the television images. We masturbate to the cadence of the video cassette. That is the very genius of capitalism: to package, to put a price-tag on men's dreams. Never to value us beyond our mediocrity. Ladies and gentlemen, the escalator awaits you. We are moving upward together. Towards better sun-tan lotions, towards a faster lawn-mower, to the deep-freeze of your wildest dreams and the stereo and white telephone next to your toilet seat. Hold on: the Holy Grail of cable-pornography for all is in sight. Look: there is the promised land, Disneyworld for all. And there are gods, Carlo *mio*, in supermarket heaven. Madonna of the sequin tights. And Maradona, he of the hand of God. Has it ever struck you how those two names . . . '

He broke off, emptying his drink at a draught. He should not have drunk that second glass. It thrust him forward. He was marooned in his own loquacity, the words thrashing about and spilling.

'The Cold War was no accident. No conspiracy concocted by power-brokers. Communism, perhaps even Stalinism, had horribly over-estimated man. As I said . . . '

He was repeating himself, he knew. Professorially. He couldn't stop: 'How accurately America has priced man, reducing him to well-being, making peace between human desires and fulfilment. Stalin starved millions. It's the truth. May he rot for it in hell everlasting. But America made the hungry, the drugged, the ugly invisible. Which is worse? It buttered the souls of men. No matter that the stuff is often margarine, oily, synthetic, golden-yellow. The colour of money. No matter. Fat-free, slim-line, daisy-sweet margarine on thirty kinds of bread. Carlo, I'm not making this up, they have *thirty* different sorts of bread over there: health-breads, croissants, seeded rolls, blueberry muffins, nut-breads, whole wheat, rye, pumpernickel, *panettone* for your dog, for your canary, all spread out in those California emporia.

'How stupid, how cruel it was of those nut-cases, of those prophets in their flea-bitten desert to make man homeless to himself. When there is Los Angeles.'

'Bullshit.'

Father Carlo said it without rancour.

'Bullshit, *Professore*. The old Party-line blood-libel on human nature and on America. About which, I mean America, you and I really know very little. To me it sounds like the society which says to every man and woman: "Be what you want to be. Be yourself. This world was made not only for geniuses or neurotics, for the obsessed or the inspired. It was made for you and you and you. If you choose to try to be an artist or a thinker or a pure scholar, that's fine. We will neither inhibit you nor put you on a pedestal. If you prefer to be a couch-potato, an auto-mechanic, a break-dancer, a mile-runner, a broker, if you prefer to be a truck-driver or even a drifter, that's fine too. Perhaps even better. Because it so happens that ideological passion and ascetic illumination, that dogma and sacrifice, have not only brought light and aid to this approximate world of ours. They have sown interminable hatred and self-destruction." And when America says, "Just be yourself," it is not saying, "Do not better yourself." It is saying: "Go after that Nobel Prize if that's what fires your soul. Or that heated swimming-pool." Not because America believes that heated swimming-pools are the Parthenon or even a necessity. But because they do seem to bring pleasure, and not very much harm. "Move up the ladder, if you can," says America, "because the desire to live decently, to give your family a comfortable home, to send your children to schools better than those you attended yourself, to earn the regard of your neighbours, is not some capitalist vice, but a universal desire." Do you know, *Professore*, America is just about the first nation and society in human history to encourage common, fallible, frightened humanity to feel at home in its skin.'

'Not if that skin is black!'

'Even that is coming. Painfully, I know. But inevitably. American democracy . . . '

'In which, even at vital elections, only about thirty per cent exercise their right to vote . . . '

'But that's the point!'

Father Carlo was almost shouting: ' "Vote if you will," says America. "Our education, our democratic system would have you vote. But if you are too lazy to bother, too ignorant, too bored, well, that's no catastrophe either. There's plenty of history ahead." It is under the Nazi boot, *Professore*, it is under the Stalinist truncheon that ninety-nine per cent of all citizens cast their ballots. Do you prefer that to American waywardness?

'I do know this, my dear friend: there are in American affairs black pages, stupidities in plenty. But on balance, America does stand as the one and only great power and community which, unlike any other I know of, is aiming to leave the globe a little better off, a little more hopeful than it finds it. Hope has, in fact, been America's main gross national product and export. Think of Woodrow Wilson, of Roosevelt. Of Lincoln, above all. Ask, if you dare, the millions who have survived under Marxism–Leninism, whether they would rather endure such a regime a day longer, or be penniless immigrants to America or even tenants in an American slum. You know the answer. It is filling the air just now.'

'A country which no poem can shake. Where no philosophic argument matters . . . '

Carlo cut him off.

'I did once hear you declare, at one of those blessed meetings of the Circle, that to exile a man because he differs from you on Hegel and on points in Party orthodoxy is proudly to honour the human spirit. That stupid enormity still drums in my poor head. I have never heard a sane man expound anything more barbaric. If learning, if intellectual argument need to be honoured at that price, if they must feed on intolerance, on condescension, on fatuous authority, to hell with them!

'Like you, *Professore*, I cannot abide rock music. My stomach turns at most television, at the plastic and porn, fast food and illiteracy that pours out of what you call "California". But I wonder whether even these things are inflicting on men a fraction of the pain, of the despair which all our Athens, all our high culture have inflicted. They rocked around the clock not long ago to raise millions for charity. They lectured on Kant and played Schubert and went off the same day to stuff thousands into gas ovens.

'America may not be for you or me. Not for a Communist dreamer and glutton for the printed word. Not for a mendicant friar. But we two are museum exhibits. Incorrigible chatterers. We are ghosts out of the dark of history or pre-history, you said so yourself, *Professore*. Don't you understand? The tidal wave across the Berlin Wall and all the way to Prague and the Pacific is screaming with life. It is the insurrection of the young, even when they are eighty years old. Your dogma, your tyranny of the ideal, pumped youth out of human lives. Under despotism children are born old. Just look at their eyes and mouths in those pictures from Romania. And if America is childish, as it may be, what a lucky failing that is! Fountain of Youth? What he found may be Coca-Cola. But it does bubble!'

'It rots your teeth. You Jesuit. You casuistical Jesuit.'

They were walking again, briskly and aimlessly, towards the southbound boulevard and the war memorial.

'We are, Carlo, a murderous, greedy, unclean species. But we have produced Plato and Schubert, to use your own example, Shakespeare and Einstein. It follows that there are differences in worth between human endeavours. *Credo*: that it is intrinsically finer for a human being to be obsessed by an algebraic problem, a Mozart canon or a Cézanne composition than by the manufacture of automobiles or the trading of shares. That a teacher, a scholar, a thinker, even, God have mercy, a priest is almost immeasurably more valuable and nearer the dignity of hope than is a prize-fighter, a broker, a soap-powder magnate. *Credo* again: that the mystery of creative and analytic genius is just that, a mystery, and that it is given to the very few. But that lesser beings can be woken to its presence and exposed to its demands. Oh, I know, on a free vote it is the bingo-hall and the dog-track that will prevail, not the theatre of Aeschylus. I know that hundreds of millions of our fellow men prefer football to chamber music and would rather become glazed in front of a soap opera or blue movie than pick up a book, let alone a serious book. Amen to all that, says capitalism. Let their choice be free. Let them stew in their well-being.

Hippos are free to wallow in their mud. Why not man? But that, Carlo . . . '

And once more they stood on the pavement facing each other.

'is to hold man in utter contempt. It is to turn history into a graveyard for used cars. Marxism tried otherwise. It filled the symphony halls and the libraries. It gave teachers and writers a living wage. What matters more, it gave them an eminent status in society; it made museums free of charge, open to all. It taught that a great theorem or sonata or philosophic principle comes nearer the bone of man, of our nascent humanity, than does the latest hit on a pop chart.'

The sounds in the air, even their own resumed motion, appeared to get busier with the imminence of daybreak.

'I agree with you, *Professore*. I wouldn't be feeling the wet pavement through my shoes if I didn't. I agree with every word, my dear orator. But I cannot see by what authority, by what right, you or I can cram *our* values – yes, they are mine too – down other men's throats. You claim to be arguing from love for the common man, from what you call an overestimate of his means. But that love is filled with contempt and oppression. The pursuit of quality, your blueprint for excellence, comes with the lash. The price is too high. We have seen that.'

'Hypocrisy, Father Carlo, hypocrisy and cant! If you honestly believed that, how could you be a priest, even half of one? How could you be a teacher, imparting knowledge to others, forcing it, as you put it, down their often unwilling throats? Every little step forward is made of sweat and mutiny. Until the insight is won, until the craft is mastered. No one has ever learned or achieved anything worth having without being stretched beyond themselves, till their bones crack. "Easy does it," says America to mankind. But easy has never done it. Never. I don't want to know how long it takes to produce a bottle of Coca-Cola or an instant hamburger or a tranquillizer. I do know that it takes six hundred years for the grapes to become what they are in those hills around us, six hundred years of back-breaking toil and silent cunning. Years in which hail almost flattens them or in which the heat is too fierce or during which they have been ploughed under.'

'Why, then, did you define socialism as impatience?'

'I don't know.'

As if at the edge of the pavement, in a stillness.

'Of late, I do get things muddled, Carlo. A slow impatience. Something like that.'

And abruptly, he seized his companion's elbow: 'I am a socialist. I am and remain a Marxist. Because otherwise I could not be a proofreader!'

The self-evidence of it burst on him. He wanted to fling his arms wide, to dance on that very spot.

'If California triumphs, there will be no need of proof-readers. Machines will do it better. Or all texts will be audiovisual, with selfcorrectors built in. Night after night after night, Carlo, I work till my brain aches. So as to get it absolutely right. So as to correct the minutest misprint in a text which no one may ever read or which will be shredded the next day. Getting it right. The holiness of it. The selfrespect. *Gran Dio*, Carlo, you must see what I'm driving at. Utopia simply means *getting it right*! Communism means taking the errata out of history. Out of man. Reading proofs.'

He was out of breath. What a queer picture they must make, Carlo pacing, he on his toes, under the first distant volley of bells. Matins and the wail of a siren from the river.

'I can't match all your clever arguments, *mio* Carlo. You may even be right about America. And I know what they would have done to an outsider like myself – am I some sort of Leninist Albigensian? – over there, in the East. But I believe in my belief. What else is there for me now?'

More bells, out of unison, querulous and booming. An early bus drove past, and he saw the tow-headed driver yawning hugely. A metal shutter was cranked up, and electric light from a kiosk spilled down the road. Sunday morning sounds thickened at every moment. A bus in the opposite direction, just out of the depot.

Carlo said: 'Look at that skylight over there. Under the chimneypots. Just over there. Morning.'

He followed the pointing finger. To see better, he closed one eye.

9

'Open both eyes, if you please. Wide. Hold steady.'

The ophthalmologist's buttery breath enveloped him.

'Keep open. Try not to blink.'

The drops had dilated his pupils. Now the harness through which the eye-doctor was peering held his chin rigid and pressed on his forehead.

'You can close for a moment.'

Darkness and a vague impression of swimming.

'Open again. Now look up. Down. To the left. Left again. Hold. Now to the right.'

The man's voice was absurdly close, but coming at him as through a rubber tunnel.

'You can relax now.'

The apparatus glided away. Dr Melchiori switched on the overhead light and returned to his roll-top desk. He scribbled. There was a stain on the back of his white coat. It must have been sizeable if he could make it out, for the room was blurred and the letters on the wall-chart quivered and merged.

'It will take a while for the drops to wear off. Be careful when you leave. There are steps. And they're digging up the road. As usual.'

He continued making furious notes and flipped once more through the card on which he had inscribed the measurements taken during the examination.

'I shall prescribe medication. An ointment and drops. To ease the strain. Three times daily. Make sure the drops reach the cornea and the corners of the eye.'

For a moment it sounded like a dismissal and the end of a routine visit. Then the doctor motioned to him to come nearer, to sit not on the narrow metal stool next to the instruments but in the chair by the desk.

'You're not a child. So I had best be frank with you.'

The doctor scrutinized his notes and seemed vexed: Profession: proof-reader, text-editor. 'A trade, my dear sir, not exactly calculated to make things easy for your eyes. How long have you been at it?'

The doctor glanced at his records and nodded.

'More than thirty-five years. As I thought. Why, in heaven's name, did you not come to me before? Why?'

He spun on his chair, aggrieved.

'You say that the morning discomforts, what you call "a burning behind the eyes", began only a few months ago. But why waste even those months? I know: we have waiting lists. The service is overrun. You'll often find me at this desk fifteen or sixteen hours at a stretch. I do realize . . . but in emergencies! When the case is acute. As yours is. I can't hide that from you. I don't hold with baby-talk. Melchiori tells his patients the facts. In plain language.

'There are no miracles. The weakness in the left eye must go back a very long way. Possibly congenital. You did say that your mother wore glasses, didn't you? And you have, my friend, been favouring the right eye far longer, far more intensely than you realize. There was going to be a problem whatever you did. But with your job and this regrettable delay . . . '

Bruno Melchiori looked at him, seeking, soliciting approbation, fiddling with the switch at the base of the desk-lamp. Then he turned back to his notes. Exasperated, commiserative.

'The fact is that there is in your left eye little but peripheral vision and that the strain on the right has already caused considerable damage. Considerable. There is a small tear in the retina, just here.'

He thrust a rough sketch across the desk.

'Had you come to me in good time, it would have been worth operating on the left eye. To remove those cataracts. To implant a lens. As matters stand now . . . '

His voice seeped away.

'You are, of course, most welcome to seek a second opinion. Perhaps you should insist on having one. In my judgement, an operation would bring only discomfort and false hopes. The left eye is going on strike, dear sir, on permanent strike. So our real problem is the right.'

The doctor half-turned away, and as to himself: 'Can you change your employment? I didn't think so. What I can do is to give you a medical authorization for a few weeks of leave. The right eye *must* rest. It is infected and must have complete rest. Otherwise . . . You do understand me? If you don't give it a rest . . . '

The ancient gesture of doleful impotence, palms upward.

'As is, I cannot be too optimistic. Plain words are what I believe in. Your sight will diminish significantly. Whether or not we decide to operate. Whether or not surgery succeeds. The problem with glaucoma and related conditions . . . But I won't bore or alarm you with technicalities. As do so many of my esteemed colleagues.'

Melchiori's chin quivered.

'With rest and regular treatment much can be salvaged. But to leave things so late . . . '

The nurse, in the swarming corridor of the clinic, helped him impatiently into his coat. When he reached the street, which swam before him in a half-light, he ransacked his pockets for the prescription. But he could not help noticing that the rasp of the tramcar brakes had taken on a new sharpness.

10

They gave him a fortnight's leave and tinted glasses. Time turned grey. As if a drowsy wasp were droning and knitting the hours.

He had resolved on method. A touch of physical exercise in the morning (a man's toes, as he bends towards them, can induce melancholy). Three solid hebdomadal sessions at the municipal library, where he would reread, so as to renew the armoury of his soul, Marx's *Eighteenth Brumaire* – how he remembered the trumpet shock of his first brush with that text. Moreover, there were the newspapers, fanned out on a table at the entrance to the reading-room. With their fat headlines and arresting pictures. The vacuous shelves and breadlines in Russian cities. The indictment of Party officials in East Germany and Bulgaria. Royalists unfurling banners in Romania. Gorbachev pirouetting for loans and hand-outs in what had been, not long ago, the Escorial of Franco. He read. He thrust the captions close to his right eye as if the Medusa held him fast in her stony smile. And then he sat at the library table, incapable of serious attention.

The winter park was no better. The thinning pigeons seemed to glare at him as if he was a rival for breadcrumbs and peanut shells. The statue of and to Garibaldi, turbaned, his curved blade operatic, with its chiselled promise of emancipation for the common man, struck him as insufferable. He played games with its lapidary syllables, substituting vowels, inverting letters. The resulting obscenities were out of an adolescent's lavatory. A passing couple, tourists, guidebook in hand and muffled against the raw wind, asked him, in halting courtesy, for directions to the Museum of the Resistance. Promptly, loquaciously, he misdirected them. Realizing, as they thankfully departed, that they were Jews, most probably Israelis on some visitation of remembrance. A numbing distaste flooded through him. Against himself, but also against the innocent. As if it was indeed the stiff dolour of the Jews, their inability to let be, which had brought the political and ideological world to its present chaos.

When he told Maura, elaborating the incident in self-reproach, she flinched. Not only then. His constricted emptiness grated on her. She was, just at this time, fiercely over-worked and, he sensed, self-sufficient.

Almost involuntarily, he drifted back to the print-works. Away from the barrens of his supposed rest. His temporary replacement – but was he only that? – tolerated his presence on a cast-off stool in a corner of the eyrie. Let him sit there while he, the young man with the keen glance, scanned the wet pages. The floor quivered to the mallet-strokes of the rotors. One night, the new man vanished to the toilets (a complaisance he had virtually sought to deny himself when total concentration was of the essence). Compulsively, he lifted from the desk one of the sheets, corrected, already initialled and ready to go. He spotted, at once, as if through antennae in his skin, as if with second or third sight exact beyond any of his failing retina, two errors: an accent out of place and a letter in a wrong font. He reached for the red biro.

'For Christ's sake,' breathed the young copy-editor who had returned behind him, cat-like up the metal steps.

'For Christ's sake.'

Not in outright annoyance, but softly, with a hint of derision.

'Nothing escapes the Owl, does it? I've heard all about you. Holding up urgent jobs for a second or third look. The perfectionist.'

He plucked the offending page and laughed outright.

'Do you know what this is? Have you bothered to look? Or don't you read but only proof-read? Have a closer look, *maestro*.'

354

He thrust the print at him.

'This is a handbill. For an auction of used farm implements and manure sacks! To be held in the co-operative of San Maurizio – God knows where that hole is – on Tuesday next. One hundred copies. To be stuck on some outhouse door or dumped in the next ditch. And you worry about an accent!'

'Desperately. Do you know what the cabbala teaches? That the sum total of the evil and miseries of humankind arose when a lazy or incompetent scribe misheard, took down erroneously, a single letter, one single, solitary letter, in Holy Writ. Every horror since has come on us through and because of that one erratum. You didn't know that, did you?'

They faced off in the thumping obscurity and stood speechless as the runner-boy stopped by and scooped up the pile of corrected, imperfect bills.

'You're no help, you know. They haven't dared tell you. The schedules are being tightened. Your sort of practice may suit printers of fine books and copperplate work. But not here.'

The next packet had just landed on his raked table.

'Not here.'

'On the contrary. It is just here that it matters more than ever before. To act otherwise is utter contempt. Contempt for those who cannot afford to look at a fine book, at quality paper or crafted type. Contempt for those who have a right under God, yes, under God, to have a flawless handbill, also for a sale of manure! It is just for those who live in rural holes, in slums, that we should do the best work. So that some spark of perfection will enter their wretched days. Can't you understand how much contempt there is in a false accent or a misplaced serif? As if you spat at another human being.'

His understudy stared at him. Neutrally. As from some later planet.

'You can sit over there if you want. But let me get on with it.'

And towards the dead hour of first dawn: 'Let me get you some coffee, rabbi.'

He startled at the epithet. He watched embarrassed as his sharer drew back to himself a sheet already initialled and read it a second time.

11

His hand loitered on her buttock. The tremor in his wrist came and went.

'Not to worry,' said Maura.

Would she say next: 'It can happen'?

She did and his insides knotted. She veered towards him and brushed his cheeks with her lips. He reached for his unaccustomed spectacles on the night-table. The one lens might, for all the difference it made, be window glass. The other was so thick that, had anyone bothered to take notice, it was not an owl they would compare him with but a frog, bulbous-eyed and groping. Maura sought to draw him back to her, gently. But the stale inside him continued shaking, like a minor bog.

'Nerves,' she offered.

He peered at the rain-sodden streak of early light under the edge of the blinds. He had woken dimly out of a punishing dream, but erect and reaching for Maura's warm back. She had nestled close. Then nothing. The branch sagging under some dead weight. Nothing. She cradled the deadness in her hand, consoling. He wanted to rip her touch away, but held the rage and the ache in his throat. And fought for breath. 'This room, the mausoleum.' The phrase chimed out of the ebbing dream. Then he made the connection.

Television, the slow killer. They had watched the midnight news round-up and review of the week. Naked under the partial tent of the bed cover. The reconsecration of St Basil's Cathedral on Red Square, with its onion-bulb cupolas and Lego-set minarets and the splotches of gold-leaf pillaged from the ancient Khans. The bells were whipping the pigeons and swifts to a frenzy. Across the square wound a slow procession of the faithful, cradling candles. The camera, inside the nave, lingered on the upturned visages, the brimming eyes and clasped hands of the worshippers. It panned across their mouths, slack with ecstasy and a queer sort of greed. Greed for remembrance, for home-coming, for the annulment of time (seventy years, was it?).

'Look at their faces. I've seen faces like that before. In medical encyclopaedias. The happy faces of imbeciles. Of the senile.'

She had not answered and he felt mired in the morass of his outrage.

'Just look: the rolling eyes of cretins, the wet mouths. There has never been any church more corrupt, more servile. None that has been a blacker censor of truth and free thought.'

The candles seemed to gather the chant and the fug of incense and the ardent breaths into a single pyre.

Why had he not turned the thing off?

On came the commentator. A woman star in the television firmament. Brushing a tear from her lighthouse eyes. 'After the long and terrifying night, after more than two generations. Treasured viewers, my friends, join me at this historic hour, here on the steps of St Basil's in Moscow. The Eucharist. Once again. Bread for the starved hearts. Who never lost hope. Never. And now we can share in their felicity. Look, just look at the light on the gilt domes. And now . . . ' A dramatic cut as the cameras swung abruptly towards a squat, lightless shape barely distinguishable under the Kremlin walls. 'Lenin's tomb.' Her voice was honeyed with victory. 'That famous, or ought we to say infamous, mausoleum. How much longer till it is shut, till the waxen figure of the despot is removed?'

After Maura had switched off the set, sleep stayed out of reach. When it came, so did the sour dreams, the flotsam of nightmare. Maura got out of bed and slipped into her bathrobe. Recently, still, its ochre and autumn-leaf pattern had moved him almost to grateful tears. Now he observed the rent at the hem and the hurried patching. He took in the cough and hiss of the toilet. He felt broken, the air knocked out of him. Maura rolled up the blinds and lit the gas-range. He tugged at himself with gross effort. The numbness eased. But staring at his naked legs as he put his feet on the scrap of rug at the foot of the bed, he suffered a sense of utmost strangeness, perceiving his feet not as his own but, through the layers of the lens, as belonging to some intimate unknown. To someone under way towards him.

12

The start of the meeting lacked elevation. Cesare Lombardi turned aggressively to the matter of dues. Had the treasurer, he demanded, taken into account the fact, 'the manifest fact', as he put it on a note of stentorian reproach, that any long-term adjournment, let alone dissolution of the Circle of Marxist Revolutionary Theory and Praxis, would necessitate – his voice underlined that hallowed word – the reimbursement of some equitable portion of the membership fees and of the subscription to both the cyclostyled Bulletin and the complete works of Plekhanov to which the *Circolo* had so imprudently (surely, members recalled his, Cesare's, cautionary dissent) committed itself?

The treasurer, one Alberto P., with a tendency to slide into a mild stupor during theoretical debates, fumbled at his notes, snapped the rubber bands and inserted a paper-clip in his mouth.

He was, opined Alberto, not altogether confident that there was anything left over in the kitty. Not after the summer outing and the replacement of the broken chair, which the school where they convened had insisted on. As to the further tomes of Plekhanov (the frayed prospectus fell to the floor), he would do his best, but harboured some blurred apprehension that the *casa editrice*, the publishing house for Workers' High-Schooling responsible for that monumental undertaking, had itself gone into recent liquidation.

Tullio laughed under his breath. But audibly. Which did not help.

Anna B.'s anguish bore on the minutes of past gatherings. These were, assuredly, of historical 'and ethical' – she stressed the addendum – import. An act of witness, a testimonial whose status would not be effaced (at which point her pudgy hands managed a gesture of peculiar desolation) by the grievous change in the fortunes of the movement. 'The movement', the way she breathed the phrase made it plain that it was not the nine members of the Circle actually present tonight, but a vast throng progressing out of time, out of perennial enslavements, the Spartacus revolt, the peasant rebellions and millenarian uprisings, the Communards and the innocent and the kneeling shot down on that grand square in St Petersburg in 1905, a column without end of the mutinous and the vanquished, giving their lives to the cause, in 1917, in the cellars of Shanghai and torture chambers of Madrid, Berlin, Santiago, singing to stay awake in the frozen inferno of Stalingrad, unquenchable then, unquenchable tomorrow. 'The movement'. To which, humble as they might be, the minutes, the chronicles of the Circle belonged.

As spoken by a somnambulist, with the faintest accent of resurrection.

But there was another side to the coin.

'One must be practical.'

Comrade Anna drove her thumb into her palm.

'Comrades will acknowledge that I have always attended to practicalities.'

No dissent from that.

'Suppose our minutes were to fall into the wrong hands. Is it not likely, indeed almost certain, that Fascism will re-emerge from the present crisis?'

Her alarm swept the room.

'Fascism in its most ruthless, mechanized and avenging guise? Aided, financed by American intelligence and the renegades scurrying across from the East. In which event there will be blacklists. Just as when Mussolini's hooligans took over. House to house. The night-visitors with their rolls of names, their truncheons and their castor oil. If the minutes of the CMRTP were to be found, everyone associated with it would be hunted down and imprisoned.'

She hovered over the prospect with some fascination.

'A clandestine organization, and that is what we will have to become, must keep no records, it must leave no betraying spoors. See Lenin, 1902. Am I right, *Professore*? We must find a truly safe hiding-place. The Fascist and the CIA pigs could nose out truffles buried deep.'

(The simile was not hers.)

But in self-conscious unison the members present murmured the shibboleth: 'What then is to be done?'

It was Father Carlo who struck the higher note. Was there not, he asked, a difference between the dissolution of the group, as it figured on tonight's order of business, and its cessation?

Let him explain. His training in dogma and church history had left him with an awed intimation of the paradigm of the king's 'two bodies'. The king's mortal flesh could die. But the incarnate identity, the essence of royalty, could not. It inhered, intact, materially immortal in the crowned effigy placed either on a special pediment or on the throne itself, an imago of a real presence to which courtiers brought daily news and food and drink till the new monarch was proclaimed. By virtue of which usage, the continuity of the institution of kingship was guaranteed. Dissolution would abolish the Circle and pronounce it defunct. Resignation of its several members – did they not see the close analogy to the royal case? – resignation for whatever reason, would ensure its survival. He was not urging a sophism or arcane paradox. An organization could endure even if, temporarily, no one chose to adhere to it. Wells dry up and the deep springs return again. Who knows what may lie ahead after this present quake?

A query which impelled even Tullio to turn towards the *Professore*.

Father Carlo's allegory had greatly moved and persuaded him. There can be no 'dissolution of a truth', of any fundamental order of human insight and proven discovery. No tearing down of a wall, no overthrow of a regime, not even the collapse of the USSR, could refute the verities shared by those whom he now addressed. On the contrary. A new phase of imperialist exploitation, racism and wage slavery, in short, an Americanization of the planet, would attest to the unshakeable foresight of Marxist theory. Short-, even middle-term prognostications had gone wrong. There was no use denying that. Capitalism had not only survived the two world wars which it had caused, it had not only weathered cyclical depressions, but had turned these to its profit. Members had, he trusted, read Hobsbawm's analysis in the last but one issue of the Bulletin. Keynes, a figure of sinister genius, had appropriated certain Marxist techniques in order to rescue capitalism from ruin. The condition of the working classes *had* improved.

At which concession, Comrade Anna shrugged grimly.

'Why shut one's eyes to that or to Marx's error concerning the ineluctable pauperization of the proletariat? No nineteenth-century mind, however capacious, could anticipate either the exponential benefits capitalism would harvest from its investment in research and development, in high technology, or the inability of the underdeveloped world to resist expropriation and insurmountable debt.'

This did *not* mean that Marxist revolutionary theory had been disproved or made obsolete. The exact opposite was the case. That theory needed to be deepened and made more flexible. It seemed to him perfectly obvious that major conflicts lay ahead: between Islam and the West, between the northern and the southern hemispheres, between inflationary capital and the debt-structure on which it cynically depended. North America was entering an accelerating spiral of recessions and bank-failures. Never had there been more need of theoretical clarity.

It might be that migrant labour would swamp western Europe. What then? To dissolve their Circle would be folly. The day would come when its membership would no longer total twenty or a dozen but hundreds and thousands thereafter!

His ardour had fallen flat. Nods all around, to be sure. And Anna put an awkward hand on his shoulder. But Tullio's 'speaking concretely' seemed immediate and undeniable.

'Speaking concretely', Tullio failed to see much use in further convocations. Even free copies of their Bulletin found no takers. The attempt to organize a workshop plus picnic in the housing estates or among the senior classes in the schools and polytechnics had aborted dismally. Humiliation seemed to lie like salt on Tullio's tongue. To him, also, Marxism was, at signal points, the truth. But not true just now. Not in the actual situation in which men and women, and not only capitalist profiteers and neo-Fascist gangsters, were living their lives. A dry season, as the *Monsignore* had so neatly put it.

'Why, then, spit in the empty well?'

Tullio had concluded. Adjournment *sine die*. A vote of thanks to the relieved treasurer (Lombardi abstaining). Maura would let the school know that the room would, for the time being, no longer be thankfully required. The *Professore* would undertake to keep the records in a safe place. Anna's mien registered doubt. Was there any further business?

They stood up. Still vexed. Lombardi knocked over his chair. Was it Maura who intoned first, in a low, trained voice? 'Arise ye prisoners of starvation . . . ' They joined hands, embarrassed. The rhetoric brought pain. But he sang. Out of tune. And this time Maura's smile to him was like warm bread.

As they unravelled, heading in different directions, Anna B. looked back and raised her fist in . . . He was going to say 'valediction'. That would have been another erratum. She raised it in promise and in terror.

13

He had taken the trip on an impulse. Probably ill-considered. Even the special excursion fare to Rome intended, he wryly noted, for pilgrims in quest of remission and absolution at the holy places, sapped his budget – one now stretched to the limit because he knew he would only be able to resume his proof-readings part-time, if at all. It was a loan from Tullio which had made possible his overnight stay in a grotty *pensione* near the railway station. Dutiful but hurried hands had assisted him down the steep steps from the carriage to the platform. He was on his own in the blaring rush of the city. As a child, he had rubbed his eyeballs to provoke crystalline star-showers. Cleaning his glasses obsessively, blinking hard, all he could produce now was an undulant mist.

He knew Rome's orange-grey and the smoky light which gave to many of its monumentalities their ghostly weight. On a much earlier visit, he had been made uneasy by the mottled air and the sepia wash which lay, day in and day out, on the august walls and arches. But this time the dun veil, which floated between himself and the illustrious sites, hung within. He walked slowly, hesitated at corners and picked at railings.

The nastiness had been reported, very briefly, at the bottom of a column of miscellaneous crimes in the national press. The plaque in the Street of the Dark Shops in Rome had been vandalized by unknown, though presumably neo-Fascist or royalist defacers.

He remembered how he had found that plaque, years ago, and how he had deposited, at the feet of the wall, a small bunch of violets. The event commemorated was one among hundreds no less atrocious enacted on those antique streets and squares between 1943 and liberation. Fifteen members of a Communist underground resistance group had been betrayed into the hands of the Waffen-SS by an elderly, observant housekeeper prone to insomnia. They had been tortured. So far as could be discovered, not one had broken and given up further names. Not the sixteen-year-old boy whose testicles they had put in a carpenter's vice. Not the three young women whose bodies had been chequered with cigarette burns. Not the old man (the name suggested that he was a Jew) whose beard they had torn out hair by hair and whose hands they inserted in a door-jamb. They then had dragged their prisoners to the narrow street, propped them against the wall and machine-gunned them. One of the victims, his legs smashed during interrogation, had slipped to his knees when the SS opened fire. Seeing him alive, they kicked him to death, slowly. For years, it was said the runnels and star-splashes of human blood could be made out like fading burns on the stone.

Standing in front of the inscription on his visit long ago, testing its lettering and the incision of the Party badge, he had, almost unawares, committed to memory a number of the names. Bartani (Adriana). Pradone (Vigilio) – the boy. Gildo (Manuele). Together with their dates of birth. Comrades. Rostagni (Marco), aged twenty-three when they strapped him to the table. Condini (Fabio), the leader of the cell who had, on the very eve of the war, published in a clandestine edition that notable essay on Marx's reading of Lucretius. Comrades-in-arms about whose courage and sacrifice there could be no question and whose doomed faith and actions had cleansed Rome of some part of its unholiness, of its self-betrayals.

Encasing these names in his memory, adverting to them on occasion, he imagined he was practising something like the Jewish rite of *kaddish*. The refusal to forget, to let death have the final say over lives which must remain living.

He was not alone. A small group had gathered in the Botteghe Oscure. The memorial had not only been smeared with the double-lightning of the SS across a star of David ludicrously misshapen, but also part of the marble had been chipped away, and a rough fissure now sliced through the column of names. Those assembled, they amounted to perhaps a dozen, stared at the damage. One or two had brought fresh flowers. These lay at the rim of the gutter amid the splinters of rent stone and the dribble of brown paint. The right brown, he noted, that of the shirts.

A very old man was shaking helplessly, his sobs out of control. He managed the name of Santori (Anna Maria).

'She was my sister. My sister. They raped her first. She kept saying

363

"Stalingrad". So they tore out her teeth. Anna Maria. I am Giuseppe Santori.'

He turned to the bystanders for confirmation.

A tall man in a sheepskin jacket, the collar raised, said, 'Bastards. Fascist bastards.' And walked off abruptly.

It was the woman just in front of him, long motionless, who turned and spoke to him.

'Now they are going to change the name of the Party. I call that spitting on the dead. Doing dirt on them greater than this. We expect this sort of shit from the Fascist swine. But now it is the Party . . . Forgive my language: pissing on history.'

She had steeled herself to say the word aloud and carried on more freely.

'My mother was one of them. She happened to be away carrying messages to the partisans in Orvieto when the SS came. Otherwise . . . '

She looked at the stained names.

'She knew who betrayed them. The foul bitch died only a few years ago. In a cosy home for the aged. Paid for by your and my taxes, *Signore*.'

The laugh was forced.

'My mother unearthed her not long after the Americans came. She wanted to have her arrested and put away. I imagine she was even ready to kill her. But the hag cringed and whined and offered Mother bits of hideous jewellery and money. Mother vomited and left her blubbering on the floor. But the Party is no better. It is betraying them all over again. I can wager that they would rather not replace the plaque. So embarrassing. Men and women done to death with the names of Togliatti, of Stalin, yes of Stalin, in their hearts.'

She shut her lips tight and turned away. He saw the slow shiver of anger and disgust pass through her shoulders. Now her back trembled. His hand was on her arm. She did not remove it but drew it more closely to her when she saw him fumbling at the edge of the steps which led to the piazza. She was, he decided, beautiful.

In the diminutive trattoria confidence flowed easily. They had agreed to share the bill, but the thin wine, he insisted, was to be on his side of the ledger. She sold plastic and fake-leather bags, belts, gloves, accessories and costume bangles in a boutique behind Via Veneto. At first, she kept eyeing her watch. Then, with shy bravado and over a second cup of coffee, she announced that she was taking the afternoon off. Let them dock her wretched pay if they chose. She detested the job anyway; the odour of celluloid and varnish, the customers pawing the goods endlessly and then complaining about their own finger-marks on the fabric.

Yes, she would take today off. In homage to the defiled dead. How her mother had feared and scorned shopkeepers, she who had been an educated woman but tubercular.

Her own existence? Quickly inventoried. A father who escaped, as into air, soon after her birth. Trade-school. The years as a receptionist in a garage and repair-yard on the road to Ostia. Oh, indeed, quite close to the one in which Pasolini had been attacked. Then, a shadow in her left lung. A less taxing employment, or so it sounded, in diverse emporia and boutiques.

No, it had not worked out. The man was of some intelligence and political decency, but restless. They had parted more or less amicably. The first few postcards had come from Tunis. Then nothing. Yes (and she was at ease reporting it), there had been episodes since. But something in the incompletion of her ways – the phrase intrigued him – seemed to exclude others. Or it might be, and her smile quickened the light all around her, that those who came too near to her, to these incompletions and jagged edges, felt – how should she put it? – superfluous or scratched. At this image she reddened and laughed into her wine.

But what of him?

When they got up, the trattoria had emptied, and the waiter was wiping neighbouring tables with palpable reproof.

Nothing like it had ever happened to him before.

With its unspoken self-evidence.

He did not recall their progress through immaterial streets, only the firm tug of her arm as she conducted him across loud tram-rails, around ruts and steep pavements. Nor did he really remember their ascent in the clanging lift. What was vivid to his recollection was her low warm laugh as she fumbled at her key-ring and failed, twice, to use the right key to open her own door. They undressed each other like children in a lost game. Her lips sped across his whole body and lingered where it was worn. The loveliness of her arched back pierced him with wonder. His fingers idled in her unpinned hair as she knelt. When he entered her and let that high soundless wave carry him, a single word rang in his unbound being: 'dormition'. He had read it in a catalogue of old masters and did not know quite what it meant. Not so he could define it. But in that motion towards and with her, dormition seemed to signify a waking sleep, a peace and rest so whole as to be on the other side, on the lit and southern side of sleep.

In the darkening afternoon they spoke of this and that. In abbreviated yet long-familiar phrases. It was only when putting on his clothes that he noticed the stack of cuttings and pamphlets on her dresser. Horoscopes, astrological charts, predictions of planetary conjunctions to come and of their portent. She beamed at him full of confident zeal.

What, exactly, were the hour and the day of his nativity? She would read his palm for that also was a science of which she had some knowledge. The desecration they had witnessed that morning and which had brought them together, Taurus and Libra, had been foretold. That is why she had turned to him so naturally. No less foreseeable was the return of the Communist Party to repute and power. When Jupiter and enigmatic Neptune were in the house of the Lion. There could be no shadow of doubt. Not for those who would see. Once baleful Saturn had moved out of Scorpio . . .

She reached for a tract and pressed it on him. What had been his mother's astral sign, her favourite precious stone?

'Tell me, please.'

They parted strangers, and he hurried to the station.

14

He was walking too fast. Twice already, he had come up hard against edges and breaks in the pavement. Now his feet caught in a discarded carrier-bag, its garish design malignantly alive in the wind. He kicked blindly at the thing.

A sentence sprayed on the back of the bus-stop shelter seized his notice. 'God does not believe in God.'

To which a lesser hand, armed only with red chalk, had added the word *our*: 'God does not believe in *our* God.'

Absurdly, a touch of fear stung him, and the momentary, deranged conviction that a deserted universe, like a house unlocked after the removal vans had gone, would sink into oblivion if he failed to carry out his present purpose. He felt the inane certitude that this enactment, so trivial in itself, was the litany of which Father Carlo had once told him, whose recitation, out of however gutted and reduced a human mouth and soul, kept reality going and coerced the tired future into its advent.

Shivering in the cold, he wiped his glasses and pressed on.

Though he knew his city well, the building was not easy to find. Instead of the customary name-plate by the entrance, he was able to make out only a bent card, illegibly inscribed, and pinned to the downstairs letter-box. The stairs lay in thick shadow and he groped uselessly for the light-switch. At the fifth landing, he found the door closed. He pulled at the bell. The sound came back muffled and distant. He pulled again and waited. He was about to reverse his steps when the door inched open. He could not really see the figure behind the crack.

What was it he wanted?

He stated his intention.

If anything, the opening narrowed even more.

Was he a practical joker? A *provocateur*?

Urgently he leaned against the door handle.

'Nothing of the kind!'

He advanced his name, the date of his original adherence, the number on his Party card. He inventoried his Party assignments and activities.

Was he babbling? The sad notion crossed his mind.

He cited the names of several comrades who could vouch for him, who knew of his purposed recantation.

A muted, theatrical laugh on the other side of the door. But the opening widened.

Innerly, to be perfectly honest, he had never left the Party. He had only sought to clear up for himself, at a time of especial internal contradictions, some theoretical conundra (it was too late to rescind that pretentious, evasive word). Certain perplexities which had also troubled other comrades. He had been wrong. He knew that now. As Bukharin had taught: deviants, however right *subjectively*, belong to the limbo of history.

Again the miserly laugh. But the door opened.

The man was in slippers and a smell of fish clung to his sweater. A pan – soup, coffee? – was spluttering behind a curtained recess. Parallel to the door, as in a second line of defence, stood a table. Printed forms, roneoed sheets, cigarette ash. Now he saw that the man held an unlit cigarette between his lips.

'You *are* a queer one, aren't you, *Professore*. Isn't that what they called you? Always talking. Talk, talk. If you ask me, that's where we made our big mistake. There's no pay-off in talk. Take to the streets. Smash their fucking skulls. Occupy the factories. That's what I always said.'

The surly recognition, the recall of his mocking sobriquet, filled him with rare joy. He was eager to debate the issue, to identify the leftist infantilism (Lenin's decisive tag) of the man's position. But he checked himself and asked with humility whether he could apply for reinstatement.

'Haven't you heard?'

The man motioned towards a scatter of cards half-hidden under a file at one end of the table.

'Those are just this past week's. Most tear up their Party cards or stuff them in the incinerator. But some do send theirs. With obscenities attached. Shall I read them to you, Comrade?'

That would not be necessary, and he heard the irony in the mode of address. Yet he flushed with contentment.

'By next month, honoured sir, there may not be a Party.'

Ah, but there would be, leaner, more astringent, better armed theoretically. The truth knows no circumstances. Tullio was wrong. If God no longer believed in God, the time had come for man to believe in man. Only Marxism could make that belief effective.

The functionary cut him off with a shrug. He drew a creased form from one of the piles and nudged it across the table. An application for membership. He would pass it on to the committee. Which had not, in weeks, succeeded in assembling a quorum. There was a small fee for processing.

He had the notes ready. The man counted them and considered him with distaste.

'The Party will examine your case. And that's what you must be, believe me. A case.'

The lame play on words seemed to trigger silent mirth. He shook his head.

'You'll hear from us.'

Then he looked down at the form which the applicant had begun to fill in.

'Don't you even read a paper? Haven't you heard? "I hereby apply for acceptance in the Communist Party." There is no such thing, my friend! There is no more PCI. *Basta. Finito.*'

Detaching each funereal syllable, he slid the flat of his hand across his windpipe.

'Gone and buried, the old whore. It is now the Party of the Democratic Left.'

He spelled out the new initials hoarsely.

'No more red star. A green tree. Look here: a bushy green tree.'

He waved the new logo in front of the *Professore*'s face.

'Is that what you want to join? Well, is it?'

It was. So precisely that the penitent could find no rejoinder, no words for his thirst. Only a puppet's quick unseeing nod.

The man cleared his throat impatiently, spat into a grey handkerchief and bade him write his address. In capital letters, if you please.

He would be receiving a summons from the district committee.

'Though only God knows when.'

God did seem much about in the city these days. So be it. The real battle with Him lay ahead.

The door shut loudly.

It was only at the bottom of the stairwell, still in pitch blackness, that he realized he had not held on to the banister. Not even once. But then one doesn't need to, does one, when coming home.

Desert Island Discs

His requests did stretch the resources, almost all-encompassing, of the sound-archive. But that is part of the game.

First he asked to hear Fortinbras's belch. The one at the end of the interminable coronation carouse. There was no use denying it: despite tireless scrubbing, new rushes on the floor of the hall, the aromatic salts expended on the long tables and logs in the chimney, the death smells persisted. They hung sweet and rancid in the corners and by the tower stairs. There had been too many corpses. Was it six, was it seven? Fortinbras the King found it hard to remember. A woman's carrion among them, bloated and waxen, with the scent of burnt almonds on her twisted lips. The surviving folk, royal cousins and courtiers, had been pleasant enough. Caps lifted, knees bent to the new monarch. General sentiments of relief. And now the King's chambers were being thoroughly aired, the arras taken down and replaced by more cheerful hangings. Still, the feast had not been unblemished. There was the thin, faintly hysterical child on the balcony, troubling the military fanfare – plain lads out of Norway, not those Danish luteners and players on elaborate pipes, most of whom had, anyway, taken to their heels at the first cannon shot. Flitting among them in her pale, nearly transparent gown, a younger sister, or so the King had been informed, of one Ophelia, drowned. And there was the good Horatio, solemn as a blind horse. Assuring the new sovereign of his insightful fidelity, of his imminent retirement, telling him that the great and dread events of which he, Horatio, had been humble witness, must be memorably noted. Horatio to Fortinbras, in a hushed, dulcet tone; the King having to strain his battle-deafened ears to catch the man's desolate, incessant drift.

The wines had been heavy, and the herring. Dawn could not be far off. Even through the thick walls and battlements, Fortinbras, the son of Norway, could sense the changing rasp of the sea when dawn approaches. He was bone-tired. Almost envious of the dead prince, who had always seemed to him like a master of sleep, and of the secrets which sleep breeds. Fortinbras belched. It was a loud, cavernous belch. From the inmost of his drowsing, armoured flesh. It was a sound the courtiers would not forget. Thunderous and replete with the promise of a simpler tomorrow.

The second recording he asked for was that of the neighing of the little horse, of the dappled grey with the cropped right ear, after it had cantered into the surrounding hills.

The journey had been hot and dust-choked. The ticks and the blue flies hammered like mad that long day. They had left the high gates and the cobbles of the town well before sunrise. But even at that hour, the air had been listless and the heat trapped underfoot. And there had been a strange unrest in the courtyard. The old woman with the pale eyes and heavy brooch had exuded a kind of quivering. The dapple had felt it in his wet nostrils: night-sweat and spilled seed. Not that the actual trip was of any danger or difficulty. They had made it often. Past the spring with its loud bucket, through the olive groves and into the baking plain. Then onward to where gaps in the burnt hills flashed with the sheen of the gulf. The old master was light in his cart and the driver scarcely more than a rude, overbearing teenager. The horse had heard him in the stables, boasting of his manhood, of his prowess with the whip, of the leaves he chewed and of the hot dreams they brought on. But the voyage should have been routine, and the shaft-horse, though patronizing (he had been to the oracle before the grey was foaled), was friendly enough.

It all happened at such speed. The horses had been half-asleep, their eyes closed against the damned flies. Out of breath with the heat and the slight rise which leads to the place where the three roads meet, the two slaves were trotting in the spare shade of the cart. The old man was humming to himself, as he often did, a lullaby to a new-born child, but breaking off, always, as on a jagged tooth. Then the harsh pull on the reins, forcing the horses almost to their haunches. The slash of the whip and the charioteer's high-pitched obscenities. The muffled call of the old man, his bony arms waving in the drumming air. And cutting through it all, a voice which the dapple would never shake out of its ears. A voice strangely like his old master's, but totally different: raw yet resonant, like that of a bronze clarion. A call so brimful of rage that it tore the skin off one's back, but knowing, with a knowledge that was like a knife.

One of the windmill strokes from the traveller's knotted staff grazed the little horse's neck. It was not a direct blow – he had heard the old man's skull crack and the death-rattle of the driver – but of a contemptuous violence. The traces had snapped like dry reeds and the grey had raced for the hills. The sharp flint had galled his hoofs and now, at sunset, the shadows ran cold. Looking back, the little horse had glimpsed a figure running desperately towards Thebes. Was it one of the slaves, or the traveller? He did not know. And began neighing, uncertain of his fodder.

His third record request was for the scratch or, more precisely, for the sibilant swerve (in G minor) of the steel nib on Rudolf Julius Emmanuel Clausius's pen in the instant in which this pen wrote the n in the exponential n minus x to the nth power in the equation of entropy.

Würzburg is not, even at its best, an ebullient town. On that early spring evening in 1863, the rain was streaming down the grimed windows. His lids heavy, Herr Clausius blinked and bent closer to his work-table. A grey film seemed to hang around the gas lamp, and when the draughts streaked through the curtains, the china globe of the lamp shivered morosely. Clausius observed with annoyance that these same gusts made his dentures throb. Unnoticing he pressed the pen-holder against his aching molar. Foxed with the damp, the off-prints of Sir William Thomson's papers on thermodynamics and Sadi Carnot's *mémoire* on the airpump lay at his elbow. Carnot's two equations, for the boiler when the piston was in position a, and when it was in position a prime, hummed, as it were, at the enervated edge of Clausius's awareness. Like two stick-insects, their brittle feelers interlocked. Somewhere in the house, and behind the splattering rain, a clock chimed and rattled. Konstanze had, again, forgotten to wind it.

To the nth power. The nib hovered over the paper, and for an idle

372

moment Clausius's attention wandered, through the armorial and dragon-maze of the watermark. The equation stood. Against reason. Against the long-drawn breath of life. In uncaring defiance of the future tense. Formally, the algebra was nothing but the proof, at once abstract and statistical, of the unrecuperability of caloric energy when turned to heat, of the degree of loss in all thermal and thermodynamic processes. That is how Clausius would entitle and describe his paper when dispatching it to the *acta* of the Prussian Academy of Science (Section IV: Applied Science). But what he was staring at – and the sensation was rather more distant, more indifferent than that of his bruised gums – was the determination, irrefutable, of the heat-death of the universe. The n minus x function would not be bought off. Entropy meant run-down and the transmutation of spent energy into cold stasis. A stillness, a cold past all imagining. Compared to which our own deaths and the decomposition of the warm flesh are a trivial carnival. In that equation, the cosmos had its epitaph. In the beginning was the Word; at the close was the algebraic function. A pen-nib, bought in a scrolled cardboard box at Kreutzner's, university stationer, had put *finis* to the sum and total of being. After the downward right-hand stroke of that n came not infinite blackness, which *is* still, but a nothingness, an unfathomable zero. Unthinking, Clausius started tracing a line beneath the equation. But the nib had gone dry.

The custodians of the sound-archive are not prudish. They know how often hearing is overhearing, and brought him his fourth disc unblinking.

A petty nightmare of a day. The first flight cancelled at Brussels Airport because of a work-to-rule by French air-controllers. Planes stacked over Europe like stale rusks in holding patterns and the fog thickening. He had rung her apartment; she must have left minutes before. Which meant she was already at the railway terminal. His change ran out as he tried to reach the station and have her paged on the public-address system (knowing how incensed she would be at the grossness of hearing her name loud-hailed, though it was a coded sobriquet, he was almost glad he had not succeeded). As through cotton wool, he heard the announcement of a possible departure to L. from the other terminal. He bounded awkwardly along the escalator and connecting tunnel, only to find a dozen other stranded passengers at the stand-by counter. When he finally took off, it was late afternoon. The hotel room had been booked in an assumed though, God knows, transparent name and she would not be able to claim the reservation. Would she have the spendthrift nonchalance to take another room in the same hotel? She would bridle at that.

With the fog slow to lift, the airport at L. was teeming and the lines at the passport-window interminable. He reached the hotel almost hysterical with exasperation and guilt. No sign of her. He lacked the nerve to enquire whether a lady of singular radiance (or so she was to him) had left her overnight bag with the *portier*.

The streets and squares of the city were awash with tawdry snow and patches of black ice. The flicker of neon lights dazzled him as it bounced off the tramcar-rails and shop windows. He circled aimlessly, back to the hotel lobby. Once more across the gusting bridge. Now obliquely and towards the cold flatness of the lake. He detested the place. He had loved it beyond words when last they had arrived there, the lights of the station underpass caught in her live hair. Now towards the hotel again, his hands trembling.

He found her. At the bottom of the unlit alley below the steps to the old town. She heard him running and turned. They stumbled, like drunks, into the solid dark of an arched doorway.

The sounds came in a soft rush. That of her fingers in his perspiring hair as he knelt. Of the buttons slipping out of the braided hooks of her long coat. The rustle of her skirt, like the leafy edge of summer, as she drew it up her thighs. And when his tongue came home to her, from above his dizzied head and shoulders, that laugh, distant at first, over-arching, then closer than his own skin. The hushed chime of her laugh (it was this he had requested from the archive) as he drank of her. A note which left his soul singing and crazy with peace.

There is, so far as is known, only one (and imperfect) tape extant of the otherwise lost Trio in F Major for crumhorn, double bass and Sumatran conch-bells which Sigbert Weimerschlund composed in the year of his death. The choice of instruments, though perhaps *recherché*, had seemed to Weimerschlund inevitable. As deputy curator of the palaeontology collection in the Atheneum in Second Falls (Ohio), he had long been spellbound by the serpentine, delicately rifled contours of certain immemorially ancient horned beasties. His heart attack in the cruel winter of 1937 – a serious hiccup, some years later, was to cause his decease – had left Weimerschlund with a singular aural vestige. At certain moments, in the face of a prairie wind, under professional stress – the Second Falls Chamber of Commerce, though sympathetic, recurrently put in question the value of the Atheneum and, more especially, of its fossil cabinets, which the new Estes Polk Memorial High School was, in any event, prepared to house – or when sheer lonesome gluttony had seduced him into bringing to his boarding-house room and consuming at one go a whole quarter-pound of chopped herring, Weimerschlund would hear, inside the echo-chamber of his ventricles, a low syncopated thrumming. A dense beat, a second beat echoing the first, then a vibrato. Tremolo and reprise sounding from the shadow-left of his heart. Though alarming, the sequence had its eerie charm, and Sigbert sometimes found himself hesitant to reach for the assuaging pills. Hence, after the crumhorn, the double bass.

The conch-bells, not bells really but nacreous, iridescent sea-shells suspended on a bamboo frame and graduated according to the pentatonic scale, did, he knew, represent an extravagant touch. Weimerschlund had never, of course, been anywhere in range of Sumatra. But he had heard the chiming glitter, the sea-arpeggios of conch-bells through a tent-wall on the night when Hubbard's Circus and Raree Show had stopped in Second Falls. Weimerschlund scarcely remembered what improbable impulse had taken him to the fair-ground. He fled in nausea from the eyes of the caged timber-wolf and the cackle of the pink-haired Tom Thumb. Looking for an exit, he heard that crystal scale; as if the wind had made the snow sing. Riveted, he pressed his ear to the muting canvas. He squirmed still at the recollection of his indiscreet gesture: Sigbert Weimerschlund, deputy curator and Shriner, down on all fours, prising loose the sodden tent-flap to peer inside. Where he glimpsed, by the sheen of a greying light-bulb, only the back of the player. It was, he later thought, the back of a boy or very young man (The Indian Rope-Trick Performed by Tamu the Blind Pearl Diver).

The precise circumstances under which the Trio had been recorded by the three brothers – he was now listening to a tape taken from the 78 – are a matter of mild musicological dispute. Nor should one advance exaggerated claims for the quality of the piece. It is, after all, amateur work. Weimerschlund appears to have overlooked that pizzicato on a double bass produced awkward effects when in counterpoint to the nasal register of the crumhorn. No, what remains memorable is the devoted performance. Zeppo manages to draw from the crumhorn not its customary sedate buzz, but a desolate and oracular hum. His breath-control, his variations of pitch and flutter, are those of a virtuoso. On the double bass, Harpo has lapses. It is not he, however, who is to blame when Weimerschlund calls for a glissando at the start of the last movement and, unreasonably, marks it presto. In Chico's hands or, more accurately, under the felt mallet as Chico wields it, the Sumatran chimes are magic. It is they who prelude, by means of a subtle rubato, the transcendent moment in the Trio: the return to the dominant, nineteen bars from the close. A moment in which the ache of the horn, the heart-thrum of the double bass, itself like a footfall on a winter path, are fused by the almost imperceptible yet rhythmically binding flicker of the bells. This, he fancied, as he listened in the studio, might well be the music played, and these the performers, in the waiting-room for the Last Judgement.

The painting which occasioned his sixth and final selection is little known. An unreliable mimeographed check-list is all that is made available, morosely, by the semi-private collection in the French Savoie in which it is hung. Labelled 'By the Master of the Chambéry Passion', it is a Crucifixion on gilded panelling which can most plausibly be dated mid-fourteenth century and ascribed to one of the workshops in the Turin area. The taut, angular grouping with St Damian at the edge, the motif of crossed lances and gonfalons against a dullish burnt-earth background and empty sky, suggest the influence either of Baldassare Ordosso himself or of one of his apprentices (a number of these are known to have journeyed the Alps into France after 1345). The torn features of Christ, the somewhat rhetorical gesture of the Mother of God – observe her heightened knuckles and the touch of sweat around her azure headband – are well executed but iconographically routine.

It is the red-headed lad in the attendant crowd, the fourth figure from the left, who arrests attention. He is whistling. On two supple fingers inserted, shepherd- or street-urchin-style, into a corner of his full lips. Whistling, either to himself or to some listener – a crony, a sheep-dog, a girl – outside the scene. There can be no mistake. The whistle is a loud and joyous one, as of a thrush on a spring upland. The whistler's firm, green-hosed legs tell us that, as does the merry swelling of his throat and cheeks. And though his lips are pursed, there can be no doubt as to the smile and dawn cheer which gives them breath. Yet the young man's eyes are on the Cross, on the twisted flesh and the petals of bright blood around the nails. The eyes are unwavering as he whistles, as the pure clear merriment rises into the paschal air.

What he asked for from the sound-archive was the recording of that whistle.

Strangely enough, it was not this request which proved most difficult to satisfy.

Noël, Noël

That one sound is different.

So many sounds at this time of year. I have noted twenty-seven. That of Father's footstep before he opens the front door. Lighter as the holiday nears. His stair-step, dragging when it's been a long day. That of his slippers, the furry scuff towards the tingle of the whisky decanter, and then the slosh in the glass. Mother's gait: quick in the dark of the morning, changing, a touch heavier after lights-on. The drum-roll of her heels, in and out. And that queer weightlessness, the pent-up breath of her first step before she enters the bedroom. I won't try to list the child-music. The scamper, right to the blown tip of her hair, when off to school. The skip at the gate. She dances to herself, at times, in her room. Tap and turn. Her laughters. Stuff my ears and I can still tell you of seven sorts. They ripple across one's skin.

There are, of course, the sayings of the house. When the heating clanks on or the rain dribbles. The flushings, the wince and quease (how would *you* put it?) of the stair-well. More door-voices than there are registers of wind. Warmth has its sound when it slides under the kitchen door. I know them all. They prickle my scalp. But this one is different.

I may be in error. Exceeding care is in order. Like that of the rat-catcher, arched and knit to hear the faintest creak, the cut whisper in the roof-beam or trestle. Error would be unforgivable. Come Christmas, sounds mix and multiply. And are shot through with smells. The shiver of the dwarf-pine with its green smell and hiss of needles; that of the post lurching through the slot in the door, heavier now with the waxen sound and scent of the glossy brochures and catalogues; the crackle of wrappings and the whole house chiming, like the chandelier. Even the lone light in the attic sounds crystal gay.

But here I must be prudent. Not only the candles in the window and on the mantelpiece give off a savour of felt and old copper; so do the electric bulbs, hung with pine-cones and holly, and on so much longer during these short days. One inhales sound and smell at one breath. Confusions may arise. (Days too soon I muddled the tide and ebb of voices from the schoolyard – Penny does not have far to go in the morning, 'Not far to drop,' says Father, at which she pretends to flinch – with that of the carollers.) One cannot be too precise. I may be in error.

Yet that sound *is* different.

When did I first hear it?

I don't remember exactly. Not exactly, that is. To which uncertainty blame attaches. Is my memory weakening? It has been formidable. Not a whistling in the street or in the house that I ever forgot or confused with any other. Last spring's early thrush, the show-off, crochet-semi-quaver-crochet and the rubato on the trill. Ask me when Father bought the new wellies, the lined ones, or Mother burned the roast with the guests – I caught Mr Blakemore's rancid breath, those dentures, even before he banged the door-knocker – with the guests (did I already say that?) at the front steps. Ask me about Penny's mumps and their hot smell in the room, and the time (it was years ago, wasn't it?) when I heard her at the top of the landing, without slippers, passing her fingers and then her braids through the moonbeams, trying to count them one two three, singsong, in her nightdress. With its odour of camphor, meaning start of school and leaves falling. Ask me. I will call up memory. How, then, is it that I don't recall, not exactly, the first time I heard the sound?

Could it have been when Mother was looking after her aunt – bronchial flu, was it? – and was away for the weekend? There are such sharp holes in the air when she is out of the house. Father and Penny had been to the movies. Four steps on the gravel. But then only two and the key fumbling in the lock. Because he was carrying her into the house, skipping, laughing. Penny was laughing too. And there were chocolate éclairs for tea, which Mother thinks bad for our teeth. So I was sworn to secrecy. 'Hi-ho the gang,' said Father and put rum in the tea. Only a drop for Penny and, at first, she wrinkled her nose and wouldn't. But then she sipped and coughed and giggled. The taste hung on our breath like warm gold. After which Father put on his favourite cassette, the *Pirates of Penzance* highlights, and he danced his hornpipe and knocked over the delphinia. So we were sworn to secrecy again and had raisin slices on top of the éclairs. Do you know what he did then? Put the raisins and bits of walnut to the edge of his lips and blew them out, in a high arc, telling Penny to catch them in her mouth. But they fell on the carpet and I was quicker. 'O Daddy, Daddy-o,' hummed Penny, spluttering and rounding her mouth. 'Daddy's duck,' he said. And she asked again when Mother would be back and why Auntie May had no one else to look after her, and couldn't Mum come home tonight. 'She would smell the chocolate éclairs,' said Father, basso profundo, and we would be in serious trouble, '*mucho* serious, Ducky.' Which made Penny giggle more.

Could it have been that night I first heard the sound?

Or was it at Nubb's Point?

I do detest picnics. Those ants; drawing-pins in my ears. But could it have been there? Consider the broad daylight. The herd of people about, squealing, snoring, licking wax-paper, huffing at one another, flying kites and screeching after them. Consider the loud slap of the lake against the piling. And the transistors. In all that squelch and flailing one can scarcely hear oneself sleep. True, there is the tunnel of shadow and of mildew behind the boathouse; and that odd thick spread of high grass and scrub downwind, away from the benches and the ices. But even there children swarm and couples cling (why else do they go on a picnic?). So it could not have been there, the sound I mean. Or could it? The time we dozed till twilight, till the early chill came off the water and Mother got up shivery. To pack the hampers, to shake the sand and dead grass out of the bath towels. Which was just when Father looped the beach-ball high and challenged Penny and me to the chase; beating us to its first bounce and punching it up again with his fist so that it arched into the late light and over the tea-stand. Where I lost them. There was muck in my eyes. I could hear them racing, breathing loud, and laughing. 'Penny for your thoughts, sweets for a penny,' Father's voice sliding away. I don't think it was then. And how could it have been, with Mother calling and starting towards the car-park? Revving motors and klaxons confuse me, like the yawp of gulls. I did say that I loathe picnics and the candy-drops underfoot.

What sound?

I find myself asking. Asking myself. Which is a muddle. Have I been imagining it, as I might certain smells? Does fear really have that scent of sodden cardboard? Is it in my head? I have seen old men tweeze out their hearing-aids and shake them bitterly, forgetting that the bat's piping is inside their skulls. It could just be, you know. I don't claim to be as sharp as I used to be. Other sounds, yes: twangings after the heavy winds, scratches as from somewhere behind my teeth, trills when I'm very thirsty. I might muddle or imagine those. But not that sound. It is too . . . Too what? I do have an especial ear. Too *other*. I don't know that that makes sense. *Other*. Like nothing else in earth or air. And there might just be something in the word *other* which is like the shape and shadow of the sound. The *O* at the outset, the soft thud and the rasp. I can't have imagined that soft scratching, like a hand through stubble. Night-beings, they say, move to that sound. Broken bits of us loosed to the air when the moon is down.

But does it matter? I mean, does it matter where when I first heard their sound? I am hearing it now. *Now.*

What a day it has been. The house caught in a bright wash of bells. The door-bell: deliveries. A registered parcel – the annual smoked ham from Father's cousin in York. Bells pealing on the radio and at Evensong, on the box, out of some vaulted nave, and those white voices of little boys chiming Latin. 'Bluebells, tinklebells, twinklebells, Santa's a-coming.' And the bird in the oven, crisping, crackling, simmering like handbells in the far wood. If only the house wouldn't ring so. It makes it hard to be certain. The door being shut.

Daddy dancing the evening long. Not literally, to be sure. But walking, turning, standing as if always on his toes. Taking the stairs at a bound. Whistling away the whisky on his breath. Not leaving me be for even a minute. Calling, rubbing his hot cheeks against mine. 'Old King Cole,' off-tune, incessant, making the sitting-room rock. That 'merry old soul!' over and over and over and Daddy-o slurping at me: 'Merry! Do you hear me, you sad brute, merry! That ole King Cole, a goner, high, on the trip of his boozy life. Jinglebells, *mon ami*. Heading for our chimney. Merry! The soul of him bursting like grilled sausage. You don't understand, do you, *mon ami*, with your sad old eyes.' I do hate it when he speaks to me in French. Dancing. I tell you the man was treading air. And those stage-whispers: 'No peeking, Katkins. Off with you. Upstairs, Penny and I have business. Wrappings to wrap. Ribbons to tie. For a certain special little lady. Off with you. I'll keep a weather-eye on the oven. Not to worry. For all manner of things shall be well. But nooo peeking, Slyboots. Not till tomorrow morning. Mummy's Christmas. Mummy's own very special Christmas. Right, Penny?' And Father swung Mother around the settee as if she were a child. I heard the light-switch clicking off as she went upstairs. But the darkness wasn't dark. You understand, don't you? It pulsed, somehow. There was no stillness in the silence. After he and Penny had trimmed the tree, I mean, and put out Mummy's gifts, the chintz housecoat, the acacia plant, the toiletries in their starry mantles and tinsel. The darkness just wouldn't go quiet. You do know what I mean, *please*.

The thread of light under Penny's door. Pencil-thin and dark pink as is the shade on her bed-lamp. At first I couldn't make out the tune, the little old record-player which they rescued for Penny out of the attic last spring being so low. Then I caught the lilt of it. The *Snow White* medley. 'Whistle While You Work'. A favourite of hers. And some-where somehow out of that soft piping, out of the filament of light under that door, came the sound, the oh-ing, so faint I could barely pick it up, the Daddy-o O-Daddy-waddy and the scudding breath, as through his mouth, the soft soft laughter, but more like a slipping out of key, sideways, out of true, the sound that is *other*. That is on the other side. Of what? I don't really know. On the other side of what can be borne. 'A penny for the guy. And mum's the word. Mum.' And this time the glassiness was out of his laughter. It was everyday. As if morning had come and the time for gifts. But it hasn't. Not yet.

My hind-legs ache. Badly. I am not as strong as I once was. But strong enough, still. When he opens the door – I love him so – I'll go for his throat. He is wearing his flannel house-shirt. The plaid one, with the broken collar button. I shall aim for his throat. And the sound will cease. I have no choice. You do see that, don't you? It being Christmas.

A Conversation Piece

A humming as of bees, distant.

'But the Master, Eleazer son of Eleazer, in his commentary of 1611 said – '

'That Akibah, may his name shine in glory, had been mistaken – '

'When he wrote that Abraham was altogether free, a man at liberty, the father of freedoms, when God, blessed be His unspeakable Name, called upon him to take the boy, Isaac, to the place of burnt offering.'

'By which Akibah meant to signify that God's commandments are spoken to the spirit of man when that spirit is in a state of sovereignty over its own truth, that commandments to the enslaved and the maddened are empty.'

'To which Eleazer son of Eleazer, he of Cracow, retorted – '

' "What freedom has man in the face of the summons of the Almighty?" When He commands, our freedom is obedience. Only the servant of God, the absolute servant, is a free man.'

' "Not so," said Baruch to me, he of Vilna. "Not so. When God bade Abraham, our father, take Isaac, his only son, to Mount Moriah, He paused for an answer. Abraham could have said, 'No.' He could have said, 'Almighty God, hallowed be Thy Name. You are tempting me. You are putting in my path the supreme temptation, which is unthinking, blind obedience. Such is the obeisance demanded by the Dragon Baal, by the empty gods with dog-heads in Egypt's temples. You are not Moloch, eater of children. What you now await from me is loving denial.' " So Baruch, my teacher.'

'The journey to the mountain took three days. During which Abraham did not speak to Isaac – '

'Nor to God. Who listened closely. Hoping for the answer, "No."

383

Whose patience was without end and who was saddened. So Baruch, in our *schul* at Vilna, where the almond tree – '

'That's crazy. God's foreknowing is total. What need had He to listen to Abraham. He knew that His commandment would be obeyed, that it was not for man to question. I knew Baruch, your teacher. He was so subtle that in his hands words turned to sand.'

'Yet God, blessed be the hem of His unsayable Name and the fire-garment of His glory, did not wholly trust Abraham.'

'Another madman.'

'No. Listen to me. God's confidence in Abraham was not total. Let me hammer out my meaning. Do not interrupt. If God had been utterly certain that Abraham would strike down the boy, He would have let the sacrifice come to pass. And brought Isaac back to life. For is it not said that God can waken the dead? By putting the ram in the thicket, by saving the child, He left uncertain the final obedience of Abraham. Did not Gamaliel the Cabbalist instruct us that there are moments, openings in the universe, during which God questions His own foreknowledge, during which the Angel of the Unknown, of the nameless, passes across the light of being?'

'Gamaliel the heretic. The witch and alchemist of Toledo – '

Many voices now, close-crowded.

'That accounts for the gloss – '

'Gloss? What gloss, chatterbox?'

'In the Talmud in the *yeshivah*. Written in by hand.'

'Which *yeshivah*?'

'Ours. At Bialik. Saying that Abraham was angry. That anger choked him all the way home. That he did not speak once from Mount Moriah back to Beersheba.'

'*Angry*? Our father, Abraham, to whom God had restored Isaac?'

'Because the Almighty had not kept faith in him. Because God had not been absolutely certain that Abraham would fulfil His commandment and strike the knife into the boy. In the night after he had heard God's voice, and during the unendurable march to the mountain, Abraham had died many deaths. His senses had frozen. His brain had become like black dust. The heart had stopped its song. There was no ground under his feet, no dawn under his eyelids. His steps were like those of a bullock when it has been stunned, when the blood is already out of its throat. Those who looked on Abraham saw death walking. The faith in him had grown so mighty, the sinews of obedience so stretched, that there was no room for life. There was doubt in Moses, sanctified be his great name and remembrance. Mutiny in Jeremiah. But Abraham, he the father of our fathers, had been made faith. All else had been purged. He was faith in bone and nerve. No hair, no hair of a hair on him or in his unkempt beard but had become faith and obedience harder than steel. The knife was softer than his hand. The blade might snap. That was Abraham's last fear. But God did not know this. He did not choose to know it. His trust in Abraham, His servant, fell short. Now the Almighty would never have proof of Abraham's infinite faith. He would never know how tight was the knot of Abraham's obedience. As life came back into the old man, as pain came home to him, so did a towering anger. That, said the gloss, is why the silence on Abraham's return journey was more terrible than the silence on the road to Moriah.'

'Error. A false gloss. For has not Jehoshuah of Prague cleared up the matter of the silence? Has he not instructed us – '

'That Abraham's anger was the very opposite. He could not at first, and may he be forgiven, find it in his heart to praise, to thank God for the saving of Isaac. The terror had been too sharp. The temptation too severe for a man to bear. Unendurable because twofold. The temptation to obey was murderous and beyond human understanding. How could God ask such a thing of Abraham, his most faithful servant? The temptation to disobey. But is there anything worse than to deny God's voice, to close one's ears against His calling? That the Almighty had saved the child did not take away even an atom, an atom's breath of terror from His commandment and the three days thereafter. And what if God *had* taken Isaac? What if Abraham's knife had struck? What then? How could the boy's resurrection make up for his sacrifice, for Abraham's act of slaughter? On the way back to Beersheba, Abraham could not speak to God. The hurt, the doubts gagged his soul. Had not the ram appeared too late in the thicket? How could Abraham live after that moment on the mountain, how could Abraham draw breath after he had carried inside him the slaying of his son? Hence the grey sweat on him during the return, hence the total silence. So Jehoshuah, whom they stoned in Prague.'

For an instant the voices dropped. But then, like a grape bursting –

'Foolishness. Foolishness. Hair-splitting.'

Almost in chorus.

'God had promised Abraham, "I will make of thee a great nation." He had promised father Abraham that his seed would be as are the stars, numberless, inextinguishable even when scattered. He had renewed with Abraham the covenant of hope. That Israel would endure, that Abraham's seed would be sown across the earth. Indestructible as is the living wind.'

'That it would endure despite –

'That the destruction of the temple and the loss of Zion –

'Despite massacre and dispersal –

'That we should not be consumed, not finally, in the fiery furnace, in the teeth of the mob, in the charnel house or the pogrom –

'That we shall endure even after they have torn the almond tree from its roots –

'Like hot ashes through the night. Alive even in death. Alive.

' "A nation and a company of nations shall be of thee," said God to our fathers, despite –

'But how then could Abraham have believed, even for a minute, that the Almighty, sung be His Name of Names, would have him slay Isaac? For without Isaac there could be no lineage, no children of Israel? Answer me that.'

'Was it all a game? Play-acting, as at *Purim*? When Haman roars through his black beard that all Jews, both young and old, little children and women, shall perish in one day, and the spoil shall be taken from them for a prey? O that black roaring. How it frightens us, how the children in the hall hold their breath and crowd close to their parents. Though we know that Esther is in the wings and that evil Haman will hang high. God and Abraham acting out the play of Isaac. To make our hearts breathless. To teach us by terror and by joy, as children must be taught. And Abraham was silent because he knew that all would be well, that he would, through Isaac, be a father to nations. Silent as was Joseph when he recognized his brethren and looked on Benjamin.'

'But where then would be Abraham's merit? Play-acting? When the being of God is, as Maimonides taught, truth. A truth so pure that

386

there is no shadow, no shadow of a shadow where it prevails. Abraham was an old man, a very old man – '

'Who might have forgotten, in the numbness of that terrible calling, the terms of God's promise, so long ago, in the land of Ur – '

'Who might have thought, in the dizziness of his fear, that God would bring to Sarah another son, a child of late evening after Isaac – '

'Who could have believed that the Lord, blessed be His Name, had changed purpose, that some other people, and not Israel, would be sanctified among nations. Because even Abraham, father of our fathers, had known sin, being a man. Or so it is argued in the commentary of the learned Ephraim of Mainz. I remember the passage.'

'And for all these reasons, or others we are too blind, too unlettered to apprehend, Abraham might have taken for the voice of God that of a demon – '

'That of Satan himself.'

'Abraham in his numbness, in his dizziness, in his knowledge of perfection, mistaking the whisper of Satan for the voice of God. For was it not said by Soloviel the Cabbalist that these two voices, that of God whom we must not name and that of un-nameable evil, are so utterly alike. That the difference between them is only that of the sound of a rain-drop in the sea?'

'It *was* the voice of Satan. God is no play-actor. Neither is *He* a sadistic tempter. How do we best define God, how do we seek to imagine Him? Precisely as one who *cannot* ask of a man that he stick a knife in the throat of his child. There is no surer proof that God is than the incapacity of our souls, of our minds, to conceive of Him as tempting Abraham to murder his son, to conceive of Him as torturing Abraham our father during the journey to the mount. Even a gentile, albeit the wisest among them, understood that the definition, the being of God, is proved by the impossibility of the commandment to Abraham. That it was Satan who confounded Abraham and seduced him to his devilish purpose.'

'A gentile? What gentile?'

'He bore a name like ours: Immanuel. He lived in Koenigsberg.'

'In Koenigsberg? I have a cousin there. Menachem the draper. Do you know him, the shop in the old town square? Do you know what has happened – '

'And having observed the confusion of Abraham, the Almighty betook Himself to Mount Moriah, set an angel to guard Isaac and wove the ram into the thorn-bush. Perhaps the selfsame bush that would burn for Moses.'

'Why then, *rebbi*, did God not intervene at once? Why did he not drive Satan from Abraham's door and take the old man out of his agony? The journey took three whole days. Three long nights Abraham lay awake with the face of Isaac before him, with that knife in his belt. An eternity. Why?'

'Our time is not His. Perhaps that ram was not yet born or the bush thick enough. Perhaps in His infinite mercy, the Almighty, praised be He, sought to give Satan a chance, to see whether the Fallen One would feel remorse seeing the sweat on Abraham, and undo his evil trick.'

'Though you are a learned man, you speak like a simpleton. You say that we know the being of God, the meaning of Him, just because He could not order Abraham to sacrifice Isaac the child, the only son. You would have us believe that so crazy, so obscene a commandment could come only from Satan. God's existence tells us that Abraham was mistaken when he took the voice of the devil for that of the Lord. You cite a wise man of the gentiles. Perhaps he was wise. But no true Christian. For is the God of the Christians not He who gives His only son in sacrifice, who let His son die in bestial pain on the Roman cross?'

A rush of voices.

'But that is not our God. Not ours. Not – '

'Our God is one. He does not beget. All men are His sons. The Nazarite was no Messiah. Only a man. Mad, perhaps.'

'Let me speak. I do not say that their God is ours, or that Christ was His child. I can attach no meaning to such words. But consider this: only Almighty God, only He who spoke to Job out of the whirlwind and slew the first-born of Egypt, could command Abraham to sacrifice Isaac. Abraham was not mistaken. His hearing was good. Listening to those terrible words, words which should never cross the lips of the living, Abraham *knew* that God was speaking. God is what He is because He alone can demand of His most faithful servant that he slit his child's throat. And it was this knowledge, this understanding beyond reason, which made father Abraham speechless on the journey to the mountain and mute on the road back to Beersheba. We who are fallen into the hand of the living God – '

Was the sound nearing? A sound slithering, like smoke across sand.

Next, a voice lime-green and acid.

'Who speaks for Isaac?'

Not yet a man's voice. Choked by the first starched collar and the bite of the collar-stud.

'Who speaks for Isaac? It was a hard march. His father Abraham walking too fast. Saying nothing, but pulling him by the hand. Black, impatient as Isaac had never seen his father before, but silent. Isaac saw the dry wood and the flint. He knew that his father was carrying a knife and a whetstone. But where was the lamb for the burnt offering? And when he asked, his father said that God would provide. But the words sounded strange, like the beads of sweat on Abraham's lips. Do you think Isaac believed him? I don't. He must have guessed. From the way in which they hurried from the house, from the way they camped in the night, hardly washing, all under one stinking tent-cloth. Oh, Isaac must have guessed and smelled the knife. And fouled himself in his fear. Marching three days with his bowels cold and loose, trying to sleep three short nights in the stench of his fear. Can you imagine their climb up the mountain? It may be that Abraham carried the wood, giving to Isaac the flint and shavings for the fire. But Isaac must have noticed the rope around the logs. Too thick, too freshly woven. A rope with which to tie a man's hands behind his back. Why did he not scream for help or run back to the young servants whom Abraham had left at the foot of the trail? Isaac's friends. The serving-men with whom he played in the courtyard of the house, who brought him the new grapes from the vine and cut arrows for him? Surely they would hide him and spirit him home. Why did Isaac not seize his father's hands and cry out for his life? Why did he not snatch at the knife and throw it over the side of the hill?'

'Because the spirit of God was upon him, because he was blessed in obedience.'

'Because Abraham's ass, the brindled she-ass whom Isaac fed, had whispered to him that he need not fear, that an Angel was beside him. There is a Midrash which says that the beast of burden spoke comfort to Isaac.'

'Fairy-tales. Lies. I will tell you why Isaac did not scream for help or run away or try to stop his father. It was because he was too frightened. It was because his voice had frozen inside him. It was because he was ashamed of the hot dirt and smell in his pants. The shame being even greater than his fear of death. But when Abraham bound him and laid him out on the altar, on that dry, sharp wood, when he heard the knife come out of his father's belt, he screamed. No one heard that scream. Because Isaac was vomiting, because the vomit was in his mouth, like a gag. But I know that he screamed.'

'Nowhere in the Torah, nowhere in the scrolls of truth – '

'But I hear the scream,' said the boy. 'All around me. And inside my head. Since we left for the station. It is Isaac's scream, which has never ceased.'

Refutation is made. But gently.

'You must be mistaken, boy. There was no scream. And even if there had been, it stopped at once. The Angel called out. And Isaac's heart leaped and sang at the great blessing: "I will multiply thy seed as the stars of the heaven, and as the sand which is upon the sea shore; and thy seed shall possess the gate of his enemies." And when they came home to Beersheba, they feasted and rejoiced in the Lord. The ass was put to pasture and Isaac the child was given the ram's horn, circled with gold, to blow on. It is that horn you hear, calling to the hills.'

'I don't believe you.' Even shriller. 'I don't believe you. I can't. It's like the sweets they cram in your mouth after you've had a tooth pulled. Do you know what those sweets taste like? You don't do you! Of blood and pus.'

'But Isaac loved Abraham. His love never wavered. It was Abraham his father who chose Rebekah for him. And when Abraham died at 165 years of age, his blessing was on Isaac and Isaac tore his hair in grief.'

'Bedtime stories. No man lives that long. Isaac never trusted Abraham again. Not for one instant. How could he? How could he forget the walk to Moriah, the faggots, the rope, the knife? The taste of his father's hand on his eyes and mouth, of Abraham's knee in his back, never left him. That is why Isaac was deceived by *his* sons, by Esau and Jacob. No Jewish father looks on his son without remembering that he may be commanded to take back his life. No Jewish son looks on his father without remembering that he may be sacrificed by his father's hand. How can there be trust or forgiveness between us? Blood and pus. Don't you smell it, you who call yourselves teachers, masters of the word?'

The young voice skidded, like a cracked pipe, soon inaudible. In the droning dark.

'And what of Sarah?'

A woman speaking. An angry chorus.

'Silence. Silence. Is it not ordained by the Law that no woman shall come to the Torah? That women, though blessed and honoured is their mystery, shall not comment on holy writ?'

'Then why are we here, behind the same closed door? You have never given us a sabbatical from pain. Never a leave of absence from massacre. Though you would have us be silent, we are branded like you. Sarah *knew*. How could she not have known? How can any mother not know when her child is taken from her to be slaughtered? Old Abraham told her to be silent, to stay out of God's unfathomable way. But she saw the wood, the rope, the knife. She smelled the cold fear in the old man's groin and the hot fear in the boy's hair. They stole away before sun-up, like foxes from the hen-house. But she was awake. She heard their lying steps on the threshold and the drowsy coughs of the serving-men. She lay awake, did Sarah, crazed with fear, her guts turning to stone. Six nights and six days, her eyes so hot with horror that she could no longer weep. And when they came back from the mountain, the men and the boy – her child, her only son – they told her to prepare a great feast, to deck the great table with fresh green, to send for flute-players and dancers from Ashod. When all she wanted was to hold the child, so close he would feel the fire in her bones, and cry out her pain. During those six days and nights, Sarah's whole life had passed before her. How Abraham had handed her over to Abimelech, king of Gerar, how he had handed her over for the king to whore with, lying to save his own precious hide, saying, "She is my sister." How other women had laughed at her, behind their fluttering hands, when she became pregnant with Isaac, how no one believed that the old frozen man was Isaac's father – did Abraham himself believe it? Sarah saw before her the years during which she had had to endure in her house, in her kitchen, in the vegetable garden, Hagar the Egyptian and the dark son she had borne Abraham, how she had had to endure the scent of burnt almonds from Hagar's skin, Abraham's scent. And even as she lay dying, Sarah heard, in Abraham's train, the chirping of women, of the concubines that came with him to Hebron. Do you really think she did not know, in her parched hollowness, that Abraham would, immediately after her death, take to wife Keturah, the girl with the good teeth? But what did it matter, what did anything matter after those days of Mount Moriah, after this boy's footsteps had been taken from the house? What could make up for that? The Holy Books report nothing of Sarah's torture. No learned commentator reports what she felt when she heard the lick of the ass's hoofs on the cobbles but dared not look whether Isaac was among the men coming home. No man, no one who has not borne a child, can imagine that. We women are not called up to read the Torah. A good thing for you. It is between the lines we would be reading, between every two lines. For in that space lies the silence of women. Who have had no say among you. It is the loudest silence in the world. Loud with the cries of labour and with the cries of all the mothers who have seen their children beaten to death in front of their eyes. But now you must hear it, you men. In this meeting-house we no longer sit and pray apart from you. Here we also are called, we daughters of silence.'

Another woman's voice, and a third: 'Dance, Miriam, dance. In this small house – '

Too small, really. Not a dancing-floor at all. Not that it terribly mattered. Men and women, oh, impropriety, young and old, were now welded so close that the merest motion, a raw breath out of a single mouth, quivered through the lot.

'A thousand years you men have argued, ravelled, spun words. You have read yourselves blind, crooked your backs, poring over the single letter or the missing vowel. A thousand years you have chanted and swayed as if truth could be caught in your fingers. You have burrowed for meaning like starved mice and pounded the words so fine they have fallen to dust. Living men, their lips caked with dust, as are the buried. You have hissed and croaked at one another, owls at noontime. We have heard you when we passed the closed shutters of the schools, we have heard you when you lay beside us in the night, expostulators, litigants, cross-examiners, word-peddlers even in your dreams. To what end? Have you found those syllables which make up the secret name of God? What pun, what game of hidden numbers has made us free? Was it all for *this*?'

'Thought is the dance of the mind. The spirit dances when it seeks out meaning, and the meaning of that meaning. Perhaps there is in the forty-ninth letter of the forty-ninth verse of the forty-ninth chapter of the Book of Books, which lies hidden in the Torah as the Torah rolls lie cloaked inside their shrine, a truth so mighty that God Himself must pause when He remembers it. The dance-steps of the soul are words, woman. The lords of the dance are we. Are we not dancing now?'

Up steps of air.

Which grew steeper and steeper.

Mountainous. Higher than Moriah.

'Dance, Miriam, dance,' said the spigot in the ceiling.

'There is no ram now and the bush is burning.'

Dancers, their mouths wide open. So that the hive swarmed into their throats. And hummed to them the slurred slow song of gas.